THE IN-BETWEE

THE
LIFE

SAGAR CONSTANTIN

Copyright © Sagar Constantin 2021
Published by BUOY MEDIA LLC

All rights reserved.

No part of this book may be reproduced, scanned, or distributed in any printed or electronic form without permission from the author.

This is a work of fiction. Names, characters, places, and incidents are either products of the author's imagination or are used fictitiously. Any resemblance to actual events, locales, or persons, living or dead, is entirely coincidental. The content of this book is for entertainment purposes only and is not intended to diagnose, treat, cure, or prevent any condition or disease. You understand that this book is not intended as a substitute for consultation with a psychologist. Please consult with your own physician if you need help. The read of this book implies your acceptance of this disclaimer. The Author holds exclusive rights to this work. Unauthorized duplication is prohibited.

Cover design by Juan Villar Padron,
https://www.juanjpadron.com

Special thanks to my editor Janell Parque
http://janellparque.blogspot.com/

facebook.com/SagarConstantinAuthor
amazon.com/Sagar-Constantin/e/B093NXD4C2
twitter.com/ConstantinSagar
linkedin.com/in/sagarconstantin
instagram.com/sagar.constantin.author
bookbub.com/authors/sagar-constantin

1
THE JOURNEY

"Excuse me, sorry." I'm running as fast as I can, and I struggle to get the words out as I'm panting hard. Up ahead is the yellow sign saying gate 122, the gate closing notice is flashing angrily, but somehow everybody has agreed upon walking in slow motion and right in front of me. If I don't make it, I won't be able to pick up Luke from Kindergarten tomorrow as promised. And even worse, I might not make it home in time for his fifth birthday.

"Can you move, please? I'm sorry." I'm squeezing my way through a group of people on a travelator as they have decided to stand on both the left and the right while looking at their phones. It seems that people have conspired to get in my way or slow me down.

Finally, I can see the check-in woman looking impatiently at her watch and flipping through a printed list. When she sees me, she puts on a forced smile and crosses me off the list.

"Late again, Ma'am...."

I'm still puffing and get out my passport and boarding card. "I'm sorry. I just had to get a present for my kid."

"Did you see anyone else running this way?" There is a small sign of a thaw in her tone of voice.

"No, I didn't look back, sorry."

I throw a glance to her list, where two people are still not crossed off.

"Have a pleasant flight, Ma'am."

"Thank you." The departure hall is deserted, and I head straight for the plane. A woman in a tight suit welcomes me, and I hurry down toward my row. A few passengers manage to move their attention from their tablets and give me the "you are responsible for the late departure" look as I pass. Luckily, I don't have to walk through the whole plane; I'm in my favorite row, number seven.

"Excuse me."

The lady at the aisle seat looks up from the emergency folder.

"I'm by the window."

She moves just enough for me to slip past, and I drop down in my seat with a sense of relief.

"This is the flight attendant speaking. Will passenger Mr. Wung and passenger Mrs. Jensen please let yourself be known to the staff?"

I reach for my diary and start flipping through it. Grocery shopping, pick up Luke, playdate with Luke, prepare for Luke's birthday. Luckily, I just managed to get him a present, a massive box of the latest released LEGO castle with warriors. A warm sensation flows through my body, making me blush. There is no way I will let Luke out of my sight for the next few days. The story I just did grew much bigger than I anticipated; I was supposed to go home last week. But it developed, and I had to stay till the worst crisis was over. Hopefully, I will cash in a big check and be able to take off work for a few days. If I'm really lucky, I might be nominated for the Pulitzer Prize again this year. It would be my third nomination, and hopefully, this time... I don't finish the thought. Instead, I cross out an appointment with John; *that's not happening*, I think to myself.

"We still need to hear from Mr. Wung and Mrs. Jensen."

So much for being the one to blame. I look around. Everybody is absorbed in their own world, watching something on their devices. The staff is busy too. That gives me a chance to call Luke.

"Hello," a tired voice answers at last. I turn toward the window so that the flight attendant can't see that I'm on the phone as she walks by looking for the missing passengers.

"Hi, it's me. Can you put Luke on the phone?"

Andreas sighs dramatically. "He's about to go to bed. Do you really think this is a good time to call? He never settles down after talking to you."

This is not the time or place to get into a brawl with my ex-husband. I lower my voice, "Just put him on for a minute. I promise I won't say anything to get him too excited."

Andreas grumbles and puts down the phone. A few seconds later, I can hear Luke's voice.

"MOMMEEEE!"

I press the phone even closer to my ear. "Hey, Luke, my love. How are you?"

"I miss you. When are you coming home?"

His voice is not as energized as yesterday, and I have to press the phone even harder to my ear to hear him. It sounds like he has given up on the question he has asked every day during my three-week trip. I wish I didn't have to go away from him so long, but the circumstances are unavoidable. After Andreas and I split up, I was forced to go back to freelance journalism. That was the easiest way for me to make a living, but it also keeps me on the move. At least tonight, I have a better answer for Luke.

"I miss you, too. But I'm on my way home; I'm actually on the plane, we will take off very soon. I'll be there to pick you up from Kindergarten tomorrow."

"And you won't be going away again?" His voice is soft, and I can hear his yawns.

"Not for a while...." My heart beats faster. "We'll have plenty of time together. Time to do lots of fun stuff. Maybe I'll even let you stay home from Kindergarten for a couple of days."

"That sounds grrreat," At that moment, Luke sounds wide awake. His voice is full of the kind of enthusiasm I wish I could bottle and bring with me on a trip like this.

He is telling me about an excursion to the park with Andreas and the Kindergarten and how they got ice cream on the way home. I'm forcing myself not to comment on it and start to explain how I interviewed some people who lost their homes in a big storm and how they managed to survive. Luke is not saying a word, but I can hear his soft breathing through the phone. While we are talking, I pull out my favorite picture that I always keep close of Luke, Andreas, and myself on Luke's last birthday. His blue eyes are sparkling. I rest my eyes, looking at his blond hair and little nose, and lean my head against the window, feeling just a little bit closer to him. When Andreas and I were together, we always went to Legoland on Luke's birthday; it's his favorite place on earth. The colors on the picture have started to fade. I close my eyes as I feel my heart expanding. I rest the stiff photo paper on my chin. Now, Luke has another birthday approaching, his fifth. Where did the time go?

Andreas is in the background, telling Luke that it is time for bed. His voice is firm with a hint of irritation. I stare out the window where workers are looking through the baggage trolleys, most likely searching for the two missing passengers' suitcases.

"Luke, I will see you tomorrow. Have a wonderful sleep. I love you."

"Bye, Mom. I love you, too."

"Bye, Luke. Can you put Dad back on the phone?"

There is a scratching sound. The phone is rattling, and a moment later, Andreas is back on.

"What's up? I need to get him settled." Andreas is clearly annoyed. There is no doubt that the call interrupted the flow of his evening. I take a quick look through the seats in front of me. The front door is still open, and the staff are chatting up front. It doesn't seem like we are taking off right now.

I clear my throat and do my best to speak calmly and friendly. "It's Luke's birthday the day after tomorrow. I thought maybe we could do something together, the three of us." Andreas isn't saying anything in response, so I continue, "You can come over for dinner. As long as you don't bring any of your new girlfriends." Again, Andreas says nothing.

"Okay, I'll come over," Andreas says at last. "I need to talk to you about something, anyway."

"We have located the luggage of the missing passengers and are now in the queue for takeoff. Hopefully, we will be on our way in approximately five minutes. We apologize for the delay." The voice sounds like a tape recording, but I can see the flight attendant moving her lips.

"Great, see you at seven. I'll make dinner."

"See you," Andreas answers briskly before hanging up.

I throw the phone in my handbag and look over at the woman next to me, all dressed in red. She is still studying the safety instructions and doesn't pay any attention to me. I better get some sleep, so I'm all fit when I get home. The past several days have been exhausting, and I've hardly slept. The images of burning houses, animals running for their lives, and people suddenly without homes are printed on my retina. I don't know how I manage to cover stories with so much devastation, but I do. It must be my ability not to feel other peoples' pain. The images get blurry, and I doze off.

"PLEASE, FASTEN YOUR SAFETY BELT." The flight attendant's voice is firm, and she walks with a fixed stare ahead. She is wearing a snug skirt with a matching tailored jacket, very classic and straightforward in dark blue with a stripe down the side. Her smile is rather indulgent.

"But we won't be landing any time soon," I reply wonderingly and sit up straight, rubbing my eyes.

The attendant has already moved on to the next row, but she leans back toward me. "We're heading toward some bad weather, but it should be over soon." With a sure step and gentle sway of her hips, she continues up the aisle to find more safety-belt sinners.

I reach for my plastic cup of water and take a sip. It's tepid. Suddenly, the airplane lurches. My cup of water slides from one side of the tray table to the other, and I just manage to put out my hand in time to stop it from falling over the edge and onto the woman seated next to me. I lift my tray and hold onto my cup of water, now half-spilled on the floor, with one hand. I try to push my bag under the seat in front of me with my foot. Another bump sends my diary to the floor. When I try to reach for it, my head is a few inches from bumping into the chair in front of me. I force myself back in the seat and pull my belt tighter. Even though it is dark outside, I can make out some flashes of light on the horizon. We must be above water or a nature reserve because there is no other source of light to be seen. It seems that we have left the bad weather behind.

I manage to drink the rest of the water in a mouthful and look over to see if the lady next to me has noticed the potential spill. She is reading the monthly horoscope in a magazine—a *believer just like my mother*. The woman holds onto the magazine so tight that her knuckles are all white. Her forehead is lined with deep wrinkles as she stares endlessly at the same page. Her red suit doesn't have a crease, and her short hair is styled as if she has just left a salon.

Then the plane lurches again, followed by a bump that makes my stomach sink. Images of Luke flash before my eyes in brief glimpses. It is like a slideshow that runs at high speed. He is laughing and waving at me. I shake my head quickly a few times and smile to myself, glad that I fastened my safety belt. If not, I might have hit the ceiling and ended up on the lap of the woman next to me.

I am not the type who scares easily, but I must admit that sometimes I can't help thinking about how I would react if something suddenly happened, that is, something critical. Would I act heroically and be the one who takes over and calms the other passengers, or would I save my skin and hope for the best?

My mother has always said that I was born under a lucky star. I think she's right. It seems like things just come to me when I am in need. Not that I just lean back and wait passively; I am not the type who goes around searching for a lucky chance. Deep down, I believe that I will be all right, and everything will be fine. That is, at least until I'm not meant to be here anymore.

There is a loud explosion, and the whole airplane lights up for a couple of seconds and then goes into a free fall. My stomach drops so that I can hardly breathe. There seem to be arms and legs everywhere. Up ahead, an older man has fallen into the aisle. The sound of screams and crying children rises like a wall around me. The flight attendant I just talked to is trying to assist the fallen man but falls herself and only manages to grab hold of an armrest a bit further down. I hold my breath.

In an instant, everything becomes white. The rumbling of the airplane is gone. No one is screaming. Everything is perfectly still.

I'm not sure whether my eyes are open or closed, and I can't feel my body. Everything is perfectly still. I consider moving or standing up, or better yet, I'll just try to raise my hands to determine whether my eyes are open. I attempt to lift my arms, but there is no reaction. What's happening? Where am I? Where is the woman who was seated next to me?

The light becomes more intense, and it is burning inside me. Everything is almost luminous white. Why can't I see anything; why can't I feel anything; what's happening to me? Thoughts fly around my head, and I can hardly complete one thought before the next one starts.

"Eva."

A voice is whispering my name.

"Eva."

A soft, warm voice is coming closer and is becoming stronger. But I still can't see anything. I feel the heat on my eyelids that is spreading across the rest of my face. It feels like the sun is melting some ice, leaving behind a new sensation on my cheeks. I can suddenly feel my lips. The warmth continues down the length of my spine and heats the small of my back.

I am lying perfectly still; that is, I think that I am lying down. Somehow, I can sense a figure coming toward me, but my eyes are not open, or to be more precise, I can't actually see anything. Everything seems utterly unreal, and my body is tense. A second ago, I was sitting on the airplane next to the woman wearing a red suit. If I could feel my body, I know it would be trembling. That's putting it mildly. As long as my eyes are closed, I feel safe. Here, inside myself, I feel secure. Just like children who don't think that anyone can see them if their eyes are closed, I am pretending to hide in my own universe.

"Eva, when you are ready, you can open your eyes," says the calm voice in a kind tone.

Yeah, sure, that's easy for you to say, I think. I'm the one lying here with no idea where I am. You are out there and know where we are. I notice that my breathing has begun to slow. How bad could it be to find out where I am? I can always just close my eyes again. Why don't I just open them? I'm not usually afraid of anything.

"Eva," repeats the voice. Now the voice is right next to me.

"Y-yes," I stammer. My mouth feels like sandpaper, and it is as if the word is stuck and can barely come out. If I keep my eyes closed, maybe the light and the voice will go away, and the friendly flight attendant will come back. Perhaps I'm just in the middle of a very realistic dream.

One... two...

I take a deep breath and hold it.

Now.

Three.

I release the air from my lungs while I slowly raise my eyelids. The light is even sharper, and I am blinded by it. I squint slightly and blink a couple of times. A tear runs from my left eye. I want to wipe it off, but my hand won't move; even when I focus on my hand, I can't budge it.

The light is overwhelming, and it is impossible to see a thing. Is it the sun? It was just the middle of the night. What's happening?

A shadow bends down toward me. I narrow my eyelids so that there is just a little slit to peek through. It feels like I am looking at an unknown world, like observing another reality from my safe hiding place.

The figure becomes more distinct, and it is almost beside me. It looks like a man, a young man. I try to focus.

"My name is Thomas."

I let my eyes widen, and the muscles around them relax. My tongue moves so that I can generate some saliva, and I try to moisten my lips. Instantly, my chin drops, and my mouth opens. He is the most beautiful person I have ever seen. Long, dark blond hair falls into natural curls along the sides of his face. His skin looks as soft as a baby's, and he has distinctive cheekbones. The crystal clear, blue eyes are almost transparent.

"Thomas," I mutter. So far, so good. How long have I been lying on the floor? I don't know. I have totally lost my sense of time and space. My eyes have become accustomed to the light, and I let my gaze wander without moving my head, but I can't find a fixed point. All of the surfaces run together, and everything seems to be out of focus. It looks like I can see the room, but there is nothing to see. I slowly turn my head from left to right and back again, but it looks the same everywhere. It is all white, and a kind of nebulous haze surrounds me.

I start to notice that what I am lying on is soft and actually quite pleasant. The floor is subtly diffuse, and the indefinable surface makes it seem alive.

"Do you feel like sitting up?" Thomas's voice is calm and smooth as silk.

He stretches out his hand toward me, immediately inspiring confidence. I look into his eyes and feel a rush inside, taking yet another deep breath that turns out to be more like a gasp. I thought that I had tried just about everything in my life. *This is, without a doubt, the most extraordinary dream I've ever had.* I want to laugh, but nothing happens.

My gaze fixes on Thomas, who is now sitting next to me. He is wearing a long blue silk shirt with a simple gold thread that forms a pattern of cascading flowers from the shoulders downward. The upper part of the garment hangs loosely, revealing his muscular body. He looks like a prince from a fairytale, which makes me confident that this *is* a dream. Thomas places his hand on my shoulder and supports me as I sit up. The room changes: it is as if the walls are moving. Am I on drugs? Have I gone crazy? *If this is a dream, I would like to wake up now and be on my way. I've got a plane to catch and a family waiting at home.*

"Welcome to In-Between," Thomas speaks slowly and clearly, looking at me and smiling so I can see his beautiful white teeth. His eyes sparkle as he talks and become even more transparent.

"In be—what did you say?" I mumble and let my eyes wander while I move my head in small jerks.

"In-Between," Thomas repeats calmly. He seems to be very understanding. "Come, I'll show you around." He leans forward and gently puts his hand on mine. It's warm and so soft.

"Stop," I say in a very firm tone and manage to raise my right hand in front of me. "Before I go anywhere, I want to know what's going on."

When I was a child, a friend taught me that I could interrupt my dream's storyline. If I were trying to escape from the bad guys, I could just say that it was just a dream and then muster up the strength to turn around and overpower them instead of running away. That is my new tactic in this dream. Whoever Thomas is, he has to learn that he can't mess around with me. I am not going anywhere until I know what is going on. Even though Thomas doesn't seem like a bad guy, I still have the right to know what I'm doing here.

"I want to know where I am and what I'm doing here," I manage to say in a small, shaky voice with much less command in it than I intended.

Thomas doesn't appear intimidated in any way. "Later. Come on, let me show you around."

"Yes, but..." I manage to stutter. Thomas has already risen and is heading off.

"Wait for me." So much for that plan. I get onto my feet but need to rise slowly since my head is spinning, and I find it hard to stand on the floor's drifting substance. I count to five before hurrying the best I can after Thomas. There is no way that I want to be left behind. Walking on the floor is very peculiar. It gives way in a bit of a rubbery manner. I can't see any doors, but there is some sort of opening in the slightly diffuse surface. The floor, ceiling, and walls are covered with this drifting substance, vague, indistinct, and in constant motion. My legs are stiff, and I shake them a bit as I start to walk.

"Hey, wait for me," I call after Thomas. "I'm coming." I feel almost like a small child trying to keep up with an adult who has much longer legs.

With careful steps, I pass through the opening and enter a large room. My eyes widen, and a shiver runs down my back. It is so bright, light, and open, but there are still walls of some kind. I can't feel my feet, and I squeeze my hands together tightly. My brain can't make any sense of this place. I don't know what it is that I'm seeing.

Thomas stops walking and waits for me to approach.

"The place we just came from is the reception area." He turns toward me when I join him. His arms hang loosely along the sides of his body, and he projects serenity. "That is where everyone who comes here lands. I am one of those appointed to receive new people and ensure that you get settled comfortably. Over here is our center, and from here, you enter In-Between and can move about freely." He points toward a large surface framed by a fine red line that marks a door and continues in a circle all around us with more indications of doors. The rest of the room is bare and rather uninteresting. Some long passages run from the doors, but it isn't possible to see where they lead.

I am still unable to comprehend anything at all and look up despairingly at Thomas. "What is In-Between?" If I continue to repeat my question, perhaps he will answer, and I will finally understand. That is my new strategy.

I notice some more colored circles on the wall. Thomas stands directly in front of me and looks right into my eyes. His crystal-clear blue eyes are so penetrating, and it seems like he can look right through me. I feel utterly naked under his gaze—like he somehow knows all about me, and I don't know anything about him. Quickly, I lower my eyes and take a step back. If only there had been a chair to sit on. My legs feel like jelly, and my hands are placed deep in my pockets.

"What is the last thing you can remember?" The light from the skylights falls gently on his face, marking his cheekbones.

My body tenses, my shoulders and back tighten, and my breathing becomes strained. I raise my head and make eye contact. "I remember sitting on the airplane." I gasp for breath. "It was nighttime and dark outside. And then there was a storm and a lot of turbulence. The woman who was sitting next to me... I remember that she was uneasy, but I don't remember anything else. Then I woke up in the other room and heard your voice." I reach out in a gesture of despair, looking around as if there were some answers to be found.

Thomas nods passively. "It's perfectly normal. The transition went quickly, and it can be quite a shock for your body."

"My body?" Now that he mentions it, I can feel every single muscle in my entire body. Places that I didn't even know could ache are shooting off little bolts of pain. I shift my weight from one leg to the other and move my hands across my face. There is nothing to feel, no cuts or scratches.

"You are beginning to feel your body." Thomas points at my legs, which are still swaying from side to side and shaking slightly. I stop abruptly and freeze on the spot. He notices everything. I have to watch what I say and do until I have figured out what is going on.

"I'd like to show you where you are, but it can be rather overwhelming." Thomas looks grave and quite firm. Such a severe expression does not seem to suit his face; it looks like it has a more playful nature. What could be so serious or frightening? Isn't this still a dream?

I glance down at myself. I am still wearing jeans and a pale blue shirt with a white sweater on top that hangs open. I have a ring on my finger and a white gold chain with a pendant around my neck that Andreas gave me when Luke was born. I put my hand around it and squeeze it tightly.

Thomas presses his hands gently together in front of his chest and slowly raises them upward toward his chin. "The way that people react varies greatly. I cannot prepare you for what you are going to see. No matter what happens when we enter, please know that I am here for you." He looks toward a door to our right and pulls up the sleeve on his long blue shirt very precisely.

I turn my head in the same direction, now starting to feel a bit nervous. My hands turn cold and sweaty. They are not usually clammy, but what Thomas is saying sounds pretty strange, and I simply can't relate at all. I fumble with the zip of my sweater. After a few attempts, I manage to zip up my shirt and feel a tremor throughout my body.

"Are you ready?"

Am I ready? Ready for what?

"Yes, sure, I'm ready," I say, regretting my words instantly.

Thomas gently places his hand on my shoulder and looks into my eyes. "All right then, we'll go in. Remember that whatever happens, I am right here beside you, and I'm not going to leave you."

I can feel the warmth from his hand on my shoulder and the subtle vibration of energy flowing through me. Hesitating, I take one step and then another toward the door... slowly, very slowly. My legs are stiff, and my feet are so heavy. There is a resounding silence here.

Thomas seems to know that I need some time to walk over there. He walks calmly by my side and doesn't let go of me. There is no way to avoid it. I know that, but even so, I feel a strong urge to turn around and go back or maybe just to keep the conversation going. Why can't he just say where I am and get it over with? Why make such a big deal out of it?

Although we only walk about four yards, it feels like an eternity. The back of my neck tightens, and my shoulders are almost up to my ears. I am panting and squeeze my eyes together to try to make out what is waiting ahead. That doesn't make it any easier. Right about now, it would be nice to call a friend or grab hold of some kind of lifeline, but Thomas and I are the only ones here.

Thomas is standing next to me, as solid as a rock. I slowly raise my eyes and lean slightly forward.

A section of the wall starts to move slowly aside, and I stiffen.

2
IN-BETWEEN

I grab hold of Thomas's arm and squeeze it tightly.

A room opens up in front of me, and enormous paper-thin screens dominate it. They cover the wall around the huge round room. I stare, and my brain is working overtime to figure out what I'm seeing. Images of the ocean where whales are playing, a city nearly covered in pollution, and a rainforest on fire. I feel myself being pressed back, overwhelmed by the images in front of me, but I manage to remain standing.

There are people everywhere, sitting in front of ultra-thin, nearly transparent hovering screens. Some wear what seems to be very high-tech headphones and are staring at their screens in deep concentration. An eruption of laughter comes from a group of people I immediately assume are friends.

I take a small step forward. The room is cool, and I keep a firm grip on Thomas's arm. Two almost floating staircases lead to a central area filled with screens and chairs. The floor is a translucent aqua. All the tables are made of black material with matching chairs that hang in the air. Everything has simple lines, giving the space a minimalist appearance. The room is made with levels coming from the center of the room, rising one level at a time. Each level has workstations all the way around.

Thomas places his hand on mine. I slowly release my grip, and our palms meet. "Come."

He gives my hand a little squeeze and starts to walk slowly down the steps. Everyone smiles and greets him as we pass, one screen after another. I cannot understand how he can remain so calm and unaffected by my anxiety. But then again, he is on his home turf. And perhaps he is used to types like me who are nervous and full of misgivings. I have to say that I am almost at the point of refusing to believe that he is real. I try to smile as we walk down the stairs looking at all the friendly faces. But my mouth feels so stiff; have I lost my ability to pretend that everything is fine?

My arm is gently guided as Thomas changes direction, heads toward one of the large screens, and pulls down a workstation from the ceiling. It simply hangs in the air with no support or cables. He touches the screen a few times, and then an image appears.

"This is your window." He looks at me gravely.

I look at the screen. A crashed plane. Ambulances. Fire engines. Spotlights are cutting through the darkness and illuminating the wreck. I stare questioningly at the screen without blinking. There is no sound, but I have a good idea what it would sound like.

My window? I manage to mumble to myself.

A child is crying. Suitcases with their contents are spread in all directions. Firefighters are slicing through the wreckage.

It gives me a start. I step right up to the screen and push my head forward like a vulture leaning toward its prey. A woman is lying on the ground. She has been flung out of the plane through a big hole in the wreck, and bits of her chair are strewn around her in pieces. The safety belt is still around her waist, and her body lies prone on the runway. I get right next to the screen and put my finger on the spot where the woman is... It is the woman who was sitting next to me on the flight. I recognize her red suit, although it is torn in several places. Her face is covered with scratches and blood.

Tears begin to run down my cheeks, and the lump in my throat swells hugely. I cannot feel my body; it is totally dead, no pain, no reaction, just tears burning my skin. The entire room and all the sounds around me seem to vanish, and all I can see is the image on the screen. I slowly take my finger off the screen and let my arm fall slack at my side. Tears drop onto my shirt, and my nose begins to run.

Thomas puts a hand on my shoulder, offering a tissue. He is standing right behind me like a solid rock.

"Thanks," there is hardly any sound in my stammering voice. I dry my nose and force myself to swallow a few times. I want to ask if that is real, but I don't dare because I am afraid that Thomas will think I am incredibly stupid or rebuff me. I am petrified that he will say that it is... real. I have to protect myself, hold myself together. The tissues are quickly soaked as I dry my eyes and nose. I am standing completely still like a living statue staring at the screen.

The image shifts and shows the other side of the wreck. There is the same level of activity. Ambulances are rushing away from the scene. People are running around in confusion with desperation in their eyes, searching for their loved ones. Children are screaming, but there is no sound. Smoke and fire come out of the wreckage, and the firemen are working hard to put it out. Airplane and body parts are strewn across a large area around the remains of the crashed airplane.

I cover my mouth with my hands. Thomas steps forward and stands right next to me. He is breathing calmly, and his gaze rests on me. I try to swallow, but my mouth has dried out.

None of the others in the room react to the images on the screen in front of me. They are all absorbed in their own business. The pictures on the screen are crystal clear, and the colors are so bright. Had it not been for the screen and the shifting angles, it is just like being there.

"What about me?" I finally manage to stutter, shifting my gaze briefly to Thomas and back. Before he can answer, the image shifts again and shows the interior of the plane. Rescue workers are treating an older man who is lying on the floor covered in blood. Seats are torn apart, and several windows are missing. A young rescue worker shakes his head and pulls a black blanket over the older man. The back end of the airplane was affected the worst. It must have crashed onto the ground first because there is almost nothing left of it. I can still make out the plane's structure up toward the front, but it is difficult.

"Can we zoom in?" I straighten up and turn resolutely toward Thomas.

He hands me a joystick. I look at it and try to focus. It reminds me of the first computer games in the eighties.

"You can use this to shift between images and zoom in and out and pan any way you like. If you press here, you can move the field of vision smoothly with this button." He moves his thumb on a button that is on the side.

I take the joystick; it is the first thing here that feels a little familiar. Quickly, I direct the area of vision toward the front of the plane. When I get to row 15, the seats are still intact. Fourteen, row thirteen is missing...

Thomas smiles at me. "A lot of airlines don't have a row 13 because people are superstitious."

Rows twelve, eleven, and ten are all gone, so are rows nine and eight. The outer seat in row seven is missing. That is where the woman in the red suit was sitting. All of what was once the roof is gone; the edges are torn into sharp points.

My hand begins to shake, and I tighten my grip on the joystick. I turn the field of vision to the left side of row seven. Thomas steps closer to me, and I can feel his body heat right next to me. He places his hand on the back of my neck, and warmth spreads down my back.

There I am...

It's like a blow to my stomach. The aqua floor rushes toward me. I just manage to put my hand in front of my face. My head jerks back, and my shoulder hits the cold floor instead. A scream tears open my chest, forced out of my body through my mouth. My hands are clenched so tightly that blood recedes from my fingers. I curl up on the floor like a fetus. Everything goes black, and I cover my face with my hands. I don't want to see anymore. I don't want to be here. Get me out of here; do something, anything.

My breath is heavy, and the sound of my scream takes over completely. I gasp for air. With every beat of my heart comes a stinging pain. The force behind the scream subsides, and I clasp my hands behind my neck. My body slumps as I start to cry. Thomas is sitting right next to me, perfectly calm. I can sense that he is there, but he does not intervene. Only small bits of air make their way to my lungs, and I keep gasping for more while I beat myself on the forehead. I don't understand a thing. How can this have happened? I am usually so blessed. Why has my good fortune deserted me?

How long I'm lying on the floor, I'm not sure. I want to run away but can't move. And I don't know where to run. Thomas places a hand on my shoulder, and I open my eyes again. My vision is blurred, and I dry my tears away with my sleeve and look back at the screen. The view is still inside the plane on row seven. Using all my willpower, I manage to put a hand on the floor and push myself up. I have to find my strength. There is no way I can give up now—I have to be there for Luke. The thought gives a rush in my chest.

At last, I find the power to reach out and take the joystick in my hands again. My hand is shaking, and I slowly put my finger on the button and zoom in on myself. Am I breathing? Am I dead? I look at Thomas questioningly.

"You're in a coma," he says serenely.

A few rescue workers are standing around me. They are conferring while pointing at me and making various gestures.

"They are afraid to move you because they do not know whether you have too many internal injuries. But they don't want to wait too long because you need treatment."

I'm not dead. I am in a coma. I AM NOT DEAD. I AM IN A COMA.

"But..." I hesitate, "I am here..." and look around the room. The images on the large screens on the walls shift—an urban scene, an empty beach full of litter from visitors, a woman carrying a child in her arms. No one in the room pays attention to the large screens or me except Thomas; they are all busy with their own lives. I feel the cold sensation from the floor on my skin and want to find a comfortable position, but nothing happens. Thomas grabs a chair and takes my hand as he helps me to get up. The chair is floating in the air and hardly moves as I sit. Right now, my brain can't comprehend anymore, and I have to focus on the screen.

A rescue woman comes into view; she is about my age. Her hair is short and dark, and the look in her brown eyes is very concentrated. She is carrying a blue stretcher. There are about six people around me, mostly young men in uniforms except for the rescue woman. They loosen the safety belt and take my pulse. The woman slowly bends forward and picks up a torn picture of me, Andreas, and Luke from the ground. Her finger brushes some of the dirt off it, allowing Luke's smile to shine through. Then she places the picture in my front pocket. Her hand reaches out for mine, and she gives it a gentle squeeze.

I feel nothing.

The rescuers look at each other and count to three and then lift me onto the stretcher. One keeps a finger on my pulse, and the others carry the sides of the stretcher. I follow them with the joystick. I want to see what happens. They lift me into the ambulance parked outside by the wreck, and the woman shuts the door from inside. The siren is turned on, and the ambulance drives off quickly from the scene of the accident.

Thomas strokes my hair gently and dries off the tears on my

cheek. I sink and let my head and shoulders fall forward. The chair somehow embraces my body.

"You are in between life and death," Thomas speaks calmly. "In-Between is a place where people come if they have left Earth before their time or if they are not ready to leave their lives there, but have been forced to, as in your case, because of an accident." He pauses and takes my hand that is cold and sweaty. "You could say that people get an extra chance here to continue their lives or to take leave properly." He looks right into my eyes, leaving me no other choice than to return his gaze. "We are a sort of reception and rest center," he says with a subdued and unhurried voice. "We receive people and give them the opportunity to continue at a suitable pace. It is important that people depart from their lives on Earth in a proper manner. Both for their own sakes but also for the sake of their loved ones."

My eyebrows are wrinkled, and I pull back my long hair. I don't believe in life after death! Slowly I exhale and raise my head. "I have a son named Luke. What about him? Does he know yet? He's with his father."

Thomas shakes his head, stands up slowly, and pushes a chair toward me. "The images you see are in real-time. It's been 45 minutes since the plane went down. The police are busy identifying those injured, so it will be a while before the relatives are notified. Your family will be among the first because you are still alive."

I hear what Thomas is saying, but I don't understand it. His words seep in, but they mean nothing to me. It is as if he is trying to convince me that this is all quite normal. The logical half of my brain has hit the wall. I push the chair back, a bit away from the screen. It rocks gently. A younger man sits down at the workstation to our right. He has round cheeks and thin, blond, spiky hair. He smiles at me, revealing his crooked teeth. I try to force a smile, but it doesn't come off.

"There's nothing you can do," Thomas looks at me. "You can observe, but you can't do anything."

"But..." I implore with my hands, "there must be a way that I can have some influence. I should have some say. I'm a mother." My voice is about to break.

"That is true, but right now, you aren't in a position to make any valid decisions regarding yours or Luke's life." Thomas shakes his head from side to side. "Right now, you are in between life and death." He reaches out and puts his warm, soft hands around mine.

"Yes, but..." I sigh and shrug my shoulders, letting go of his hands.

"I know that everything is overwhelming right now. There is a lot that you still don't know or understand." Thomas places a hand on my shoulder. "Let's go for a walk, so I can try to explain more about this place. Come." He stands up and helps me get to my feet.

The room seems smaller, and I can see people's faces more clearly. I notice a man with wrinkles that make deep lines across his forehead and a woman with dark glasses covering most of the top part of her face. They all look completely normal and absolutely real. My legs are tired. They feel like jelly, and I have to support myself on the table to keep my balance. For the first time in my life, I feel like I have to entrust all responsibility to another person and be confident that whatever will be will be. I feel like a piece in a game that I don't understand. It's as if someone has forgotten to tell me the rules, and I am being moved around without knowing what the game is all about.

We leave the control center through a different door than the one we entered. In fact, there are several doors, each with a different color —red, yellow, blue, and green. Everything is simple and stylish. It seems somewhat secretive or, more precisely, mystical. We enter another large room. I let my hand glide slowly across the wall, covered with a subtle, light veil of mist and hard without being solid. The chill from the wall makes me draw back my arm. My eyes try in vain to find a point to fix on, but there is no furniture, nothing. *Boring*, I think. They could have at least provided a chair so I could sit down.

The ceiling consists of a circle where all the walls meet and what looks like frosted glass in the middle of it. The silence is absolute. Thomas has gone over to the opposite wall. There are more tiny colored circles, and he put his finger on the blue one. A low humming noise starts, and the whole wall slides to the side. I take a step back.

"Come over here. It's perfectly safe." Thomas laughs and waves me over. Every move he makes seems so elegant, like an easy dance. His long blue tunic flows loosely as his muscular body turns.

I step forward carefully. There is definitely something strange about this floor. It is a bit springy, and no sound is produced when walking on it. The air in here is dry and feels very fine and pure. I try to act like I'm in control, bite my teeth together, and run my hand through my long hair. In my pocket, there is a hairband, and I pull my hair back in a ponytail.

Behind Thomas, an enormous closet appears, filled with shoes, shirts, jackets, pants, socks, gloves, and headgear.

"You should put on some other shoes." Thomas waves a pair of black boots. "Size eight and a half?" he asks appraisingly.

"Uh, yes, eight and a half." They look heavy and remind me of the high-tech walking boots that were in style in the 1990s. Thomas hands me the boots. They don't weigh a thing. I can't help but laugh but hold back when I realize he is looking at me. This is a strange place, and nothing is as I expect it to be. I bend to take off my sneakers and almost lose my balance. The room is spinning, and I place my fingertips on the floor.

"Wait." Thomas touches the red circle with his finger, and a section of the floor slides open, and two red chairs and a small black table appear. "Let's sit down for a minute."

Though its design appeared purely functional, the chair encloses my back, and I start to relax. It is soft and warm. I push off my shoes and put on the boots. They are made of a very soft, pliant material and fit perfectly. Thomas stands next to me, giving the impression that he has plenty of time.

"The shoes are made especially for outdoor wear so that you can stand firmly. We wouldn't want you to fall anywhere. You've had enough falling for a while." His smile is enchanting and makes me smile back. Our eyes meet, and I keep the contact much longer than I usually would. I'm not sure if he actually enjoys my company or is great at pretending that he does.

"Here, you'd better put on a jacket too. There's a very strong wind today." The jacket is bright red and ultramodern. It fits snugly and is deliciously silky smooth. I look around to see if there is a mirror. It would be nice to see how I look before we move on. But all I can see is the white moving walls.

Thomas offers a hand, "Hold on to me tightly." He has put on a long black coat with golden buttons down the front and long black boots with golden laces. Before I get a chance to wonder too much about his boots, a cold wind hits my skin. The wind plays with the golden straps that are braided over the shoulders of his coat and hang loose at the end.

We are walking on a white mass that feels firm enough to walk on, but the surface is constantly moving. On both sides, there is a kind of railing also made of the white mass. It is a kind of footbridge that links one unit to the next.

"Where are we?" I yell at Thomas.

He turns and smiles, the wind blowing his hair directly behind him. "Are you afraid of heights?"

"Afraid of heights?" I look down, and at first glance, there is nothing to see. This white mass is like a featherbed. It looks cozy, and I feel like touching it. I bend down to let my hand run through the white billowy air. It is cool and floats past my hand. It is hard not to grin because it is incredibly liberating to be outside in the fresh air. I fill my lungs until they can't take in any more air. As I stand up, a gulf opens up next to the footbridge, almost directly under me. It gives me a jolt, and I want to step back but fall over my own feet and try to regain my balance. My legs start to shake, and Thomas just manages to grab my arm before I fall on my bottom. He chuckles, implying with his laugh that he has seen many others do what I just did. I try my best to smile back at him. I don't want to come across as unsettled, but it is strained. The footbridge is gently swaying, and far, far below, I can catch a glimpse of something. It is—I rub my eyes and squint—it looks like.... No, it can't be. I lean carefully forward; yes, it is—land. Fields, houses, cars... I am slightly nearsighted, so I blink a couple of times and try to focus again. Land? I am seeing visions; how can it be land? I look over at Thomas. There is no reaction to see on his face—not even a fraction of surprise or fear. Thomas maintains one of his long and very patient silences, standing there with relaxed eyes and hands folded in front of his body, so annoyingly calm. At the same time, my brain works under high pressure, trying to find a way to categorize this experience. But no boxes fit, not even the one saying weird dreams. My eyebrows are so puckered that it hurts. "I..." The fresh air fills my lungs to the point of bursting, and my eyes tighten. "I don't understand. Are we up in the clouds?"

Thomas nods serenely. "That is exactly right. In-Between is located in the clouds. Haven't you ever wondered what was inside the clouds and what they feel like?" He smiles at me as the wind blows his long hair in front of his eyes.

I lean slightly forward and look down again. "But..." I shake my head and clench my teeth. There must be a logical explanation.

"You can walk on the clouds because you are wearing those boots." Thomas points and smiles mischievously. "I would strongly advise you not to go outside without them on." He winks at me and then looks down at Earth to make his point.

I look at Thomas in all seriousness. "Listen. I don't believe in life after death! And..."

Thomas looks mysteriously at me. "Since when has it been a question of belief?"

I hold my head still and pull a face. Point taken.

"And you are not dead, are you?" He keeps looking at me with this intriguing look in his eyes that makes me insecure but warm inside.

"No, but..." I hold back and kick some of the white clouds that have surrounded my feet. It's morning, and the sun is rising above the horizon. I feel closer to it, and the bright orange and red penetrate my body. "Does that mean that we're constantly moving?" I turn my head and look at Thomas questioningly.

"Yes. We are a floating unit. When we're on autopilot, we just drift along, but we can also choose to steer. Up here, we have an overview of the whole planet. In the control center, you saw that we could tune in everywhere in the world."

A loud rumbling sound is rapidly approaching.

"Hold on." Thomas takes my hand and puts it around the railing. Suddenly, a large airplane flies through the cloud in front of us and is heading our way. I grip my hands tightly around the railing and crouch down as I hide my face behind my arm. The cloud we are standing on moves aside so fast that it makes my long hair rise in all directions. The airplane cruises past us, and the noise recedes into the distance.

"Can I let go now?" I spit some strands of hair out of my mouth and rise again.

Thomas nods. "Yes, it's gone now."

"What would have happened if it had hit us?" My voice is trembling.

Thomas leans nonchalantly against the railing as if nothing is more ordinary than a jumbo jet passing by. "Nothing. It can be a little distracting, but in principle, nothing actually happens."

My head is spinning as I'm struggling to understand this last bit of information when I hear someone addressing Thomas from behind. I turn to see a man in his early twenties. He is chubby, and his shirt is untucked. He approaches us rapidly, out of breath.

"Thomas, they need you." He trips over his own feet, and two deep dimples appear on his cheeks when he smiles at me.

THE LIFE

Thomas nods to the man and then turns toward me. "I have to go, but I'll come back soon. This is John."

John waves at me as he keeps smiling.

"He can show you to your room. Try to see if you can get some sleep. A lot has happened to you. Your inner self is working at full throttle."

I don't know whether to laugh or cry. A feeling of being left, abandoned, and rejected at the same time flows through me.

"Come." John stands next to me, fidgeting and still panting. "I'll show you where you are going to stay."

I feel Thomas's hand on my arm, and he pulls me softly toward him and hugs me. My body is stiff. I am not used to getting close hugs, and Thomas keeps standing there with his arms around me. It's not that kind of hug with three pats on the back, and then it's finished. I try to relax but find myself stiff as a stick. Finally, Thomas slowly releases his embrace, puts his hand in his pocket, and brings up a little round device. It's about the size of the palm of my hand and three-quarters of an inch thick.

"This is a transmitter and a sort of computer." He holds it between his index finger and thumb. "As long as you have this, I can always find you, and if you want to reach me, just press this button." He points to the side of the device. "It does other things as well. You can use it as a telephone, a camera, and a music player, for instance. We call it a Skycon."

He hands me the Skycon, and I turn it around to examine it. It's weightless and made out of a material I can't recognize. The surface is kind of black but still a bit transparent.

"Don't hesitate to contact me. If you need me, just call. And if I don't hear from you, I'll come by in a couple of hours. But please try to relax. That will make everything easier. All right?" Thomas leans his head a tiny bit to the side, his eyebrows are so straight and narrow, and there is no sign of age on his face. I nod with my lips pressed together and force a little smile. Thomas leaves, and I am standing alone next to John. I can feel the tears coming but turn to prevent John from seeing them.

"That's all right." John glances shyly and avoids much eye contact. "Just take it easy. I was new here once too, so I know how it is." He looks toward the clouds hanging on the horizon. "I cried for days and struggled against everything that I was told. I refused to come to terms with being here and not having any say in the matter."

"Everything is so...." I stammer.

"And more. But it's all going to be okay. Let's go find your room." He raises his eyes and glances at me briefly. "This way..." He takes the lead.

We walk across the footbridge. The wind bites at my jacket, and I support myself on the railing. From here, all the houses beneath us look like dollhouses with toy cars moving around. It is like watching a fantasy world from above. But the funny thing is that down there is real, and I'm in the fantasy part. A sliding door captures my attention as it opens in front of us, slowly and silently.

John touches the green circle inside the hallway with a short chubby finger. In a matter of seconds, the wall slides aside. We enter a small, bright room with a lot of numbers and letters on one wall. 1-10A, 1-10B, C, D, E. My eyes run across the numbers and letters.

"You are in the A section." There is not much room here, and John backs into a corner. The door closes slowly, and it startles me, so I bump into John.

After a few seconds, a part of the wall moves aside, and we step into a long hallway. On one side are large, oblong windows, and on the other side, small circles and screens are placed at regular intervals as a part of the wall. The floor is light in color and material, and a thin red line runs the length of it under the windows. John must be familiar with this place because he does not even look out the windows but just continues purposefully. The view outside the big windows makes me walk closer to the wall. We are hanging and floating in thin air. As far as I can see, there are only clouds like a majestic landscape.

"You will be staying here in number 110," John says as we reach the end of the hallway. "You use your fingerprint as a key—just put your finger in this circle. If there are any messages for you, they will appear on the screen." He avoids eye contact and looks down.

The screen is soft and gives in slightly when I touch it. The words "Welcome, Eva" appear.

John wets his lips and looks at the ceiling. "I'm sure you have a lot of questions, and you will definitely get the answers. Save them for now, though. The best advice I can give you at the moment is just to stay calm." He puts his hands in his pockets.

I look at the screen and place my finger inside the green circle. The door glides open. A room much larger than I anticipated appears in front of me, and I step tentatively inside, holding onto the doorframe. The room is simple. Sunlight shines on one wall, making a reddish half circle. On the right side is a bed. I take another step inside the room. I turn toward John; he is waving at me as the door slides shut in front of him.

"Thank you..." I manage to say before he is gone. The bed is practically floating in the air, and I bend down to see whether anything is holding it up, but there isn't. I can't help but smile. At the end of the room is a window with a view that stretches to infinity. Next to the window are a table and chair also floating in the air. On the table is something that looks like a folder.

"Welcome, blah, blah... Eating: There are several places to eat in In-Between; the largest one is the café which you can find using the map feature on your Skycon. You are also welcome to order in; here are a few suggestions for meals... You place the order on the screen in the closet, and the meal will appear within seconds."

I definitely have to try it out. A bit further down, it says: Washing, you can place your dirty laundry in the basket in the closet, and fresh new clothes will be replaced in your cupboard the following day.

That sounds great. I wonder if I don't have to clean either; it's hard not to smile at the thought.

I take another step forward and catch sight of more small circles on a wall to the left. My fingers are itching to push all of the rings, but my eyes are so tired that I can hardly hold them open, and my feet hurt. With a sigh, I recline on the bed, which is soft and airy. My eyes close slowly, and I inhale deeply as I sink into the bed. My body yields to the mattress, and I vanish into oblivion.

3

THE NOTIFICATION

The doorbell rings. Andreas instinctively looks at the clock on the wall in the kitchen. Who comes to the door at seven in the morning?

"I'll get it," Luke calls from his room, where he was playing with his LEGO knights before leaving for Kindergarten. Small steps are heard in the hallway and fumbling with the lock.

"No, no, I'll do it," Andreas says, drying his hands and rushing out of the kitchen. He doesn't want his son to get in the habit of answering the door for anyone who would knock this early. As he gets to the front entrance, Andreas can see two uniformed men through the door's glass panes. Luke has gone back to his room and collects some knights he wants to play with in the living room. Andreas opens the front door tentatively.

"Good morning, Mr. Lancaster," says the older of the two. "We're sorry to show up unannounced at this time of day."

Andreas looks from one officer to the other and back again. He looks them over as he leans against the half-open door and nods slowly, without replying. The older officer is bold and has a scar above his left eye. The younger has a buzz cut and seems uncomfortable, holding his hands firmly on his back.

It's my mother, Andreas thinks. Though he hasn't spoken to her in a very long time, one of Andreas's cousins recently mentioned that his mother is very ill.

"May we come in?" The older officer leans slightly forward and gestures toward the door with his arm.

Not realizing until that point that he's been blocking the way, Andreas steps aside. "Yes, of course."

The older officer extends his hand to Andreas as he passes. "Peter Taylor."

Andreas shakes the officer's hand and introduces himself, though the men obviously already know who he is. The younger officer says that his name is Josh Black and avoids eye contact. Andreas looks from one officer to the other. He wishes they would just get this business, whatever it is, over with in the hallway. But the officers don't seem inclined to say anything while they stand there. Finally, he gestures them toward the living room, stepping over LEGOs, toy cars, plastic dragons, and a variety of other playthings he'd been too tired to pick up after Luke last night.

"Sorry for the mess," he says as he pushes a path clear. He must be quite a sight, barefoot and still wearing his striped pajamas. His tall, slim body seems thinner in the loose clothes, and his gray hair is sticking up randomly.

"Can I get you anything?" He looks from one officer to the other.

"No, thanks," reply the two officers simultaneously.

Luke comes in at that point, stares at the officers for a moment with moderate interest, and then starts playing with his toys. Within seconds, he has immersed himself in some drama involving knights and trolls. Andreas directs the officers to the sofa, and the men sit with straight backs and their hands resting on their knees. The living room is not that big. A couch, chair, table, and TV just fit in. On the wall behind the officers hangs several pictures of Luke, Eva, and Andreas together.

Now, can we just deal with this, Andreas thinks as he sits in a chair across from the men and looks briefly at his watch. He has his first appointment in his clinic at nine. Just then, Luke turns away from his battlefield and announces that he is thirsty. His blond hair has grown a bit long and reaches down over his blue eyes.

"Excuse me," Andreas looks at the officers and nods in the direction of Luke. "Just a second, and I'll be right back." He goes into the kitchen that is right next to the living room. "What would you like to drink, Luke?"

"Milk." Luke is distracted by a troll that is sneaking up on one of his noblemen.

Andreas takes a glass from the dishwasher, opens the fridge with a tug, and pours the milk into the glass so hurriedly that it spills onto the table. "Damn. Stupid carton," he mumbles to himself and dries the glass off with his sleeve. On his way back, he hands the milk to Luke and sits down again. "Please, go ahead." He nods at the officers.

Taylor inches forward slightly on the sofa and speaks in a firm, somber voice. "We have some difficult news about your ex-wife."

"Eva?" Andreas begins to bite the nail on his thumb. A shudder he hadn't anticipated runs through his body. He glances swiftly at Luke, who seems in another world entirely, and then back at the officers.

"The plane she was on last night crashed." Taylor rocks back and forth slightly and rubs his hands together.

Andreas stares at the officers. He hears the words, but it is like they won't connect to reality. The room starts to tilt. "Eva..." He can't seem to find a suitable grimace.

"She's alive, but she's in a coma." Taylor forces the words out without any feelings attached. Still, small drops of sweat appear on his upper lip.

Andreas can barely make out the words the officer is saying. He opens his mouth to speak, but no sound comes out. At that moment, the living room feels confined and as if there is no air left to breathe.

"She was taken to St. Jude's Hospital last night," Taylor continues with a calm and almost collected voice. "The plane crashed at 3:58 a.m. It is too early to say more about her condition. When you get to the hospital, the doctors will be able to tell you more. Counseling is available. You can ask about it at St. Jude's. They'll take care of everything." He wipes his upper lip and pulls down his uniform.

Andreas makes eye contact with the older officer and looks at him as though seeing him for the first time. "Yes, okay…" Eva is in a coma. What does that mean? Will she be awake in a couple of days, or is it more serious, one of those cases where the person lingers in this state for years? He can't cope with the thought of losing Eva and shifts focus. His mind flashes on the conversation they'd had that spelled out the beginning of the end for them. Eva had wanted a brother or sister for Luke, and Andreas knew he didn't have the energy for another child. The crestfallen look in Eva's eyes haunts him now.

"Dad, I'd like some granola for breakfast, okay?" Luke's words cut into Andreas's thoughts, and he looks over at his boy. Luke is sprawled on his stomach, surrounded by fantasy figures. Many warriors have fallen, and the good ones are close to victory.

"Sure. Can you get it yourself?" Andreas sits utterly still and looks blankly into the air.

"No, I want you to do it," Luke replies instantly.

Andreas stands and turns to the officers. "I'm sorry, but we have to get on with our day. If there's nothing else, I'll see you to the door."

The two officers stand and straighten their uniforms in unison. "Just introduce yourself at St. Jude's reception. They already have your name and will be ready for you when you arrive." Peter reaches for Andreas's hand.

"Fine. I'll go there right after I drop off Luke at Kindergarten."

"We can find our way out. You have enough to see to." Josh offers Andreas his hand, which is slightly sweaty.

"By the way," Peter has reached the hallway but turns around. "We've tried to find Eva's other relatives but haven't been able to. Do you happen to have her parents' telephone number?"

"I have Eva's mother's number. I can tell her myself."

"I'll note that in the report."

"Bye, Luke." Josh watches Luke, engrossed in a decisive battle, and only gets a preoccupied wave in response.

The sound of the front door closing makes Andreas drop onto the sofa, leaning his head back and closing his eyes. He fills his lungs with air and sits motionless. Why Eva? Just when everything is going somehow smoothly, and Luke has accepted that his parents live separately. Damn it. He kicks a toy car on the floor, so it takes off and bumps into the sofa's wooden leg, leaving a small mark. Why does she have to travel so often? Can't she just stay at home? He sighs deeply and rubs his eyes. None of the stories he has heard in his career as a psychologist compares to being the main character in a drama. He bends forward to take a sip of the coffee that's on the table and spits it out again. It is cold. "Damn coffee," he mumbles and pushes it away, so it spills on the table.

"Daaad. I'm hungry!" Luke's tone of voice leaves no room for doubt that he means it.

Andreas sits still, closing his eyes and willing himself to avoid letting Luke see the turmoil running through him. He refuses to allow himself to think about Luke losing his mother before his fifth birthday. Tomorrow. Eva is strong. He knows better than anyone that she is a fighter. If anyone can emerge from something as dire as this, she can.

"Dad! I *am* hungry!" Luke's thin voice is strained and cuts through the room.

Andreas slowly rises from the sofa. "I know; I know." He goes into the kitchen. "What do you want to eat?"

"I already told you—granola. Can I have some?" Luke tosses the knights aside and throws himself onto the sofa.

"Coming right up." Andreas absently pours the cereal and adds milk. His eyes are empty. Everything around him has a feel of unreality. It is simply that he can't believe his ex-wife's plane has crashed in the middle of the night; it is that he can't believe that even simple things like getting his son breakfast are possible right now. When he comes back to the living room, Luke is fiddling with the remote control.

"I want to see the one with the knights and the wizard." He turns on the television.

An image of devastation fills the screen. Ambulance lights cast red shadows over the scene. "It is not yet known whether any of the victims will survive," says a female voice-over.

Andreas rushes to the sofa, tossing the granola on the coffee table with such disregard that the cereal spills over. "Luke, this is not—"

"Look, an ambulance." Luke hops on the sofa excitedly.

"Give me the remote." Andreas reaches his hand toward Luke.

Andreas's only concern at that moment is changing the channel. What if they somehow flash on an image of Eva? It will be tough enough to break this news to Luke; he doesn't want the morning news to do it for him. Andreas finds the show Luke wants to watch and settles on the sofa as knights and wizards start their television battle. Rain is pounding on the living room windows. The sky outside has darkened entirely, and the only light in the room comes from the screen. Andreas pulls his son close to him, wrapping an arm around his thin shoulders. He reaches out for his coffee and takes a sip, only to realize that it is still cold.

"I'll let you watch the whole thing today, even though it's going to make you late. But then you need to get dressed and get to Kindergarten."

Luke's eyes are riveted to the TV. "Be quiet, Dad. I can't hear anything."

Andreas hugs Luke tighter, which causes him to wriggle. After watching the first ten minutes, he gets up and goes into the kitchen to pack lunch. Right now, the best thing to do is to make the morning seem as familiar as possible. He grabs his laptop and cancels his first three appointments of the day, and then reaches for his cell phone. He might be able to reach Eva's mother while Luke is preoccupied. Her phone rings and rings, but no one answers. She probably left her cell in the house; she always does that when working in the garden.

Andreas comes into the living room just as the closing credits are showing. He goes over and turns off the television, tossing some clothes to Luke.

"Time to get dressed, young man."

"Why do I have to do it myself?"

"Because you're a big boy who is going to be five years old tomorrow."

Luke stands up unwillingly and puts on his clothes. "What's happened to Mom?"

The truth. Andreas ought to tell the truth, but he doesn't know what the truth is right now. He picks up Luke's shirt.

"Here, let me help you." He pauses, takes a deep breath, and runs his hand through Luke's soft blond hair. "I don't know what's happened with your mother, but I will tell you as soon as I know more. Is that a deal?"

The shirt slides over Luke's head, and he nods.

4

HOPE

The drive to the hospital seems unusually long—as if there is more traffic, and everyone is driving slower than usual. Andreas is driving the car in silence. Typically, the radio would be playing, or he'd be talking on the phone, but not today. He is absorbed in his thoughts and stares blankly out the windshield. The autopilot is turned on, and the other drivers just seem like extras in a film.

A tear runs down his cheek, which he hurriedly dries off. He moved into Eva's apartment shortly after they met, and they were always together after that. At the time, he only had five boxes of belongings. Eva wouldn't stop making fun of him about that. Her apartment was full of all the newest gadgets and electronics, many of them he didn't even know the purpose of. She got that from her trips around the world. He fell in love with her instantly and very, very hard. He admired her strength, but even more a little-seen part, the sensitive and feminine part that only came out on the rare occasions when she felt comfortable enough to let all her defenses down.

Andreas smiles at the thought of her as he shifts into fourth gear. She was completely the opposite of him: outgoing, driven, and insatiably social. Andreas preferred to stand in the background, observing.

Glimpses of the huge apartment they moved to after Eva quit her job in television comes back to him. Her furniture disappeared in the apartment's big white rooms with stucco ceilings. For many years, he didn't know what he wanted to do in life, and it was only because so many people told him he was a great listener that he decided to educate himself. He graduated as a psychologist at the age of thirty-eight, six months before he met Eva. So, they lived on her savings and the occasional work he got as a consulting psychologist. The arrangement turned Eva's world upside down; she was a firmly established journalist with a promising career ahead of her. She told him that the TV station's CEO said that she would one day be his successor. But they wanted a life different from the one they could lead when she was in such a high-profile media position.

He turns the corner and speeds up a little, overtaking a small red car with an older woman with a tight, bright yellow scarf tied around her head and enormous dark glasses behind the wheel.

It was in that huge apartment that they started a new business together. They combined their expertise in their respective fields to create a life coaching business that could help people and businesses reach their goals. Eva drew on her experience as a journalist and her ability to always accomplish what she put her mind to, and Andreas contributed his professional knowledge. She worked day and night, trying to get publicity and people attending the seminars they created. Andreas would sit opposite her, listening to all her ideas while playing a solitaire game on the computer, its screen hidden from Eva's gaze.

The light goes red, and he stops abruptly.

He kept lots of things hidden from her—mostly his ambivalence about the venture that so excited Eva. Andreas admitted that the seminars were a good idea, but they required a commitment and discipline that he didn't possess or couldn't find. Or wouldn't make an effort to find, Andreas thought, remembering.

When he thinks of Eva, he feels that he has grown as a person—more tolerant, perhaps even more decisive. Eva taught him how to live out his passion, at least on occasion. They'd hardly had an easy relationship; they argued often and regularly seemed on the verge of breaking up. Yet before they knew it, they had spent two years together, and Eva was pregnant with Luke. From there, they slowly started to drift apart.

He moves his hand over his stubble, pulling a hair, so it stings. An angry driver's horn blasts startle Andreas. The light has turned green while he's been lost in thought. He makes an apologetic gesture with his hand to the driver behind him and mumbles. "Would you relax?"

Three more traffic lights, and then he's at the hospital. The last time he was here was when Luke was born.

"Eva isn't dead," Andreas speaks in a low voice as he gently tugs his hair. He knows that the doctor's report will probably not be very encouraging.

The last thing to do is to find a parking space. He drives toward the main entrance and hopes to find a spot near it. That was another thing he adopted from Eva. She always made a competition out of getting a parking spot as close to an entrance as possible. Now, he does it too. It has begun to rain again, and he is just not in the mood to get wet. *Yes!* Someone pulls out of a space near the door just as he turns the corner. He focuses on the tangible. First, park the car. Then find someone who can tell him where Eva is and what her condition is.

He turns off the engine, takes the keys out of the ignition, bends forward, and sighs. The rain is pounding on the windshield, and Andreas looks out through the drops. He is alone, completely alone. It is a sharp contrast to the day that Luke was born, and they were going home together like a happy little family. It was Luke's first day in the real world. This moment feels anything but real. That day had been the best day he'd ever shared with Eva. And even though they'd split permanently, he'd anticipated sharing many special times with her in the future as Luke grew. Now, he wasn't even sure if they'd share another word.

Inside, the hospital is filled with people. All the chairs are taken in the reception area, and people have settled on the floor. A nurse comes running past, and a woman is crying. Andreas heads directly to the reception desk. The woman sitting behind it is in her mid-fifties and is wearing red glasses and a light green shirt under her white uniform with the light blue St. Jude's logo on the chest. She looks at him and smiles.

"Who are you looking for?"

"Eva Monroe" His voice is nervous, and he hopes that he will be informed that there has been a mistake and that Eva has not been admitted. The woman leafs through the lists on her desk, occasionally glancing at a computer screen. All the lists are filled with names, including many that have been crossed off. Some of the names have comments beside them, but Andreas can't read them upside down.

He looks around the reception area. There is a swarm of people, and their conversations produce a constant drone. Most of them look somewhat confused.

"She's in intensive care. Go down that hall over there and turn left at the end. Ask for the attending surgeon when you get there. His name is Dr. Johnson."

"All right. Thank you," he says, not sure if he means it.

She is on the list.

This is real.

Andreas walks briskly and purposefully down the hallway. His gaze is fixed firmly in front of him. He puts his hands in his brown anorak pocket and finds a coin that he repeatedly turns over in his hand.

Am I going to be a single father? Can I handle that?

The nervousness makes him walk faster. He was forty when he

became a father, and even though it is wonderful, there are also moments when he feels dejected and inadequate. It is good to have Eva to lean on. Women seem to be somehow born with a motherly instinct that comes forth when giving birth to a child; something opens up inside them. He doesn't have it, but he's doing the best he can. Every bit of parenthood took so much effort from him. If he truly has to have full responsibility for Luke...

Andreas is unable to complete the thought.

In the hallway, stretchers are being wheeled back and forth, doctors are rushing, and people are sitting and crying. The atmosphere is frenzied. Everything seems unreal—like entering an animated world where he doesn't belong.

He stops at the entrance of the intensive care unit and looks through the window. He waits and takes a deep breath before pulling the cord that opens the doors. He has never been in the intensive care unit before. There is a discomforting silence—a glaring contrast to the activity level he came across in the hallways.

Andreas looks around searchingly to find someone who can help him.

"Excuse me," he says to a gray-haired woman who is sitting with her back to him, filling out some forms. She turns around and looks up. Her wrinkled face has friendly eyes.

"I'm looking for Dr. Johnson." Their eyes meet. The hallway is empty, the pictures on the wall hang a bit crooked, and several used cups are on a small round three-legged table. He tucks his hands back into the pockets of his jacket and flips the coin.

"He's at the end of the ward. What do you want to see him about?" She smiles kindly as if it is just another day at the office.

"My ex-wife is supposed to be in this department. She was on the plane that crashed this morning." He tenses the muscle in his jaws.

"Just a moment. Please, wait here while I get him." She disappears down the long hallway. Andreas paces back and forth while biting his thumbnail all the way down. On the wall hangs a bin full of used napkins, and on the floor, there is a circle where the colors have been worn off by the people before Andreas who have waited in despair.

Eventually, he sees the woman coming back, walking next to a man in his fifties. He is tall, fit, and is wearing his rectangular glasses propped on his forehead.

"Dr. Johnson, I presume." Andreas leaves the circle and extends his hand.

"Yes, I am the attending surgeon of this department and have received all the victims from this morning's crash." Dr. Johnson has a firm grip and speaks rather frenziedly in a deep voice.

Andreas nods and remains silent.

"And you are...?" Dr. Johnson pushes his glasses a bit higher on his forehead. His eyes wander from Andreas toward some other people who have taken over the circle down the hallway.

"Oh, sorry. I'm Andreas Lancaster. My ex-wife, Eva Monroe, was on the flight."

Dr. Johnson smiles warily at him and indicates a door further down the hall. "Let's sit in there for a minute. If you'd like a cup of coffee or anything, then you can get it over there. I need to check on a couple of other patients first."

"A strong cup of coffee would be great." Andreas tries to smile but fails.

The doctor disappears down the hallway, and he steps into an alcove and pours a cup of coffee in the last remaining clean paper cup. The smell is comforting, and he sighs. Dragging his feet over the floor, he enters the office.

The walls are pale gray, a couple of colorful abstract paintings are hung on the wall to the right, and there's a sofa in the far corner. He walks over to the window and notices that the windowsill's paint is beginning to flake off. It's still raining, and the dark clouds are overlapping with each other. It doesn't look like it will clear up today. He takes off his jacket and throws it on the armrest of the sofa. His shirt has significant wet stains under his arms.

"Have a seat." Dr. Johnson gestures toward the chair at the desk and brings a chair from the hallway for himself. The door closes with a creak behind him, and the bare walls seem to reinforce the silence. Had it not been for the window without bars, it would have been more reminiscent of a prison cell. The doctor glances down at a long list of names and turns a couple of pages before he looks up at Andreas and tries to find a pleasant expression.

"There is a lot to keep track of today. Let me try to give you a summary of the situation."

Andreas leans back, eager to find a comfortable position. The chair is both hard and worn out. It must have carried too many broken hearts. He sits still, trying to breathe softly.

"The airplane that Eva was on crashed at 03:58 this morning. A powerful bolt of lightning struck it, and all the engines failed. The pilot was forced to attempt an emergency landing. It was partially successful." Dr. Johnson clears his throat and takes a sip of water. "I have been informed that the circumstances were extremely unfortunate because normally, only one or two engines would fail." He shrugs his shoulders and adjusts his glasses. "The plane landed so that the back of it hit the ground at high speed, and most people in that section died instantly. Many people were flung out of the plane, and parts of the plane were scattered over a quarter of a mile. Eva was the only person in her row who survived; the other survivors were seated in some of the first rows. Some had only bruises, and others were more seriously injured." He pauses and swallows.

Andreas is stroking his stubble intensely. He looks out the window, but there is no comfort to be found.

"Maybe you've already been told that Eva is in a coma."

Andreas looks back at the doctor and crosses his legs and arms. Rain starts to hit the window with a loud noise that drowns all his thoughts.

"At present, we can't say if she's going to make it. We are examining her for internal injuries and...."

Andreas straightens up quickly and makes a despairing gesture with his arms. "What does your experience tell you? You must be able to say something?"

Dr. Johnson shakes his head slightly. "Every person is unique. It could go either way. In part, it depends on whether she chooses to fight her way back or if she gives up. We can't say anything more at this point." By the tone of his voice, he gives Andreas the impression that he wants to get this over with.

"Eva is a strong soul, and she loves life...." Andreas goes over to the window and leans against the window frame. "She *knows* that Luke, our son, needs her." He turns and looks earnestly at the doctor. "She won't leave him. If she has a choice, she'll fight her way back. Eva is very close to Luke. They've always had a special connection. Would it help to bring him here?"

Dr. Johnson frowns. "It is very intense for a boy to see his mother in a coma. How old is he?" He flips through the papers.

"Four, he will turn five tomorrow." Andreas toys with the half-dead plant on the windowsill. He pulls a dead leaf off and crushes it in his fist.

"Hmm. It's your decision. If you think that he can handle it, then it could help bring Eva back." Dr. Johnson pushes his glasses further up on his forehead. "If she doesn't make it, it would be the last image that Luke has of his mother. That is a decision only you can make. I can't help you with that."

Andreas puts his hand on the window frame for support and looks up at the sky. Still black, and now, there are also a few flashes of lightning on the horizon.

The doctor looks steadily at Andreas. "Eva can't breathe on her own, so she's on a respirator. At some point, we'll check to see if she can begin to breathe on her own. But there are still many unknown factors."

There is a draft by the window, and Andreas heads for the sofa and slowly sits down while he continues to listen. He wants to ask so many questions but can't think of any. The sofa is just as hard and uncomfortable as it looks.

Dr. Johnson straightens up in his chair, lets his glasses fall to his nose, and looks down at the papers in front of him. "Do you have any more questions?"

Andreas winces slightly at the doctor's sharp tone, a tone that leaves no opening for further conversation. He takes a deep breath and finally finds a question to ask. "How long can a person remain in a coma?" Without thinking of it, he fidgets with his stubble.

The doctor crosses his arms and leans back. "That's a good question. In my experience, there is some kind of shift after six weeks. I can't explain it, but the physique often changes after that point." He shrugs. "But we have had some patients who have been in a coma for longer periods and have still come out of it. Some come out of a coma after a few hours, and others can lie there for years. It also depends on whether the body can function on its own."

He pulls out a watch from his pocket and flips it open. He throws a glance at it and puts Eva's file on the table between them. "If you can think of any objects that are meaningful for Eva, you're welcome to bring them here and arrange the room to your liking."

Andreas takes a sip of his coffee, which is tepid and weak, but at least it has some warmth to it.

"This department of the hospital operates somewhat differently than the rest, as what we do here is so extreme." He writes a few comments in the file and ticks off a few bullet points.

"How many survived the crash?" Andreas's hands brush firmly across his stubble.

"Thirteen."

"Out of how many?" He clears his throat and raises his voice.

"Four hundred and eighteen. Most were brought here to St. Jude's, as we have the best crisis facilities, but all hospitals in the area have received patients. We have seven in intensive care. The rest are spread out in different departments." Dr. Johnson takes a deep breath and holds it for a moment. The rain keeps beating against the window. The light from the ceiling doesn't offer much clarity as it is covered in a lampshade made of what was once white glass now covered with insects. "I have to warn you that Eva has a number of injuries on her face and body. They will heal with time. Her body is functioning relatively normally. She is fed food and liquids through a tube, and the first series of tests don't show anything critically wrong." The doctor maintains eye contact with Andreas. "...But we need to wait a bit longer for the results from some of the tests before I can say more. Her body seems to be robust."

Andreas starts to bite a nail on another finger. "Yes, Eva has always been physically fit, and she plays many sports." That couldn't be said about Andreas. Eva tried so many times to persuade him to come running with her. She never succeeded. It was as if he was glued to the couch if he sat down. Eva's willpower made her run in all kinds of weather. He always admired that so much and wished he could have borrowed some.

"That will benefit her now." Dr. Johnson smiles, and his eyes liven up. "Should we go in to see her now, or is there anything else you'd like to ask?"

"No, there isn't. Let's go see her." Andreas grabs his jacket and follows the doctor. As long as there is hope, he will do everything he can to bring Eva back, for Luke's sake.

And for his own.

5

MY NEW HOME

I wake with a start and raise my head.

Where am I? My eyes search the room—white walls, no pictures, a desk, clouds...

In-Between.

As the words come back to me, I realize this is not a dream. I fall back onto the pillow and notice that I am still wearing my clothes. Now, I remember...

My new boots.

Thomas!

I remember it all.

There is no way I'm getting up now. I want to rest some more. My body is heavy and sore in places I didn't know it was possible to notice. I pull the quilt over my head, and everything is dark. It feels safer under the covers; the world seems smaller, and now I can take it all in. I can feel the warmth spread, and the air becomes thick. Sometimes, it is best just to stay in bed and let the world take care of itself. Perhaps everything will go away again, or they will forget about me if I just keep lying here.

I still don't know much about this place in the clouds, and I'm not sure I want to know much more. I just want to go home. Even though it hurts a bit, I let one arm out from the quilt and reach for my pants, fumbling my way into the pocket. It's empty. I forgot; the photo of Luke is not here.

A prickly sensation arises in my heart, and I try to shift my attention away from it. I clench my teeth, so it hurts. Maybe I should go back to the control room and see if I can tune in to see how he is doing. I wonder if he has been told about the crash and already knows that I will not pick him up from Kindergarten today. The present I bought him was probably scattered to the winds when the plane went down. I kick the quilt to get some air in, wondering how long I've been sleeping—did I sleep through the night, or is it still the same day that I arrived? An insistent pain runs through my body every time I move, reminding me that In-Between is for real.

With my right hand, I cautiously fold back the quilt just enough to look out and see the ceiling. It is white, just like almost everything else here. Things are simple and well-arranged without seeming clinical or sterile. On the contrary, it is actually quite calm and cozy here. I wonder where all the others are. It's so quiet; there are no sounds to be heard. The quilt envelops my body, and the pillow supports my head and neck in a very gentle way.

The sunlight starts to pour into the room in quick flashes; it must be daytime or at least morning. I turn onto my side and see clouds breezing past my window. Crazy! Like something in a bedtime story I would make up and tell Luke. Unfortunately, I'm in it. It's not made up. And I'm not sure that my imagination would go this far either.

The room is smaller than I first perceived, but it seems spacious because there is not much furniture. I can see some sort of folder on the table next to a lavish bouquet. The folder is black and extremely thin. Maybe there is some paper inside it like there usually is in hotel rooms, so I can make a list of practical things I need to do and jot down a few questions.

I lift my head from the pillow and am reminded of the stiffness in my neck. On the wall opposite me, I catch sight of the red, blue, and green circles, which are the only things that interrupt the white surface.

With discomfort in every part of my body, I sit up. It's a wonderful bed, wide, soft, and firm, inviting enough to spend the whole day in it. I fill my lungs with the thin air and rub my eyes as I ease my legs to the edge of the bed and place my feet on the pale floor. It's warm.

Slowly, I walk over to the table and put my hand on it to support myself when my legs suddenly give way. There are clouds above and below me, and I tighten my grip on the edge of the table. I pull out the chair with a firm tug; it is slender and made of fibrous material. I open the folder on the table and skim the top sheet of paper, reading aloud to myself. Welcome, general information, no television, no computer games, no fun. What do they do here? I shake my head, slam the folder shut, and push it to the back of the table. This place seems more like a prison than a hotel.

I turn to the wall with the buttons, ignoring my body's attempt to scream at me. My fingers glide over the red circle. Part of the wall slides aside, and a smaller room appears behind it. It seems like a hallway and is just as simple as the room I'm in. There are some more circles on the wall inside, but no furniture. At the end of the room is a tall oblong window that faces infinity. I stare, and my vision stretches.

Next to the red circle is a green circle. I let my finger glide over it, and it opens the closet. How incredibly organized. All of the clothes are my size. "They are well-prepared," I say to myself, carefully holding back a grin. I run my hand over a row of dresses, jackets, pants, and shirts; the different fabrics are pleasing to my touch. There are shoes and belts as well. I can't help but smile at how much they seem to know about me. There is a whole shelf with sunglasses and another one with watches. My hand runs over the surface of the watches, examining them. One in the back catches my eye. It is white with a circle of crystals around the edge. I pick it up and put it on my wrist. It suits me. The time is ten past ten.

There is one last circle, and when I put my finger on it, more shelves appear. They are full of something that looks like a laptop computer, small gadgets, a few things that resemble clocks, and more things that look utterly unfamiliar to me are lined up next to each other in perfect order.

My fingers itch to touch it, but there is no movement in my body. I stand completely still and focus on breathing calmly. Maybe I just need to find the bathroom and give my body a chance to catch up with the help of a warm bath.

I drag myself into the room that the red button opened and put my finger on a circle in the middle of the wall. A bathroom appears—big, bright, and gorgeous. Perfect. I step on the almost transparent floor. It has a soft, almost silky surface that tickles under my feet. The heat and a sweet fragrance make the small jabs of pain drift away, leaving me in a state of relaxation. There are mirrors all the way around. In fact, I realize that the entire room is mirrored. The bathtub is built into the end wall, just like a little cave. Above the bathtub are rows of small lights covered with crystals that form a circle. It looks amazing. Anywhere else, I might have thought that it was in poor taste or excessive, but not here. It suits the surroundings. There is shampoo, conditioner, toothpaste, and a toothbrush. The towels are thick, immaculately white, and look like they have never been used. There is a small "IB" embroidered in the corner with a thin golden thread. I have seen a lot of hotel bathrooms over the years, but this one surpasses them all.

The mirrors reflect my body from all possible angles. I can't stop myself from smiling as I lift my shirt and turn a bit. There are no visible bruises or sores. They must have picked me up before the plane hit the earth. I peel off my clothes and let them fall slowly onto the transparent floor. Bath or shower? Bath. I turn the faucet and let the water fill the bathtub.

As the water is running, I stand naked in the middle of the floor and examine myself. I can't think of the last time I did that. I usually shower, brush my teeth, and talk to Luke at the same time. I am thirty-four years old, but I think that my body has become more beautiful with age. My looks have improved. When I look at pictures of myself from when I was young, I realize that I look younger but not as beautiful as I am today.

I can see myself in all the mirrors. My body is fit, and the pounds sit in the right places. My legs are long and thin. The belly has a slight, feminine curve, and my shoulders are pronounced. My face shows my age, not to mention the gray hair. There's no getting away from that. Knees still have a few scars from my childhood falls, and my thighs have marks from when I was pregnant and gained weight.

The bathtub is filled, and the steam from the warm water makes the reflection disappear. I dip my big toe into the water. It is divine. I let my body slowly sink, and the water envelops me. The warmth penetrates every single cell. I lie down and rest my head on the edge. Eyes closed. Completely relaxed. I take a deep breath and slowly exhale through my open lips.

Thoughts begin to fill my head. It is hard to be at peace. There are so many who talk about meditation and inner silence. My head is more like a marketplace where there is a noisy crowd of people pushing and squeezing past each other. It is not chaos, but there is a lot of activity. Questions begin to come. Is there money? How many people are here? I can't help but wonder if there are others from my flight. I don't know if I could recognize them, probably not, because I only really noticed the woman sitting next to me. I wonder if she is here.

Maybe I can go exploring on my own. That's a good idea. Nothing can really happen. After all, Thomas said that I could call him if I needed him, not that I couldn't go around on my own.

I smile and slowly open my eyes.

6

EXPLORING

"What are you doing here? I don't think I've seen you before."

I turn around, and a sense of guilt hits me at a hundred miles an hour—just like I've been discovered with my hand in the cookie jar. And I have only reached the end of my hallway and gone through the first door.

"My name is Annabel," says the woman standing in front of me. She has green eyes and slightly wavy, shoulder-length blonde hair. There is something about her that arouses my curiosity and makes me lower my defenses. I smile and don't know what to say—feeling like an undercover agent on a secret mission. Right now, I have ventured into an unknown area and crossed a border that perhaps I am not supposed to—precisely the sort of feeling I remember from my investigative journalism assignments. I swallow once and keep on smiling till it hurts.

"Hi, my name is Eva," I try to say it as if it was the most natural thing in the world. Annabel looks at me, and it is clear that she has seen right through me.

"When did you arrive?" Her voice is enthusiastic, and her body language engaged.

"Last night, I think." I lower my voice and take a small step back, leaving a bit more space between us. The hallway suddenly seems awfully long and immense. The shining red stripe on the floor runs right by my foot, and I step on it.

She moves forward and closes the space I just created. "Who received you?"

I lower my gaze. "It was Thomas Leander." I sense that she is looking at me, but I am trying to avoid eye contact.

Next to us are windows filling the whole wall on one side, and on the other side, there are small screens by a row of doors, just like my hallway.

Annabel puts her hands in her back pockets and arches backward. "Well... hmm."

"What do you mean by that?" I look up, and our eyes meet. My voice is firm, and I am about to fold my arms across my chest, but I change my mind and put them in my front pockets instead.

"I think that you were lucky. He's very handsome, isn't he?" Her eyes are sparkling with a curious look.

"Yes," I manage to say and notice her sensitive charisma.

"Coma or dead?"

She makes it sound like heads or tails.

"Coma." I almost whisper it as if saying it aloud would make it become more real.

Annabel maintains eye contact. "Do you want to join me, or would you rather be alone?" Her body is continuously moving, so full of energy that she can hardly stand still—like a fire burning inside her beaming warm energy.

"Company would be nice." The words fly out of my mouth. Somehow, Annabel makes me feel safe, like I am in good hands. After all, what can happen when I'm almost dead anyway? "Do you know this place well?" I force a smile and look out the huge window; a large flock of birds drifts by in slow motion as the wind carries them.

"Yes, pretty well. I've been here for some time now." Annabel clasps her hands together. "Let's go…."

I hesitate, and she is already one step in front of me when I say. "I don't know what day it is or precisely how long I've been here." I chuckle and step on the red line before I hurry and catch up with her.

She hadn't realized that I was left behind for a moment. "Let's go over here. There's a beautiful garden. Has Thomas shown it to you?" Annabel walks at high speed, and I must make an effort to keep up.

I shake my head no; he hasn't. I didn't explore very much before Annabel showed up. All I've seen so far are hallways and the control room.

We go down some hallways that all look the same—light and simple. How will I ever find my way around here?

"Take a look at that stripe that runs along the wall. It tells you which section you are in." Annabel points to the floor and smiles so that the fine lines around her mouth get visible. The stripe has gone yellow. She grabs my hand. It is soft like a baby's skin and warm. "And if you do get lost, you can always use your Skycon." She winks at me.

We make a couple of turns and reach a dead end. A section of the wall glides aside, and I can feel the fresh air on my face. It refuels my system, and the tension in my body is released. The birds are flying around freely, and the air is so subtle and pure. The sun is shining, and the weather is mild. The garden is encircled by the sky. Ahead, small low bushes form a maze.

I look at Annabel. Her loose hair flutters in the breeze, and she heads toward the center of the maze. There is something about Annabel that seems familiar, but I can't work out what it is.

"How long did you say you've been here?" I am walking right behind her, still trying to keep up.

"I didn't say," is her prompt reply. "I don't pay such close attention to it because I am not in a coma." Annabel hums quietly while her way of walking nearly turns into a dance, swaying her hips and arms to the sides.

I realize that I am watching her swaying backside, and I look away resolutely. She is not what you would call beautiful in a fashion magazine, but she is beautiful. Annabel has a unique quality that comes from within; I feel it but somehow can't relate to it. In addition, she has great charm and a lovely fragrance about her.

She stops, turns around, and looks into my eyes. "What do you want to know? I have been here longer than you, so you are welcome to ask me about anything you don't know yet. I'm sure that Thomas hasn't told you everything."

I smile and can feel my cheeks become warm. I let my mouth open.

"Are you married?" she asks.

I don't get to ask a single question before she raises another one, and I shake my head no.

"Children?" Her voice is playful, with a touch of seriousness. She reaches out and picks one of the small flowers on the green bush. "For you, welcome to In-Between—a world of wonders." She laughs and continues walking.

This time, I can keep up, and we are walking side by side toward the middle of the maze, not making any wrong turns. The sun blinds me, and I use my hand to shade my eyes. "I have a son. His name is Luke, and he's four years old."

"Do you miss him?" Our arms brush each other. The path is narrow, and the bushes are nearly the same height as me, making it hard to see where we are going.

Do I miss Luke? That's a good question. At that moment, I suddenly feel a stab in my heart that forces me to stop. Being here has been so intense that I have completely forgotten about him for a while. I cover my face with my hands, trying to rub the thoughts away. The pain in my heart grows like a wave of small arrows trying to force their way through my veins. I force myself to move on.

Annabel stops. We've reached the middle of the labyrinth. "I know it." She takes a step closer to me, a little too close for comfort, but I just stand in place.

"I have a son too. He's two years old." Annabel seeks eye contact. "Sometimes, I also catch myself and realize that I haven't thought about him for the entire day." She shrugs her shoulders and starts to walk again. "Your priorities are different now, and you can't avoid that. It doesn't make you a bad mother. You are living in the moment, and that makes you a better person."

I lower my gaze and sigh. A sensation of emptiness fills my body in no time.

The center is full of flowers in different colors. There is a wooden table with two benches in the middle, and where there would typically be gravel, there is a floating, light mass.

Annabel takes hold of my shoulders and shakes me slightly. "Don't take it so hard. Even though you feel a sense of guilt about not being there for Luke, remember that life goes on." She smiles as if what she is saying is completely natural. "The sooner you can surrender to the circumstances, the easier it will be, and then you can enjoy your time here. You don't have much choice...." She leans against the table where names and dates are scratched into the wood.

Something vibrates inside my pocket. Annabel smiles, "Someone's trying to reach you."

I put my hand in my pocket and take out the Skycon that Thomas gave me. His voice sounds clear and distinct, and an image of him appears on the small screen. With a simple touch, Annabel reaches out and pulls up the picture in front of me and steps aside.

"Hi, Eva." Thomas waves at me. "Are you enjoying yourself?"

"Yes," not sure what face to make, and realizing that the statement is true, I feel almost overwhelmed. I can't hold back a smile that is coming all the way from my stomach. "Yes, I am."

"Would you like to meet in half an hour in front of your room? There is something that I'd like to talk to you about." Thomas's long dark blond hair falls along the sides of his face. His luminous blue eyes are lighting up the picture that is hanging in front of me.

"That's fine. I'll be there." I nod eagerly.

"Perfect, see you in a bit." He waves and the picture fades out.

"Well..." Annabel takes my hand, lifts it, and then holds it between her palms. "It was very, very nice to meet you." We stand facing each other, looking into each other's eyes. "I hope that we meet again. It was a pleasure. Too brief, though...." She looks at me, smiling so that her eyes light up.

I stand completely still; my mouth drops open, but no words are coming out. She pulls me toward her and hugs me. I can feel her body against mine, her breasts, belly, and legs—so feminine and gentle. Our bodies are close, and heat rises between us. I try to step back a little and tighten my grip around her to let her know hugging is over. Nothing happens. It was the same with Thomas, very intense without coming on too strong or being uncomfortably intimate. I sense that they mean well and move my feet a little to stand more grounded. It is not at all intrusive or vulgar. Her hands move down my back, and I can feel the warmth through my blouse. Since Andreas and I got divorced, I have only had very few male acquaintances. Standing so close to Annabel, I feel attracted by her womanliness—to that fragrance that I can sense in her but not find inside myself.

I try to take a step back but can't. Our bodies have melted into each other. Her head glides slowly to the side so that our cheeks meet, and I feel the warmth from her soft skin. We stand there holding our heads against each other. Her hand smooths my hair, and I look into her eyes. Their green color gradually becomes light brown and makes a very delicate pattern. I'm taken by surprise and can't establish any of my defense mechanisms in time to get out. I let my eyes close and fall into the encounter and its intensity. It is new, totally new for me to allow someone to come so close and so quickly. I can't help but snicker for a second, and I open my eyes to see if she reacts. She doesn't. Annabel keeps standing with closed eyes so silently and calmly. I want to move my hand, but it won't respond. Instead, I turn one foot slightly and feel her hand stroking my cheek and caressing my skin. My face tightens somewhat, but as her hand glides across my skin, I relax little by little. I move my hand cautiously on her back. I wonder if it's a good idea to reciprocate her touch so that she knows that I am enjoying this. Because I must admit, I am.

Suddenly, I feel her breath near my mouth. There isn't a sound out here. It seems to be secluded, standing in the middle of these bushes. My breathing seems heavy and noisy.

Relax, relax.

At that moment, I feel her lips against mine. I am caught in the moment. I can feel her breath right next to mine, and the warmth from her lips sends a jolt down to my knees, so they feel like rubber. I hope that no one comes. Instantly, I look to the side without moving my head. All I can see are the tall bushes with tiny flowers. Nobody can see us here in the middle of the maze. I hope.

The tip of her tongue touches my lips and pushes gently past them to meet my tongue. It is as if it is exploring. Her hands hold my face loosely while caressing my skin. A powerful sexual heat flows through me, and every part of my body is tingling. I am panting for breath and smiling inwardly. I surrender and dive into the experience. Thoughts disappear for a while, and I am filled with her sensitive touch and the warmth of her body. Our bodies are like two magnets that are attracted to each other. Lips are playing, and our tongues are dancing an intimate dance. Sometimes, I have wondered what it would be like to kiss a woman, but I have never even been close. Now, I know that it is very beautiful, intense, and exclusive. I wonder if this is also how men experience it when they kiss women. Our lips glide away from each other, and we look into each other's eyes again.

"See you." Annabel smiles at me. She lets go of me and dances her way back into the maze, where she disappears.

"Yes, see you," I say after she's gone. My eyes are blinking frantically as I try to reach out for the table. It is too far away, and I take a step sideways and only just manage not to fall over. A newspaper headline comes to mind, "Woman in coma kisses another woman." Absurd. It might turn out to be a very interesting period here in In-Between.

Slightly bewildered, overwhelmed, yet filled with energy, I go back to my room, following the colored lines on the floor. I can't help laughing; my body is bubbling. What just happened?

I am not a lesbian, a voice in my head shouts. Not that I have anything against lesbians or gays, some of my best friends are gay—but I have never seen myself as a lesbian. This is a tough one. It sounds like I am in denial, but I refuse to be labeled by society. I just want to be me. It doesn't matter what color my skin is or what I believe. When people label me, I feel like my freedom is taken away, and others are judging me. But maybe I'm judging myself? Maybe I'm not as free as I believe.

My head fills with nonsense. It was just a kiss, and I couldn't help it. So, what is the big deal? She started it. I wonder if she prefers women. I'm probably in over my head. I don't want to admit that I enjoyed kissing her, but it was just a kiss, an innocent kiss. Would I go further? I don't think so.

On the other hand, if anyone had asked me 30 minutes ago if I would ever kiss a woman, I would have said no, quite convincingly. I try to calm myself. No one saw us, and no one knows it or needs to find out about it. Maybe I'll never see her again. What if she does that with everyone she meets? I suddenly feel taken advantage of, that I am just one of many. Is she playing games with me? Is she testing me?

I have reached the door to my hallway and stop to take a deep breath.

Relax, I say to myself. It was just a kiss, and she happened to be a woman. Maybe all women here act like that.

I begin to laugh again. I'm far out, or should I say, far up.

THE LIFE

THERE IS THOMAS, already waiting outside my room. He is standing relaxed, looking out the huge window, wearing his long black jacket with golden buttons and slim boots with gold laces up the front. I smile and wave at him. He turns and waves back. Funny how the hallway doesn't seem to be very long now. I pass by the rooms, each with a touch screen outside the door placed in level with the wall, elegant and Zenlike. Mine is the last one at the end of the hall. It is nice and warm with the sun shining through the large windows. I walk down the middle of the hall and feel like I'm almost floating toward Thomas.

"How are you doing?" His blue eyes shine, and his straight white teeth show as he smiles.

I can feel the warmth in my cheeks and can't help but laugh. "Well, it's going fine."

"Have you settled in?" He takes my hand, and I look down at the floor shyly.

"That's a good question. I think I'm getting there."

"Good. Just remember that everyone leaves here at some point."

Why did he say that? I look up. Has he seen us?

Huge clouds are building up outside the windows, and the bright light from the sun is replaced by the light that comes from within the hovering white mass in the ceiling.

"It can be very overwhelming in the beginning." He stands in front of me and takes both of my hands in his. "It is important to focus on the reason you are here."

"And what is that?" The mood I was enjoying quickly vanishes, and I feel left in the dark—again. Do I have a mission that I am unaware of? Did I miss something? I briefly look down the hallway to see if we are still alone. We are.

Thomas is composed, speaks quietly, and smiles at me. His face has a warm glow. As he runs his hand through his long hair, I notice that he is wearing a thin golden ring with small marks around his long finger—thin as a thread that has been tied around his finger. "You are here because you have an opportunity to develop yourself, to evolve. You need to find out whether you are ready to continue on your soul's journey or if you want to return."

I don't understand a thing. Is he saying that I can come back out of my coma? That I have a choice? I look at him searchingly and try to find a suitable expression and end up crossing my arms.

"If I can return, why don't you send me back now, immediately? I'd like to go home now." My tone of voice is a little more determined than I intend, and I bite my teeth hard together.

It is quiet in the hallway. Even though the clouds are moving by quickly, there is no wind to be heard. I look over at my touch screen by the door. It is turned off.

Thomas shakes his head. "You aren't ready to make this decision yet, and it can't be done right now."

"Does this mean that it is my decision if I want to go back or not?" I take a step back, now looking right into his looming blue eyes.

"Yes, when the time comes, it is you who will make that decision."

"When will that time come?" I stare at him as if I could pull the answer out of him.

A door opens a bit further down the hall, and a woman with short black hair and a black dress comes into view. I keep my eyes on Thomas.

"Not yet," he says effortlessly. "You have plenty of time." He turns the ring on his finger and looks at me with the friendliest look.

I step back and fold my hands behind my neck, biting my lower lip, not letting any words slip out. His answers are always diffuse and sometimes ambiguous. Maybe it is because he is better at evading than I am that it irritates me. Why won't he just answer what I ask him? The sound of footsteps disappears, and we are once more alone.

"There are more things that I want to share with you." Thomas extends his hand toward me. "Shouldn't we find someplace where we can sit alone in peace and quiet?"

"That sounds like a good idea." My voice is determined, and the words can only just make it past my clenched teeth. My arms are still crossed in front of me, and I force a smile to cover the battle between anger and despair that I feel inside.

"Follow me." His hand is still extended toward me, and I go along with my hands deeply buried in my pockets.

Just as long as we don't go to that garden where I just came from.

And just as long as we don't run into Annabel.

7

A CRY FOR HELP

"Eva. Eva." Andreas's voice fills the room. He is standing next to Eva's bed, and Dr. Johnson is right behind him. It's almost like seeing a dead person, but she isn't dead because the respirator is helping her breathe. The bed is placed against a pale yellow wall. On one side of it is a blue upholstered chair; next to it is a table with nothing on it. The room is long and narrow, so there is just enough room to get past the foot of the bed. The curtains are pulled back from the north-facing window so that daylight can enter, but not much does. On the wall is a picture of a man running on a beach with the sun setting in the background and the words, "Live in the moment" underneath.

There is an I.V. in Eva's arm, a mask covering her mouth and nose, and some machines behind the bed. Andreas has no idea what they are for. He carefully places his hand on her chest to feel her heartbeat. His hands are shaking, and a trembling is running through his arm, vanishing into his body. The heat in his body rises, and tiny pearls of sweat appear on his forehead. His eyes are fixed on Eva. It cuts through his heart to see a person that he used to share his life with being lifeless. The last six years flash by—her smiling face, her playfulness when she was with Luke, and the puzzled look in her eyes when they first met.

"Eva..." There is a discordant timbre to his voice. He has to be stronger than ever. He is thinking of the whole scenario. How can he tell Luke that his mother is in a coma and might never awake? Slowly, he empties his lungs of air.

Dr. Johnson steps forward and stands beside Andreas. His voice sounds tired and almost as mechanical as the machines whose screens and printouts he is glancing at.

"I don't know how busy you are, but it would be ideal if someone could be here with Eva, especially in the beginning. That's when there is the greatest chance that she will come out of the coma. Do you have any contact with her family?"

Andreas keeps staring at Eva and can't take his eyes off her. It's an effort for him to find words. Dr. Johnson starts to flip through the papers on his note board.

"I've tried to get ahold of Eva's mother," Andreas finally says. "But I haven't been able to reach her yet. I'll arrange for people to be here with Eva. I can make my own work schedule, so I'll take time off if necessary." He pauses and keeps staring at Eva. "But I don't know yet if I want to bring Luke here." His hand slides into his pocket, and he brings out his wallet. There is a picture of Luke, Eva, and him together, and as he holds it, he gulps down a sob. Very hesitantly, he sets it on the table next to Eva.

Dr. Johnson looks up from his papers and steps aside. "You don't need to decide right now. Maybe you want to talk it over with others who are also close to Luke first. And remember, if there is a scent, a sound, or anything else that you know that she especially likes, then those are the sorts of things it would be best to bring here."

Andreas looks around the room and nods mechanically. It will not be hard to make the room seem more familiar.

Dr. Johnson continues in his firm, almost monotone voice. "You can do almost anything you want here, except for painting the walls.

Candles and plants aren't allowed in this unit, but you're welcome to bring more photographs, music, and other things. You have our total support as far as doing what you think will help Eva come out of the coma. The only thing that we ask is that you refrain from moving her." He places his glasses on his forehead and puts the note board under his arm.

Andreas bends forward, lifts Eva's hand, and presses it against his cheek.

The doctor's voice softens up a bit and sounds almost human. "You can touch Eva carefully," he raises his eyes, and a tight smile flickers across his face, "but we don't know yet if she has any internal injuries. Her body is very likely in shock after the crash. It affects her body even though she is unconscious. Does that make sense?"

Andreas rubs one of his eyes, nods, and places her hand gently alongside her body.

"Now, all that's left is to wait and hope for the best." He places his hand on Andreas's shoulder, pats it a few times, and then leaves.

Andreas sinks into the chair next to the bed and looks at Eva. Somehow, he can't stop staring at her. He tugs at his hair and looks up at the ceiling.

Why?

Why Eva?

He knows that he can't find an answer, but he doesn't understand it. Why does it have to be Eva? With billions of people in the world, it seems so unfair. He hits his fist against the railing of the bed.

The machines' sound produces a constant white noise in the room, and an old clock supplies a regular rhythm that is almost like a heartbeat. Andreas wants to surrender himself to that sort of sensation, to the blankness of white noise. But he knows that he can't. He has to pick up Luke soon. There is still time. After he dropped Luke off at Kindergarten, he canceled all his appointments for today and tomorrow. Maybe he should try to phone Eva's mother, Janet, again. He reaches for his cell and opens his favorites contacts. He punches her icon. It rings and rings. What is she doing? Why doesn't she answer? He turns off the phone and throws it on the table.

Now that he is sitting here looking at Eva, he realizes how much he has missed her. She is so beautiful. There is no time for regrets, but still... He should never have let her go. They had been a fine little family, the three of them. It could have worked. He could have tried harder to make it work. He swallows and tightens his fist until his fingernails bite into his palm. Maybe they should have had another child. What if they had and the marriage had still failed? Then he would have to fill the role of both parents for two children. Even that thought terrifies him. Despite everything he's done while Eva is on an assignment, the idea of being the only parent full-time seems incredibly daunting.

She has to wake up.

Andreas leans forward, resting his arms on the railing of the bed. He has always believed that things happen for a reason—that there were lessons to be learned even from life's harshest moments and that growth is always possible. In his work as a psychologist, he has seen people rise from life crises and find a strength that he doubted that they had.

Now, he is questioning his own preaching. Andreas has lived his whole life believing that if he can ever find the strength to take full responsibility for himself, the universe will respond by helping him and showing him the way. Now, the way seems foggy.

In some way, it is contrary to his convictions, but he folds his hands and says, "Whoever is out there, please bring Eva back. We need her. She is Luke's mother. Please, help us."

He sits completely still, pressing his forehead against the cold metal of the bedrail. "Please, help me," he whispers. "If you are there, I need your help. Anyone."

The door opens behind him without him sensing that someone has entered the room.

Carefully, he places his hand on Eva's chest and gradually lets his eyes open. A pulse flows through his arm, to his hand, and over to Eva. He feels a hand on his shoulder and lays his other hand on top of it without knowing who it is. Andreas breathes deeply while taking in the warmth from the unfamiliar hand. He can't hold back his tears. No matter how he struggles against it, he can no longer resist the pressure building up inside him. It feels like his heart has been stabbed with a knife, and he doesn't know how to remove it. The tears flow over, and he breaks down in sobs.

"Help me." Andreas's voice is full of tears and fills the room.

"Please, help me."

8

THE ILLUSION

I tilt back my head, and my whole body relaxes. The sky extends into infinite space above me, and a sense of freedom flows through my body.

"There is a reason for everything." Thomas turns his head and looks at me. "It just isn't possible to understand when we are right in the middle of it."

We sit down, looking out over the water, where the sun is hanging like a fireball out on the horizon. Golden light is shining down on us and our surroundings, bringing pleasant warmth.

Thomas speaks deliberately, and I have to concentrate in order not to think about anything else.

"In my experience, when people become sick or die, it happens for a reason. There is something we must learn. If we listen and learn and enter into the experience, then we can develop." His voice is smooth as silk.

I turn my head, and our eyes meet.

"You are here because it is uncertain whether you will leave your mortal life now or not. There may be more for you to learn on Earth."

Other than Thomas's voice, the only sound is the whistling of the wind. We are outside on a ledge a short distance from the reception area and control room. There is no furniture, so we are sitting directly on the cloud. It is solid without being hard, cool without being cold. Thomas is wearing his long black coat over his blue tunic and black boots tied with gold laces. The wind starts to play with his loose hair. I am seated, wearing my red jacket with a high-necked blue shirt under it. My legs are extended, and my hands are resting on my lap. The sunglasses in my hair keep it from blowing into my eyes.

"But," Thomas looks at me, "...it may be time for you to continue on your journey. A soul's journey is long. We take with us the experiences that we can use from previous lives." He smiles archly as he looks at me. "Have you ever wondered why some people find it so easy to learn new things? Isn't it odd?" The light makes his eyes twinkle, and before I can come up with anything to say, he continues. "We all carry something with us from previous lives. Before a soul finds its new destination, it chooses its challenges. It sets a goal for what it would like to learn in its next life on Earth. Whether it reaches its goal is up to the individual."

A cloud drifts in front of the sun, and the warmth goes away. I shrink into my short red jacket and raise the collar so that it covers the back of my neck.

"What's my challenge?" I can't help but smile and feel the innocent stream of bubbles running through my stomach.

Thomas laughs loudly. "You're pretty quick." He leans back and rests his hands on the cloud so that we are sitting shoulder to shoulder.

I'm staring into the distance, still far from convinced of the existence of previous or future lives, but I'm saying nothing to Thomas. I force myself to concentrate. His words will drift by on the wind, devoid of meaning if I don't. The concepts and experiences here are coming at me so quickly. I need time to take it all in. There is a sense of loving care and openness from Thomas, even from In-Between itself, but my brain is trying to hold onto what I know. But I find it harder and harder to hold on. Sometimes I have to fight just to see an image of Luke in my thoughts. What is happening to me? A knot in my stomach tightens. The idea of losing myself, my real self, frightens me.

I sigh and clench my teeth slightly.

Thomas observes me without saying anything. His eyes are relaxed, and he is breathing evenly. I can't help but wonder where he gets all of that tranquility. Part of me fears that he will quickly tire of me and my uncertainties.

"Let me put it like this." He cocks his head slightly. "There can be many different reasons that people come to a standstill in their lives or never pursue their dreams or whatever it is that they long for. It takes a lot of courage to dare to look inward. But we all have opportunities to develop, to learn something new, and to let our souls advance." He pauses and looks out at the horizon where clouds build up and form a beautiful landscape in many different shades of red. "There are some who choose to take what we call a 'resting' incarnation; that is, they don't have major goals for themselves. Others give themselves almost inhuman challenges."

A resting incarnation is certainly not what I had chosen for this life. I pull my legs up under me and put my arms around them. I have been busy my whole life. It is like sitting and looking at an enormous painting—clouds with their indefinable forms, the rays of the sun trying unremittingly to break through, and the clear blue sky as a background. Why can't I just relax and enjoy it?

"Are you telling me that everything is predetermined?" I shake my head, grimacing.

"No, but the opportunities are there. It's up to you to take advantage of them."

"Yes, that's easy for you to say." My words come out more harshly than I intended, but I'm not offering an apology.

Thomas seems unaffected by my sharp tone of voice. "Let me put it like this. You may find that your life goes in circles. You face the same challenges repeatedly as if you are a needle stuck in a groove on a vinyl record and the record just keeps spinning round and round. You attract the same types of people, and the same sorts of things keep happening to you."

The simplicity of the image seems to make sense to me. I manage to speak evenly and without an edge to my voice. "Hmm. Let's say that you're right. How can you get out of the groove?" I stretch my legs and cross my arms over my chest. When Thomas looks at me, I quickly let my arms fall along my sides.

"First, you must be aware that you are stuck in the groove. Then you need to be ready to let go of what you already know, whatever thoughts and behavior are long-established and secure in your life." He speaks evenly in a low voice. "...Only then is it possible for you to get out of the groove. You can do that in many ways. It isn't until you achieve a deeper understanding within that the changes will manifest outwardly, such as moving to a new home, finding a new job, or meeting a new friend or a lover. Changes can appear in many forms. What is characteristic is that before changes take place, you must learn something and begin a new way of living."

He leans forward, turns toward me, and looks directly into my eyes.

"There is something else that is important."

I remain seated by his side. Actually, I would like to hear what he has to say, but I also feel like I have an inner warrior who just wants to fight with Thomas, contradict him at any cost, debate, or refute his claim. This warrior has taken over me and is ready to attack first rather than risk relinquishing any of my fundamental beliefs. The warrior has wrapped me in a suit of armor to ensure that I won't get hurt. I would very much like to turn so that I am sitting face to face with Thomas, but I can't. My legs simply won't obey me. Thomas lets me be and doesn't try to change me but calmly continues with what he was saying.

"For something new to enter your life, you need to be thankful for what you already have." His words are hanging in the air like small crystals before melting.

That makes sense. I know so many people who complain over the slightest things, especially that nothing is happening in their lives. They live vicariously through the people they see on television, on the internet, or in magazines.

"Take you, for example." He pauses. "You have a choice every single moment. You can choose to focus on the fact that you are not with Luke, or that you would like to return, or that your body is sore. You can also choose to be thankful that you were on board that airplane, that you are here now, and that you have the opportunity to get to know yourself even better."

I sit with a stone face, not offering Thomas any reaction. What he is saying is very logical and actually quite simple. But I can't see why I should be thankful I was on that plane. I would rather go home. And my body is sore; that is a fact.

A small cloud passes over us, and for a second, we are completely invisible. It is cool, and I have to wave away the mist with my hand to see Thomas. He is sitting there passively.

"Every single moment of our lives, we have a choice. We can choose to focus on the negative or the positive. To a great extent, it depends on our attitude toward life. We can choose to enter each experience with the intent that something exciting can happen and that something can benefit us. Alternatively, we can expect that it is going to be a bore, that we are wasting time, or we can feel unfairly treated."

Thomas keeps his eyes on me, and I nod to indicate that I'm following what he says. He leans over and reaches behind me, where he molds a backrest out of a piece of cloud.

"It's very simple. We attract everything ourselves, often unconsciously." He leans back.

"Are you trying to tell me that it was my fault that the plane crashed because I wanted to die?" I don't move an inch.

"What do you think?" The expression in Thomas's eyes is intense, and I quickly lower my eyes.

"I don't know." I place my hands under my legs and run my teeth over my lower lip.

"Are you sure?" he asks with a quizzical expression.

The sun's rays blind me. I close my eyes slightly and can feel a powerful white light from within. Is he saying that I know it? Is he implying that I am lying? I lean to the side and am surprised by the support the cloud backrest offers.

"All right." I look up. "Let's say that there is a higher purpose, that I am here for a reason, and that I unconsciously attracted it." What I am saying seems beyond belief. "What happens with this spinning record and the groove if I learn whatever it is that serves this 'higher purpose'?" I indicate quotation marks with my fingers. "Do I get to go home then?" I draw a smiling emoji in the cloud between us.

"When you are close to completing a groove, the challenge you are about to learn will increase. You will feel that the heat is on." He pauses and looks at me. "If you have learned what is needed, then the tonearm moves a notch closer to the center in a new groove, and you come closer to yourself and what you truly long for. You begin to live in the next groove until you have gone all the way around, and it is time for you to enter a new groove inward, closer to your center; that's how life goes on." He draws a circle around my emoji eyes and mouth, completing the face. "You can see that there will be less and less time between the repetitions in your life because the circles become smaller, but it is also easier to shift because you become more insightful as you approach what it is that you long for."

The cloud we are sitting on is moving at a faster speed. Now, all I can see beneath us are treetops. The words keep spinning in my head and are on repeat.

"Come," Thomas rises. "Let's walk for a while." He extends his arm toward me and helps me to my feet. My whole body is stiff.

Right above us, sunbeams penetrate the diffuse edges of the

THE LIFE

clouds, making them change color. "Here." Thomas points toward a building where I can make out a small path. There is no one else in sight. I have Thomas all to myself; a warm sensation runs through me, and I smile. He takes my hand, and we stroll along the path around the building.

"You have been given an opportunity to view your life from a distance. Very few people experience this. Remember, it is only those of you who enter a coma who have a chance to go back and continue your life where you left it." He releases my hand and puts his arm around my shoulder. "Those who die suddenly or commit suicide cannot go back and continue their lives. They are here for the same reason, to learn from their lives and also to bid a proper farewell to their mortal lives. After that, they continue on their souls' journeys."

"Are you trying to tell me that I'm fortunate?"

Thomas smiles at me. "What do you think?"

"Thomas," I look down and dig my thumbnail into the side of my index finger, so hard that I can feel it all the way up my arm, "there's something that I want to ask you."

I'm trying to find the right words, but it's not easy, so I speak out flat and bluntly. "I simply don't understand how In-Between functions, I mean...."

Thomas stops and folds his hands in front of his chest. "Let me try to explain it as simply as possible. When you leave behind your life on Earth, a kind of duplicate of your body is made, just as it was before the transfer happened." He gestures that we should continue walking. "That is the body you have here. Basically, you don't need to eat, sleep, or do other earthly things. But, to keep the transition from being too abrupt, a certain frequency has been encoded around In-Between, which means that you experience your body and the surroundings here in the same way that you did on Earth."

Thomas reaches out and pinches my arm.

"Ow," I exclaim, then begin to laugh.

"See, you can feel it... but your body won't age while you are here."

I rub my arm a little and frown. The sun has broken through again, and I can feel the heat on my skin.

Thomas continues to walk at a leisurely pace. "I eat, sleep, and follow the rhythm of the sun more or less. It suits me well. But if you are ready, you can let it all go and concentrate on your personal development."

I stare in amazement at Thomas, and the corner of my mouth pulls up in a half-smile. Can I really stop eating and sleeping? Incredible!

Thomas smiles at me. "In-Between functions like a true copy of life on Earth—with a few advantages."

"Advantages?" I raise my eyebrows and kick a hole in a little cloud that has settled by the side of my foot.

"Well, we don't need to pay for food, for example. And we can utilize certain frequencies to transport ourselves quickly. But if you give up eating and sleeping and then choose to return to Earth, the transition can be too abrupt."

Thomas points at my boots. "And those?" He chuckles. "It's all in your mind," he taps his forehead, "but wearing the boots helps you to accept it."

Far below, I can see the surface of the ocean. It looks like a dark mass filled with popcorn that is rolling rhythmically. Now it's just a matter of making the most of this opportunity. I turn and look back toward In-Between. The path has vanished behind a cloud.

"I'm not sure that I fully understand what you are saying. My soul has plans for me. Surely, I should have some influence?"

Thomas rests his hand around my shoulders, and we walk synchronously. "That is correct. What often happens, though, is that people identify themselves with their goals or with their ways of living and then can no longer see clearly." He pauses. It seems to me that, for once, it is Thomas who is searching for words. Thomas always speaks so correctly and convincingly. Somehow, he makes me forget my critical attitude. He swallows and continues, "They forget to be aware of their feelings and of life itself. In that way, they shut themselves off from themselves and others, and then there is a struggle to obtain or achieve something that they believe will make them happy."

That statement strikes home. I have pursued many goals in my life—first in school and later as a journalist—as a mother, as a wife, at least so long as I held out hope for my marriage to Andreas.

Where did my feelings fit into those goals? Did I even consider such things, or was I too busy with my goals themselves to see what they were doing to me? Were they even my own goals—or simply reflections of others' expectations of me?

Thomas is still speaking, and I make myself pay closer attention to his words.

"The hope that we will become happy once we have reached the goal is what keeps us going, but when we cross the finish line, a new goal appears. The finish line is moved the very moment that we are about to cross it. And so, it keeps going in life."

We have reached a large, open ledge. The vast cloud in front of us resembles a mountain. I listen to Thomas's words and try to take them in.

"While you are here, you have an opportunity to go back and learn from your life. In the control room, you have access to a personal development program that is set up especially for you. You can watch situations that occurred in your life from a distance and learn from them. As you make progress, you also have an opportunity to join group sessions and meditation." He stops and turns toward me. "The time you have here can become very valuable, and you might discover a thing or two about yourself."

"And when I complete the program, can I then return home?"

Thomas can't hold back a laugh, "No one has ever completed the program."

I guess I will be the first one then, I think to myself. I will show them how it's done. I cross my arms and look straight ahead.

"There is one last thing that may comfort you." Thomas stops and turns toward me. "In my experience, when things in your life are going well and come easily to you, then you are on the right path. When you begin to struggle, and things work against you, then it's time to stop and listen."

The mountain formed of clouds dissolves as I watch.

9

LUKE

Andreas is standing outside Luke's Kindergarten, unable to move. The wind is blowing and tugging at his brown anorak. He doesn't know what to do and has no desire whatsoever to pick up Luke. Right now, he is happy not knowing what has happened. Soon, Luke's life will change, and it is Andreas who has to give him the bad news. Wishing he could simply stand in the wind forever, Andreas finds the strength to take hold of the heavy iron gate, open it, and go inside.

"You look a little pale." It is Ingrid, one of the older teachers in Luke's ward, who has noticed Andreas. She is sitting next to a little girl with blonde braids who is playing in the sandbox. The wind lifts Ingrid's gray hair, and she tucks it behind her ear so that her wrinkled face is visible. "You're not sick, are you?"

Andreas shakes his head no and tries to smile the best he can. "No, I'm not sick, but this isn't exactly the best day of my life." He doesn't want to talk to anyone about the accident at this point, afraid of not being able to control his feelings.

The teacher nods and points to the playground. "Luke is in the back over there."

"Thanks." His breathing seems labored, and he walks with heavy footsteps. A couple of mothers are talking near the back of the building. They look relaxed and don't pay any attention to Andreas as he passes by.

"Did you see the footage from the plane crash this morning?" The woman speaks with a high-pitched voice. She doesn't look busy at all.

"Yes, that was terrible. Practically the whole plane was destroyed." The other woman nods eagerly. She is wearing a sweatsuit and looks like she has just come from a run. "I heard on the news that there were a lot of foreigners on board."

Andreas looks at them soberly. He feels a stab in his chest, and he runs his hand over his forehead a few times. He still hasn't seen any images of the crash. He's not sure if he will ever see them.

"Vroom." A little boy with fair, curly hair runs past, holding a stick in the air. "Here comes Captain Hook and his flying ship. And they're landing; they're landing, vroom... They made it."

Andreas wipes his hand lightly across his left eye. His shoulders sink as he walks over to the slope where Luke usually hangs out with his friends.

There is a ringing sound; he reaches for his pocket and pulls out his cell. "Granny" flashes on the display. He turns around and hurries down the slope again, hoping that Luke hasn't seen him, keeping his eyes on the little hill as he answers.

"Andreas! Have you heard? Eva... Eva." Janet's voice is strained, and there is a long pause.

He kicks the dirt with the toe of his shoe and catches a glimpse of Luke on the slope. "I've been trying to reach you all day."

Eva's mother interrupts again before he can continue. "I saw the crash on television when I came home a little while ago, and, and...." She pauses. He can hear her making a slight smacking sound with her lips. She always does that when she is nervous. "I knew that was the flight that Eva was on, so I called the police." Her voice is just about to crack. She stops.

Andreas looks up at the sky and struggles to hold back his tears. It has somehow become more real now that Eva's mother also knows.

"I'm just picking up Luke from Kindergarten," Andreas speaks with a low voice.

"Oh, God. What did you say to him?" She sounds a bit accusing.

"Nothing. I haven't even seen him yet...." Andreas paces back and forth, making a track in the dirt, keeping an eye on the hill.

"Don't say anything to him. Don't get him worried." Her voice begins to waver.

Andreas tries to keep calm and tightens his grip on the phone. His whole body is tense, and irritation starts to build. Slowly, he walks over to the building and leans his back against the wall.

"Listen, I have to say something to him." Andreas's voice becomes firm. "Luke knows that something is wrong. He was already aware of it early this morning." He stamps his foot lightly on the ground and swallows once. "We're going to drive to the hospital to see Eva either today or tomorrow, depending on how he takes it. Listen, I have to go now. We'll talk again later tonight after Luke's gone to bed." He snaps the phone shut and slides it into his pocket.

"Daaad!" Luke comes running toward him. "My dad's here!"

Another dark-haired boy follows on Luke's heels. Andreas lifts Luke and gives him a big hug. "I'm so glad to see you."

"Dad, will you swing us?" Luke squeezes his face together between his small hands.

"No, Luke. Not today." Andreas sets him down, and Luke bends his head and stomps a couple of times. Andreas has no time for a dispute. "Come on. We're going home now. Where's your jacket?" Andreas looks searchingly around the playground.

Luke tugs at his arm and points at a tree behind them where the jackets are hanging side by side. Andreas reaches out and takes a blue coat.

"No, Dad, that's not my jacket. This one is mine, and here's my lunch box."

Clouds gather fast above them, and the wind starts to build up. Luke puts on his jacket and is about to run off again. Andreas grabs hold of him and lifts him in the air while he is turning around. "Where do you think you're going, young man?" He pulls him close as he starts to head for the car.

"Please, set me down, Daddy...." Luke chuckles.

Andreas slows his pace but does not put Luke down. Instead, he draws him more deeply into his arms and holds him tightly.

In the same moment as they get into the car, Luke asks. "Why didn't Mom come to get me?" His confused look is so earnest that it feels like a knife in Andreas's chest. "She promised that she would pick me up today."

The air is damp, and the rain is beginning to drum on the windshield. The windows fog up, and Luke runs his hand over the window next to him. Andreas nods slowly. "There's something I want to talk to you about."

He turns from the front seat, so he's facing Luke and strokes his hair.

"Mom isn't coming home, is she?" Luke looks down and kicks the back of the seat in front of him.

"Yes. Yes, she is. Actually, she's already come home...."

"Hurray! Where is she?" Luke lights up with a huge smile and leans forward in the seat. "I want to see her."

Gravel is crunching as several other cars pass by on their way out of the parking lot. Andreas tries hard to keep his focus on Luke.

"The thing is," he swallows and starts to pull at a whisker. Mom is sleeping." Andreas looks down and tries to hide his despair.

Luke's legs start to move like drumsticks, like the rhythm of a heart beating. "I'm great at waking people up. I just tickle the bottom of their feet, and then they wake up, right, Dad?" He bounces in his chair and draws a smiley face on the window next to him.

Andreas smiles as he reaches to undo Luke's harness. "Come here." He takes Luke in his arms and squeezes him tightly. "I wish it were that easy." Another wave of tears is building up inside him, and a lump forms in his throat. He swallows against them and looks at the ceiling of the car to avoid any tears from running. "Mom is in something called a coma. That means that she is sleeping, and no one knows when she will wake up."

Luke eases out of Andreas's embrace and climbs back into his seat. He places a fingertip on the window and tries to follow a raindrop running down. Eventually, he turns his head to his father. "When can I play with her? What about my birthday?"

Andreas shakes his head slowly while looking down. "She's sleeping very deeply. It isn't even certain that we can wake her, but we're going to try. Do you want to help?" He forces himself to look at Luke.

Luke wriggles in his car seat. His smile is nearly powerful enough to pull out the knife in Andreas's heart. "I think she'll wake up when I tickle her, don't you, Dad?"

10

APPRENTICESHIP

The sun has gone down, and darkness is falling. My first day here in In-Between is coming to an end.

"Are you cold?" Thomas turns his head toward me.

I am not and shake my head. We are at the edge of a cloud lying on our backs, looking up at the starry sky. Thomas is relaxed with his legs outstretched and his hands folded on his chest.

"How long have you been here?" I ask, smiling a little self-consciously.

"I've been here for seven years." He looks at me with the same bland expression that I'm growing accustomed to. "I've been receiving new arrivals for the past two years."

"What did you do before that?" I roll onto my left side and rest my head on my arm.

"For a period after I arrived, I was an apprentice, and I had other duties as well."

"An apprentice?" I ask in surprise. "What kind of apprentice?"

"It's a long story." Thomas turns so that we are facing each other and have eye contact.

The air is chilly, and I can feel the coolness from the cloud begin to penetrate my clothes. Luckily, Thomas brought two white blankets. He hands me one of them. It is incredibly soft.

"Let me start by telling you the short version." He pauses. It's so quiet here. These lulls help me enter a silent place within myself. I used to hate pauses and always hastened to interrupt them, but right now, I am enjoying the calm, the silence, and the space to breathe in the middle of the stream of words.

"In-Between is made up of lots of different departments. Many people are needed to make this place function because a great number of souls come through here." Thomas is perfectly still and maintains a calm expression while he speaks. "To become an apprentice, it is essential that you have the necessary insight. Some of the souls who come here are selected and invited to stay if they wish."

I use Thomas's silence to frame one of my many questions. I'm determined to learn how In-Between works—and who or what directs its operation.

"Who selects the apprentices?" I move a little closer to Thomas. My voice is eager. "Who instructs them?"

He rolls over and faces the bright stars that are hanging over us as a lighting blanket. They reflect small white dots in his clear blue eyes. "It is the Master who selects and instructs people. He is the liaison between the Panel and In-Between."

"Master? Panel?" I mumble and raise my eyebrows, and I lie on my back too. My finger traces a question mark in the mist of the cloud we are lying on. Every time Thomas answers one question, it opens up to another one.

"You can consider the Master to be the head of this place. The Panel is made up of those who have a sort of grand overview of us all... They are not here." He cannot hide a smile and casts a glance at me. The sky has become dark, and the stars seem closer than before. Shining brightly, they appear inseparable from the sky.

I start to count the brightest stars and imagine what sort of being would qualify to sit on a panel with such influence and so extensive an overview of the entire world. Perhaps the whole universe. I'm wondering how I can be considered for a position like that. It's hard not to smile.

"Who is selected to be on such a Panel?" My tone of voice is cunning, and I turn my body over once again, hoping Thomas will do the same. He stays on his back and moves his hands behind his neck.

"Haha. You'd like that, wouldn't you?"

Can he read my thoughts? I have to be careful. I adjust my position but find it hard to find a comfortable way of lying here.

"It's very simple. Before you can be considered for the Panel, you have to be enlightened. That is, free of your ego, just as the Master is."

I move a little closer to Thomas and can feel the warmth of his body.

"Can I meet the Master?" I whisper in his ear.

Thomas turns to look directly into my eyes. "Would you like to meet him?"

A rush of excitement bubbles through my body. "Absolutely."

"Why?" He keeps on smiling and gets a mysterious look in his eyes that I can't decode.

That's a good question. My toes start moving up and down inside my boots. And I make a few curlicues in the mist of the cloud. "Can I think about it before I give you my answer?"

It is completely deserted here at the edge of the cloud—no sounds, no people, just us. Thomas nods. I sense that it makes an impression on him that I don't just say something clever. But that wouldn't be right just now. We are in another place.

"Would you tell me more about the Master? Have you met him?" I am deeply grateful to be here together with Thomas. Although the cloud is cold, warmth spreads from the blanket throughout my body. I pull it a little further up under my chin.

"Yes, I've met him." He breathes calmly. Even here in the

starlight, Thomas's blue eyes shine. "The first time was when I had been here for four years."

"FOUR YEARS?" I blurt out. I'm definitely not going to wait that long.

Finally, he rolls over, and we lay facing each other. "Yes." He pauses, and I begin to think he only does that to stretch the time and my curiosity. "I was invited by someone who was acting as the Master's right hand at the time. Unlike you, I didn't care to meet him. Meeting the Master wasn't anything I was particularly interested in then. I was more absorbed in my own process. The invitation took me by surprise."

"How was it?" I turn onto my stomach and let my elbow rest on Thomas's chest, completely forgetting to blink.

He smiles and raises his head slightly. "I will leave it to you to experience yourself if you are ever invited. I can't tell you what the apprenticeship is about either. It is confidential, sorry to say."

I hit my hand against his chest, and I squint my eyes together slightly.

"Who knows? Perhaps you'll be called one day." He smiles at me, raises his eyebrows a couple of times, and turns his gaze back toward the stars. I turn onto my side and sink into his embrace. The sweet scent of his body pleases me, and we lie together perfectly still without saying anything. Although we are drifting on a cloud, it feels like we have made a safe little space out of a much bigger space. I take in a deep breath and feel at ease.

Thomas raises his arm and looks at his watch. It's ten past ten. Time flies. It only felt like a minute ago that the sun went down.

"Very few people can become free of their personalities," Thomas speaks quietly, and his soft voice has such a reassuring effect. "Most people are busy trying to get others to compensate for their shortcomings or whatever it is that they long for, and they are never happy."

I try to think of Andreas, but as with my pictures of Luke that are getting harder to see, the image of Andreas is fleeting, gone nearly as soon as it formed in my memory.

"When we get others to fill in our emotional shortcomings—you can also call them emotional holes—then we become dependent on them. Then, if they suddenly no longer want to be with us, it can be very painful because, without them, we feel our pain again, and then we begin to struggle."

I pull down the blanket and place my hand on Thomas's chest. Andreas made me feel safe and not so alone; was that an emotional hole? The thought of Andreas drifts away like a feather blown by the breeze. I don't try to hold onto the thought.

The moon rises from below. It is a great, luminous orb whose cool, white light glows on us. I close my eyes and listen to Thomas's words.

"Very few people can figure out how to be alone without shutting off life or how to be together with another without being dependent or having a relationship based on ownership and love contracts."

Is he talking about me? I try to act nonchalant. But I can't help taking a quick peek at him.

Thomas looks at me. "We become fixed in our ways of being and often come to a standstill because it is so nice when others fill our emotional holes. But they are still there."

I knit my brows and raise my elbow that is resting on his chest. "Well, I guess everyone should probably look inward. Can we avoid it?" The statement was the best I can do. I'm not sure if I believe it myself.

Thomas continues, "The great majority of people never look inward but blame others for everything, or they don't know or believe that it can be different. So, they take on an attitude that they are satisfied with what they have. The great challenge is that they are never truly happy and have a hard time letting others in." Our eyes meet. The moon is reflected in his eyes, giving them greater depth. He is lying on his back with his arm around me. I can feel his heart beating and the heat from his muscular body. His coat is made of some kind of incredibly soft material that goes warm when he's cold and cool when he is warm.

"When one is enlightened, there are no emotional holes left. There is no acting, and there are no unconscious patterns of behavior. You are whole, and the role-playing is over." Thomas places his palms together and lowers his head slightly.

He falls silent.

I don't say anything, but instead, I'm aware of how the silence fills me and makes every little muscle in my body unwind.

"Do you still think that it's a coincidence that you are here?"

That's what I call a leading question. "I've stopped believing anything." I shut my eyes and breathe the cool air in through my nose. "Right now, I don't know what to believe."

Should I tell him about my experience with Annabel? I let my mouth drop open. No, not now, maybe later. I don't even know what it's about. Perhaps it was just a one-off and nothing more. I smile inwardly. This is certainly a strange and fascinating time.

Thomas raises his head slightly. "There's something you're not telling me."

I nod. That's the closest I'll come to the truth tonight.

11
CONTACT

The atmosphere in the control room is excited and noisy. Curious, I edge my way over to a group of about ten men forming a circle around a screen and stand next to a tall, thin man with very short, dark hair. He glances at me and smiles, acknowledging that I want to join the circle. Everyone's focus is on the screen. I place my hand on his shoulder for support to balance on my tiptoes and see what's going on.

"Yes, do it," yells a man in his thirties. He is bouncing with enthusiasm and clapping his hands.

"Do it; do it; do it."

"Nooooo." The man next to him holds his head with his hands. His hair sticks out in all directions, and he looks like a real teddy bear the way he's standing there. The others clap and howl, and their mood is elevated. I can't see what's on the screen and try to move a little closer to get a better view.

"Come on. Do it."

"Yes, yes, yes. Look now."

They are all shouting simultaneously, and soon everyone from the control room is gathered around the screen.

"What's going on?" I whisper to the man standing next to me.

He laughs. "Come stand in front of me so you can see it better. They've all bet on whether the boy will discover the hint they've given him." He steps back and makes room so that I can see the screen without support from his shoulder.

"Hint?" I frown slightly.

"Yes. We are not supposed to contact those on Earth, but it is hard not to do it once in a while." He smiles at me briefly and looks back at the screen. "It's become a sport to see who can do it without being caught. Ian is the one standing over there with the dark brown ponytail and the red sweater." He nods in the direction of five men on the right. "It's his son on the screen."

I turn to look at Ian, who is totally absorbed. He is staring at the screen and clenching his hands in front of his body.

"He's written a word on his son's soccer ball, their secret code word, and now everyone's waiting to see if the son notices it."

My frown deepens, and I shake my head in confusion.

"The important thing is to be inventive. It's easy enough to leave clues and messages, but it has to be done elegantly so that only the person it is intended for gets it." He turns back toward the screen, not taking any notice of my furrowed brow or strained smile.

I can contact Luke!

At once, my body is like a fireball, filled with energy. If Ian can contact his son, then I must be able to contact Luke.

What am I waiting for? I have to find out how to do it.

I glance at the man beside me, but he doesn't look like he wants to be interrupted anymore. He, too, is completely absorbed by what's happening on the screen. I have to find someone else. I look around the control room. Everybody is standing here being entertained. Then, I realize.

Annabel!

Annabel must know how to make contact. She seemed to know

quite a bit about In-Between and how the place works. Thomas is a bit too correct; I better not ask him.

I turn around, find my way through the circle of enthusiastic men, and head directly toward the door with quick steps. Just last night, I was wondering whether I would ever see Annabel again. Now, all I want to know is how to find her. Surely there must be some kind of telephone directory somewhere or other. I stop at a screen and press it. It comes to life. There are numerous icons, and one says directory. I press it and start to scroll down. A, Ann, Anna.... I don't have to look far.

Annabel. There are five of them, but only one has been here for over a year. It has to be her—number 3723.

It is only eight in the morning, but somehow, I'm sure she is a morning person.

Swiftly, I pull the Skycon out of my pocket and start punching in the numbers. When Annabel answers, my stomach jumps.

"Hi, it's Eva." I only just manage to get the words out of my mouth.

"Well, hello." Annabel's voice is cheerful. "Where are you, and what are you doing?"

"There's something I'd like you to help me with," I say in a grave tone.

"Oh, it sounds serious." Annabel laughs gently. "Okay, let's meet in thirty minutes. Do you know where the library is?"

"No, but I'll find it. I'll be there in thirty minutes then." My heart is beating so fast, and a heatwave rushes to my head.

Did she wink at me before she hung up?

A rush of nervousness runs through my body. Do I really want to see her again? Maybe she misunderstood the reason for my urgency?

I chase the question from my mind. This is no time for distractions. I have half an hour to be at the library, but I have to find my way there first. For a moment, I think of asking someone in the control room for directions. I glance at the screen where I've found

Annabel's number. Perhaps I can scroll down to the L's and find the library's code.

Then I remember the Skycon. Carefully, I push the small letters. Even though it is so thin and soft, it doesn't bend when I touch it, and the small screen seems much bigger than it is.

L-I-B-R-

The Skycon's screen flashes, and a map appears. A small green dot saying 'Eva' glows in the lower-left corner of the screen. In the upper left is a bright blue star labeled library. A dotted line is connecting the two with other buildings and landmarks marked for reference.

A satisfaction from working it out all by myself fills me like finding the answer to a riddle.

I start to walk, glancing from time to time at the Skycon, pleased to see that the little green dot representing me moves as I do, and even more pleased to see that every step of the way, I remain on the right path. I'm right on time and will arrive in twenty-seven minutes.

WHEN I REACH THE LIBRARY, Annabel is standing there waiting for me. Her hair is up, making her face stand out more distinctly. A long patterned skirt in bright colors covers her legs, and she is wearing high-heeled sandals.

"Hi," I say as Annabel swiftly steps closer to me.

I get a big hug and a kiss on the mouth as if it is perfectly natural to greet each other in that way. Caught a bit off guard, I feel a little uncertain. My eyes are blinking fast, and I try to keep calm and stay focused.

Annabel looks at me curiously. "What is it that's so important?"

There are many people in the hallway, and I take a step closer to Annabel. "Do you know how I can make contact with Luke? I was in the control room, and some of the guys there were leaving messages for their children." My words come out, not leaving any break between them.

Annabel sighs softly. "Come. I think that we should sit where we can have some peace." She takes my hand, and the door glides open to reveal a large room. All the walls are covered with shelves filled with books that are kept behind glass. The ceiling is high, the floors are pale marble, and the style is simple and pure. It isn't the decor I usually associate with a library, but it is welcoming, with a unique blend of old and new. There is no sign of librarians or other staff.

"Sit down here." Annabel points at a red sofa that is situated on a black carpet. At first, the couch does not look very inviting because it is rectangular, and I hesitate.

"I can help you," her voice suddenly seems so serious, "but there's something you need to know first."

A tug of fear pulls inside me, but I draw a deep breath against it as I sit on the sofa next to Annabel. It is so soft and comforting. She touches a discreet button on the sofa's arm. The nearest bookshelves slide back to reveal a fireplace where a gentle, warming blaze appears. I refuse to be distracted by yet another of In-Between's marvels.

"Tell me," I look straight into Annabel's green eyes and don't blink even though my eyes start to get dry.

Annabel speaks in a heartfelt manner, "If you make contact, it will be impossible for you to make a choice." She rests her hands in her lap and sits with her back straight.

"Choice?" Thomas has also mentioned this choice. But for me, there's no doubt that I must return as soon as possible. Why all this talk about a choice?

"Yes," she takes my hand and looks me right in my eyes. "*Your choice*, the one no one else can make for you. You have been given a chance to make progress, to learn things here that you will apply to your next life. Or you can choose to return to your life on Earth and live with Luke and the rest of your family. That's your choice, Eva."

I sit passively, taking in her words. Her hand is slight and warm. The sound of voices in the hallway comes and goes. We have the library to ourselves. It's like my thoughts fill up the whole space. There are so many books here, with so much knowledge, I guess. If only I could leave my thoughts in a book for now and close it, so I could have peace of mind just for a little while. Maybe that would help me to think clearly.

She leans forward and whispers in my ear. "There is no doubt that there is more for you to learn on Earth, but there is also a reason that you have come here."

Has everyone been brainwashed so that they all say the same things? Is there some kind of conspiracy here? I am somewhat skeptical and pull back my hand. My judgment has never failed me as a journalist. Was it wise of me to contact her? What if she tells Thomas? Can I trust her? Is anyone eavesdropping on us even now? I look around to see if there are cameras in the ceiling or on the walls. There is nothing to be seen—just books in cupboards from floor to top and aisles that reveal more books.

"What reason?" I say in a flat voice. "What's the reason that I've been brought here?"

"I don't know why you are here." Annabel lets herself fall back against the sofa. "But, if you begin to contact Luke, you will reestablish the emotional contact you have with him, and he will also be able to feel it."

I take my time, reading between the lines of Annabel's words. *Reestablish emotional contact.* Something about this place, something about In-Between itself, or the experience of being brought here had put distance between me and the emotions I feel for Luke. My throat tightens at the thought of being manipulated in such a way. I don't want to be. But somehow, I can't fight it.

Annabel tilts her head slightly. "Soon, Luke will be able to sense that your soul is not one hundred percent in your body. He is a boy, and he will do anything to get his mother back, but who knows?

Maybe his great life lesson will be something he has to learn by losing his mother."

"That is so far out! That is not a lesson to be learned. That is inhuman." I push Annabel away with my words and cover my face with my hands. Everything goes dark, and I close my eyes. The best thing for me to do is to go back. It is my duty as a mother. How could I do anything else? I simply cannot understand why they keep talking about it as if it were a choice. In my mind, I don't have a choice; it is only a hypothesis.

Slowly, I lower my hands and open my eyes. "Have you been in contact with your son?"

Annabel shakes her head. "I have been close so many times, but I haven't done it. Besides, my son, my mother, father, and brother are still alive." She moistens her lips and speaks quietly. "I have never contacted my family. That doesn't mean that I don't keep an eye on them because I do. It's hard to let go completely. Especially the first weeks I was here, I watched them every day. But now, some time can pass between viewings."

I can't help thinking of my mother, father, and sister. What if I never get to talk to them again? Then, my stomach sinks. It is Luke's fifth birthday today. An explosion of guilt, anger, and fear presses so hard on the inside that I feel like throwing up. How could I forget? I always sing for him in the morning, bring him presents, and make my very special pancakes together with my mother and Andreas. I try to breathe to make the nausea go away. It doesn't help. Annabel is sitting calmly next to me, not knowing that I'm drowning in guilt inside.

I have to do something...

I try to make my mind blank as I stare at Annabel. She straightens up on the sofa and reaches toward me. I put my hand in hers and feel the warmth flow into my cold fingers. The logical part of my brain tells me that it is still only morning. There is time to check in with Luke later, or even better, send him reassurance that I'm alive. My feelings keep flooding me with waves of guilt.

Annabel's eyes widen as our fingers intertwine. "There has been a shift inside me. I have resigned myself to being here. Most of my time, I use to focus on my process so that I can prepare myself as best I can before I move on." Annabel's eyes shine with increasing brightness as she speaks.

"When are you going to move on?" I ask curiously, still looking into her eyes.

"When I am ready." Annabel looks down. "Would you still like to contact Luke?"

I nod. "I miss him so terribly. He is my little boy." My sight grows blurry. I can't make up my mind whether to tell Annabel that Luke turns five today or not. So, I don't. If I say it out loud, it somehow becomes more real, and so does the guilt of forgetting.

Annabel kicks off her sandals and pulls her feet under her. The glow from the fire makes the room cozy and warm. Annabel waves her hand effortlessly over the table. A part of it moves to the right, and a tray with glasses and water becomes visible. She pours water in two glasses and hands one to me. "I know that feeling myself. I know it so well, that bond. It is the strongest bond a woman can have. It's hard for us to let go of it."

The water is ice cold and fills my mouth. "Then you'll help me contact Luke?"

She smiles cautiously at me. "Let's wait until tonight so that there aren't so many in the control room, and it's easier to give it a try."

It can be done! A surge of excitement runs through my body. Almost immediately, I feel an equally powerful rush of worry. Is contacting Luke the right thing to do? Right for Luke—and right for me? It is hard to admit it, but I'm not sure anymore. One moment I feel that all hope is gone, the next as though I have been given the keys to the universe. What is this place, and what is it doing to me?

I take a deep breath, and I look at Annabel. "Thanks..."

She places her hand on my cheek. I lower my eyes and can feel her hand glide down my skin and under my chin. She lifts my face slowly so that our eyes meet.

"There's so much going on inside me," The words tumble out of my mouth. "I'm just so confused and afraid. I don't know what's right or wrong." I hold my breath before I continue. "What's best for Luke, what I should do—or what I shouldn't. And... and it's his birthday today." Tears start to run like a river that has been held back for too long.

Slowly, Annabel places her hands on my chest. The warmth of her touch is like a circuit being completed. My tensions, nervousness, even the questions that most concern me begin to drain away. I have a connection with Annabel that I have never before experienced with another woman.

"I don't have any friends that I have been as close to as I am to you now. It is so new for me, to be so honest." I give a wry smile and try to excuse myself. Why am I compromising myself in this way? I hurriedly look away. But Annabel continues to sit there, holding my hand without saying anything, and she doesn't seem particularly put off by my announcement.

I have always thought that women were weak—that needing others was some kind of failure and that it is best to fend for yourself. But, as I am sitting here, I realize that I can't fend for myself, that I do need others. It is a painful insight because it means that I have to open up and ask for help. What an admission of failure.

Throughout my whole life until now, I have been independent and relied only on myself.

She hands me a napkin, and I dry my face. The longing to accept my vulnerability and let another person through my armor is so great that it feels like a part of me is awakening in Annabel's company, a part of me that has been closed for many, many years. To me, vulnerability has always been equal to weakness.

I take a deep breath and let myself lean carefully against

Annabel's chest. When I relax against Annabel, I find myself wrapped in a sensation of warmth and softness, strength, and confidence. I drink in her scent, and bit by bit, my entire body relaxes. It seems like a part of me is growing and being healed as I sit here—like the vulnerability becomes a strength and allows me to connect. I feel like a young bird nestled next to its mother's breast, safe from the whole world.

I want nothing more than to surrender to that feeling, let Annabel care for me, and take my other cares away. Despite my desire, though, the armor I have carried for so long remains in place. The fear of being rejected strikes me like lightning and spreads throughout my body. What will happen when she leaves? What if she thinks that I am too clingy? I take a deep breath. Am I just filling one of my many emotional holes?

She strokes my hair in a loving, motherly way—can she recognize my worries? Her loving touch tells me I have nothing to worry about. I sit up. We look into each other's eyes, and I see that there is an incredible depth and clarity about her. She has something quite remarkable that I have never encountered before or perhaps have not been open to.

"I've never kissed a woman before." Annabel looks at me with a straight face.

"What?" I raise an eyebrow and smile at her. She seemed so confident, so experienced.

She smiles back. "It took me by surprise yesterday when I kissed you, but I felt extremely attracted to you. It seemed so natural, and I just couldn't help myself." She leans forward. "Can I kiss you again?"

I can't help but smile. At record speed, blood rushes to my face and warms it. I look down a little shyly and nod yes. Her face approaches mine, and we lose ourselves in an intense kiss. Our bodies fall onto the sofa, pressed together. We lie still, and I take in her feminine scent and let it penetrate every little cell in my body. It's like a key that opens a door inside me that I never knew existed.

I run my hand over her body; we have the same form, curves, and softness. I have been with many men over the years, and, in some ways, I know the male body better than the female body, which seems somewhat bizarre. I'm curious and want to go further into the space that has opened inside. My hands slide down her back.

"Aren't our clothes in the way?" I whisper in her ear with a voice soft and warm.

In a swift motion, Annabel removes her dress, and I follow. Without a word, we lie together naked. I rest my head on her chest, and she brings her arms around me. Her scent is mild, intense, and intimate. And her skin is like silk, soft and inviting. I succumb and let the sensations fill me. I don't have to do anything—just allow her to hold me, feeling like a new woman.

My life is expanding.

12

A NEW CHALLENGE

"This is where Mom's sleeping."

With one hand in Luke's and the other on the door, Andreas carefully pushes open the slightly scratched wooden door to Eva's room. Luke jumps up and down and pulls Andreas's arm.

"Come on, Dad. Open the door, push it... I haven't seen her for years!"

It's hard for Andreas not to laugh, but he manages and gives Luke's hand a soft squeeze. "That's nearly correct; it's been three long weeks." Before he opens the door entirely, he takes a moment to run his hand over Luke's hair. "Remember what I told you in the car; she can't hear or see you."

"Right, Dad," Luke puts his tiny shoulder against the door and roars as he gives a good push, just enough for him to see Eva's bed come into view. He squeezes through the opening.

"Mom!" His frail little voice is filled with hope as he runs to the bed.

The room is looking cheerful. Andreas has brought pictures, a small water fountain, and a light brown carpet for the floor to make the space more inviting. A selection of songs that they used to listen to together is playing at a low volume. Andreas doesn't know what music Eva is listening to these days, but he hopes that familiar melodies can help bring her out of the coma.

Luke is already at the bedside, jumping with enthusiasm. "Mom! Mom!" But there is no reaction. Then he takes her arm and shakes it. "Mom, wake up now. We have a playdate. It's my birthday; you have to wake up."

Eva is lying there perfectly still. With slow and heavy steps, Andreas walks over and stands behind Luke. He places a hand on his shoulder and runs his other hand over his stubble again and again.

"Just keep on calling her. We don't know what she will react to. She's sleeping very deeply."

"Why can't we just wake her? I want to show her the new toys that you gave me." Luke turns and looks expectantly at Andreas with his big blue eyes.

"I know you want to. But right now, it is impossible to say when she will wake up." It is too hard for him to maintain eye contact with Luke, so he shifts his gaze, looks out the window, and blinks a few times. Dark clouds are building up in the sky; it definitely looks like it will rain later.

It doesn't seem to affect Luke; he stands very still and stares at his mother. Before Andreas knows it, he crawls up on the chair next to the bed, leans down over her, and kisses her. "Mom, I miss you. Will you please wake up now?" He grips the railing and shakes it gently.

Andreas runs his hand over his face to wipe off the tears that are rising. Luke is such a brave boy. How could he be expected to understand something like this? He feels a shiver run up his spine and looks around, feeling like someone is watching them. Just then, the door opens, and Dr. Johnson comes in. He must have been glancing at them through the partially open door.

"Do you have a moment?" the doctor asks.

Andreas turns toward Luke, "Do you want to stay here with Mom?" He doesn't react. "Luke, I have to talk with the doctor. Will you stay here with Mom? You can touch her but not anything else, all right?"

Luke answers without looking at Andreas. "Yeah, Dad, I heard you."

Andreas steps outside the room with Dr. Johnson but leaves the door open.

"We have the latest results from the lab." Dr. Johnson holds up a sheaf of papers and printouts. Andreas says nothing. "There's not a lot to report. We continue to monitor, to look for signs of improvement or... To monitor." He looks through the pile of papers. "And we look for other things that might reach her through the coma." He clears his throat loudly and pushes his glasses up onto his forehead. "I have a sensitive question. Do you know anything about Eva's private life? Since your divorce?"

Andreas shook his head. "No, since we split up, we haven't seen very much of each other. It's been over a year. We still have contact because of Luke, of course. Other than that, we don't see each other often."

"So, you don't know if she is in a new relationship?"

"Relationship? What are you asking?" Andreas looks back at Luke to make sure he isn't listening. He is fully absorbed in telling Eva about his birthday so far.

"Is she—romantically involved with anyone?" Dr. Johnson turns over another page.

"What difference could—" Andreas falls silent, then speaks slowly, irritated. "No, Doctor, I don't believe she is in a new relationship. I think she would have told me. Or Luke would have. What difference does it make?" His tone is starting to sound a bit irritated.

"Probably none," Dr. Johnson replies. "But we—I—thought that perhaps if there were someone new... well, that person... that person's voice, his presence might be another way of reaching her, of trying to reach her."

Andreas feels his stomach knot, mostly in anger at the doctor's intrusion into private matters, no matter how well-intended, but also with a sharp stab of jealousy, so sharp that its intensity surprises him. He leans his back against the wall and rests his head. Eva has never spoken to him about anyone, and he has no illusions that she wouldn't see other men, just as he has seen other women, but thinking of it so clearly, having the issue raised so bluntly, caught him off-guard.

He glances briefly at Luke to make sure he still isn't listening. Then closes his eyes briefly before replying. "No, Doctor. As far as I know, Eva wasn't seeing anyone." Andreas starts to run his fingers over his stubble.

The doctor is frowning slightly, making a checkmark next to a line on his paper.

"You've contacted her mother, of course. If you think of any other relatives or close friends whose voices Eva might recognize... well, you understand what I'm saying."

Andreas said nothing. After a moment, the doctor closed the folder. "If you think of anything...."

"I will," Andreas pats him on the shoulder. "Thank you."

Dr. Johnson leaves the room, ready to see the next patient, and the door closes behind him. The machines' sound makes a constant noise in the room, like a humming sound combined with the wind. Andreas doesn't move for a long moment. This whole situation just made everything so complicated. He'd been planning to tell Luke about the news in his life for some time now, and he had finally been ready to tell Eva as well. Now, he doesn't know if he will ever get the chance.

He feels the dull ember of frustration inside him and tries to ignore it. Eventually, it dwindles enough for him to return his attention to Luke, who is singing along with the music coming from the soundbox. He takes a step toward his son and his former wife, unable to shake off the feeling that someone is watching them even after the doctor's departure.

THE LIFE

I STAND THERE WATCHING Luke with tears rolling down my cheeks. The control room is nearly deserted, and there is no one in the same row as Annabel and me. The huge screens hover from the walls, showing pictures of a forest burning, a demonstration between black and white people, and a mother with her dead child in her arms.

I force myself to breathe deeply and rhythmically, almost in the same pattern as the machines supporting my body in the hospital bed. There is so much to take in, not just the images of Luke—how tiny he looks and how deeply I want to hold him and run my hand through his hair; how I want to smell him; how my body is connected to the medical, technical technology; and the images of Andreas.

There is something about him; I have rarely seen him so tense. I saw the reaction on his face when the doctor asked his question.

I look down at Annabel, who is sitting right next to me. She reaches for my hand and gives it a slight squeeze. "He has been keeping something from you."

For once, I feel that I have met a completely honest person. Nothing gets wrapped up. She is entirely straightforward, always with a loving intention. I look at her beautiful green eyes and her soft white skin and feel the love and care she resonates.

"By the way Andreas reacted when he spoke to the doctor, he could still be in love with you." Our eyes meet briefly.

I make a rejecting facial grimace and look back at the screen. Andreas is standing right behind Luke next to my bed. "No, he is not. I'm sure of that."

"Are you—?"

"—Yes, of course, I am." I grit my teeth and press my tongue hard against the inside of my teeth.

"I was going to say, are you still in love with him?"

I turn my head quickly and look straight into Annabel's eyes. "NO. Why would you even think that?"

Annabel just smiles.

"He's a good father to Luke," I add quickly, then catch myself. "He wants to be, anyway. Always has. He can be."

"And now he has no choice; not really," Annabel looks at me with an imploring look in her eyes. It brings a sense of realism with it. She moves her chair even closer and pushes a chair over toward me. It is made of a simple black construction also hanging in the air. "There has got to be something good to say about him," she gives me that teasing look.

I let myself fall into the chair that rocks softly. "Sure, he is very charming, a great listener; he is fun to be with and easygoing; when I went too fast, he got me to slow down… I guess we were each other's antipole."

I can feel Annabel's eyes resting on me as she continues. "In my experience, the greatest challenges provide correspondingly great redemption. But only once we've made it through to the other side can we see that." She keeps looking at me, and I keep looking at the screen, where Andreas is still standing behind Luke next to my bed.

Annabel is right. A part of me knows it. Andreas has a good heart, and he is under a lot of pressure right now. Honestly, I don't know I would react had I been in his shoes. At least I know I will wake up soon; he doesn't.

Although more and more people are gradually coming into the control room, it remains silent. A young girl with hair down to her hips sits down close to us. Her eyes are bloodshot, and she is squeezing a tissue so tight that her knuckles are white. Further back, an older man is holding up his palm, nearly touching the screen. There is a respectful atmosphere here. Annabel is sitting close enough for our legs to touch. She squeezes my hand and moves her arm around my shoulders. I slump in the chair and let her warmth fill me up.

The picture on the big screens shift. Now, photos of dolphins playing in the ocean and several other images from the great barrier reef show. Some parts of the reef are still alive, and some are not.

"How many days do you have left?"

I lean back so that my chair rocks. "What do you mean? How many days do I have left?"

"I mean... how many days have you been here?" Annabel sits still as if it was the most ordinary subject to discuss.

I shake my head a bit instinctively. What kind of question is that? "I haven't counted them, but not very many. I mean, I only got here yesterday." I try to look calm, but inside me, there is nothing calm. My heart beats faster, and I pull off my sweater.

"Well, fine." She cannot hide a smile, "Then you have time to think about it. Now, do you still want to leave Luke a message?"

I draw a deep breath and shake my head. Maybe now is not the time, even though it's Luke's birthday. Somehow, he is seeming to cope, but making contact could make it worse and more challenging. And by the look on Andreas's face, he is not the best support for Luke at this time. "Not now." I bite my lip, feeling a twinge of pain shoot through me.

Annabel runs her hand gently over my chin. "There's no hurry. Remember that I'm here for you. Just tell me what you need."

What I need is a good question. A part of me just wants to sit here, being held. But another part of me feels like being alone, taking it all in. "I think I need to go lie down," I hesitate a bit and hope Annabel doesn't see it as a rejection.

"Anything else you need?"

I look up, "I lost my picture of Luke. Is it possible to get a new one?"

"Nothing to it." Annabel presses the screen and brings up an image of Luke playing with his LEGOs and smiling broadly. "Is this okay?"

"Perfect."

Annabel reaches behind the screen and hands me a copy of the picture. I immediately press it to my chest. "Thank you."

"Do you want to be alone, or would you like some company?"

I can feel her question is sincere. No agenda. It is a relief. I don't have to satisfy her or be concerned about her needs.

"I do want to be alone. But can we meet tomorrow?" I look back at the screen where Luke is busy drawing at the table next to my bed.

"Of course, we can. Whenever you wish, just call me. I'm properly busy sorting some stuff out. But just call, then we can arrange to meet." Annabel kisses my hand, and I move it to my chin and close my eyes for a moment. I just want to take her motherly energy in and let it fill me for a moment.

"Thanks." I let go and press the screen to shut it off, only to find that I am turning up the sound. The girl with bloodshot eyes looks over at me, and I try to make the sound go away.

"Here, let me." Annabel taps the screen, and the picture of Luke and me fades away. "Shall we walk together some of the way?"

"Yes, I'd like that." I stand up, and the chair moves softly back. I reach for my sweater and manage to suppress a sigh.

She takes my hand, and we walk out of the control room together. It's wonderful to know that there's another person who's there for me and that I can be myself without being afraid that she's going to leave me.

13

THE MASTER

I wake up early the following morning, filled with energy. My room is bright, and the sun is rising over the horizon. It is tempting to lie here a little longer without moving, thinking of what I saw in the control room, thinking of Annabel's words. Andreas is hiding something from me, and this is not the first time. But this time, I'm not the only one sensing it. My heart starts to beat a little faster. Why would Annabel suggest that I am still in love with Andreas? Maybe it is Annabel who has not come to terms with her relationship and is projecting it onto me. I rise on an elbow and throw back the covers.

Sunbeams peek over the windowsill, blinding me. I blink a couple of times and turn my head to look at Luke's picture that Annabel gave me. It is sitting on my desk next to the bed. His smile reminds me of the times we have laughed so hard together that we both got stomach pain. He was so brave yesterday. The way he was sitting next to my bed singing, waiting for me to wake.

I reach out for the picture and let my fingertips slide over it, just to make sure it is real. Everything that I am experiencing right now is so surreal. Maybe I'm going crazy. I close my eyes. It could be that something just clicked in my mind, and I am actually in a psychiatric ward, and all of this is only happening inside my head.

The quilt seems suffocating, and I kick it off. Insanity has always terrified me; my body tenses at the thought, and I stiffen. It seems as if I have experienced being on the fine line between sanity and insanity, leaving me with a great fear of going mad. What would happen? Would it be possible to return to a state of good mental health after losing it? I press my fingernails into my palms, hard enough to hurt. Then I blink a couple of times and let my eyes rest on the flowers on the table next to Luke's picture. Their colors are luminous—bright red and yellow. Are they supernatural? Of course, what around here isn't? Slowly, I lean forward and press my face against their petals, hoping to drink their scent. But there isn't any.

Deep inside, I associate being insane with totally losing control, letting go of my energy and everything that comes with it, and disappearing into another universe, a place where I have no control over time or space and maybe not even over myself. I breathe deeply and slowly so that the sound of my breath fills my head.

The thought of being locked up makes me wince, and the idea of others controlling me or declaring me incapable of managing my affairs scares me even more. It feels like the heat has been turned on inside of me, and small pearls of sweat build up on my chest. When it comes down to it, I am all alone.

The sound of my laughter surprises me. Better to laugh about it than cry, I try to convince myself. When my laughter subsides, I touch Luke's picture once more. I don't know why it surprises me that it is still cold and hard.

Something is missing inside me. I can't fight it anymore, this empty place that I worked so hard not to feel all my life. It feels more extensive and more pervasive than ever before. I sit up on the bed and try to breathe softly, but my breath comes short and ragged. At that moment, I realize that not even my love and responsibility for

Luke can fulfill that hole inside me. But then what can? Could the answer be out there, somewhere in the vastness of In-Between?

The Master.

A sensation of a flutter of butterflies in my stomach overwhelms me. What if I can find him? He must live here somewhere, and maybe he holds some of the answers to my questions.

I stretch, loosening my muscles, and then reach out for the green circle on the wall. The doors open gently, and I find a pair of jeans and a blue sweater. "I believe I will go exploring," I say aloud. "I will have an adventure." A smile fills my face and is followed by a sensation of excitement.

It took Thomas four years before he met the Master, but it won't take me so long. I smile in satisfaction and feel ten years younger.

A light touch on a button, and the wall slides open, revealing the cabinet with all the technical equipment. On one side is a big screen with a lot of options to select from. There must be a map or something I can use to get an overview of In-Between. My finger glides down the screen, and I press different buttons that bring up images with names, workstations, a calendar, contacts, and an overview. Excellent, there it is. I press the screen softly, and a large keymap of In-Between appears.

The flatscreen map reveals a far more spacious campus than my Skycon had when it guided me to the library. "This place is huge," I say aloud. "Where am I?" There is a tiny red dot flashing. My fingers touch the screen, and it zooms in, and I move the map gently with my fingertips. Section by section, I go through the chart to localize the area I would like to explore today. I can't help but smile when I see the library and the place where the maze is.

There are many places I have yet to discover. I'm not sure where to start. Down in one corner, it seems like the map just stops. There is a little notch that doesn't make sense when the rest of it is so symmetrical. All the other corners are rounded—this one is vague and ill-defined, as though the territory hasn't yet been mapped.

Or as though what's there is off-limits.

I feel a tingling sensation in my gut.

There is a knocking sound outside my door. I look and wait to see if it continues. But it is quiet. Maybe it's just in my head. I stand perfectly still and realize that I'm holding my breath. A happy voice says hello, followed by more words that I can hear. It is the guy next door. I laugh nervously and shift my focus back to the area on the screen.

Could there be some unmarked territory? I zoom in on that area, but no information comes up. It seems like a large area is missing, that there is something that hasn't been drawn onto the map. I run my lips over each other and get a feeling like a little child at Christmas. This is where my adventure will begin.

Quickly, I put on the clothes I chose and fetch my Skycon from the table beside the bed. I tuck the photo of Luke in my pocket, and, after a few fumbling moments, I figure out how to sync the Skycon with the larger display, copying the map into the smaller device. Then I trace a path from my location's flashing red dot to the grayed-out area in the map's lower corner. A dotted line appears just as it did when I sought the library. This time, the difference is that no matter how hard I try and how firmly I tap the screen with my finger, the dotted line will only approach the grayed-out region, not enter it—another mystery.

Clinging to my Skycon, I leave the room and set out.

The area around my room is familiar now, and I walk through it quickly. The sun is high in the sky and is fully visible in the hallway. It feels like a sauna, and I take off my sweater and put it around my waist. A few people are standing ahead of me, and they greet me as I walk past. I am beginning to recognize more people here, but so many new people have arrived that I am no longer one of the latest arrivals. On the contrary, I am about to become one of the old hands in such a short time.

It suits me properly, a bit more than I like to admit. It's nice to be someone others turn to when they are confused. A warm sensation showers inside me when I think of helping a newcomer. It reminds me of the warmth I have drawn from Annabel or Thomas—a sensation like love itself—like a fragile scent that you can sense but not touch. It gives a sense of lightness to my body as I move ahead into the next hallway.

The red stripe has become green. The hallway still looks the same; doors on one side and large windows looking out over the horizon where clouds are hanging like an endless landscape on the other. I am approaching the area on the map where that strange indentation is. At the end of the hallway, I slow down my pace so I don't appear suspicious. I look at the names on the touch screens that I am passing, but there aren't any that I recognize. Outside the window, another cloud is passing by at high speed. A small portion of it breaks off. It is shaped like a lion, and I can't help but smile.

Suddenly, it seems like there are more people in the hallways than usual. Maybe it's just that I am a little paranoid, afraid that some of the people who greet me are also spying on me. Three more doors, and then I should be at the end of the map. Heat rises in my body, and a delicate tremble lies under my skin. I look back over my shoulder and slowly move toward the door. It slides open, and the stripe is yellow here. My feet come to a standstill. What if someone sees me? Nonsense. I haven't done anything against the rules, and I can always say that I got lost. Two doors, and then I will be in the missing area. Maybe I should have asked Annabel if she would come with me. My laughter resonates in the hallway. Am I such a coward when it comes down to it? I have been at the worst hot spots in the world with war and natural disasters, and I survived. If anybody asks, I'm just out looking around.

Just then, the beep from my Skycon startles me. I pull it out of my pocket and accidentally hit the on button.

"Hi, it's Thomas," says a voice, and then his image comes through. My heart skips a beat. I look eagerly up and down the corridor and turn so all Thomas will be able to see is the clouds behind me and my face.

"Hi, Thomas." I hesitate.

"I just wanted to hear how you're doing. I ran into Annabel, and she seemed a bit concerned when your name came up. Has anything happened?" I can't tell where he is, only that there are many people around him. Still, his voice comes through clearly.

"Oh, no. Um, well, yes, actually," I stammer. "But I'm out for a walk right now. Can we meet later?"

Two bold men dressed in jumpsuits pass by me, and I nod to them in a friendly way as I step aside. There is a little niche across from the door where I can stand undisturbed.

"Yes, fine. How about eating lunch together?"

"Lunch? Sure, good idea." I nod eagerly, making sure to hold the Skycon so that Thomas can't see the line's color on the floor.

"Great." Thomas smiles so that fine lines around his eyes appear.

"Good, then it's a date." I am fidgeting with impatience because I want to end this conversation.

"I just wanted to be sure that you're all right." He is looking right into the camera, and it is incredible how his eyes burn through that little screen.

"I'm fine. See you at lunch at one o'clock." I start to wave.

"Fine, see you." Thomas waves back at me. "Oh, by the way...."

Now what? I hastily look to each side to make sure no one is approaching.

"How about meeting at the café?"

"The café. Fine. See you." I don't have a clue where the café is, but I'll save that concern for later. Quickly, I break off the Skycon and put it in my pocket. That was close. I exhale in relief. For the last few days, I have had all my meals in my room. I was so amazed at the speed it arrived and how delicious it was. I have ordered burgers, salads, and dishes I have never heard of before. Fast and easy, just my liking. Apart from that, I needed time by myself. At least that's what

I'd been telling myself, but I must admit that I also hate sitting alone in a restaurant. This will be a great way to expand my knowledge of this place.

At the end of the corridor is the last door. I start to walk and don't look back. Not knowing where to go when I reach the door, I get out my Skycon, but the screen is blank. I thumb the device into call mode but get no response. It has gone dead. With nearly silent steps, I walk over to a window and hold up the device. Still, nothing happens. Maybe it is the batteries; for sure, this place isn't perfect. I shake my head and backtrack a bit, holding the Skycon in front of my eyes to catch even a flicker of life on its screen. Finally, I shut off the device and return it to my pocket. I know where I am, and I know how close I am to the area missing on the map. For sure, I can make it the rest of the way on my own. How hard could it be?

One more door, and then I am there.

As I get closer to the door, I hear the sound of footsteps approaching from behind. I continue walking straight ahead. Ten more steps and I am at the door. The corridor seems extremely long right now. The sound is getting closer, and I hear someone picking up the pace. I keep on going and pretend that nothing is the matter, but it is difficult. I feel a cool wind on my skin and notice a section of the wall pushed to the side, revealing a small terrace with a cloud beside it. At that moment, there is a careful tap on my shoulder. My body gives a little jump, and I stop, frozen in place.

"Hi. Sorry if I startled you."

I turn around to face a bald man with deep eyes that penetrate. He smiles at me, flashing his crooked yellow teeth.

"My name is Frank."

I don't say anything, just look at him. He is not someone that I have seen before. His face is covered with small scars, and he is a head shorter than me with broad shoulders. I keep looking at him without saying anything. He continues in an extremely friendly tone that borders on being sickeningly sweet. "What are you doing here?"

Right now, I wish I could take a step back, but the door is right behind me. Instead, I hold my breath.

"People don't come here very often." His tone of voice is unctuous and too sweet.

I lean sideways and look down the corridor behind him. It is empty. Who is he, a guard? A tremble builds from my legs, and before I know it, my hands are also sweaty. My muscles are tense, and I bite my teeth hard together. "I'm just going for a walk." I have to test him to find out who he is and if it is a coincidence that he has come here. If he is a guard, then I know that my intuition was correct and that I am close to the Master's residence.

The clouds outside the window gather at a menacing speed, and the sun disappears entirely. I grab my sweater and pull it over my head without losing eye contact in a swift motion.

Still smiling, he puts his hand on my shoulder and chuckles. "It's really nice to meet you."

Warning lights begin to flash in my mind. He is just a little too nice. There's something suspicious about him. I smile tensely and let the words slip out between my clenched teeth. "What are you doing here?" It's always good to respond with a question. A technique I have often applied as a journalist, and it has been useful to me in many interesting situations.

"I needed to pick up something in building A4, and this is a shortcut." He points at the door in front of us. "You still haven't told me what you're doing here."

I'm not familiar enough with this area to work out whether it is, in fact, a shortcut, so I look down at the floor. My mind is working overtime. "Does it matter what I'm doing here?" I answer in a firm tone that cannot be mistaken. There can be no doubt that I don't appreciate his presence.

"No, it doesn't. I was just asking out of curiosity."

All of a sudden, rain bursts out of the sky, and water pours into the hallway. Frank quickly puts his finger on a red circle, closing the

THE LIFE

door to the terrace. Now, I definitely want to get rid of him. I have no desire to stand here and chat. If only I could take a side-step, easing around him and gaining access to the long corridor.

"Well, I have to get going," I try to smile, but it's a bit forced. "Nice to meet you." That I should never have said; why do I automatically act so pleasing?

"Yes, maybe we could have a cup of tea together sometime. I didn't catch your name yet."

"Uh, yes." I clench my fists and bite my lower lip. "Let's see...." That is the last thing I want to do right now. But I am incapable of saying what I mean. Frustration is beginning to boil within me as violently as the storm beyond the window.

The rain turns to hail and hammers down on the window, filling the hallway with its intrusive sound.

Frank steps closer, and his kindness seems artificial. How can he just go on and on with that smile? He is standing there waiting, practically compelling me to say my name.

"Eva." I force a smile.

"It's so nice to meet you, Eva." He raises his voice and lets his hand slide down from my shoulder and stroke my back. It sends a freezing cold shudder down my spine. I want to shout at him to get his clammy hand off me. If there is anything I can't stand, it's when men try to be extra nice, thinking that all women are crazy about them. The isolation of the deserted corridor only makes matters creepier and more threatening.

"I have to get going too, but you can walk with me if you like. It seems we are heading the same way." Frank moves his hand up and down my back. Even though I want to move to get rid of his touch, I stand frozen. But I manage to reach for the Skycon in my pocket.

"Sorry, I have to make a call." I press my hand firmly around the Skycon as if it was my lifeline.

Frank keeps smiling. "Well, it won't work here." He is pointing at my hand that is turning white as I tighten my grip around the Skycon.

"You need to go back up the corridor or through the next door. There's no signal here." He nods in the direction I came from.

"Thanks." I force a smile, turn away from Frank, and walk back down the corridor, hoping that he will leave me behind. When I reach halfway up the corridor, I stop. The signal is indeed back.

The rain subsides, and the sunlight is beginning to break through again. The air is heavy in here.

I wait until I'm sure that Frank has disappeared at the far end of the corridor. Then I turn around and hurry back to the spot where I was when Frank interrupted me. My sense of mission is stronger than ever, and I won't let a creepy guy like Frank get in my way. When I reach the final door, I'm out of breath but don't hesitate even a second before placing my finger on the green circle beside it. It opens, revealing a narrow hallway with three more doors. I take a step forward, and the door closes behind me. Which of the three new entries should I choose? Light is shining down from a skylight, making the room feel bigger than it is. Three small pictures hang on the door in front of me. They are very simple, with faint lines that intertwine, forming a wavy design. Apprehensively, I put my finger on the green circle in front of me. It gives a jolt in my finger, and I pull my hand back.

A long corridor opens in front of me, a wide passage covered with nothing but mirrors. I stand still and stare. There are only very fine grooves between the mirrors and no one in sight anywhere. Carefully, I step forward. The floor is made of pale marble. The light in the ceiling is pronounced, somewhat overwhelming, yet somehow a natural part of the design as a whole. The corridor seems long, but nothing enables me to estimate its proportions, nothing that breaks my line of vision. I tiptoe very slowly and quietly. There is no sound in here and nothing but my breath to be heard.

I must be close. My intuition can't fail me. Otherwise, why would there be such a change in the style of the interior? All the other hallways have windows, white walls, and there is always a colored stripe on the floor running parallel to the wall. There are no stripes here. I am about halfway down the hallway. To my right, a tiny ring on the mirror catches my eye. It is almost invisible. I step closer, right up to the mirror, raise my hand, and put my finger on the mirror. Nothing happens. Maybe I'm just seeing things. My hand runs smoothly over the mirror without leaving any trace.

My pocket starts to vibrate, and then the Skycon rings again. Quickly, I glance at my watch and see that it is ten past one. It is most likely Thomas calling me. I should have been at the café ten minutes ago. There is no way I can answer because whoever is on the other end can see where I am.

Reluctantly but quickly, I make my way from the mirrored corridor, filled with regret at having to break off my quest when I was so close and yet so far away.

14

A FRAGMENT OF THE WHOLE

The café is full, and I don't see Thomas anywhere. Outside is a huge screen full of the names of the people who have arrived and those who have departed. Before entering, I let my gaze run over the new ones; maybe there is someone I know. There isn't, and on the departure list, I don't know anyone either. I guess that's good. I start to work my way through the crowd of people.

On the right is a bar that serves food and beverages. It's like a rather large island with a lot of personnel stationed there. They are all smiling and seem to be having a great time. Above the bar hangs an oval light fixture that gives the space a more exclusive air. The bar is encircled by a high counter made of some sort of transparent material with a turquoise tinge. Windows cover the entire end wall all the way up to the arch. My first guess is that about 200 people could be seated at the tables; some are tables for two, and others are large and round. At the far end, there are sofa arrangements with tables and chairs placed next to them. On the walls are light formations in different colors and shapes that look like they can be modified when desired. I catch sight of Thomas sitting on one of the sofas in the back of the café. He looks at ease, lifting his cup in a graceful movement.

His shirt has a silver thread that draws a pattern from the shoulders and down, some kind of ancient symbol that I have never seen before.

"Hi. Sorry, I'm late." I am slightly winded when I make it over to him.

"That's all right. Don't even think about it. I just tried to reach you to see if you were on your way." Thomas stands up and opens his arms to hug me. There is a bit more room in this part of the café. Although some people are seated at the table next to ours, it seems like there is more space here.

"I heard the ringing, but I couldn't find the Skycon in my bag." I am obliged to lie, even though I'd rather not. Lies are the worst, but it just rushes out of my mouth. It's only a half-lie. I try to smile naturally at Thomas, but it seems pretty artificial.

I'm sure he can sense that it isn't true but doesn't say anything. He just smiles at me and gestures at the chair across from him. "Sit down. Can I get you anything?"

I shake my head. "Noo, yeah, I mean…." I'm off to a great start. Why can't I just act normal? He is standing there waiting as he looks at me with the most patient gaze. "I'd like a glass of juice," finally comes out of my mouth.

"Fine. Let me get it." He goes up to the bar, giving me a little time out. Take a nice deep breath and relax, I tell myself.

The rain has died down, and I can see far out on the horizon, but not below it because the clouds have settled under us like a goose-down quilt.

Why is it so hard to tell the truth? He won't kill me. I don't think that I've done anything wrong—I've just been out exploring. It is easy to smell a lie a mile away, which isn't always an advantage. I used to be obsessed with proving that I was right, and I wouldn't give up until I had made the person who had lied to me admit it. Good thing that Thomas isn't like that. Now, he's coming back. I sit back on the chair and smooth my hair. Apparently, I am not yet fully enlightened.

He places a large glass of freshly pressed orange juice in front of me. The color is brilliant, and the ice cubes rock gently on the surface.

"I brought some food too. Are you hungry?" He smiles at me and sets a salad plate in front of me.

I am. My secret mission and the rush back to the café have used up my reserves, so food is a good idea.

"The café has the most delicious food—vegetarian or meat it is up to you. You can also get salads, vegetables, and the most delectable dressings. You can get anything that you can imagine, but most people stick to what they know. Isn't it interesting how we like to think that we are impulsive, brave, and ready for change? But when it comes down to it, we prefer everything as we know it." He smiles and pushes a plate over to me. "The human species are the most adaptable individuals on Earth, and still, it is very hard for us to surrender to change." He pauses and looks at me with his intense presence.

"You've been here for several days now, Eva. Are you settled in?"

I nod eagerly and put some salad in my mouth. The taste explodes in my mouth like a bright, colorful painting.

"That's good. Is there anything you need or that you don't think has been explained well enough?" The tone of his voice is so calm and caring. His presence is intense, and he makes me feel like the most important person in the world at this moment.

"Noo...," I say after I finish chewing. I'm wondering if that is another outright lie or just a way of avoiding the real truth that I have dozens, hundreds, and thousands of questions. I swallow and put down the fork on the edge of the plate. I take a breath and say, "That's not quite right, as you can imagine."

Thomas's gentle chuckles allow me to overcome my hesitancy.

"There is actually something I would like to share with you."

He leans back and holds his gaze on me.

I make an effort not to talk too fast as I tell him what I overheard in the control room—about my meeting with Annabel and my decision not to leave a message for Luke just yet, despite the fierceness of my desire to do so. Even though it is hard for me not to speed talk, I control myself and make sure I tell the story clearly and accurately. It is important that he understands me.

Thomas waits until I finish my account. Then, with devastating accuracy, he asks the question I somehow feared he would.

"Eva, what's the real reason you left no message for Luke when you wanted to so badly?"

"Because—" Tears are piling up in my eyes. My voice trembles and is just about to crack. "I don't know." I shrug and look down. A tear runs down my chin, waiting to let go. "I wanted to; it's just that...." I pause, and the tear is about to leave my chin and fall into the unknown. "After being here, I feel like I'm falling apart. Everything I knew before, everything I believed in, I don't know...." I wipe away the tear before it falls.

"Try to look deeper, Eva," Thomas urges gently. "See if you can let go of what you think you know."

More tears begin to flow freely. "It's not just about me and what I want." My voice starts to tremble. "I have to go back. For Luke." This time, I let the tears run down my chin and fall upon my sweater.

We sit together quietly, looking at each other without saying a word. There is a long interval of complete silence. I feel like I'm losing myself in the depth of Thomas's eyes; they are overwhelmingly deep and full of mystery and clarity at the same time.

When I get a grip on myself, I almost whisper. "I'm in a hopeless situation, and I feel so lost and disoriented." Closing my eyes for a moment, I blink away my tears.

Thomas reaches out for a tissue and puts it in my hand. "Now, it's my turn to tell you a story."

I open my eyes as Thomas begins to speak, and I dry off the tears piling up in my eyes.

"Once upon a time, over 2,000 years ago, when the Chinese philosopher Lao Tzu was alive, a story was repeated again and again. Let me see if I can remember it. It goes something like this."

Thomas looks at me, squeezes my hand gently, and says, "Come and sit next to me on the sofa."

I push back my chair and stand up slowly. He moves over and makes room for me. When I sit next to him, he puts his arm around my shoulder. My whole body relaxes into his arms.

"There was an old farmer who lived in a village. Even the king was envious of him because he had a beautiful white horse. No one had ever seen a horse like it, with such beauty, elegance, and strength."

I let my eyes close and shut out everything but Thomas's voice.

"The king offered to buy the horse from the farmer for a great deal of money, but the farmer wouldn't sell it. He said that the horse was not a horse for him, but a person, and how could you sell a person? The horse was a friend, not a piece of property. It wasn't possible for him to sell it."

The warmth from Thomas's hand pours into my body, and I sit completely still, thinking, if I don't move, we can sit here for a little longer.

"The farmer was poor, so there were many good reasons for him to sell the horse, but he never would. The king was disappointed because he was sure that the horse could have won many prizes and could certainly have made a poor farmer rich."

The sound of his deep voice makes me relax throughout my body. The story fills my mind, and I feel my body settle down. I open my eyes a tiny bit, just to make sure that nobody is watching us. He doesn't seem to take notice of me and continues.

"All the neighbors shook their heads at the old farmer. They said, 'You hardly have enough food, and you could make a fortune by selling your horse, and yet you keep it. What is it with you?' The farmer replied, 'You do not understand.'"

Thomas pauses and leans forward to take a sip of water.

"...One night, there was a terrible storm. When the farmer woke the next morning, the horse was gone. The men from the village came running. 'Oh, no, your horse has been stolen. See, you should have sold it when you had the chance,' they said. 'How can a man as poor as you care for such a valuable horse? You could have had whatever price you wanted for it. It would have been much better if you had sold it. Now, the horse is gone. What a scandal. What bad luck.'"

The sound of a glass shattering on the floor makes me turn my head. The café is still filled with people. It's like nothing can distract Thomas, not even me.

"The old farmer shook his head. 'Say only what you know. You're going too far. Be content to say that the horse is not in the stall. That is a fact, and everything else is supposition. If it is lucky or unlucky, how can we know it? How can you judge it?'"

My body is right next to Thomas's, and I can feel his chest moving slowly in and out. His shirt is soft, and his smell is sweet.

"'...The people said, 'Don't try to fool us. We may not be philosophers, but you don't need wise men to see that you have lost a fortune. That is bad luck.' The old man said, 'I will stick to the fact that the stall is empty, and the horse is gone. I don't know more than that. If it is good luck or bad is only a fragment of the whole. Who knows what will happen?'"

I straighten up and move even closer to Thomas, if possible. He squeezes my shoulders. This must be the best place in the whole café.

"The people laughed." Thomas continues in his warm, calm voice. "The old man must have gone mad. They had always known that he was strange; otherwise, he would have sold the horse, made a fortune, and lived like a king. But he lived from hand to mouth, at the edge of poverty. Now, it was certain that the man was a fool."

I am captivated and listen intently.

"After fifteen days, something happened." Thomas's voice becomes more intense. "One night, the horse came back. It hadn't been stolen but had run out of the fence and into the wilderness. And not only did the white horse come back, but it also brought a herd of wild horses with it. People came and gathered around the old farmer.

'Old man,' they said, 'you were right, and we were wrong. It wasn't bad luck, and the horse wasn't stolen. It was a blessing. We are sorry that we were so insistent.'"

My eye wanders off outside the window, where the sun continuously struggles to break through the clouds that have formed a massive ring around us. I blink a few times and look back at Thomas, who is fully present.

"The old man said, 'You're going too far again. Let it suffice to say that the horse has returned and brought some other horses with it. Whether it is good or bad luck is only a fragment of the story. Unless we know the whole story, how can we judge? If you only read one page from a book, how can you judge the whole book? If you only read one line on one page, how can you judge the whole page? If you only read one word in a sentence, how can you judge the whole sentence? Life is so vast, yet you judge all of life with only one page or one word. You have only a fragment, and you have already judged the whole. Do not say that it is a blessing because no one knows if it is. I am content with my ignorance. Don't bother me with what we don't know.'"

Thomas stops to see my reaction. I smile. He takes another sip of water before he continues. All the tables in the café are occupied, but the sound doesn't travel in the room. We have created a confined space for ourselves.

"This time, the other men didn't say very much, thinking that perhaps the old farmer was right. They kept quiet, but inside, they were certain that he was wrong. Twelve beautiful horses had come back with the farmer's horse. With some training, these horses could be broken and sold for a great deal of money. The old farmer had a son who began to break in the wild horses. Just one week after he started, he was thrown off one of the horses, and his leg was broken. People gathered around the old farmer again and started talking. 'You were right, old man. You were right again. The horses were not a blessing. Look what's happened now. Your only son has fallen off a horse and broken his leg. He may never be able to walk normally again. Your son was your only support, and now he can't help you. Now you are poorer than ever.'"

A young man comes over to the table and takes away our plates. Thomas finishes his water and passes the glass to the young man. He smiles back at Thomas and places a candle on our table before he disappears over to the next table.

With a soft voice, Thomas continues. "The old man said, 'You are still obsessed with judging. Don't go so far. Say only that my son has broken his leg. Who knows if it is a blessing or a curse? No one knows. Again, it is only a fragment of the whole, and you will never know more. Life comes in small fragments, and you mustn't draw conclusions about the whole.'"

Thomas pauses. He is sitting so quietly, looking at nothing in particular and breathing evenly. It feels like he has all the time in the world.

"...After a couple of weeks, all the young men from the village were recruited to become soldiers in a war. Only the son of the old farmer didn't have to leave because his leg was broken. The people gathered around the old farmer, crying. 'You were right,' they said. 'God knows you were right. Your son may be crippled, but at least he is alive and with you, and he will be able to walk again. Perhaps he will have a limp, but he will be all right. But our sons are gone forever.'"

Thomas leans forward and clicks his fingers right above the candle that lights up.

"The old farmer said, 'It is impossible to talk with you people because you go on and on with your judgments. No one knows anything. Say this and only this: Your sons have been forced to go to war, and my son hasn't. But no one knows if this is a blessing or not. No one will ever know it. Only God knows.'"

Thomas looks at me. "Does the story make sense?"

I nod. There is no reason to say another word.

15

A GLIMPSE AT PERSONAL DEVELOPMENT

It's nighttime, but I can't fall asleep. I am just lying in bed, staring at the sky. Starlight casts a dim shadow on the ceiling. Thoughts fill my head. I miss Luke terribly. It comes in flashes and has become stronger over the past few days. I'm thinking of the morning that I left when he begged me not to go. His eyes were trying to persuade me to call off my assignment. I told him that the time would go quickly, and I would be home again long before his birthday. He tried to be brave and hide his tears as I waved from the car. The pain of my separation from him is like a pinch that won't go away. I've never felt like this before. When I have been away on assignments, I have always been so engrossed by the task that I forgot everything around me. Once, I forgot to call him as promised, and after that, I had to schedule my calls with Luke. Now, the up and down cycle of intensity and longing, and then the periods when the wonders of In-Between and the people who live here take over the forefront of my thoughts and feelings, is becoming my daily reality. Each side of the equation has grown stronger over the past few days. Right now, my thoughts are of Luke and nothing else.

THE LIFE

A hard knot in my stomach feels like it's going to explode. I didn't know that it was possible to miss someone so much. The pain from my stomach moves up into my chest, leaving me with a feeling of a heavy weight that has been placed on my chest, making it hard to breathe freely. Then I close my eyes and see more flashes of Luke before me. So many times, I told him that I just needed to finish work, then I would be with him, but then I had to cook, or the phone rang. Something always came up. Work, friends, and family all expected something from me, counted on me to come through for them. I was always unwilling, or unable, to say no, to risk letting anyone down.

And Luke would just stand there, waiting for me.

I didn't see him. Sometimes, even when I looked at him, I didn't see him or see who he really was and what he needed from me; all I cared about was myself and what others thought of me.

Lying in bed, I swallow hard and have to gasp for breath. I can't stop the images and thoughts that assail me, the memories of what has been, and ideas of what might have been. Suddenly, Luke was one year older, and gone were all the teddy bears. Where did that year go? I remained preoccupied, busy with work. Why didn't I go and play? Why didn't I make him my first priority?

My body is tight, and the memories and regrets make me feel as though I am in prison. My whole life, I've been in prison—a prison filled with emotions that I have tried to maintain and others that I have been avoiding. Every single moment of my life, I have been busy doing something to avoid feeling the emotions.

Should a feeling of guilt slip through the mound of prison walls, I would shoot it down right away. I have been caught up in reaching my goals, trying to control my life and being accepted, getting success, and being seen.

Right at this moment, I feel how much I love Luke. A warm sensation spreads from my heart out into every little cell of my body. I have taken Luke for granted and also had a hard time surrendering myself to him. There were always things that needed to be done. He is a human being, a little boy, and he needs me. Work can do without me, so can my friends. But not Luke. When I look at myself, I see a woman in control on the outside, too busy to feel anything. The knot is back in my stomach, and bursts of pain shoot through my body.

I'm breathing hard, almost panting. Then, I open my eyes and turn toward the picture of Luke. I reach out and let my hand glide over his image. After I left Thomas, preoccupied with the story he told me, I stopped by the control room, found a viewing screen, and tuned in on Luke while he was sleeping. New toys were spread all over the floor in his room, and a little light was turned on by his bed. Next to the light stood a picture of me in a golden frame. It was almost unbearable to watch him without being able to touch him, smell his hair, and feel his body. He is so little but looked so calm and at peace. His features were wholly relaxed; no bad dreams were troubling him. His duvet was lifting up and down following his breath. Part of the experience of having children is watching them grow up, but not from a distance. I want to be there together with him, not watch him through a cold, lifeless screen.

I am hot and pull down the quilt. Maybe it will help if I lie on my side. I feel torn in two. Part of me has accepted being here at In-Between for a short period, and part of me struggles against it and wants to go back now at any price.

It is impossible to sleep in this heat. I want to go back; I want to go home! But first, I have to find out how I can return. If there is a way in, there has to be a way out. It's just a question of finding someone who knows someone.

Tomorrow, I think, maybe I should resume my search for the Master. He must be able to help me. I was so close; I know it. My thoughts fade away, and I fall asleep.

"COME HERE," says a voice. The voice belongs to Thomas, but I don't recognize him immediately because his clothes are different from what I am used to seeing him wear. Looking down at myself, I see that I am dressed in a simple white gown like his. I am wearing sandals too, and an orange shawl that is draped over my shoulders and fluttering in the wind.

Thomas has something in his hand, a necklace.

"This is for you." He looks at me intently. The necklace is made of small wooden beads with an incredibly powerful violet stone pendant shaped like a diamond. The color is almost infinitely deep and with a nearly invisible pattern scratched into it.

"The stone is said to bring out the potential in the person wearing it so that you cannot keep from following your own path. It is also a stone that opens the heart for love, a Sugilite."

He takes a step closer to me and raises the necklace with both hands. I bend my head, and he hangs it around my neck. At first, it feels cold, but almost immediately, it begins to emit heat.

"It looks good on you," he smiles.

"Thank you," I return his smile. Carefully, I touch the stone with my fingertips and feel the energy from the stones streaming into my hands.

"These stones have been handed down from one searching person to another for thousands of years. Now, the necklace is yours." Thomas looks at me with his characteristic calm gaze, as if presenting me with this precious gift was perfectly ordinary. I reach out my hand to thank him, but he places his palms together and bows slightly.

"Come. Let's go over to the others." Thomas gestures somewhere behind me.

I catch sight of a group of people sitting around a bonfire. We are high up on a mountain peak. The air is so fine, very thin, clear, and cool. Thomas takes my hand, and we walk toward their circle, where there are two free spaces. I hesitate, not very confident about the situation, and hold back. Thomas squeezes my hand, and the warmth from his hand makes my shoulders drop. I sense that he already knows the others. The heat from the bonfire does me good. It is getting dark, and the temperature falls with the sun as it sets below the horizon. I look around the circle, lingering for a moment on each face: a bold elderly man, a slight woman with thick black hair, and a tall man with a broad nose and a rather square-shaped head next to her. Thomas is seated, and I am standing there rather awkwardly and considering the situation before I finally join the group.

They know me, no doubt about it. Gradually my uncertainty fades away, and I come to feel one with the circle. My eyes go blank, and the others resume their conversation. We are having some kind of meeting, and though I am listening to what they say, it doesn't make sense. It is like watching a film that already started a long time ago.

Thomas leans over and whispers in my ear. "Soon, it will be your turn."

My turn, I wonder, having no idea what he is alluding to.

At the same moment, all their attention is directed toward me. I look around. They are waiting patiently. What do they expect of me? There must be a mistake; they must have confused me with someone else. I look at Thomas, and he nods encouragingly as if everything is going smoothly.

"Hmm," I clear my throat. "Umm." I look around at the others, who are sitting there, not speaking. "Yes, well...." Words come out of my mouth very slowly, almost randomly. "Hmm." That's the most intelligent thing I can come up with. I close my eyes and fully expand my lungs with the pure mountain air. I hold my breath briefly and then release the air through the crack between my lips.

And then, something inside me breaks through, a light. My eyes open slowly again. I begin to remember these people who are sitting in this circle. I don't know what's happening, but a stream of words begins to flow out of my mouth.

"...I am on the way. But there are still some things that I can't relate to. I need your help to reach the next level...."

I fall silent and look around the circle. The older man, who looks to be around seventy years old, somewhat wrinkled and not very tall, takes over.

"Each of us has some things to learn before we are ready to meet again. In due time, we will reunite, and together, we can carry out the mission."

Mission?

My shoulder hurts, and the mattress feels hard. I start to shake. The image of the circle disappears, and my body cramps up. My teeth are chattering uncontrollably, and a sharp coldness spreads throughout my body. I am in a state between being asleep and awake, conscious enough to realize what is happening but powerless over my body.

With effort, I turn onto my side to try to stop the shaking, but it continues. I feel like a frightened animal that is paralyzed and is trying to shake off a bad experience. Pain shoots from my lower back to the base of my head, and my head and spine form a taut bow. I am cold even though sweat is gushing out of my body, and my nose is running. My whole system is straining, and I am just an onlooker.

If this is the point of no return, if I must depart now, then let me get the best out of it once and for all; let me drop the reins and go along for the ride; let me leap over all the borders and into the unknown.

I surrender to my body, and the force of the movements becomes more intense. It feels like I am being shaken by stormy weather, and there is no use fighting it.

Suddenly, there is a shift; the coldness turns into heat, and I am boiling. My bed covers are soaked, and my quilt could almost be wrung out. Eventually, the heat and the shivering in my joints wane and finally go away. "Ahhh," I hear myself moan.

I fall into a deep sleep again, and when I finally awake, I can hardly move. My body is exhausted, and I cannot lift my legs. My covers are still wet, so I do not doubt that what I experienced was real. Still, I haven't the faintest idea what has happened to me. Slowly, I try to sit up in bed but give up and let myself drop back. It's only six o'clock, but I can't sleep anymore, although I am completely spent.

SOMETHING INSIDE ME HAS CHANGED, but I cannot exactly determine what it is. I maintain a state of silence. Inside, I feel completely at peace, as if something has vanished and left some extra space behind.

I am aware of my body and the space that has been made inside of me. My eyes open briefly, and I look around my room, which seems bigger and brighter than usual.

Then, I start to play back last night's experience in my mind to see if I can make sense of it. First, there were the events that took place on the mountain that seemed so real. It was not just like a dream—I *was* there. I can still feel the air and remember its scent, which was so sharp. And the episode with the shuddering—was I ill? Maybe my body has picked up some sort of virus, but still, it was different from anything I have ever experienced.

My arms spread out to the sides. Usually, I would feel lost, but, to my surprise, at this moment, I feel very centered and calm. It seems like something has fallen into place inside of me, or rather, something has opened so that my body is not a physical barrier for my energy. My energy can now expand far beyond my body.

I close my eyes, aware of the sensation of the cold, damp sheet against my body.

The Master. I must find the Master. He must be able to help me understand what has happened. If only I can muster up the strength to get up... I remain on my back a bit longer, staring up at the ceiling. My breathing is calm, and there is no tension to be found in my body.

Although I would like to understand what I experienced last night, I am deeply confident that everything is as it should be. Interesting.

Before I know it, I fall back into a state where I can make out sounds but can continue to rest. I breathe deeply. If only I could always feel like this. All former worries are gone, and there is plenty of space inside me, plenty of space and light.

16

A JOURNEY DOWN MEMORY LANE

I have tried to find the Master several times, but with the same result. Therefore, I have decided to look into the personal development program that Thomas mentioned earlier. I might as well; there is no point chasing down a ghost that might not exist after all. Maybe the Master was something Thomas made up to come across as more interesting. He wouldn't be the first man in history to use that trick.

As I enter the control room, I notice that the people here are concentrating, watching their screens. It is like they are inside an invisible bubble where they are not disturbed. I head for the workstation where I sat with Thomas the day I arrived. It turns on when I sit down, and I get to choose between a live signal or my learning program. I press the learning program—better get it over and done.

Level one, it says on the screen.

Next to me is a young woman, she is pale, and her hair is greasy. She is looking at images where she gets beaten up by a fat man who spits as he shouts at her. I look briefly away; maybe it is not for me to see. She doesn't seem affected by the images. Even though it is hard to watch, I look back. There is no doubt that her lesson is standing up for herself. I turn to my screen, where pictures from my childhood appear. This can't be that hard; I smile to myself. I'm in the garden with my sister. We are building a castle out of milk cartons. She is two years older than me and always a bit cleverer. Her castle is both bigger and more detailed—the picture shifts. Now, I'm in school. My face is tense and all red. The teacher asked me a question I can't answer. I hated that so much, I recall. The image shifts once again. This is just a situation from my last day on Earth. What does that have to do with the rest? On the screen, I'm checking all the details in my story before I sent it off and making sure I got it all right.

I lean back and look around. People of all ages and colors are here. They all look so concentrated. Is this really all they do here? To my left sits an ordinary-looking guy with a polished appearance in a suit and tie. On his screen is a woman searching through the kitchen cupboards. Behind the garbage bin, she finds a bottle. Instantly, she put it to her mouth, but it is empty. She starts to put her tongue down the opening, but there is nothing left. She throws it on the floor and continues her search in the rest of the cupboards. The guy doesn't react at all. The images change. He is a lawyer in a big office, looking really successful. A colleague comes over and asks him a favor; instantly, he gets up to help and leaves his own task behind. Maybe he should start to take care of his wife before looking after everyone else?

It is strange to look behind the scenes in other people's lives; somehow, it doesn't seem to bother them that other people can see it too. I shift focus back to my workstation. Somehow, it is more fun to watch other people's stories and work out their challenges.

The next image on my screen I remember perfectly. I hate that situation. It's like I can still feel the powerlessness as if it was yesterday. I was at the local leisure center after school with a friend. We were training, and before getting changed, I went to the café to ask if they had found a shirt I forgot there the week before. I had to get it back; otherwise, my dad would be really upset. There was no one to be seen at the counter, so I leaned forward to see if anyone was in the back. Then, on my way to the changing rooms, the manager called out for me. I turned and was happy to see him—maybe he could help me out. Instead, he started to accuse me of stealing candy from the café. He said that someone saw me reaching over the counter and stealing. I was devastated. The leisure center was my second home. I went there every day after school and loved my sport. I didn't know what to say. The manager was a very tall man, and he was furious. He shouted at me, and I just stood there, numb. Everything inside of me shut down; I couldn't feel anything. I was just waiting to get away from the situation. He tried to force me to admit that I stole the candy, but I kept shaking my head. And every time I did so, he became even more furious.

"No one steals from me," he shouted.

How could I convince him that I didn't do it, that it was a mistake? He wouldn't listen to me. He grabbed my arm and started to shake it. The more he shook me, the more stubborn I got. I wasn't going to admit to something I didn't do.

I lean back. It is hard to breathe, and it stings underneath my skin. I don't know what to do with this experience. I press "Finish" on the screen, and a message comes up. "Continue," "Save for later," or "Find a suitable group." I press the last one, and several suggestions come up for groups starting shortly. Without thinking too much about it, I hit the first one. It says to meet in section S, room 7. Instantaneously, my pocket vibrates. I pull out the Skycon, and it offers a suggestion on how to get there.

I get up and leave the control room behind. I follow the instructions on the Skycon, and within ten minutes, I stand in front of the session room. It is already full of people, and I start to wonder if it would be better to come back tomorrow. Before I get a chance to sneak off, a woman comes toward me and welcomes me. I get seated with the others, and she begins to explain how we will do different exercises that will bring us closer to understanding our lives and releasing some of the pain we carry. This is definitely a mistake; this is a place for my mother, not me. She always believed that there is a greater meaning to life. Or maybe Andreas would like it here; he must have done something similar in his studies. I don't want to get too much attention, so I stay seated.

The session starts with a meditation where we are supposed to go back in our lives and find a situation we want to dive into. I pick the one from before since it is at the top of my mind. After some time, she asks us to imagine that if we are dealing with another person in the situation, he or she is entering the room. Suddenly, my heart start to beat faster. I try to laugh a bit. That is so ridiculous; why is my heart beating faster just because I'm thinking of a situation that happened over thirty years ago? My eyes are shut, so I can't see if the others are experiencing the same thing. All I can hear is the woman guiding us.

"Now, imagine that the person is walking toward you."

The temperature in my body rises, and my mouth dries out.

"Remember to breathe...."

Breathe, I empty my lungs at once. Now, I can see the tall manager in front of me. He hasn't changed a bit. But before he starts to shout at me, I get up and am just about to tell him the truth.

"You can now talk to the person. Tell the person what you couldn't back then. Now, as an adult, you have the strength and power; it is time to stand up for yourself."

I am already standing and looking right at the man. I can see his torn face full of anger. *I didn't take anything from you*, I say inside myself.

"Say it out loud; say it like it is the most important thing you have ever said," the woman encourages.

"I didn't steal from you," I say and keep looking at the man with my eyes closed. He starts to open his mouth, and his eyes get more tense.

"I DIDN'T TAKE ANYTHING FROM YOU!" I shout out loud. It feels great, and since more people follow and start to shout too, I keep repeating myself. The man looks at me and closes his mouth. "You took away my trust in other people, my innocent trust." Where the words come from, I'm not sure, but I know it is true. "You made me shut down and control all my emotions." My hands are hitting the air, and I'm shouting with all the power of my lungs. For how long this goes on, I'm not sure. But somehow, it feels great to let it all out.

"Finish what you are saying and sit back down," says the female voice. "Take a moment to breathe and let the experience settle."

I suddenly realize that this incident has led to so many other actions in my life. Maybe this is one of the roots that I have based my choices upon. I see myself as a child; I'm about fourteen years old. I steal money from my father's wallet. He never noticed that a few coins were missing, so I steal some every day and buy sweets. I hear a voice inside my head saying *nobody believed me anyway; they thought that I was a thief. So, I might as well be one. It doesn't matter.* A tear runs from my eye. In my adult life, I have always felt numb whenever people talked about lying or cheating; now, I understand why. And I also understand why I always worked so hard not to get in a similar situation again. With my stories as a journalist, I could always prove everything, and I kept airtight notes for years. I open my eyes and look around. The other people have already left without me realizing it. The woman is still here. She stands up and comes over to offer me a glass of water.

"Is it your first time?"

I nod and drink the whole glass in one go.

"You are welcome anytime." She smiles at me and folds her hands in front of her chest, and bows.

17

TIME HORIZON

"How long have you been here?"

"Eleven, no, twelve days." I hesitate for a moment, a little uncertain because I have just stepped out the door and run right into Annabel. She is wearing a pink dress, and her long blonde hair is loose—looking like someone who just came from a bar on the beach.

I have been going to the sessions every day. A part of me hates it and makes up so many excuses not to go there, but when I get there and start to dive back in time, another part of me really likes it. In the personal development program, I have made it from level one to level five in no time. From here, I can tell it gets a bit harder, or maybe it doesn't. If what Thomas told me about the record and the turn in the grooves is right, it will become easier the closer I get to my center.

"Twelve days? Wow. Then you only have thirty days left. They are going to fly by. Before you know it, you'll be on your way!" Annabel reaches out for me and pulls me toward her. I frown and stiffen a bit. My eyes are wide open, watching some men who are standing together further down the hallway. They're in the middle of a discussion and are making broad gestures with their arms.

Clouds are forming several thin layers outside. The sunlight shines from underneath, producing a chaotic pattern on the ceiling.

"What do you mean?" I'm still tired, and my brain isn't quite running yet. My thoughts were fixed on setting off for another day at the control room with the rest of the people here. I break out of Annabel's embrace and step back so we can make eye contact.

She smiles and looks surprised. "You do know that you have forty-two days here, don't you?"

The three men are coming toward us, smiling flirtatiously as they pass. I force a polite smile and can feel sweat running from my armpits and down the sides of my body. I don't move.

"No! Forty-two days?!" I whisper with a reproachful voice when the men have passed us. I can't comprehend it, and my brain shuts down. What is she saying? I'm in a state of disbelief. "Forty-two days?" I say, shaking my head back and forth in denial. I must look like someone waving an S.O.S. flag because Annabel reaches for my hand. A tear is about to lose its grip in the corner of my eye, but I manage to blink it away.

"Eva, listen, it's the same rules for everyone who's in a coma. You have forty-two days to decide whether you will go back or go further in the system. This period allows you to turn over the matter in your mind and see things from a higher perspective, so to speak." She strokes my cheek. "I've said all that I can and more than I should."

"But," I stare at her, "you're not in a coma."

Annabel shakes her head. "When you're ready, as I'm ready, you'll know there's only one way to go." She moves her arm like she is flying toward the sky.

I wobble backward. Annabel is leaving me, and I have to stay forty-two days. I look down at the floor; the red stripe is not shining as brightly today.

"Yes, well, I want to go back now, immediately. I thought that I was only going to be here for a brief period...." The pain shoots from my lip as I bite it. At that moment, reality hits me, and the loss of Luke overwhelms me.

"I want to go back. That many days is too much for me to cope with. I can't handle it." My hand runs through my long hair frantically. Outside the window, a large bird is sitting on the ledge, watching me. I make a face at it, but it doesn't react.

Annabel doesn't move. Patiently, she looks at me. Maybe she doesn't get how serious I am. How hard can it be? I want to leave now. I raise my eyes. The sense of peace I had just found is completely vanished just because of Annabel.

"Come, let's go and have some lunch." She extends her hand toward me.

"Listen, I have other plans." I feel betrayed and know that it isn't fair to take it out on Annabel; after all, it isn't her fault. My jaw is tense, and the back of my neck hurts. What I want to do is run off screaming and get as far away as possible. The bird outside the window spreads its wings and flies off with no effort.

"Other plans, um-hmm," she says in her wily way, with a sparkle in her eyes that could make anyone melt and confess everything. But, before I can submissively apologize and admit the truth, she breaks in. "Don't say anything. I want to hear it from you when you're ready to tell me about it. We'll get together later. Take care of yourself." She gives me a peck on the cheek and strolls down the hallway with a light dancing step.

I LOSE INTEREST IN EVERYTHING. What is the point of me being here for so long? What is the point of that stupid program if I can't speed up the process and go back and see if it worked? I can't see any reason for it. Thirty more days—an entire month. It feels like I've been thrown into a black hole where all hope is gone, and there is no reason to do anything because it wouldn't do any good anyhow. I am alone, all alone. My back leans against the wall, and I slide down. The floor is ice cold.

If only someone would rescue me right now—free me from these feelings of wanting to give up and not being able to see the purpose in anything whatsoever. I look down the hallway and don't see a soul.

If I can't go back to Luke now, what reason is there to stay? What good can come of this? Why am I here? I feel more and more hopeless. I want to scream, but I don't feel up to it. I want to cry, but there are no tears. I feel like a four-year-old girl who would do anything to get her mother's love and care. But there is no one I can reach out to. I've just sent away the only one who is here for me, rejected her. Smart—very intelligent, I sarcastically think to myself.

The hallway seems annoyingly long, and the chill from the floor seeps into my bones. I stare into thin air. Someone is laughing inside one of the rooms. That is so annoying.

I have a choice, a small voice says in my head. Either I let myself sink further into this black hole, or I can pull myself together and move on. It's too exhausting—all this pain. I must muster up some energy. There has got to be a meaning in all of this. Of course, I can go back.

The Master, if he is real, I *have* to find him.

Pulling myself together, I manage to mobilize the energy I have and force myself to my feet. I reach for the Skycon in my pocket and call up the map from the other day. My solar plexus is hurting, and my whole body is tense. "Forty-two days," I whisper. Why hasn't Thomas told me that? An intense tense sensation builds up inside me, and my hands are clenched.

An elderly woman passes me and comments cheerfully, "What beautiful weather we have today." Her voice is frail, and most of her teeth are missing. "Have you noticed how many layers the clouds have formed?"

I nod and smile the best I can. Many layers—what about it? Slowly, I start walking down the corridor, staring at the map on the

Skycon. Thomas has kept it from me, hidden it. Maybe he isn't as fantastic as I've built him up to be. It's impossible to concentrate on my mission. I have to find him. Now. The ache inside me rises from a point between my ribs to my upper chest. He tricked me. I thought that I could decide how long I would stay here—that I would be ready to leave in a couple of days—at the latest! My finger punches in Thomas's number on the Skycon. He doesn't answer, which seems out of character. However, I know that at this time of day, he can usually be found at the café.

I walk down the hallway in determination, and when I enter the café, I catch sight of Thomas instantly. He is sitting in the back, speaking with someone. Not many people are here at this time of day. Empty cups and plates are still on top of some tables, indicating that it was busy earlier in the morning. My steps are quick, and I couldn't care less if I interrupt them. This is important. Anger is simmering in my body and is just about to boil. I push aside a chair that's in the way, and it falls over. It hits the floor with a loud bang. A girl with dark brown eyes and smooth black hair looks up at me. She can't be more than seven years old. That makes another little pang in my heart.

Thomas hasn't seen me yet. There are only three tables between us. I stop. He is talking with Annabel. It is too late to turn around because he sees me and waves. Annabel turns in her chair and brightens up when she sees me. "Hi, Sweetheart, you came anyhow."

"Yes," I say curtly and emphatically. It is impossible to hide my anger.

Thomas looks at me. He is sitting on the sofa with his back to the large window behind him. The clouds are still dense. Thomas's blue shirt makes his eyes appear even bluer, and it fits snugly so that his muscular body stands out. The collar is short and stands up stiffly around his neck, and a few buttons run down the front. I can make out a necklace under his shirt that I haven't noticed before.

"You two probably need some privacy." Annabel looks from me over to Thomas.

"No, you can just stay." I wave my hand and pull over a chair beside her, with my gaze directed toward Thomas. "Why didn't you answer when I called?"

He is leaning back on the sofa, looking at me serenely. I lean over the table and raise my voice a little. "You didn't tell me that I have to stay here for forty-two days!" My tone is very sharp and accusing.

A young couple comes and sits at the table next to ours, so I moderate my voice.

"Why haven't you told me that, even if I'm ready to leave, I have to wait for a whole month more?" My voice cracks, and I am having a hard time controlling it.

Thomas patiently waits for me to give him a chance to speak. My body begins to tremble, and my shoulders are almost up to my ears. Feelings are welling up inside me, shifting from anger to sorrow and then back to anger, like a pendulum swinging from one extreme to another. I look at him sharply. "Say something! Stop sitting there like some holy idiot."

Annabel doesn't say a word. She is sitting still by my side. Thomas breathes calmly and takes a sip of water. I wait and grind my teeth.

"Is there anything I can get you?" A young man with a ring in his nose and wispy brown hair is standing restlessly next to our table.

Thomas smiles at him. "No, thanks. We're fine."

"A return ticket to Earth," I mumble.

"Sorry..." the young man looks at me.

"Nothing."

"Cool." He goes over to the table next to us.

Thomas sits up and leans toward me, placing his hand on top of mine. I pull my hand away and lean back.

"Right now, what is most constructive is to observe how not knowing that you would be here for forty-two days affects you.

Whether I am an idiot, a liar, or anything else doesn't make any difference. The difference is within you. So, how does it affect you?"

It's like being hit in the head with a boomerang. My anger hits me in my stomach, making it hard for me to breathe. Tears form in my eyes and start to run down my cheeks.

"I'm so angry," I snivel, "and confused," I say, looking down at the table where teardrops are forming a small puddle. "I thought that I would be here for a brief period. Now, it turns out that I'm going to be here for thirty more days. I don't know if I can stand it."

The warmth from Annabel's hand on my back helps me to relax.

"I miss Luke terribly. I'm scared too. What will happen if I stay here for so long? Will Luke forget me? Can I just show up there again? What if I am not meant to return? You've told me that I might continue on my journey. What's all of this about?"

Words pour out of my mouth in a steady flow. From time to time, I feel something like small electric shocks in my body. Thomas and Annabel are listening to me quietly with their full attention. My fingers trace patterns with the puddle on the tabletop. I throw a glance out the window; it doesn't look like it's going to clear up today. The clouds are practically fixed in layers.

"If you continue on your soul's journey, you will then proceed to the next level, which is a place where souls stay while they are waiting to be incarnated again," Thomas speaks evenly in his low voice. I fix my gaze on the patterns I have traced on the table and try to shut out everything else. "That is to say; you would leave your mortal life and travel on to new challenges. It takes time to have a mind clear enough to make such an important decision."

Time. What do I need time for? I want to go back, and that doesn't take very long to decide. Not a single moment since I got here have I been in doubt.

Thomas smiles at me. "While you are here, you gradually stop identifying with your life and the family you have on Earth. That makes it easier for you to make your heartfelt choice."

Annabel lets her hand slide down my back and rest on my lower back. I really feel like moving, but I don't. Several small groups of people are sitting in the café. An intrusive sound of laughter and conversation fills the room.

Thomas pauses before continuing. "There is no decision that is right or wrong. You will make the decision you need to make when you are ready." He sips his water. "In our experience, forty-two days is the amount of time necessary for people to prepare to make this decision or for those who are moving on to be ready. During this period, you will learn what is essential for you to continue in whichever place you choose."

I look up at the ceiling.

"What is it I have to learn? You keep saying that there's something I have to learn," I yell as I stand up and pound on the table. Annabel's glass is nearly knocked over, and the little puddle is destroyed. Those sitting nearby seem to be unaffected by my behavior. I sit down again, biting my lip and running my hand through my hair.

"You are learning it now, and you haven't done anything else since you arrived. That is, you are learning to be true to yourself and your feelings. That is one of life's greatest qualities and challenges." Thomas is utterly composed, as stable as a rock that doesn't budge, no matter how fierce a storm is blowing around it. "Most people live with major compromises, with a variety of reasons as to why they don't live the life they would like to live, why they don't tell the truth or listen to themselves. They never make progress; they're stuck in their webs of lies and false ideas. They do not truly live. They're waiting to die. Yet, at the same time, they are afraid of dying, so they will do whatever it takes to avoid death because death is synonymous with being alone, and that is the worst."

I take a deep breath. I don't want just to survive anymore. I want to live....

Thomas looks into my eyes and places a hand on the middle of my chest. "You are on your way back to yourself, and that is what you have been experiencing in the short time you've been here. Your life is beginning to seem clear; you have gained insights and have perhaps had feelings that you have never encountered or expressed before."

I look at Annabel, and she smiles at me. I nod and can't help but smile through my tears. What Thomas is saying is so simple, but it feels so complicated inside.

"But, but..." I try to verbalize. "I feel so alone. I don't even know what I feel anymore." The negative energy in my body is waning. I am no longer angry. The sense of inner calm that I felt this morning is returning to me. Out on the horizon, the sun begins to break through the layers of clouds.

"I have to go now." Annabel stands and takes back her hand. "There are a few things that I have to see to, so I will say goodbye."

Thomas stands and hugs Annabel. Slowly, they separate and establish eye contact. Thomas bows slightly forward. Then she turns toward me. "Beautiful woman, your inner diamond is about to break through. That is so amazing. I love you."

I am overwhelmed and smile at her. I cannot express what I feel and know that it is impossible to surpass her words. Instead, I take them in.

18

LIVING IN THE PRESENT

The next few days fly by, quickly becoming a full week.

This morning, I am sitting on a ledge a short distance from the reception area, a place that I found on one of my many walks. Here, I can give priority to my thoughts. Tulips are blooming all around me in red, yellow, and bright orange colors. I let my head fall back and look up at the infinite blue sky and stretch my arms over my head with open hands. The sky is filled with huge clouds today. They are unmoving, forming a mountainous landscape that spreads out further than the eye can see. My stomach rumbles, but it is only a little past ten. I pull my legs up under me and rise. It's time to get on with the business of the day.

INSIDE, the control room is humming with activity, and all the sections are full of people. I have my own workstation and spend a good deal of time here or in the session rooms. On my way to it, I greet the others. On my left is Allan, who always wears a shirt with "Alabama" printed in big red letters. I said hello to him the other day when we were the only ones in here. He's been here for five weeks and has five girls at home. I learned that he is working with his fear of being left out. When he was a kid, his father forgot to pick him up at school more than once. And he also shared with me how the other kids bullied him at school because of the color of his skin. He lived in a neighborhood with many white people; his mother is white and his dad black. He struggles with low self-esteem, always thinking other people are more valuable than him, and erases himself in his company, especially with white businessmen in suits. I look at him; he has the most gorgeous brown eyes and short, curly hair. How could anyone not like him?

On the other side is Heidi from Sweden. She doesn't say much, but I was standing next to her in the café recently, and she told me that she came three weeks ago and is in a coma but didn't say why. Her skin is pale, her hair always greasy, and she wears braces. She is still struggling with boundaries and standing up for herself. Her father used to beat her mother, and that formed her understanding of how love is. In her whole life, she has attached to men who have abused her and been violent. She got violence mixed up with love and is trying to reframe the primer in her brain. It has taken her to a place of nothingness where she doesn't know how to love or be loved anymore. She is re-educating her mind and soul.

I pull out my chair and reach out for the screen. As I take a seat, I pull up the sleeves on the white top I'm wearing over a loose brown dress. For some reason, I feel a little awkward and insecure. The top feels reassuring somehow.

There is Luke, sitting and drawing at a long table with the other children in his Kindergarten. Toys are spread across the floor, and one of the teachers is tidying up. Luke looks very concentrated. He is drawing some very tall trees that go up to the sky. That is me lying on the ground next to a tree. My heart beats faster.

He is concentrating intently, drawing fine lines. His skills are improving sharply. Far from being frightened or traumatized by the fact that I'm in a coma, Luke is rising to the occasion and the challenge, coping more capably every time I look in on him, which is a least twice a day. He seems to be handling things better than Andreas. More than once, I have seen his example of calmness and determination stop Andreas cold, reminding him to be calm too. When they are cooking, and everything burns. Or when they are late, and Andreas gets upset with the other road users. Then Luke is just sitting in the back seat laughing. It's as though he is inspiring Andreas to be a better man.

I smile to myself and feel proud of Luke—and uncertain where he finds such strength. Not from Andreas, surely, I think, mildly regretting the insight. Just as surely not from me, I admit to myself, still smiling. Until now, I have most of all been a mother driven and preoccupied with my career, by other pursuits, by appearances. Yet Luke seemed to be coming through it all with amazing poise and strength. We must have done something right. As I reach for the screen, I cross my fingers and press them softly against his picture.

It is so hard for me to look at him for too long. I am feeling even more desolate at the possibility of never holding him again. At the same time, I have to acknowledge something I've been extremely reluctant to address: if there were no In-Between, no possibility that I could return, and if my other body did not wake up, Luke would be all right. He would live and grow and be whole—without me there.

The thought causes a mixture of deep pain and soaring pride in my son's ability to survive and even thrive without me. I try to keep it at arm's length as much as I can.

I press on the screen a couple of times, and then my mother appears. She is in her garden, picking some red roses. Her hair is rumpled, and she is wearing her rather dirty green garden outfit. All the roses are blooming, and the whole corner of the garden is full of roses in all colors, yellow, red, white, and orange. More than once, I thought about how thrilled she would be with all the beautiful flowers that they have here. However, she would miss the scent. I move the joystick and zoom in a bit. Her eyes are swollen, and she looks pale. Whatever pleasure she takes from the gardening that has always sustained her isn't nearly enough to compensate for her obvious worry about me.

I run my hand through my hair and try to keep the impressions from getting to me. With a light touch, I bring up Andreas on the screen. It isn't fair to spy on him, but I can't help myself. He is walking hand in hand with a woman. I turn the joystick a couple of times, and the perspective changes. It's that long-legged woman who once participated in one of the courses we offered. We once fought about her because I was convinced that Andreas had been flirting with her. He'd protested so strongly that I finally gave in. Clearly, I shouldn't have. If I had any respect for Andreas left, it is fading fast.

I shut off the screen with a firm push and stand up. Allan from Alabama looks up and chuckles, but I have no reason to smile. I force a slight movement of my lips anyhow. There is no air in here. I have to get out.

A SHORT DISTANCE from the control room is a pavilion set up for quiet contemplation. I walk in, take a pillow, and sit down. The silence is absolute. I am one of the last ones to come. An older woman with long, medium-blonde hair smiles at me and shuts the door behind me. The room is bright due to the large windows that reach from floor to ceiling. She is wearing a pale gray button-down sweater. When she smiles, wrinkles fan out from the outer edges of her eyes. The space is full, and everyone is sitting with closed eyes.

Before I came here, I thought meditation had something to do with sitting in a lotus position and doing nothing. That couldn't be further from reality. There are numerous forms of meditation; some are active, with jumping, dancing, and shouting. Other kinds are still, like the one I am practicing today. There are so many different possibilities to grow here, a cornucopia of self-development.

I close my eyes and relax my shoulders, back, arms, and legs. A sense of calmness fills me as I listen to the woman's voice.

"Breathe slowly..." Her voice is frail yet deep. She has an extraordinary ability to make me relax. When I know that she will be leading the meditation, I always come. I feel at home in her presence.

It seems like a light is becoming brighter, and I observe a sense of love spreading throughout my body. Slowly, I forget about the others in the room and feel centered in my own energy.

At first, I was surprised that so many people came to these meditations because, like me, most of them had never meditated before. I had always associated it with something flighty. Now, I can see that, like so many other things, I have kept it out of my life with a rather arrogant attitude. I never even allowed myself to try it before judging it as superfluous, along with spiritual people who I also thought were too much. In that way, I have cut myself off from many experiences and qualities in life.

It seems like I have just shut my eyes when the woman rings a bell to indicate that the meditation practice is finished. I stand up, walk outside in silence, and sit on a bench to enjoy the last of the sun's warmth. A couple is walking toward me on a little path. It is Annabel, holding another woman's hand, and they are laughing as they walk. I squint my eyelids, but I don't recognize the other woman. I shift my weight in discomfort and feel some tension right under my ribs.

"Hi, Eva." Annabel waves at me with a huge smile across her face. "Just wait; I'll be there in two seconds."

My smile is strained, and my hands grip the bench. She hugs the other woman. I want to leave, but before I can stand up, Annabel is in front of me.

"Eva, I'm so glad to see you!"

Her friend is walking away. I don't say anything but move over a little to make room for Annabel.

"What's going on?" She takes my hand.

I press my lips together and look in the direction of the other woman. "Who was that?"

Annabel's face lights up. "You're jealous!"

"No, I'm not!" My tone is firm.

Annabel leans back on the bench, takes my hand, and kisses it. "Beautiful woman, it's fair enough to be jealous, but remember that it can only happen when you lose contact with your womanliness."

I lean back, too, somewhat against my will, so we are sitting shoulder to shoulder. Many of the others from the meditation practice walk past us in silence, not paying attention to us.

"Something I have experienced is that when I lose touch with myself, I begin to compare myself with others and become envious." Annabel strokes my hair. "The more we dare to share our love with others, the more love we have at our disposal."

It feels like an admission of failure to concede her point, but there's no denying it. I turn toward her. "But how can I come back to myself? It came so suddenly when I saw you. Before that, I felt fine!"

Annabel breathes effortlessly. The sun is setting, and the warmth is going with it. Around the bench are small dots lighting up like stars in the white mist.

"When that happens to me, then I use my body to get back in touch with myself. I might paint, go for a run, meditate, or do something else to get back in contact with my body."

We look deeply into each other's eyes. I know that Annabel will be leaving soon, moving on beyond In-Between to the next stage of her journey. It is just so hard to imagine not being able to see her again. She has enriched my life and opened the door to my womanliness. Because of Annabel, I have reconnected to a place inside myself that has been lost for years, maybe lifetimes. Yet, I know that I can't change that she has to leave, despite the dependence and love I feel.

"Very few women, or men for that matter, know what it means to be womanly." She caresses my cheek. "But your womanliness is about to break through."

I swallow and feel self-conscious. Recently, I have begun to experience higher levels of sensitivity and openness that are entirely new for me. It feels like walking on ice without ice skates.

"Eva, I have to go now. There are some things I have to put in order."

I stand, and we give each other a tight hug.

She places her hands on my face and looks deeply into my eyes. "Eva, take care of yourself. I love you."

19

AN UNEXPECTED GUEST

I feel like I've just met Annabel, and now she is gone. Feeling completely dumbfounded, I stare in shock at the thin black screen that posts important information. It is placed at the entrance of the café and is impossible to overlook when you enter. We had agreed that we would have no formal farewell. Annabel had said that our love was so deep and connection strong that it wasn't necessary. She wouldn't tell me the exact day for her departure either. Now, I am standing here, and she has left.

"No need to say goodbye, beautiful woman. We will always be together—just in ways you don't yet understand," she said the other night when we were having a drink together in the café. The words come back to me as I stand there looking at the cold screen with the devastating facts.

That precise day and time were this morning, two hours ago, according to the notice. I am aware that people are moving around me, but I remain paralyzed.

It goes without saying that our friendship is, or rather was, extraordinary. She is the only one of my girlfriends that I have been so close to and the first woman I have ever really let enter my life. She has seen me at my worst—posturing, egocentric—all aspects of me. She has been allowed to see me as I truly am. And now, she is continuing on her journey.

I stand there, staring at the screen, hoping it is a mistake that will be corrected in a minute. Nothing happens, and I try to accept that she is gone while instinctively distancing myself a bit.

IT IS twenty past two in the afternoon, and I am standing in front of the door to the room where Annabel's coffin is. The door is closed and enveloped with cool air. Further down the hallway, clusters of people are having a pleasant time. I want to be alone.

In ten minutes, the ceremony starts. It isn't one I am familiar with. Here, they celebrate that the soul is continuing its journey. Although In-Between is a stop on the way, it isn't until the soul is prepared to move on that the full transformation takes place. The hallway seems overcrowded, and I stand restlessly, trying to muster up the courage to enter. My legs are trembling in nervousness, and I don't know what I'll see on the other side of the door.

Losing Annabel is like losing a part of myself that I only just discovered. I'm determined to keep the door to that delicate feminine essence open. Still, at this moment, it feels like it is made of steel, and I am not sure I can keep it open by myself.

The warrior inside me is ready to seal the door and take control so that I don't feel anything anymore and go back to being busy and disconnected, back to a life without worries.

But she is not going to succeed. That is something my brief time with Annabel has taught me.

I look upward, trying to hold back my tears that are piled up in the corner of my eyes. Some aspects of life here are so similar to life on Earth. This always happens to me. As soon as I get close to someone, they leave me or vice versa. As a young woman, I would never let anyone through my warrior and into my heart. I would pretend they were close, but now I can see they never made it. She had the key to open my heart; now, I have to figure out how to keep it open. If anyone got too close, I would move on. Andreas was the first one I didn't leave. He made me feel safer than I had experienced before, and somehow, I think that he could feel the place Annabel opened inside of me.

I hold my breath and think of Annabel. Somehow, it feels like she is embracing me. At the same time, I'm thinking of all the things she has taught me. One of them was to remember to take a deep breath when I'm under pressure. It helps. Slowly, I'm regaining the calmness inside.

This is to be a celebration of Annabel's transformation, and I am determined to celebrate with joy, warmth, and love. I owe that much to Annabel, though I know Annabel would deny that I owe her anything.

Now, with Annabel gone, I have to take responsibility for my own progress. I can't lean on her anymore and drink from her feminine fountain. She showed me how In-Between could strengthen and support me on my way to finding myself and my path.

In-Between has become much more than just a countdown to the day where I need to make my decision. It has become a part of me.

A smaller group of four people walks past me. They hold each other's hands and head for the door, which slides open upon their approach. I look down to avoid eye contact with them. My dress is black, and I have a pink silk scarf draped loosely around my neck. Annabel loved pink. This is my secret gesture to her.

Slowly, I walk to the window and look at the sky. The moon hangs like a soft shade above the clouds. With my eyelids shut, an image of Annabel appears to me, and I get a whiff of her scent.

In a way, In-Between is a gathering place for impermanence because there is always someone who is about to leave or someone who would rather be somewhere else. I can't avoid the fact that, before long, it will be my turn to decide whether I want to continue my journey or go back to Earth.

I take a couple of steps toward the door. It slides open, and a blast of cold air hits me. The first thing I see is the casket displayed in the middle of a large red fabric that is spread out. My hands contract into fists, and I step carefully into the room.

There are already many people here. Most of them are sitting with their eyes closed, and a few are staring ahead, expressionless. Bouquets ring the casket, and a few single flowers have been placed inside it. I knew that Annabel had been here for some time, but I had no idea how many people she knew. Over in the corner are some musical instruments. The ceiling is transparent, and light is shining into the room. Candles are burning all around the room in tall candlesticks made of gold shaped like a thin leaf.

My lips are dry, and I bite them softly between my teeth one at a time as I enter the room. I have never seen a dead person this close before. With heavy steps, I approach the casket and shut my eyes briefly. I put my hands on my chest and feel my heart pounding rapidly. When I open my eyes, my stomach drops. The casket is empty. A quick look at the others standing around the casket ensures me that all is as it should be.

The space is filling up, and I step back to make room for the others. I need to find a tissue for my nose; otherwise, the ceremony will seem very long. Fortunately, there are some on a nearby shelf; I take a few and then find a place to sit in the first row.

The musicians rise and begin to play. A section of the wall above the casket slides aside, and the most charming picture of Annabel appears. She is laughing, and her green eyes are shining. Tears begin to run down my cheeks.

Annabel!

If only I could say one more word to her, hold her one last time.

The atmosphere is very intense, and it seems like her soul is present. I can't help but wonder if she can somehow sense us, or maybe she is already beyond awareness of this place.

Is the ceremony for her or us?

The woman who is singing is charming. She is one of those people who has been here for a long time. I guess she has a special agreement with the place so that she can decide for herself when she wants to move on. She has extraordinary female energy around her. I have no idea what she's been through before she came to In-Between, but there is no doubt that she has worked with herself. The energy around her is so soft and free. She looks relaxed and like she is not carrying any luggage. Her long gray hair hangs loose, and every now and again, she closes her eyes and disappears into the song. She is not very tall, but she exudes a powerful unique feminine energy, a bit like Annabel.

Although the ceremony has begun, people continue to enter. I move aside to make room for a middle-aged man, looking for a place to sit.

Thomas is the last one to enter the room, and he lets the door slide closed behind him. He takes a seat in a corner near the casket.

Music fills the room and trickles down my spine. I am sitting absolutely still as I take in the lyrics. From time to time, my eyes shut, and I enter a space beyond thought. No thoughts, nothing that disturbs me. I'm one with the experience. The sound of music gradually fades, and the room becomes silent once again.

The silence is broken by some murmuring when a door slides open and an older figure enters. The older figure walks, nearly levitating and slowly forward, smiling at everyone he passes. Two women precede him to ensure that no one is in his way so that he can be led forward without difficulty. When he reaches the casket, he smiles and folds his hands together up toward Annabel's picture.

Can it be? No, it can't. I've heard stories about this Master, but I was gradually beginning to wonder whether they were pure fabrication. I haven't seen a single picture, and people don't talk about him. Thomas is the only one I know who has met him.

But it is the Master.

The music starts up again, playing loudly and more intensely. People begin to dance. Surrounded by moving bodies, I stand up too. The energy is so lively that it is impossible to stand still.

The Master turns toward us and looks me right in the eyes. I am struck by a bolt of energy and am about to fall backward, but I do what I can to remain on my feet. He laughs at me and moves on with folded hands.

A few seconds later, he is already out of the room again.

I gradually find my balance but remain shaky, overwhelmed by the Master's appearance's intensity and then sudden departure. Suddenly, he was there, and now he's gone again. I am convinced that I will meet him again. It cannot be a coincidence that he gazed so intently at me.

The music slowly dies out, then Thomas begins to speak.

I compose myself, ready to be comforted by Thomas's soothing voice and wise words. But all he says is, "Everyone is welcome to join us outside for a piece of cake and something to drink."

He smiles and gestures toward the hallway. He is dressed in a white tunic with a very fine pattern traced in silver thread, his hair is gathered at the back of his neck, and he stands with his palms pressed together in front of his chest, greeting everyone as they exit—the same way the Master did, I notice. The musicians start to pack their instruments, and almost no one is left in the room.

As the last few people leave the room, I go and stand like a statue in front of Annabel's picture and have no desire to move; I just want to stay here and drink the last few drops of her scent. The door closes, and the sound of mumbling disappears. It is dead quiet. The room is still full of light that falls from the big windows above. From the corner of my eye, I can see Thomas moving toward me. He embraces me with a soft touch from behind. Tears start to fall from my eyes. I can't help it. It's like pressure from inside that makes my body give in. I am not sorry that Annabel has gone away; it isn't that. It's more the feeling of being left behind.

I don't even dare imagine how painful it would be for Luke if I abandoned him.

Sensing Thomas's solicitude and presence brings up a deep longing from my childhood. I feel defenseless, alone, and have a great need for some love. The greater my pain is, the more love I need. It's like a massive hole inside of me that needs to be filled in order for love to run through it.

As I stand here, leaning against Thomas's warm body, I can feel how lonesome it has been, looking after myself and shutting others out, closing my heart out of fear of abandonment. It seems like years of pain are being released when something inside me is letting go, and a part of me is surrendering.

The energy inside the room has changed since I arrived. I'm not sure if I can sense that Annabel's soul is here or has been here, but something is definitely different now. Tranquility reigns. I turn around and clasp Thomas to me. As we stand there, I feel like we are as one, merging. My heart opens, and I feel boundless love flowing through me.

In such a short time, I have met so many people whom I love, whom I will never forget. My hand rests on my heart. I'm so grateful for everything I have experienced here and the people I have met.

"Next time, it's your turn," whispers Thomas.

I sniffle. "Somehow, it must be easier to be the one who goes on a journey than the one who is left behind."

Thomas shrugs his shoulders. "We'll never know."

"Did you ever doubt that you would stay?"

He moves his head up and down, so it brushes against my hair. "I doubted it right up to the last moment, but then I realized that deep inside, I had made a choice, and it was a question of whether I dared to listen to it."

I give his hand a soft squeeze, walk right up to Annabel's picture and stand on my tiptoes to kiss her on the forehead. Quietly, I whisper, "Thank you for everything. I will never forget you... You are beautiful, and I love you too."

"Thomas," I turn back to him and make eye contact. "You are not going to leave here suddenly, are you?"

He shakes his head, no. "I'm going to stay. The question is: Are you?"

20

THE LION AND THE LAMB

Luke has just arrived at the hospital with my mother. She holds his hand as they walk down the long aisle to my ward. I frown a bit when I realize that he is wearing the same clothes as yesterday. Quickly, I turn up the volume a little and put on my headset. The control room is a bit crowded today. Allan from Alabama is sitting next to me, wearing his Alabama shirt. Apart from him, I don't recognize anybody. I turn my attention to the screen.

Luke is singing while taking the largest steps he can. My mother is quite tanned, and her skin sets off the silver frames of her glasses. Her short gray hair is casually styled and has grown too long for her to manage. She is wearing a purple scarf around her neck. She walks slowly, smiling at Luke.

"Do you think Mom will wake up today, Grandma?" Luke pulls her arm and stops right outside the door.

She looks at him and forces a smile. "I hope so. That would be so wonderful." She runs her hand over his hair and removes a few tufts in front of his eyes.

He puts his arms as far as they can reach around her waist and squeezes her. "Will you pick me up from Kindergarten again tomorrow?"

My mother nods and strokes his hair. "I can pick you every day if you want. But I will talk to your father about it. He will come around later."

She pushes the door open. It's the same ritual every time. Luke runs over to the blue chair next to my bed and climbs up. He whispers in my ear, "Mom, won't you please come back?" and caresses my cheek.

It melts my heart. Although it's a few weeks since I've spoken with him, I feel like I'm closer to him than ever before. If only he knew that I was watching over him.

At that moment, he raises his head and looks up. Could he have heard me? "Grandma," his voice is filled with hope, "do you think that Mom can hear us?"

Her eyes are smooth as a mirror filled with tears.

"Yes." She is standing right behind Luke with her hands on his tiny shoulders. "I'm sure she can." Her voice trembles a little. She gives Luke's shoulder a gentle squeeze and reaches for a handkerchief in her handbag.

My mother has always been interested in spiritual topics. When I was younger, I thought that she was too extreme. All her stories about angels and UFOs, and she does not need scientific evidence for things to be explained. It was too far out for me.

I sit up in my chair and take a sip of water—another day at the office. I can't help but smile at the thought. People are walking in and out of the control room. Some faces are new; others I start to recognize. Allan waves at me and leaves. I wave back. Now, I have this corner to myself.

"Luke," my mother continues in an easy voice while fiddling with her scarf. "There are many things that we don't understand, but wherever your mother is right now, there are some people taking care of her."

Luke turns to look at my mother. "Why do you think so, Grandma?"

"I can feel it." Once again, she reaches for her handbag. This time, she takes out a small spray bottle and sprays purified water around the room; it hangs in the air like small pearls.

It has to be one of my mother's healing herbal concoctions. She probably would burn incense in the room if the hospital allowed it.

"But Mom is *here*, and we are taking care of her...."

My mother smiles, and her wrinkles stand out. "That's right. Have you ever heard of angels?" Her bag is like the Tardis; you can pull an infinite number of things from it. This time, she produces a little waterfall and places it on the table. She grabs a bottle of water, pours it on, and turns on the waterfall. A small blue light flashes, and then the water starts to fall from the top. An undulating sound fills the room.

Luke shakes his head. "I know who God is!"

"You do? Who told you that?"

"I don't remember, but that's who invented the computer game. Pretty cool, huh? I think he lives in China because you can get anything you want from China, Dad told me." Luke sets his elbows on the edge of the bed.

My mother tries to keep a straight face and continues, "Yes, but an angel is someone who can help us throughout our lives."

"Stop, stop. He's only five years old. Give him a chance." I sit forward and knock lightly on the side of the screen.

Sometimes, my mother doesn't have the best intuition. She can tell Luke the most incredible things, like when she said he was coughing because he was wearing clothes with a synthetic iron-on transfer. There may be something to it, but her communication wasn't very well-timed. From that moment on, he refused to wear any clothes with iron-on transfers, which meant that all of his pajamas and most of his other clothes had to be packed up and given away.

She tends to impose her personal beliefs on Luke instead of talking things through with me first. Mothers....

She sits down behind Luke. "An angel is invisible to most people, but sometimes, we can tell that they are here with us."

Luke scratches his head and makes a face. "Is it like an elf?"

"You could say that. An angel would do anything to help us."

"Then I think that Mom should have an angel." He puts his head on my belly and shuts his eyes.

"Angels," I mumble to myself. What's next? Shifting my weight on the chair and looking around the control room, I must admit that it's quite pleasant here. A few more people that I know have turned up. There are many of us with the same routine, so we know each other's peculiarities by now.

My mother hasn't had an easy life. Her posture and wrinkles tell the story of a woman who's been working hard. I think that she can see and sense things that others, including me, don't understand. Because of this, she has never really fit in with the rest of society. She is quite sensitive but has learned to protect herself by keeping others at a distance.

Watching how she sits there behind Luke, I sense her love and desire to give him the very best. Perhaps I've been judging her too harshly.

I lean back in the chair and tuck my legs under me. The chair rocks softly. Some marvelous images from Africa on one of the vast screens bring to mind a story Thomas told me the other day that made quite an impression. It was about a lion cub born into a flock of sheep and grew up believing that it was a sheep. How could it think anything else? One day, an older lion came by and saw the flock of sheep. It was amazed that a lion was living among sheep and acting like them and that they didn't react to its presence.

I take a deep breath and shut my eyes to envision the story better.

The older lion became curious and chased after the young lion. The younger lion ran off with the rest of the flock, and it took a lot of effort for the older lion to catch it. The young lion began to cry for its life like a sheep would. But the older lion said, 'Stop that nonsense,' and dragged it to the nearest waterhole. It forced the younger lion to look at its reflection on the surface of the water. The moment the young lion saw its reflection, it roared like a lion. The older lion didn't need to do anything; it was enough for the young lion to recognize itself for it to transform.

I sense someone passing by me and open my eyes briefly. Heidi from Sweden just sat down next to me. I smile at her and notice that Nelson Mandela is speaking on the big screen now. I'm thinking of the lion and the flock from which it had emerged. Thomas didn't tell it without reason.

He said, "Every time a lion breaks out of a flock of sheep, it gives rise to uncertainty among the rest of the flock. They will do anything to get the lion back, to preserve peace and good order. It is disagreeable when a sheep leaves the flock because that leads to insecurity and raises questions among those left behind. It reminds them that there is another way of living and that they might also be lions if they dared to look...."

Luke sits quietly, looking at me. "When will Mom wake up, Grandma?"

It's hard on my mother. She doesn't know what to answer and strokes Luke's hair.

"If Mom is sleeping, is she still inside her body?" Luke's voice is so fine and smooth. "Maybe she isn't even here anymore." He looks up to see my mother's response.

My arm slips off the armrest, and I fall to the side. Why did he say that? Did she give him that idea too?

My mother forces a little laugh. "Mom is sleeping. It won't be long before she wakes up; you'll see."

Luke puts his hands in his pockets and sits back in the chair.

An irresistible urge to say something to him builds up inside me. I sit up straight and start to rock back and forth in my chair in agitation.

What can I do to show him that I am with him? I have no idea and don't know what he would understand.

At that moment, Andreas steps through the door to greet my mother and is on his way to Luke when he bumps into the side of the bed.

"Aw. Stupid bed," he mumbles as he reaches out for Luke and hugs him. He turns toward my mother. "There's something I'd like to talk to you about."

She smiles and answers in a light voice, "Yes?"

"Should we step out there?" He strokes Luke's back. "Luke, we're just going to sit in the hallway for a minute."

This is my chance. Luke is alone, and I can contact him now. I scoot forward on the edge of the chair. I take a quick look around the control room; no one is watching me. All sounds are blocked out, and I stare at the screen. "Luke," I whisper, "Luke, I want you to know that I am here for you."

He doesn't react; he just sits there, watching me. I shut my eyes, and with all of my energy, I focus on my index finger.

I hear a scream and open my eyes at once. It's Luke.

"Daaad, Dad! Mom moved her finger."

I cover my mouth with my hands and am about to fall off the chair, hoping that I haven't done anything stupid.

Andreas comes running. "What is it, Luke?"

"Mom moved her finger." Luke points eagerly at my finger. "That one. That's the one she moved."

Andreas rushes to the side of the bed and looks down at me. I am lying perfectly still, and there is no sign of change. "Luke, do you think you might have bumped the bed, and then she moved a little bit?"

"No, I didn't. I saw her move her finger."

"All right." Andreas nods and smiles. "I'm going back out in the hall with Grandma. You call us if anything happens again."

Luke nods and keeps his eyes on me.

THE LIFE

I look around the control room. No one has seen what just happened. I sink back in the chair in relief. Maybe this isn't the best way to make contact. I have to be more cunning. The guy I saw here once—he must be able to give me some useful suggestions. Ian, his name is Ian. I remember what he looked like, at least sort of. There is no doubt that I need some professional help here.

Before I go, I want to see what was so important for Andreas to talk about with my mother. They are in the hallway, and I zoom in on them.

Andreas is looking at my mother very seriously. "I know that it isn't ideal for you, but I need to."

"You have to think about Luke." My mother looks at Andreas a little accusingly. The hallway is empty and completely quiet. They are standing next to a window. There are a couple of chairs next to a table with a stack of old gossip magazines on top. The pictures on the walls are hanging a bit crookedly, and their colors are fading. The activity level has slowed down compared to the days just following the plane crash. Several of the patients have either been moved to other wards or have been discharged. Now, it's back to the daily rounds.

"I *am* thinking of Luke," Andreas is controlling his voice. "But I also have a life."

"What is he up to?" I stand up, pushing my chair back. My voice is loud and stern. I look over at Heidi, and she nods in acknowledgment.

"That is such a radical change. It would be too much for Luke right now. Can't you wait?" My mother makes a pleading gesture with her arms.

Andreas shakes his head. "No, I can't wait. I need to move on with my life. I need help, and so do you—help with Luke, with all this."

"But it's so soon—too soon." My mother's voice is quivering.

"You'll never think it's a good time. I was going to tell Eva, tell

Luke...." It is evident that Andreas is struggling. Whatever it is that he is telling my mother, it is important.

"Don't you dare write her off. She can still come out of the coma."

Andreas tries to hide his irritation but does a poor job of it. He always had a hard time with my mother's tone.

"That's the way it's going to be, and there's no room for discussion." He looks at my mother with a determined expression.

21

AN UNEXPECTED MEETING

If I am lucky, I may spot Ian. I don't know where he hangs out because he isn't someone I usually see around, and it doesn't seem like I know anyone who knows him.

Maybe he isn't here anymore. The thought passes through my mind. I am sitting at my usual spot in the back of the café, where I have a good view over the room, sinking into the sofa and trying to get comfortable as I look around. The café is full today, and I see both new and familiar faces. My glance shifts from one person to another, hoping that Ian will be one of them. Until now, he is not.

The patterns of light on the walls draw my attention. They are constantly moving slowly and create beautiful red, blue and green shades. Behind me, the sky is blue and infinite. The sun will set soon, making it one day closer to when I have to make my decision.

The thought of being able to go back to Earth next week is so unreal. I wonder how it will happen. Will I just wake up in my body, and that's that? Will I be able to remember anything from here? In some way or another, my stay here must leave a stamp on me. There must be someplace in my system where these experiences are stored.

A large group enters and begins to move some tables together, so my view is partially blocked.

What is it that Andreas has decided? Has he given up on the possibility that I will come out of the coma? I know that we are no longer a couple. Still, we have Luke together, and he can't make significant decisions without consulting me.

The large group of people moves to the bar and creates a long queue. I'm not in the mood to wait, even though I would like another cup of tea. Instead, I pour some water into my glass and take a sip. Many newcomers hang out at the bar, talking to the bartenders. Somehow, they seem to help people with all their questions, and they also have access to different small colorful bottles with liquor frequencies. The blue one helps to gain clarity; the green one is calming.

It's getting harder to keep an eye on everyone who enters the café because some of them go behind the bar and take a seat at the other end, but I have plenty of time. There are two places to eat at In-Between, this café and a small restaurant, so there is a fifty percent chance that Ian comes here.

A dark-skinned woman with short, curly, black hair walks past me carrying her tray. She looks sorrowful and probably hasn't been here for very long. Her eyes are lowered, and she is sitting by herself at the table across from me. I catch myself judging her based on her appearance, based on my first impression. But what is it inside me that makes me draw these conclusions? I look over at her again. She is sitting quietly, eating her salad. Her eyebrows are furrowed, and one of her hands is trembling. What could be happening inside her? Is she actually grieving? What do I really know about her? I can see her body reaction, but am I projecting my pain onto her? From all the time I spend at sessions, I have learned how easy it is to judge others instead of looking at yourself. And even though I'm aware of it, I still do it without noticing before it's too late. I have reached level seven in the personal development program now. Out of how many levels, I'm not sure. I noticed that it is the same things we all struggle with, just in a different story. The fear of being left out, laughed at, feeling stupid, or making mistakes. And we all cover it up with perfectness and control. It doesn't matter how we look on the outside; the feelings inside are all the same.

Darkness begins to fall, and the lights in the café are turned up. Lamps that are built into the ceiling emit a very pleasant, soft light.

I look around.

Just a second—no, it can't be.

I lean forward and then to the side so that I can see past a man who has moved into my field of vision.

A woman is standing by the bar; she reminds me of a friend I had years ago, Lucy. It must be at least six years since I've seen her. When I met Andreas, I lost contact with many of my friends because I got enough out of being with him. Our relationship was so full that I simply didn't have the surplus energy to maintain contact with my circle of friends.

I squint, but it doesn't help. It looks just like her. Quickly, I stand up and take a careful step forward. We've always had unbelievably fun times together. She is probably the person I have laughed with the most over the years. Just thinking of her makes me happy inside, and my stomach is full of bubbles of excitement at the memory of her. From the first time we met, I felt as if I had always known her. We never needed to put things into words.

I keep staring at the woman. She looks exactly like Lucy. The same height, golden-brown hair, and muscular body. It's hard to see her face clearly because she is standing with her back half-turned. I make my way through the labyrinth of tables and head straight to the bar. She hasn't seen me yet.

If she reacts, it's her. If not, I'll just pass by.

She's standing alone at the end of the bar and is about to order.

I stand right behind her. "Lucy?"

Surprised, she jerks back so rapidly that her hair swings around. She looks right at me.

"EVA! This is too crazy!" The words rush out of her mouth with great enthusiasm, and she can't stand still. "What are *you* doing here?"

We double up with laughter because we know very well what we are both doing here.

The guy behind the bar smiles at us and places two ice-cold glasses of beer in front of us. "I guess you could use these...." The glasses fog up, and foam runs down the sides.

We throw our arms around each other. I get three pats on the back before she lets go of me.

"Thanks," I look over at the bartender and smile. He bows to me. "Come!" I grab hold of Lucy's arm. "Let's sit down."

"Yes, of course. Let me bring our beer...." The glasses leave a little splash on the bar.

Lucy follows me. We laugh all the way to my table and find it hard to stop again. This is just too bizarre. I have to admit that this is probably the last place I would expect to run into an old friend.

"Over here." I point to my table. "Sit down. Do you prefer the sofa or a chair?"

Lucy sits down on a chair, and I throw myself on the sofa and grab hold of one of the loose pillows.

"No way. This is just too strange." Lucy holds onto her head and ruffles her tousled hair. "I haven't seen you in six years," Lucy looks at me in wonder, "and now I meet you up in the clouds. Halloo, what is happening?"

I lean toward her and feel the warmth spreading throughout my body. Calmly, I tell her the whole story—about Andreas and Luke, my work, and the flight. Then I pause and drop my eyes. Lucy doesn't say anything. I take a sip of beer and feel the cold stream run down from my lips to my belly. "Cheers." I look into Lucy's eyes and blink a few extra times to make sure this is real. "Lucy, it is so wonderful to see you, and the timing is perfect. I only have six days left before I have to make my decision."

"Six days? That's great. Then you can go back to Luke. But why have you waited so long?" Lucy's voice is trembling with excitement. The people at the table next to ours look over, but that doesn't seem to bother her.

My elbows are resting on the table. I raise my eyebrows. "What do you mean?"

Lucy spreads out her arms, bumping the glass so that the beer slops over. On the other side of us is a middle-aged man. His facial expression is cold and tight. I try to smile charitably in his direction.

"Why didn't you go back a long time ago? Isn't that what you want to do?" Lucy gulps her beer.

My jaw drops open, and I stare at her blankly. Is she insinuating that I could have left before the forty-two days are up? My heart begins to beat faster. The crabby man next to us stands up and leaves. On the other side of us, the young couple is so involved with each other that they have forgotten all about us. Outside, the wind is blowing strongly and whistling through the window. I pull down my sleeves and cross my arms as I lean forward.

"Come on; you're usually a go-getter and know all the right people." She reaches over and shakes my shoulder.

I can't help but laugh. "Yeah, maybe," I manage to say, but my expression is blank. I'm not sure that I heard her right.

Lucy pulls her chair forward. "You're the biggest flirt I know, and you're so lucky that no one else gets a chance...."

I smile because she is properly right. The light on the walls shifts patterns—greener and a few lines here and there. It looks just as confusing as I am.

"Remember when we used to go out? You were always the one who had the wildest night. You went all out and got a taxi home. Somehow, you ended up bringing home as much money as what you went out with. I never understood it. People lined up to pay for you."

I laugh superficially but remember those nights she is referring to. It even surprised me back then.

"Well, since you're the luckiest person in the world, how come you haven't met the man with the repatriation code?" She raises her eyebrows and smiles lopsidedly.

A small steam cloud rises above the bar, where one of the new ones is trying her skill at the cappuccino machine. I shake my head a bit and shift focus back to Lucy.

"Repatriation code?" I ask in wonder as if she has said a Russian word that I ought to know.

Lucy widens her eyes. "Come on. You can't expect me to believe that you've never heard of it!" She throws herself back in the chair. "Everybody here knows! Haven't you talked to the bartenders? They know all the important stuff, you know, everything you are not told officially."

I sit completely still and must look frozen. Maybe I am naive, or perhaps I've just resigned myself to being here; I'm not sure. A young woman is going around wiping off tables. I signal to Lucy that we should quiet down a bit, but she just continues talking.

"Well, okay." She leans across the table and whispers rather loudly, "There's a guy who has cracked the code and can send people back earlier." Lucy is looking at me in all seriousness. I feel like a not too bright student who has to have the teacher explain something seventeen times before finally understanding it.

The young woman smiles at us and takes our empty beer glasses. She has long, fair braids and a slender body. "Would you like anything else to drink?" she asks in a shrill voice.

I glance at Lucy, but she hasn't even heard the girl's question.

"It doesn't seem to be a big secret that the code exists, but it's not something that's discussed freely. I mean, if you want to go back, there's always a way. Didn't you used to say, 'where there's a will, there's a way'?"

The girl is waiting for an answer, and I wink. "No, thanks, we'll just have some water." She moves on to the table next to us, and I direct my focus back to Lucy.

"Yes, but…" It is almost impossible to find something witty to say just now. I feel so stupid, so naive, blind… "I didn't know that it was possible to go back before the designated time. I've always been told that I should wait." I'm speaking in a faltering voice and am aware of Lucy's upper hand in the conversation.

The rain suddenly starts pounding on the window behind me, startling me.

"Who do you hang out with?" Lucy asks incredulously.

"Thomas Leander." Since Annabel left, I don't spend time with very many others.

She smiles with a superior attitude. "He's not exactly someone that you should talk to about this."

Point taken. I reach for one of the pillows and let my fingers trace over the fine thread in the circular pattern.

"It's so great to see you again." Why am I trying to change the subject? Suddenly, I feel hot and take off my sweater.

Lucy looks at me and continues, "But maybe you don't want to return?"

That makes my stomach ache. "Why do you say that?"

"It was just an impulse." She smiles slyly.

"Of course, I want to return." I look down at the table and push the pillow away from me.

"I want to be off as soon as possible." Lucy is practically dancing on the chair. Her body is full of energy that is hard to contain sitting down. "It's really very beautiful here, but I prefer life on Earth. All of this silence and looking inward isn't me in the long run." She laughs out loud.

Lucy looks at me, and when I don't say anything, she continues.

"I've met the man of my dreams, Tim. We've moved in together in my old apartment." She pauses and then launches into an enthusiastic summary of what has happened in her life over the past six years.

The café is full, and people are having a cozy evening. The new bartender seems to have better control over the machines, and the queue is gone.

Lucy looks at me. "I want to have a child. I think that I'm almost ready for it. That's why I want to go back. That's something I want to experience in this life. And Tim is still down on Earth. He is devastated with grief over losing me."

I look out the window. The storm has passed, and my body temperature has returned to normal again. I turn back toward Lucy. "How did it happen?"

"It was a car accident. We were coming home from a restaurant when a young man who'd been drinking ran into our car from behind. I wasn't wearing a safety belt and was thrown through the windshield. Tim was driving and was injured, but not seriously. I had to go into intensive care and am still there now. Are you too, or what?"

I nod. "Yes, I've been there for a while now. It's so strange to see yourself lying there, unable to do anything."

As I sit there, looking at Lucy, she looks just like she always has, not a day older—the same smile, brown eyes, and spontaneity. It doesn't seem like there has been any agony or sorrow in her life, but everyone has their struggles. She just looks so happy, but it is also possible that she doesn't have to examine any of the major questions in this life. Maybe she is going through one of those so-called "resting" incarnations. At any rate, she is someone who brings me joy and laughter, and that is always a relief.

If what Lucy is saying is correct, I can leave now and wake up with Luke tomorrow morning. In that way, I could also find out what is going on with Andreas. The thought absorbs me.

I can leave In-Between.

But can I leave In-Between without looking back?

The relief I feel at Lucy's laughter fades as quickly as it had come. I feel a pang in my heart and try to pull my shoulders back. It doesn't help. The pain is persistent and makes it hard to breathe.

"This guy you know who can send someone back." My foot is pumping up and down under the table.

Lucy looks at me and smiles. "Yes?"

"Is there any chance that you'll be meeting up with him later?" I ask cautiously, drumming on the tabletop with my index finger.

"Yes, I'm supposed to meet him in an hour. You can come with me."

22

AN OPPORTUNITY

I am standing outside Lucy's door and am about to knock. She is staying in one of the yellow hallways. There are only seven doors in this hall, and down at the end is a way out to a small ledge. No one is in sight. We are meeting with her contact person in fifteen minutes, and I've promised to stop by to pick her up. I raise my finger but hesitate for a moment. Is what I'm doing right? Do I want to meet this person with the code? What if Thomas finds out about this? I only have six more days, so maybe I should just wait it out. My whole body is tense. There is no reason not to meet him. What if it's true that I can go back before my time? *Don't be such a coward*, I tell myself.

Determined, I place my finger on the red circle, and it begins to blink. The sound of steps on the other side of the door is getting louder, and Lucy opens it. "Eva, are you ready?" She looks super in her snug, black outfit, her hair pulled back in a ponytail, and her eyes accentuated with a bit of make-up. She smiles, revealing her slightly crooked teeth.

"Yes, I am." I nod and put on a smile. My feet are antsy, and I bury my hands deep down in my pockets, feeling a bit clumsy next to her.

"Great. Let's get going. We have to meet my contact out in B5." Lucy smacks the door shut and starts walking quickly. I keep up as well as I can, wishing my legs were a bit longer.

In-Between is so huge and is getting bigger all the time. "B5," I say, "That's all the way over on the northern point," remembering the area from the map I had studied so carefully when I was determined to find the Master. It was next to the unmarked area.

Double doors slide open at our approach, and we walk through them into a large, plain outdoor area that appears to be barren. The wind is blowing hard. The sun went down an hour ago, so there are only stars and moonlight to guide us. Offhand, I would estimate the area to be the size of a football field, but it is hard to see precisely where it ends.

"Maybe your contact person isn't going to show up." I look at Lucy and take a step closer to her to stand shoulder to shoulder.

"Of course, he's coming. Are you getting cold feet?" She winks at me. "Have you ever been all the way out at the edge?" Lucy has always been one to challenge everything. I shake my head and zip up my red jacket.

"Come on." She starts to run and pulls me along. We run as fast as we can on the white mass. The wind pitches at us from the side, and we're about to fall—pieces of cloud whirl up around our feet, reflecting the moonlight. Lucy spreads out her arms and lets her head drop back, running as fast as she can. I follow after her. This must be the closest I've ever come to flying. My feet are almost skimming the surface of the cloud. It seems immense, and we run and run.

Suddenly, Lucy tugs on my arm. We stop, get on our knees, and pause for breath.

"Look." Lucy points. A bit further ahead is the abyss. We stand up and walk slowly forward. The wind is even more forceful here at the edge, and we must be careful. Even though I still swear by my boots, I can't be certain that the wind won't blow us down. With small, precise steps, we reach the edge.

We lie down on our stomachs and slither over the last stretch to have as much physical contact with the cloud as possible. Not in my wildest dreams could I have imagined that I would one day lie down on a cloud and look down at the Earth. It is so exhilarating.

The sound of the wind is the only thing that breaks the silence. The air is so clear that we can plainly see the Earth under us. We lie there, looking down without saying a word. No words could describe it anyhow. Underneath us is a sea of light. We must be above a major city because skyscrapers are stretching up toward us. Calmness fills me inside as if I have become one with the cloud as I lie here. In the distance is a grumbling sound and some blinking lights. An airplane is approaching. The sound increases dramatically, and I feel my whole body vibrate. The next instant, it is passing under us. The pressure affects our bodies, and we are lifted above the surface. Our eyes meet, and we begin to laugh as we land softly on the cloud. Lucy waves down at the airplane and looks at me. "Do you think anyone saw me?" Her face is one big grin.

"There's no telling." I am bubbling with delight, and all my worries seem to blow away for a while.

In a smooth motion, the cloud is drifting with us. Looking down at the lights from cars, houses, and streetlamps, it's like watching it on a vast film screen, only better. Squinting my eyes so that there is just a thin line to peep through, I feel like I can almost reach out and touch the lights below.

Imagine all the people going around down there. Each of them is doing something, living their lives. Someone has just met the man of her dreams; another has just broken up. Someone has just won the lottery; another one has lost a job. Someone steps onto a street and is hit by a car, and somewhere else, a child is learning to walk. I could easily become addicted to this.

We crawl back from the ledge, and when we reach a safe

distance, we stand up and walk back to the bare, open area. The air is cold, and the wind blows some clouds toward us. Everything is bare. Someone is standing by the door. A spasm of pain runs through my body, and I am pulled out of my dreamlike state.

He waves, and Lucy waves back. "He's right on time. Come." She pats me on the back and starts to run over to him.

"Hi," he says when we are closer. "I was beginning to think that you weren't here."

Lucy laughs. "Of course, I'm here. This is Eva."

"I know." He smiles in an unctuous way. "We have a date for a cup of tea that I haven't taken her up on yet."

Frank! Of all people. I have avoided him in the café because there is still something about him that I don't like. I can't put my finger on it yet; it's just a gut feeling.

"Hello," I say, disappointment overshadowing my mood. Frank is probably the last person I would like to ask for help; he seems so sticky that he would be hard to get rid of if you let him too close.

He hugs me. "Hey. It's so nice to see you again."

The small scars on his skin stand out, and his eyes seem even deeper. He is wearing a strong aftershave, and I can't help coughing a few times.

"There's a place over there where we can sit in a shelter. Come." Frank points toward a wooden niche by the building. He takes his Skycon out of his pocket and looks at it as we walk. *Of course.* Now I realize that the Skycon can't reach us out here because this is beyond the frequency range. That's why we were supposed to meet here.

"This is fine...." Frank stops and puts his arms akimbo. He is very casually dressed in jeans and a white T-shirt that is too tight around his belly. It doesn't seem too cold for him, even though the wind is biting my skin. There is some sort of wooden annex along the wall. I have no idea why it should be here. Does anyone come here on a daily basis? Very peculiar.

"Good." Frank looks at Lucy and then looks me up and down. "Is it one or two of you who will be sent back?"

"One."

"Two."

We speak at the same time. I say one, and Lucy says two. We look at each other. If Frank weren't here, we probably would have burst into laughter, but we don't say anything.

Frank smiles as he looks at us. "Well then, let me start by explaining how it works, and then we'll see if you can work out the rest." He leans toward us with slightly bent knees and folded hands.

"In order to go back to Earth, you need a repatriation code. Exactly who has access to the code is classified information." He pauses, smiling in self-satisfaction. I begin to feel uncomfortable, and my eyes start to wander. Hopefully, no one comes. I don't like standing here with Frank. He doesn't show any sign of noticing my mental absence.

"There's a loophole in the system. Every night between 23:59 and midnight, when the system is being updated, it is possible to enter a code and send someone off without it being registered." He speaks in a slightly suggestive tone that strikes me as being affected. Although he tries to act like a man of the world, something doesn't add up.

"Furthermore, the code changes from minute to minute. That is to say; the code must be solved and entered into the system in that minute before midnight. It requires a great deal of precision."

He stops. "Are you with me, Eva?"

I can feel his penetrating gaze and look up. "Uh, yeah, the code." Why did I look away just then? Frank nods at me and responds with a superficial smile. The wind whips my hair around, so I step closer to the wall to get more shelter.

"The code is the first step. The next step is to gain access to the dispatch room. And that can be a greater challenge." Frank maintains eye contact with me and nods slowly, smiling and running his fingers over his chin. Although he is a bit shorter than I am, he positions himself so that he can look down at me. I feel compelled to keep looking at him because he is keeping a close eye on me. "They have changed the way to enter the dispatch room, so the system is more complicated now. I haven't worked out how to break the new code yet, but I'm close. When I solve it, then I can send the first of you two off."

"Perfect." Lucy is totally absorbed by him. "I'd like to leave as soon as possible, better yesterday than today. What about you, Eva? When would you like to leave?" She claps her hands. "This is something, isn't it?"

"Uh, yeah." I look from Frank to Lucy and back again. How do I get out of this situation? "I don't know right now. I need to think about it."

Frank nods knowingly at me. "You just take the time you need, and if you want to talk it over with someone, just let me know."

I force a smile in his direction. He is not the one I would seek if I wanted to talk about it.

"There's something else you should realize." Frank pauses and looks into my eyes. "If you are sent back before your 42 days, you cannot come back here ever again. Officially, we are supposed to learn something while we're here." He snorts, "but I believe that we should make decisions about our lives and know what is best for us. So, if you want to go back before the designated time, it's your choice."

My arms are folded, and my body is tense. "Why haven't you gone back yourself?"

He leans with his back against the wall, puts his right foot on the base of it, and looks me in the eyes. "I'm going to." I notice a "K" that has been carved into the wood over his head. It looks like some ritual letter.

Lucy stands restless, "Great, Frank, but not until we're off, right?" A cloud passes in front of the moon, making it almost totally dark.

Frank pulls out a sort of torch from his pocket that lights up the space between us.

"Give me a couple of days." His voice grows louder and more determined, and he won't break eye contact with me. "When I have broken the code to the dispatch room, then we can make the final arrangements."

I step back. His haughty yet friendly attitude irritates me. "Why do you do it?" My mouth is tight, and I am biting my teeth together.

He smiles and chuckles. "Right now, I'm the only one who can keep cracking the system's new codes, so I feel like it's my duty to stay and help others leave. I believe in free choice; no one should be in charge of us. No one!"

Lucy waves her arm and interrupts. "Good, then it's all settled. Frank will let us know when he's ready, and Eva will think it over."

I bite the inside of my lower lip and rub my thumb over my index finger again and again.

"Should we have that cup of tea together now?" Frank pushes off the wall and puts his hand on my shoulder. I have a feeling that I can't escape this. Part of me is also curious to find out what it is about Frank that makes me so uneasy. It isn't very often that I react like this toward other people. It doesn't seem like Lucy has anything against him. Maybe it's just me.

"Yes, let's." Lucy rubs her hands together and tightens the belt on her coat. "Are you coming, Eva?" She pats me on the back.

"There's just one more question. Is there any risk associated with being sent back before the designated time?" I stare without blinking.

"Risk? No, I don't think so. It's like I said, you can't come back here, but I don't suppose you want to if you're leaving?"

"What about my soul and its continuing journey?" I don't move an inch.

"Come on," Lucy is getting restless. "Let's get something to drink and have a good time."

I'm not moving an inch. Frank is looking at Lucy and tries to force a smile. I don't react.

"It is way too cold to stand here. Let's continue the conversation inside." Lucy is jumping on the spot and getting mad at me. I still don't move.

Frank looks down and kicks at a cloud that has formed around his foot. "Eva, I'm offering you an opportunity. If you don't want to take it, then that's up to you." He struggles to speak calmly and act relaxed, but his right eye starts to tic. He looks down.

"I just want an answer to my question. It's very simple."

Frank looks up. "It does not influence your soul's journey." He blinks his eyes and looks away again.

"Okay... Are you sure of that?" I keep staring at him.

"Yes, otherwise, I wouldn't say so. Let's go inside." Frank puts his arm around Lucy, and we walk back, taking a direct route back to the center of In-Between.

THE AIR in the café is thick, and it's so packed that people are standing all the way around the bar. We press our way to the middle.

"Hey..." It's Allan sitting at one of the round tables. He's wearing his usual T-shirt and has on a matching Alabama baseball cap today too. "You can have this table." He pushes back his chair and rises.

"Super. Thanks a lot." I smile at him and give him a quick hug.

"See you." He puts on his jacket and squeezes my shoulder.

"Right. See you in the control room later." I move the empty glasses to one side and sit down.

"That's the way!" Lucy gives me a high five. "You aren't the worst one to hang out with." Her smile is up to her ears.

Frank returns from the bar with three cups of tea and sits down next to Lucy.

"How long have you been here, Frank?" I take off my red jacket and hang it on the back of the chair. I wish that my regular table was free because I feel more comfortable there, but at least we have a place to sit.

"Here, give me your cup." Frank smiles at me. "Now, you have to try this tea. I drank so many cups of tea before I found out which one was the best." He passes me the cup. "Close your eyes and smell it first."

I raise the cup to my nose. He's right. It is very delicate, with a slight floral scent combined with something sweet. I blow on the surface and taste it.

"Hmm. Yes, it's good." I nod at Frank.

"You don't want to go back, do you?" His eyes have grown more piercing. He wears a slick smile on his lips as if he's been waiting for this moment.

I could have boxed his ears; how dare he suggest that I don't want to go home. I feel like shouting out loud so that everybody in the café can hear it, that all I want is to return home and be with Luke—be his mother again.

I restrain myself.

The question is, can I say it convincingly? Is it my destiny to be Luke's mother? I push the cup of tea aside so it spills. He does not get to question my decision. Not Frank.

My silence is too much for Lucy; she taps me on the shoulder. "Hello. In-Between to Eva," and she laughs. "What's going on?"

"Nothing. That is, I would have... you know..." I stammer, still staring intently at Frank. He seems to be enjoying the situation with no intention of removing the smirk on his face.

"Never mind," Lucy interrupts. "Don't worry about it. You're not obligated to tell us anything." She puts three lumps of sugar in her tea and pokes at them with her spoon.

Lucy has always been so easygoing, and it seems that In-Between hasn't changed that in any way.

She places an elbow in my side, and I can't help loosening up a bit and laughing. "Lighten up and enjoy—what else can we do? *I'm going home soon. And soon after that, I'll have a baby! Let's celebrate!*" Lucy is one big grin.

My tea is still hot, and I blow on the surface before taking a sip. People are moving around us, looking for a place to sit. I keep my focus on Frank, who is still sitting there with his sneaky smile. There must be a way I can divert the attention away from me. A counterattack is the best defense.

"What about you, Frank? Do you have children?"

"Yes, I have a daughter, but she isn't my biological daughter. My sperm count isn't good enough, but I am raising her as my child."

My tactic has worked. Frank goes on talking about himself. Clearly, it's one of his favorite subjects. I've lost all desire to sit here and would like some time alone. Today, a lot has happened, which means one less day to think things over before stating my decision. Why should having one less day here bother me when I can leave when I want to, once Frank cracks the code? I frown into my tea, aware of both Frank and Lucy staring at me.

There is a beep from the pocket of my jacket, and I reach for my Skycon. It is Thomas.

"Sorry, I've got to take this call." I stand up and walk away from the table before answering.

"Hi, Thomas." I feel like a heavy cloud is easing off inside of me. Is it because Thomas is calling or that I'm getting away from Frank and Lucy?

He smiles. "I just wanted to hear how you're doing."

"Super." I know that he can tell it isn't true, but I act neutral and try to keep up the facade.

"Can we meet tomorrow? There is something I'd like to talk over with you." He looks rather serious. I squint but can't see any details behind Thomas's image; I don't know where he is. The man sitting at the table I am standing next to stands up, brushing against me as he passes. He is compact with pitch-black hair that must be dyed. I smile to indicate that it doesn't matter that he bumped me.

"Oh, yes. Sure, we can meet." I nod eagerly and feel relief in my body. It's always nice to talk to Thomas. I bring the Skycon a little closer, so it's easier to see the picture of Thomas on the screen. I don't want too much attention here. Briefly, I glance toward the table where Frank is telling one of his many stories. Lucy is listening with her mouth wide open.

"Would you like to have breakfast together at seven?" Thomas's expression becomes remote when someone approaches from behind him and whispers something into his ear. *Oh no, it can't be.* When Thomas shifts his Skycon, I catch a glimpse of the whisperer and a hint of their location.

A cool sensation runs down my spine. I turn around and look in the direction of the bar. The man whispering something in Thomas's ear is the same man who just bumped into me. Thomas is standing in the crowd of people by the bar. Are they spying on me? What's going on? I turn around, looking desperately for an empty chair to sit on, but there aren't any. Has Thomas seen me with Frank? Please, no. What if Thomas realizes that I'm considering leaving before my time?

Thomas nods, acknowledging what the man is saying, and turns back to look at me through the screen. "Is that a date, Eva?"

"Yes. See you tomorrow morning." I shut off the Skycon and look over my shoulder to see what Thomas is doing. They are still talking. The other man is big and muscular and looks more like a bodyguard than anything else. I scope out the whole café to check to see if anyone else is watching me. It doesn't seem like it. Now, they are leaving together. The coast is clear. I return to the table where Lucy and Frank are engaged in their conversation. They haven't noticed a thing.

My tea has cooled off, and I drink the rest of it while standing. "That tasted delicious." I look at Frank. In some ways, he is nice.

Maybe I'm just paranoid. My head is full, and I need some time by myself to think things over, so I push the chair next to the table.

"I need to go now, but we'll see each other some other time."

"Too bad, just when we finally found each other again." Frank smiles and takes my hand. A shiver runs down my spine again. I avoid his gaze and try to find a suitable facial expression. He gives me the creeps.

"Remember what we've agreed." Frank stands up to hug me. I get it over with as fast as possible and look at Lucy.

"See you later, all right?"

"Definitely." I open my arms, and she stands to hug me. "Now that I've finally found you again, you won't get away so easily."

23

A HINT

Eager to erase the irritation Frank's smugness has caused me, I stop by the control center, intending to spend a few minutes watching Luke's delightful and cherished energy.

On my way to the workstation, I unexpectedly catch a glimpse of Ian.

He looks very concentrated at one of the workstations on the middle level. His long, dark hair is gathered neatly in a ponytail, and he is wearing a black sweater and black pants. I hesitate for a moment and try to keep the thoughts away. I run my hands through my hair a few times and raise the collar on my blue shirt. Never before have I seen the control room this full. I glance around the room to see if anyone else I know is here, but there isn't. I draw a deep breath and walk directly up to Ian. He is moving around some images on a screen. I tap him on the shoulder.

"Excuse me."

He turns around and raises his eyebrows. "Yes?"

I sway slightly. "Uhh, my name is Eva. I saw you one day recently when you were giving your son a hint, I think...." He looks at me without saying anything, and I continue. "I was wondering if you would be willing to help me. I have a son too, and I've tried to give him a hint, but it didn't really succeed...."

Ian leans back in his chair, smiling with his eyes so that they wrinkle a bit. "Well, it isn't so hard. You have to be very deliberate because those young brains are very sharp these days, and they'll know that it's you, even if the adults won't believe them. Look. Let me show you something I think is fun." Ian walks over to another screen that is larger and has more buttons on the side panel.

"This is the best station to use. The other ones are only meant for monitoring or personal process. At this one, I can combine several functions that allow me to have physical access to Earth, in a way." He pulls a chair over for me and indicates that I should take a seat.

"Look at this. There are so many things that humans don't understand. They get hints all the time but are too busy to listen." He laughs and rubs his hands together. "Let's take a random person. Here's a young eighteen-year-old woman who is traveling and is thinking about her mother. Over here, we find the mother, and now we connect them." Ian draws a fine green line between the two windows. "In just a little while, one of them will have an urge to contact the other, and they will both say, 'How strange, I was just thinking of you too.' Have you ever had that experience?" Ian turns toward me with a satisfied smile, knowing very well that I have.

"Let's take another one." Ian can hardly sit still on the chair. "Here's a guy who's longing for someone to share his life with, daydreaming about his one and only. Look, there he is now on his way to the train station, and voila, in one minute, he will coincidentally bump into 'her.' Isn't it funny? If he's on the ball, he'll get her phone number too."

My mouth drops open in shocked silence. I look from side to side, but no one seems to be paying us any attention. Ian doesn't seem afraid that someone will find out that he's playing games with people down on Earth.

"Here is an easy one—finding a parking spot. People send out wishes all the time, and why not help them? Something else I love to do is award lottery prizes to people who don't need it or don't know how to appreciate it." He weaves his fingers together, turns his palms outward, and stretches them out in front of him. "Tada! We have a winner." He laughs.

It seems like he has his own little set of playing rules. I sit there staring at the screen and don't know what I should say.

He frowns, looks at me seriously, and says in a deep voice, "Is there anything more annoying than a lottery winner who says," Ian makes a face and makes his voice shrill, "'I'm not going to change anything major, maybe a bouquet for my wife, but we don't need a new car; the old one is just fine.'" He laughs again, this time even louder, and enjoys his sense of humor and the fact that he has found a niche here. "Then there's also the question of what becomes popular or trendy. Have you ever wondered why a song or an object suddenly catches on all around the world?"

"But is this allowed?"

He stops the flow of speech and turns to me. "It's okay, I think. There's a fine line that I do not cross. Anyway, you wanted to learn how to add some more natural hints to your... was it your son?"

I nod and frown. "Only if I can do it without it affecting my choice later."

Ian glances around, casually, it seems, but I notice how sharply he looks at the room and the others working in it.

"Right now, it's about as risk-free as it ever is," he says, looking back at me. "But no guarantees."

"Do it," I say without hesitating.

I give him Luke's day of birth, and before I get to think it over, Luke appears on the screen. He is home at Andreas's apartment, playing with his knights.

I look from Ian to Luke. "Draw a mouse."

Ian looks at me and wrinkles his nose. "A mouse?"

I can't help but laugh.

Ian zooms in on the knight and gives me the pen so I can draw the mouse.

"I always draw this mouse for Luke when we play together."

Ian smiles wryly with a gleam in his eye.

Luke continues playing and suddenly catches sight of the mouse. He is startled and starts to look around the room.

Was this a good idea? Annabel warned me. But when I saw Ian, I totally forgot all about it.

Luke keeps looking at the drawing and tries to rub it off. It seems like he doesn't believe it. Then, he continues with the game he was playing.

Ian looks at me. "It can take some time before you can get a dialogue with him going, but he seems ready. Take it nice and easy. It's best not to overdo the messages in the beginning. By the way, you're not in a coma, are you?"

I nod. "Yes, I am."

"Hmm... Then I shouldn't have shown you that. Well, never mind, but keep a low profile until your time has come. It can be confusing for those on Earth to receive messages from you when your body is still there. It gives them hope." Ian turns back toward the screen and shuts down some of the windows. "It's better for those who aren't in comas because then the relatives have no more hope." He leans back, and the screen behind him turns off. "Oh, by the way," Ian raises his finger, "you haven't learned this from me." He winks, and of course, I understand his innuendo. "You just let me know any time you need some help. You can find me here at this time almost every day."

"Thank you. I appreciate your help." I smile and lower my gaze.

Ian takes up my hand and kisses it.

I blush and bring it back to my side.

24

THE QUESTION

The corridors are empty when I arrive at the café the next morning. I stop outside for a moment and look in. Typically, the café is filled with people. But not today.

Thomas is already sitting at his regular table in the back and rises to greet me. We hug each other and sit down. Light is streaming in through the large windows behind him. The morning sun is deep orange, a perfectly round fireball rising above the horizon. There are two bowls of fruit salad and some freshly squeezed orange juice on the table. He knows my preferences by now.

Thomas is radiant. His long hair is hanging loose, and he is wearing a blue, patterned tunic. The sunlight creates a backlit, luminous silhouette around his figure. I am wearing my favorite pair of jeans and found an Indian-inspired blouse in my closet that makes me look more feminine than I feel.

"You wanted to talk about something." The words fly out of my mouth as soon as I sit down. I wonder if he has found out that I considered the option of going back early. What did the dark-haired spy overhear yesterday, and has he told Thomas?

Thomas finishes chewing a piece of pineapple before replying. "There is something I'd like to ask you about."

"Thomas, sorry, but I have to tell you something first."

I take a sip of my orange juice. It is ice cold, and I press my lips together. I haven't talked with Thomas since Annabel left us, and I need to vent my feelings. I feel like I have been going around with a constant burden that I have to come to terms with. Things are accumulating inside me, and meeting with Lucy and Frank hasn't made it any easier. I am too proud to share my worries with anyone, thinking that I should handle them myself. I don't want to come across as weak either.

Thomas looks at me and waits for me to say more.

I take a deep breath and force the words out of my mouth. "If you had had the opportunity to leave here before your time was up, would you have done so?" I hold my breath.

Thomas reaches out and places his hand on top of mine. "Eva, you have to do what you feel is right. Don't be controlled by what others think or do."

My leg begins to twitch nervously. I look around the café and see that there are still no other guests. Suddenly, the place seems so big and confusing, and I feel so small. My throat tightens, and I can only get small gasps of breath into my lungs. "What if you came across some information? Would you tell anyone about it?" My words nearly wipe themselves out.

Thomas nods in acknowledgment. "Eva, In-Between is built on trust. Not everyone who comes here is equally aware, but there is room for everyone."

My heart is hammering, and my hands are beginning to sweat.

"It is the Master who makes the major decisions here. He pays attention to everyone and everything." Thomas smiles kindly at me, "Was there anything else on your mind?"

I run my lower lip through my teeth rapidly.

"It is a little more complicated than you think." I begin to shift my weight on the chair. Why couldn't I just keep my mouth shut? Why did I have to start to say something? It was going fine, just handling things on my own. I look up and directly into Thomas's clear blue eyes.

"I think I'm a lesbian."

Thomas breaks out in laughter and chokes on a piece of watermelon he just put in his mouth.

"What's so funny about that?" I ask and sit back as I push away the plate in front of me.

"You're a lesbian? Aha. Since when?"

I am shaking my head in confusion. I had expected that he would answer me sensibly, but not at all; he is laughing aloud so that the few people entering the café look over at us.

"Well," I try, "I have kissed a woman, and I am very attracted to women...."

Thomas dries his eyes and holds onto his stomach. "Okay, okay. I hear you. You think that you are a lesbian because you feel attracted to women?"

"Yes." My tone of voice is irritated. This is a serious matter. How can he just sit there and be amused by it? It has taken me a long time to work up the courage to say it aloud. Maybe I should have just kept my mouth shut. Apparently, he isn't the right one to talk to about it. This chair isn't as comfortable as usual today, and I can't get settled.

Thomas lifts his hand in a sign of peace and smiles at me. "Eva, what is important is what's happening inside you, not whether you are one thing or another. Those are just boxes that others would like to put you in. Gay or straight, black or white. Tall or short. None of it is changeable."

I'm confused. What makes him say that just when I had become so clear about it?

"It's wonderful that you are attracted to other women. That is completely natural."

Natural? What does he mean? I remain expressionless.

"You have evolved a great deal since you arrived here. There have been great changes inside you, and your feminine side is about to awaken."

Thomas smiles, and my shoulders drop down a bit.

"The best way of helping your inner woman arrive is to associate with others who are like you. Some who have perhaps already opened the side of themselves that you are longing for, the feminine, the womanly." He leans forward and lowers his voice a bit. "So, when you are attracted to other women who are guaranteed to be beautiful, sexy, and feminine, that is because they can show you the way home to yourself."

I lean to the side and look out the window behind Thomas, where the sun is golden-orange, and the morning light is so clear. It can make you see everything from a new perspective.

"Annabel was one of them." Thomas winks as he leans back and eats another piece of melon.

My gaze drops down to the table, and I notice my thumb rubbing back and forth on my hand.

"Annabel was an incredibly beautiful woman. There are many here. You should just go on looking until you are finished. Take it easy. All women, and men, for that matter, have that longing. It is just that very few of them are aware of it, and even if they are, they rarely go after it."

I listen and swallow a couple of times. It feels sort of like I am being accepted. I nibble on my lower lip; the tension in my body is waning. I swallow once more. "Are you also attracted to men?"

"Sure, I find some men beautiful and very attractive. But that doesn't mean that I want to sleep with them. Remember that all people have both feminine and masculine qualities within them. If we dare to use them and experience them, then life becomes more thrilling."

"I think there are enough thrills for now," I can't hold back a shy laugh.

He pauses and smiles, so the freezing sensation I have inside starts to melt. We still have the café almost to ourselves; only a few tables are occupied.

"Was there anything else you wanted to tell me?"

"No, there's nothing else." I take a mouthful of my fruit salad. The taste of summer and joy spreads in my mouth.

Thomas continues. "Are you ready to hear what I'd like to share with you?"

I nod as I chew. "Yes."

Thomas smooths his tunic and tugs the sleeves precisely. A woman sits down at the table next to us, and I scoot a little closer to Thomas.

"Once a week, we hold a meeting. Internally, we refer to it as the 'Inner Circle.' It is a group made up of people who are closest to the Master, who ensure that all of the guidelines he sets for In-Between are carried out." His voice conveys a degree of seriousness that I haven't witnessed in him until now. "Our meetings include topics such as who should carry out various duties, whether In-Between is facing any challenges, or if there are any policies that need to be changed. We also spend some time on our development. It is very intense."

He pauses, and I remain silent as I reach for a strawberry.

"Yesterday, we discussed you."

"What? Me?" I drop the fork on the table, and the strawberry falls on the floor.

"Yes, you." He sits totally calm.

I pull the chair even closer to Thomas and glance quickly at the woman next to us. It doesn't seem like she is listening to our conversation. Thomas remains unaffected by her presence.

"As you know, everyone in a coma has forty-two days to either decide whether they want to go back or continue moving forward. Those who die suddenly or commit suicide are sent off when they have finished processing the life they have left behind. People who die naturally don't come here; they have had the chance to take a proper farewell in time."

I nod eagerly, reaching for a new piece of fruit with my fingers.

"Thomas! Thomas!" John comes running toward our table. Thomas keeps his eyes locked on mine.

John puts his hand on the table and sets down a white scrap of paper. His shirt is hanging loose, and his eyes are wide open. "Thomas, I was asked to give you this message...." He is gasping for breath, "but I couldn't reach you on your Skycon." His face is all red, and his short hair is sticking out in all directions.

Thomas nods calmly. "Thanks, John."

John looks at me and smiles so that his dimples show and his eyes light up. "Hi, Eva."

I smile back. "Hi, John."

"Well, I have to get going." John straightens up and hitches up his pants. Thomas nods at him appreciatively, glances at the slip of paper, then looks back at me.

"We need a lot of people to keep In-Between running, and for that reason, we select some who are given the option of staying here longer. For those in a coma, it can give them a little more time to make their decision and perhaps let go of their mortal lives. Some of the people who stay will be found working here in the café; it is a popular place for those who stay a little longer to work. Apart from working here, they take care of the new ones who come here. Many people find it comforting to talk to someone like themselves, and is there a better place to do that than a bar?"

The café is filling up quickly, and I glance at my wrist; the time is almost half-past seven.

Thomas speaks, if possible, a bit slower than usual. "There's one last thing. Some people are offered the opportunity to be apprentices and have an open ticket. That is, they can stay here as long as they like, but they may never return to their previous lives. If they would like to leave In-Between, it must be through a new life."

I stiffen, and my eyes lock on Thomas. Is he going to offer me the opportunity to stay here longer? That doesn't make sense. He knows that I only have five days left. I take a couple of quick bites of a piece of melon and chew eagerly.

"Before we offer anyone an open ticket, they must first try to get an idea of what it would be like to work here. We do this to test the persons concerned. It is not the kind of test where you answer questions. Instead, we observe those who are selected to see if they are qualified to stay on here."

I stop eating and put the silverware on the table. "Exactly what is it you want to ask me?"

Thomas looks me straight in the eyes. "Eva, we would like to offer you the option of staying here."

Everything goes silent. Time is standing still. I look at Thomas without saying anything and ease myself back against the chair. I am dumbfounded and stare ahead blankly. It is like he has tossed a bomb next to my feet, and I am completely paralyzed, watching the fuse become shorter, and it is all happening in slow motion. The bomb will go off in a minute, and I don't know what that will mean.

Thomas breaks the silence. "I know very well that you only have five days left before you can go back, but the Master would like to test you. He would like to offer you the opportunity to become an apprentice if you pass."

I blink a couple of times quickly and run my fingers through my hair. The girl at the table next to me looks at me. We make eye contact, and she smiles at me.

"How does the Master know who I am?" I lean forward and look at Thomas with a side glance.

"He knows who everyone is." Thomas is as composed as ever as if what he is telling me is completely ordinary.

I still haven't fully comprehended very much of this and don't know what to say. No matter what I say, it would sound crude in this context. I feel like I have been thrown into an empty room without windows, and I can't find the door and the way out. I am fumbling around blindly.

Thomas is not affected by my state of confusion. "If you would like to be tested, then you can work with me tomorrow in the reception area. Trying it out is not binding. You can come along and then decide later. There are no expectations, except for those you may have yourself."

That sounds too good to be true. No expectations? They must have some expectations. I push back the chair and sit on the edge of the seat.

"How is it possible not to have expectations?" I pick up another piece of melon with my fingers and let it slide into my mouth.

Thomas's chest rises and falls steadily, his face is calm, and his hands are folded together on the table. "When there are no ambitions, there are no expectations. We have no ambitions, goals, or desires for you or on your behalf." He picks up his glass of water and takes a drink. "Therefore, it is absolutely and entirely up to you. But you will surely have many thoughts about how we will test you and whether you will pass. You may observe your thoughts and reactions."

My brain is working overtime, and I am struggling not to interrupt him.

"Remember, you can only make the decision that's right."

That is an interesting viewpoint: all of one's decisions are correct in the present moment. Who decides what is right or wrong? I have often believed that others had a certain preference; therefore, I made choices based on what I thought they would like. When it all came down to it, I could see that it all took place in my head and that they hadn't even thought about what I was assuming. I had just looked at them and evaluated their facial expressions and comments. I took it for granted that they meant what I interpreted.

I clear my throat and support my chin in my hands. "Then my decision is right no matter what I choose?" I frown. It puts me under even greater pressure because it would be easier if others had an opinion I could rely on. In that way, I could also disclaim some of the responsibility if things do not turn out as I hope. I look quizzically at Thomas while running my finger back and forth over my lips.

Thomas is not pulling his face. "We would prefer that you make the choice that is right for you."

"What if I say no, then what?"

"Then we wait until someone else is ready," Thomas answers serenely with a kind expression.

"When do I have to decide?" My teeth are clenched, and my lips clamp shut.

"If you'd like to join me tomorrow, you can let me know anytime today. If so, we can meet at seven tomorrow morning and see what happens."

I must look quite suspicious; my tone of voice is for sure, "What am I going to do?"

"If new people come in, then you will help receive them. We don't have a fixed way of testing people, so we just see what happens and take it from there. If you'd like to give it a try, just come. Remember that trying it is not at all binding." He reaches for the second to last piece of fruit on the plate.

I nod. "That's understood. I'll have to think it over. Is that all right?"

"That's just fine."

Actually, I feel a little bad that I am not incredibly excited about the opportunity, but I am simply not. Something is holding me back. Maybe it's because I wasn't one hundred percent honest with Thomas. Should I have told him about Frank? Even though he might already know, I hate it when people are reserved while being offered a special opportunity, and they don't just throw themselves into it and let their energy loose. And now here I am, a little bit shook, a little bit calculating, and I don't know what to do or say.

Thomas places one hand on mine and waves the piece of paper

that John gave him with the other. "I have to go now. A lot of new arrivals have come this morning, and they need me. You'll let me know later, right?"

"Yes, I'll contact you once I've decided." My body sinks back into the sofa.

Thomas stands up, and I am left with all my thoughts. It is only eight in the morning, but I could use a real drink—something to calm my nerves. This is not something that I would typically do—not even back in the wild days with Lucy. But I am really tested now. I push the chair back with a firm movement and go up to the bar and order rum and Diet Coke.

The guy behind the bar smiles at me. "One of those days, huh?"

I nod and go back to my table. I'm not in the mood to talk to a stranger, even though he might be a great support.

What would Annabel have done? What is it that made her continue on her journey? Suddenly, she was just gone. There must have been something that influenced her decision. I wish that she were here now so that I could speak with her. Besides Thomas, she was the only one here who I felt that I could depend on and really trust.

I turn my back to the café and stare out the window. The view from here is incredible, and it is hard not to be lost in contemplation. The luminous sun is constantly changing color and its position in the sky. It appears to be light and cheerful, as if nothing can knock it off course. The alcohol is beginning to work, and I am loosening up. Fortunately, I have the whole day to think things over.

"What's that you're drinking?" I hear Lucy's voice right behind me.

"Hi," I turn around. "Sit down." I indicate the spot on the sofa where Thomas just was.

Lucy sits down and continues. "I have great news. You can go home tonight. Frank's broken the code. It wasn't as hard as he had thought. So, you can wake up tomorrow together with Luke! Isn't that wonderful?"

I don't say anything but take a sip of my drink.

"What are you drinking?"

"Rum and Diet Coke."

"*Rum and Coke*? At eight in the morning? What's going on?" Lucy's eyes widen, and her mouth opens in surprise.

"Not Coca-Cola—Diet Coke."

25

TAKING RESPONSIBILITY

It's four in the afternoon. I'm staring out the window of my room. On the table is a half-empty bottle of water and a glass with melting ice cubes. It feels like my head is going through a larger renovation. I am not used to alcohol anymore and definitely not in the early morning. My hair is hanging loosely around my face, and my legs are up on the table.

I've just come back from the control room. I intended to make some progress in the personal development program, but nothing made sense. Instead, I watched Luke and couldn't help myself from taking a peek at Andreas too. He is going to move in with that long-legged woman! They were walking hand in hand. I am confident that this is what he was discussing with my mother. An explosion of anger filled me, and I had to run back to my room. Now, I'm sitting here, more frustrated than ever. I can't abandon Luke and let her step into my place. That is unthinkable. I have to go back. The sooner, the better.

In two hours, I'm meeting Lucy and Frank. Then we will make the final arrangements and get things clarified. I have to fill the time somehow; otherwise, I'll go crazy. If I agree to Frank's offer, I will never be able to return to In-Between. Then, if there is one last thing I need to do before leaving, what would it be?

The Master.

I have hardly thought of him since Annabel's memorial service, but at the same time, oddly, it is as though he's been with me all the time. I want to find him. That is going to be the last thing I do here before I return home.

I PACK my things and get some aspirins from the cupboard. The route is familiar. I quickly reach the mirrored hallway and enter. It is just as empty as when I was here last. The hallway is cool and seems to be larger than last time somehow. I can see every little move I make reflected from all directions.

Slowly but securely, I approach and find that small section where the crack between the mirror plates seems wider than on the rest of the wall. There is a very faint circle in the mirror, and I put my finger on it. My heart is beating quickly. Nothing happens. I let my hand glide over the surface of the mirror without touching it. There isn't a spot on the mirror. Still, nothing happens. I stand there, looking around. Can I have been mistaken? Isn't it here, after all? Disappointment is mounting through my body, spiced up with the feeling of unfairness. Maybe this is just the wrong part of the hallway. I go further down the hall, but there is nothing more to see. This is the only place that is different from the rest.

Help, I think I need some help.

A slight clicking sound makes me turn around. A section of the mirrored wall has opened. I stand completely still and look in through the crack. Has anyone seen me? It is empty, so I cautiously step into the room behind the mirrored wall, and the door closes behind me.

I am standing in a narrow corridor; I can either turn right or left. It is silent, and the air is still cool. Right or left, which way should I go?

Left.

At the end of the hall, it looks like there is another door. The walls are so subtle and nearly transparent. Everything is so pristine and grand. I can't help but wondering if I should remove my shoes. I approach the door slowly.

My breathing is audible, the only noise I can detect. It is almost impossible for me to match such utter silence. What should I do? Try to open the door or knock on it? I can't permit myself just to walk in. What if someone lives here...? There is nothing to see from the outside, only a blank plate that marks the end of the hallway—no circle, no nameplate, nothing.

I am tingling with excitement and can feel my heart hammering against my chest. I must be close to something. Could it be true that the Master lives on the other side of the door? That's an amazing thought. If only there were a little bell or something that could take me further.

I am gripped by doubt. Is it a bad idea for me to be here? Why did I come back? Carefully, I turn on my heels and begin to walk down the hallway again.

There is a clicking sound behind me. I stop. I turn around tentatively and look back at the end of the hall where I just was.

The door is ajar.

It makes my pulse race. Does someone know that I'm here? Is this an invitation to come inside?

With small, cautious steps, I walk back. When I am in front of the door again, I can see a room through the tiny crack. I pull my sleeve over my hand to avoid leaving marks on the door and push the door open carefully. It inches open, and I can see a large room with very pleasant, subdued lighting.

My heart is pounding with excitement. This is incredible. What if the Master lives here? It is perfectly silent. I take a quiet step forward. The room is nearly empty. The only piece of furniture is a large bed with a dark wooden frame and white bedding. It looks inviting. The style is extraordinary, bordering on being excessive yet very elegant. A crystal lamp hangs from the ceiling in the corner, and there is a wall of cabinets.

I catch sight of two more doors but can't see what they lead to—one more step. There must be a reason that the door opened, but no one is here. What if someone comes? I am almost inside the room and pause to look around. My curiosity drives me to take one more step. To my right is a giant bookshelf that covers the whole wall.

A powerful light is coming from the opening on the left. I walk painstakingly and as soundlessly as I can through the first room, heading for the opening. There is a room in the middle of a garden. There are windows on the walls and ceiling. The entire room appears to blend into nature outside. It's unlike anything I've ever seen before. The plants are so green and lush, a swan is floating by on a lake, and birds are chirping. The light is warm and pleasant.

There is a writing desk, and on the desk are three pens, all decorated with rubies. Normally, I would consider that to be kitsch, but not in this case. Something about these unique pens makes them seem appropriate here. On the table lays a piece of paper. My stomach drops when I see what's written on it.

Eva.

Nothing else.

I don't touch the paper.

What is this place?

More importantly, who do these rooms belong to?

The marble on the floor is a darker shade than what I have seen elsewhere. Otherwise, there is nothing in the room besides a table and a chair. They are placed so that the back of the chair is against the wall facing the garden. It is elegant and exquisitely simple—perfect down to the last detail. I turn around to go back to the first room.

As I step back into the first room, I catch sight of a nook at the end of the room that I hadn't seen the first time I entered. There is an ultra-slim screen and a high-backed chair with a table next to it. It is showing a feature story on the storm I went to cover. The catastrophe has grown bigger, and more people have lost their homes. If I had stayed, I might have been able to get the Pulitzer this time, and then....

I am taken aback and freeze in place. Someone is sitting in the chair. I cannot move; my legs are completely stiff. What should I do? It is silent, but my breathing suddenly sounds like I am suffering from an asthma attack. Relax, I try to tell myself; relax, no one is going to kill you. The worst he can do is to ask you to leave. Maybe I should run off and act as if nothing has happened, just walk out and hope for the best.

But I remain standing there. I cannot budge. My feet feel like they are nailed to the floor.

"Ha, ha, ha, are you all right, Eva?" The person speaking sounds cheerful and at ease. I am about to wet my pants but control myself.

"You've come to ask about something. What is your question?"

"My question?" I am a total blank. Somehow, I don't have access to any of my thoughts. They are shut off, and my brain has short-circuited. What do I do? This is what I've been waiting for. Now, I am standing here with the opportunity to ask about anything, but I can't come up with a single question. I stand there, staring with my eyes fixed on the chair. I can only catch a glimpse of a bit of his head and one arm, but I know that it is him, the Master. His long white beard and slender body cannot be mistaken.

He leans forward and turns slowly in the chair, and then he looks at me. He is wearing a kind of golden cloak with a black edging. On his wrist is a watch covered with gleaming diamonds. His white hair is thin, and his skin has a warm glow. He smiles in a friendly manner.

It is him, the Master.

The light grows even brighter.

When his deep brown eyes meet mine, a surge of energy rushes toward me, so intense that I am about to faint. There is such a force of clarity, like a sword cutting through a stone, and I am that stone. My legs begin to tremble. I am paralyzed and feel like I am standing in a blast of wind with the force of a hurricane pushing me backward. I use all of my power to remain standing and then look down. I cannot maintain eye contact. It is simply tremendous.

After a while, I have no idea how long it takes me, I look up again. "I would like to know if I should remain here or return to my life on Earth."

The Master fixes his gaze on me.

"When a challenge is great, we must look into our hearts. That is always where the answer lies. If you dare to listen and follow what you hear, you will never go wrong." He speaks slowly, even more slowly than Thomas....

"But remember to look through all of the layers of your personality. Only after you have done so will you be able to listen to your heart. There is only *one* who knows the answer. I look forward to hearing your answer." Slowly, he raises one hand in blessing and then gestures toward the door, nodding slowly. "Go now and return when you have found the answer. Now, you know where I am."

He smiles at me, and his eyes flash.

I stand there in awe, trying to take in his words—only *one* who knows the answer. The words repeat in my head—only *one* who knows the answer. I turn around slowly toward the door that I entered.

"There is one more thing, Eva." I stop.

"There is a reason for everything. If you can recognize that, then life will give you infinite insight."

"Thank you," I stammer. "I will return."

He leans back in the chair, and I know that the time has run out. There is nothing more to say. He has said what needed to be said.

Now, the rest is up to me.

The door closes behind me, and I go down the hall and back through the hidden door. There is still no one out in the big, mirrored hallway. The door slides back into place, and I check to ensure that I haven't left any traces that would allow others to find their way in.

I stand completely still, allowing my breath to slow down to its normal rate again. The sensation inside me is extraordinary, so profoundly affected by this encounter that I have reached a new state of being. There is a certain freshness about me, an impression of something greater. Part of my universe has expanded; there is more space inside me, and my energy capacity has increased. What I want to do most of all is go to my room to be alone and fully experience this state of bliss. It feels like love is flowing through me. It is great and has no direction. No one need ever receive it or see it. It is simply there and fills up my entire being. If I were true to myself, I would go straight to my room and forget everything about meeting Lucy and Frank. I take the Skycon out of my pocket. I'd better wait so that they can't see where I am.

I exit the hall of mirrors and step into the next hallway, waiting for the signal to come through. My brain is working overtime, trying to come up with various excuses. Should I say that I am sick? No, that is a poor excuse and easy to see through.

There is nothing I want more than to reunite with Luke. That is what is best for him, and he is my first priority. That is the right decision. I believe that with all of my soul.

The thought of what the Master said about listening to my heart roars in my head. I can't hear anything right now. It wasn't my ambition to leave right now, but Lucy's. I went along and ignored myself. I didn't want to spoil her excitement. Somehow, it was easier to go along than to say no.

Deep inside, I had hoped that Frank wouldn't crack the code. Then, I wouldn't have to make the decision. Now, I'm stuck with it. It is real. We have to meet, and departure is tonight.

I won't be leaving, and I don't want to meet them. There is something about Frank that makes me uneasy. I just can't pinpoint it. It is a sensation I need to listen to; that much I have learned here in In-

Between. Outside the huge window, a part of the cloud breaks off, and I can see a massive abyss beneath us. I step back and walk to the other side of the hallway.

How can I express it, and why do I end up in these situations?

I will have to take the plunge and just say it like it is. I stamp the floor with my heel and make the call. Lucy is there right away.

"Hi, Eva. Good thing you called. Frank's right here, and everything's ready for tonight. We're just sitting here waiting for you. Are you on your way?"

"There's something I have to tell you," I stammer out. Instantly, the sentiment on the other end changes from being sincere and forthcoming; Lucy becomes reserved.

"So many things have happened, and I don't feel ready to leave. I... I need to wait. I'm sorry, but I can't leave tonight." I feel a lump in my throat and tighten my grip around the Skycon. "I know that I should have told you this a long time ago, but I haven't truly realized it until now." I hold my breath.

There isn't a sound from the other end.

"I'm sorry," I repeat, biting on my lip.

"Yes, well, I am too." Lucy's face on the Skycon is tense. "I was going to let you go first, and Frank has been slaving away to be ready for tonight. If I had known this any earlier, I could have said goodbye and been ready to leave myself."

"I know that, and I'm really sorry."

"That's of no use to me now." Lucy rolls up her eyes in irritation.

Nothing I can do can save the situation, and I don't have to, anyhow. I feel a sense of relief for having stood up for what is right for me.

"Okay." Lucy looks at me. "Then Frank and I will go on with it. Take care."

I nod. "Thanks. You, too. Sorry." I shut off the Skycon and put it in my pocket. Now, I want to go to my room and relax. Before I get to put away the Skycon, it rings.

It's Thomas. I've forgotten to give him a message.

"Hi," I say in a reserved manner.

"Hi, Eva. I was just wondering if you've made a decision yet."

I shake my head; I'm not going to make any more decisions until I'm sure they reflect my true desires and wishes. "I'm under a little pressure right now," I say, not offering Thomas any explanation. "Can I call you later?"

"Do you know what? Why don't we say that if you'd like to try, then you come to the café at seven, and if you aren't there, then I'll understand that you don't care to come? Then you can sleep on it tonight and find your answer when you wake up in the morning."

I agree and close the Skycon. Thomas's picture fades away.

I am exhausted. In no time at all, I brush my teeth and am under the quilt. Alone at last. My back is pressed flat against the mattress, and the quilt covers me loosely. This room has been my refuge ever since I came here. This is where I can retreat and allow my vulnerability out. I take a deep breath and drop off.

"ANNABEL? IS THAT YOU, ANNABEL?" I walk over to the woman on the bridge. She is looking out over the sea.

"Annabel!" She turns and looks at me. I stand in place, holding my breath. Then I run the last few yards and throw myself into her arms.

"I've missed you so much. It is just wonderful to see you."

"Same here."

If only I could hang onto this moment for a bit longer.

"There have been so many times when I've wanted to ask for your advice, but you've been away."

"I know it. I am here now, just in another way. I am part of you, and you always have access to me."

The image begins to change, and suddenly we are walking in a desert. The air is scorching, and the sand red-hot. As we are walking, we pay no attention to the heat; it is just there. Annabel is dressed in light clothes that hang loosely from her slender body. She is so incredibly beautiful. I had almost forgotten just how beautiful she is.

"Can I ask you something?" I keep looking at Annabel.

"Yes, of course." She takes my hand, and we walk side by side.

"Why did you leave In-Between so suddenly?"

"It wasn't suddenly. My time was up, and I was meant to leave. I asked if I could stay, but it wasn't possible. I know that the only reason I wanted to stay was to be with you."

The sand under my feet is soft, and sunrays prick at my skin.

Annabel looks at me. "If I had stayed, it would have led to an imbalance in your decision-making process, so I had to continue on my journey. But I couldn't say goodbye to you. It was too hard for me."

We stop and face each other.

"...And now it is your turn. You have to make your choice." Annabel caresses my cheek. "Remember that even if I am not there on the physical plane, I am with you all the same."

I place my hand on my chest. "I know it."

"We'll meet again. Take good care of yourself and listen to your heart."

Annabel disappears, as does the desert and the scorching sun.

There is only darkness left.

26

THE TEST

I gradually awake, slipping from one state of being into another. My body is rested, and I am lying on the bed, looking up at the ceiling. Sun rays are shining on the wall and not in my eyes, so I can enjoy it without being blinded. I love waking up and feeling the strength of the sun, being fully charged first thing in the morning.

There are only four days left. That isn't much time. I start, and I tumble out of bed. I almost fall, but I manage to put my hand on the floor before I hit it.

The time. What time is it? Quarter past seven.

My body shakes.

No! Thomas will think that I don't want to join him.

Where is my Skycon? I grab hold of my pants and search the pockets. It isn't there. I move around objects and papers feverishly, and some of them end up on the floor. There it is. In a snap move, I enter Thomas's number. It rings and rings, but there is no answer. He's probably left. There's no time for a shower. Normally, I would have whipped on the clothes that were on the floor, not caring if they were dirty, but they have been replaced by clean ones in the cupboard. I grab a pair of jeans, a shirt, and my favorite jumper. Then

I place the Skycon in my pocket and run out the door, down the hall, and toward the café. *Please let him still be there, somehow able to sense that I am on my way.*

The café is filled with people, and I search for Thomas with evident agitation. The sound of my breath is loud, as if someone placed a heavy weight on my chest, preventing me from breathing freely. Small drops of sweat run into my eyes, making it hard to focus. He's nowhere to be found.

I gaze at the big clock above the entrance. It is half past seven. Why should he be waiting for me? On the message board is only the list of new arrivals and departures. We had an agreement. I rush over to the bar, where there's a lot of activity.

"Excuse me." I hit the bar impatiently.

"Just a minute," says a tall, somewhat skinny guy behind the counter, who's explaining how the café works to a new guy.

"It's important." I stand on my toes and try to get his attention. "Sorry to interrupt, but I need to know if you've seen Thomas Leander this morning."

The guy nods at me, realizing that I'm not just one of those irritating customers trying to get served first.

"Thomas just left two minutes ago."

"Which way?"

He points at the door that leads to the west wing.

"Thanks," I say over my shoulder, already running out. Several people are turning their heads to look at me as I race past them. When I am almost at the door, someone grabs my arm.

"Where were you yesterday?" It's Frank.

"Not now!" I wriggle out of his grip and start to run as fast as I can. He is the last person I want to spend time with right now.

The west wing is a maze of halls, and I have no idea which way Thomas went. I try to open a door and run down the first random hallway. There are two ways to turn, right or left. I take a left. Two young men are walking toward me.

"Excuse me. Do you know who Thomas Leander is?" I gesture with my hand that he has long hair.

"Yeah." One of them nods and frowns slightly as he tightens the knot on his red tie.

"Have you seen him?" My voice is about to break, and I'm out of breath too.

He shakes his head. "No. Not today."

I turn around and start running back. He must be here somewhere. It can't be right that he has gone very far. I have to find him.

A young woman walks down at the end of the hall. I yell at her. "Have you seen Thomas Leander?"

She is walking in her own thoughts and jumps, startled. "Yes." She points. "He's over there."

My heart starts pounding faster, and I run at full speed down the hallway where she pointed. It is empty; nobody's there. Maybe he's just gone into one of the rooms. There are six doors. I stop to look around. The hall is wide and has high ceilings. My movements are fast and sudden; I'm in high gear and am about to lose my head.

All is quiet here, and there is nothing to be heard from the other side of the doors. I rush to the first door. It's locked. The next one too. A disheartening feeling fills me. This can't be, just because I happened to sleep a little late. I felt so at peace when I first woke up. Now I can't think clearly. Although I'm asking myself what I should do next, everything is chaos inside me. Heat rises in my body. This can't be happening. I must find him.

I reach for the next door only to find a cleaning supply closet. There is only one more door at this end of the hall, and it's locked too. What is this place? Why are all the doors shut? I run over to the other side of the hall to the second to last door—locked. Now, I'm at the very last door. Please, please, let him be there. It doesn't make sense that I can't find him.

The door is unlocked, and I cautiously push it open. There are many machines inside the room, but I can't see Thomas anywhere. It looks like some kind of server room with screens and hard drives everywhere. I leave again, and at that moment, the door across the hall opens. The guy with black hair who reminded me of a bodyguard comes out. I gasp and call over to him, "Have you seen Thomas?" My voice is shaky and sounds uncertain.

"Thomas? Yes, he's in here." He points at the door behind him.

I walk briskly through the hall toward the man. "Thanks. Thanks a lot." He smiles and no longer seems so threatening.

"Eva, you're Eva, right?" His voice is deep, and he bites the ending of the words as he speaks.

I look at him in surprise. "Yes."

"Thomas is in there waiting for you. Just go inside."

A sense of happiness and relief rushes through me. He's waiting for me. Warmth flushes my cheeks. Maybe it will all work out after all.

I edge past the guy by the door and enter a small, dark hallway with no furniture and nothing on the walls. Thomas is in the next room, and I head toward him with quick steps. He catches sight of me at that moment and comes forward to greet me.

"There you are," he smiles and embraces me. My whole body relaxes in his arms, and I feel grounded again. A sense of peace spreads through me, and it feels like it's putting out a fire inside me. The overheated energy going in circles around my head and upper body is being diverted down through my feet, and I feel a bit more grounded.

Thomas releases me. "Should we get started?"

"Yes, let's," I say with a smile.

Slowly, he walks over to a large screen that is full of information. "This is our monitoring screen. We use it to observe anywhere in the whole world." He makes a large, broad gesture with his arm.

The screen is just one of many. Some are large, some smaller, and all have control buttons along the sides. Two oval-shaped sofas form a circle in the middle of the room. The floor is pale, made of smaller squares that divide the large surface. The color scheme is kept to shades of black and white; only the images on the screens bring life to the room.

Thomas goes to the middle of the screen and pulls down some graphs from a transparent screen.

"Our system runs on energy waves. That is, we pick up energy from people, and in that way, we can see where they are in their lives."

My eyes widen, and I take a step back.

On the screen are graphs, people in various situations, and a great deal of other information that I cannot comprehend.

"Here." Thomas glances at me and moves around a couple of images. He is wearing a black tunic made of a thin fabric that falls loosely from his shoulders. His body looks flexible, and he moves gracefully. He is so elegant to watch. It strikes me every time I see him.

"This is how you log on. Are you listening, Eva?" He checks to see that I am following the process.

"Yeah, yeah…" I hurry and step forward.

Excitement mounts inside me. This is the real thing. I blink a couple of times and nod. The room seems huge but not cold or empty because of all the screens.

"When we log on, the assignments are divided between us, according to what has been encoded into the system about us. The information includes where we come from, how long we have been here, and which security clearance level we have been assigned."

So far, so good; that doesn't seem too complicated… He talks slowly with a great deal of passion. I nod eagerly and only let my gaze shift for a second when the sun starts to pour through the long, oblong windows in the ceiling.

"Before I let you loose in the system, I just want to explain our work to you."

Thomas walks over to another large screen that has a great deal of information on display. He raises his arm and points at the screen, "We have different warning categories. Yellow is for those who are at risk of getting into an accident or who are considering suicide. Orange is for those who are seriously attracting accidents or who are planning suicide, and red is for those who are actively attempting it."

"Let's sit down here for a moment...." He takes my hand and puts his arm around my shoulder. We sit down next to each other. The sofa is soft, and I pull my legs up under me. Now that I have a better overview of the screens, I am impressed by the enormous amount of information and innumerable images available.

"What happens is that we typically prevent an accident if someone falls asleep at the steering wheel on a highway or if a child runs onto a street where there is traffic. So many innocent people could be affected by the actions of others." He speaks calmly. I move over, so there is a little more space between us.

"Sometimes, someone is trying to take their own life, but that is not always what that person truly wishes to do at all. He or she most likely has more to learn on Earth, so much more life to live. In those situations, we can try to intervene, if possible." Thomas straightens up on the sofa and brushes back his hair. "But we must be careful not to get involved because we want to save the world. That's not what this is about."

I keep looking at the screens, remembering a time when one of my girlfriends jumped out in front of a train. The conductor managed to stop before it hit her, and she got off with just a few bruises. I could never understand how the accident was avoided.

Thomas moves his arm and turns, so we are facing each other. "Some people are prepared for something to happen. They just don't know when or how. We can unconsciously wish that something would happen to us, but we cannot determine how it will take place."

"Are you saying that on a deeper level, we attract everything that happens?"

"In a way, it can be intimidating, but it is also liberating, don't you agree?"

I don't reply. The words go through my head—we attract everything ourselves. I am reminded of a time when I was working abroad. I was miserable, had had enough, and just wanted to go home, but there were two weeks left in my work contract. I was too stressed and felt that I should get away, that it was unhealthy for me to remain there. One night, I was out to eat with some colleagues, and when we were about to return to the hotel, I was getting into the back seat of the van with a sliding door on the side. Not thinking, I held onto the frame between the front door and side door. One of the men was irritated about something and slammed the front door shut extra hard, crushing my hand.

An X-ray revealed that I had four broken fingers. I got to go home. At the time, I did not doubt that I had asked for it somehow, but I just couldn't foresee the result. I could have probably found a less dramatic way, but it wasn't meant to be.

"Come over here." Thomas rises and walks over to a screen. "This is an overview of all the countries in the world. They are divided between us based on where we were last, so we can better relate to the different cultural backgrounds that people have."

I have to concentrate to keep up with Thomas's explanations. He walks over to the left side of a screen that fills an entire wall and is divided into many smaller screens within the large one.

"We can watch people over here and accidents over there. Everything has been very accurately encoded so that we have complete control over everything and everyone."

I am surprised by how advanced and precise the technology is. Still, I can't resist asking, "What if the technology fails? Don't you have software or programming errors? It must shut down sometimes?"

"Now, your thoughts are back on Earth again," Thomas laughs. "We are beyond those difficulties here. The frequencies we work with cannot be compared to those on Earth." He smiles and goes over to a smaller screen. "When new people arrive, you get a message here and on your Skycon."

I put my hand in my pocket and take out my Skycon. There is now a new window called reception status. A warm sensation flows to the core of my body.

"When you are new, you receive people who fall under the red category. Those who are clear about where they stand on Earth and therefore do not require as much experience on our part."

I nod eagerly and feel the tickling from a swarm of butterflies in my stomach.

"Because you are with me, today I am connected to the red level. It isn't possible to go to a level higher than the one you have been cleared for, but you can go lower."

That is reassuring. The sunlight is warming me like a warm hand on my back, and I take off my jumper.

Thomas takes a sip of water. "It is important that we are in balance ourselves and are prepared to take on people as they are, so, if there are days when we are working on personal matters, then we don't log on." He places his glass on the table and stands relaxed with his knees slightly bent. "This isn't a nine-to-five job. There are no expectations for you. We look at it as an exchange of energy. You give your energy, and you are paid back with energy."

"That sounds very clever, but there must be some who misuse it." I can't help but be a bit critical and cannot hide a smile.

"If you misuse it, it will only rebound. Everything is connected, and in one way or another, it will come back to you."

I look down and am aware that my lower back is taut. Was what I just said dumb?

He places his hand on my shoulder, and I lift my head so that our eyes meet.

"Part of the test today is also to see if you are ready to work here. It requires a certain degree of insight and understanding."

I feel a headache coming. I run my fingers back and forth across my face and massage my temples. I'm not sure if I feel ready for this. How can I look after a new person when I am not at peace with myself? I'm not able to relate the things the way Thomas can—not at all. He is always perfectly calm and reliable. If a new person meets me, it isn't certain that they would feel like staying. I know that they have to anyhow, but I would like to do my best.

"Now, it's your turn." Thomas takes one step back.

My eyes widen even more, and my body trembles.

"You are logged on now. Why don't you spend some time exploring the system? That's the best way to get to know it."

Thomas brings a chair over and indicates that I should be seated.

"Just relax; you can't ruin anything." My body tightens even more, and I try to force a smile but have no luck with that and accidentally snort.

He goes over to another screen on the wall opposite, and I sit down and begin to move around some of the windows on the screen. "Search" is written on one. I quickly type in "Eva Monroe" and press enter. Images of my whole family appear. My mother's image is marked with a red dot.

"Thomas," I call him in a low voice as I move around the other images to see if they also have colors. They don't. I begin to feel anxious and swallow thickly.

"*Thomas!*"

I can hear him behind me and point at the image of my mother. "Why is it red? Can there be a mistake?"

He pulls up a chair next to me and moves around the images. A live signal to my mother appears on the screen. She is cleaning in her living room. Her eyes are bloodshot, her skin pale, and she is walking with heavy steps.

"It looks like you being in a coma has been hard on your mother. Now, she is in the red group, so it is hard to reach her. She's under a great deal of pressure."

"We have to do something." My voice is very emphatic and emotionally charged. "We can't let her go so far. Thomas, *do something*."

"I can try to send her some clear white light and see if that will help." He presses a couple of buttons and traces a ring of clear light around her.

"*More*," I stare at Thomas, "give her more!"

"I can't increase it. Right now, she is receiving the maximum amount she can bear. If I turn it up, it could short-circuit her nervous system, which means she could fall into a state of insanity. Then, we would lose the possibility of reaching her."

I sit paralyzed, eyes fixed on the screen. A tear is running down my cheek, and I quickly dry it off. She mustn't give up, not now. Luke can't do without her. Of course, it's problematic that I am in a coma, but that doesn't mean giving up is an option; it just isn't. Why does Andreas have to move too? Can't he wait? It's putting my mother under extreme pressure.

"I have to go back," my voice is wavering. "I am the only one who can save her. Thomas, you have to help me go back now." I look straight into his eyes. There is no doubt that he knows that I mean it. "I want to go back now," my voice is now flat and no-nonsense. "I *know* that it can be done. You just have to access the system. You, of all people, must have the repatriation code. I know I'm supposed to stay here for forty-two days, but I know you can send me back now. There are only four days left. It can't possibly matter if I go back a few days earlier if it means I can save her life, can it?"

27

LAYERS

I am sitting on a chair with the screen in front of me. Although I am looking at it, I can't see it. My expression is vacant and resigned. We can send people to the moon, but we can't find ourselves. We can develop and produce medicine and vaccines globally, but we can't figure out how to live life while we have it. We desire all the things we don't have and overlook essential things in life. We treat symptoms instead of looking at the causes and aspire toward goals rather than living in the moment. Is there any reason to do anything? We are going to die at some point, anyhow. The surest thing in life is death. I cannot see the purpose of anything at all. Everything seems meaningless right now. There is no hope; there is no God. Nothing makes any sense whatsoever.

After sending the white light down to my mother, she calmed down and went to bed, but I have a feeling that the danger hasn't passed yet. When Andreas moves, Luke will not see her as often, which will be hard on both of them. I am the only one who can change that. If I had gone home yesterday, none of this would have happened. The opportunity to leave here last night was right in front of me. What is the matter with me? Am I losing my common sense?

Am I getting too ambitious? What is it I think will happen for me at In-Between? My family is on Earth, not here. Thomas comes in, carrying our lunch. I close my eyes briefly and gulp.

The sunlight is gone, and I reach for my jumper. Thomas places a plate with potato salad in front of me. The countless images on the screens seem perplexing, and I can't make sense of them all.

"Thank you. It looks delicious." I would like to smile, but it is impossible.

"Would you still like to leave?" Thomas sits next to me, and I nod.

"I have no choice. I am the only one who can save my mother and Luke." I cut the potato, and it splits in two.

"What makes you think that they need to be saved?" He takes a glass of water and places it in front of me.

"Well, just look at my mother. She is at the end of her tether about losing Luke and me. Luke is just a child. Now, he will have to leave his Kindergarten and start at a new one where he doesn't know anyone. On top of that, he'll have to learn to relate to that long-legged woman instead of me, and *I* am his mother."

"Who says that anything needs to be changed?" Thomas speaks with an easy voice.

I slam my fork so hard on the plate that a few potatoes roll onto the table. "I don't understand what you're implying. I have to help them. I can't just leave them in the lurch." My voice is choked up. "It is my duty to help." I look at Thomas intently. Doesn't he understand what I am saying?

He looks right back at me. "The question is whether it is, in fact, a help that you go back, or, if you would simply postpone something that your mother, Luke, and Andreas have to learn in this life. You could deprive them of the opportunity to develop."

"No. Stop it right now." I am seething. "You can't just answer that there is a deeper meaning of life every time I ask a question. We can't resolve everything by remaining passive. I need to take action." Blood rushes to my cheeks, and my whole body feels like it's boiling.

Thomas remains calm. He is bent forward slightly. "Try to look deeper." He makes a slow downward gesture with his hand. "There are several layers in this situation, and right now, you are looking at the top layer. Try to see if you can see beyond this layer and look at the next one." He moves his hand in a way that indicates that there are many layers below each other—like a pile of pancakes on a plate.

My body is tense, and I sit back with folded arms without saying anything. Running my fingernail into my index finger as I bite my lower lip distracts my attention a bit.

"I understand the layer you are looking at. That is the one we have learned as humans living on Earth. Your mother and father and their parents have lived in this way too. That is logical, and that is what we relate to. But there is more, much more."

Thomas leans back. Hesitant, I turn a bit, and we sit facing each other. "Do you remember the story I told you about the man and the horses?" I nod, and Thomas continues. "Right now, we know that your mother is doing badly. Andreas wants to move, and Luke will move with him. We don't know more than that."

Against my will, I nod again.

"We don't know what it will lead to or how it will affect their lives. We also know that you are in a coma. But we don't know if you will come out of it or not because you will not decide until four days from now. A lot can happen in those four days, both for you and your family."

I keep biting my lower lip and pull my knees up under my chin. Thomas is sitting peacefully, as always.

"We don't know whether it is good or bad that you are in a coma. Whether it is good or bad that Andreas is going to move, we don't know either. What we do know is that whether we do something or not, things will happen. If we remain passive, then that is also an action, in the same way that doing something is an action; it is just the opposite with just as great an effect."

I lower my eyes and clench my teeth. Thomas folds his hands together.

"That is, if you choose to stay, something will happen, and if you choose to return, something else will happen. But there is only one person who can make this decision, and that is you."

I jump up, gesticulating. Thomas indicates with his finger that I shouldn't say anything.

"To make this decision, you need to be emotionally detached. As long as you believe that you can save your mother and Luke and feel guilty if you don't, you cannot make a heartfelt choice. The choice will be made from an emotional state, and we can't think clearly in that state."

"What should I do then?" My tone is accusatory, and my arms are folded firmly across my chest. I start to walk back and forth behind Thomas. He takes a mouthful of his salad and turns toward me.

"Right now, the best thing is time. If you can give yourself time to disconnect from these feelings, you can once again see things clearly and make your choice. Whatever it is, I will help you to realize it."

I am deeply thankful for Thomas's support. He is right. When I am on this wavelength, I can't think clearly or be sure of my emotions. I am affected by my surroundings, and all the old programming still active in my head, which tells me what I ought to do and how to do it. I am experiencing feelings of guilt for not doing something. This is truly heavy baggage to carry.

I lock my hands behind my head and look up at the ceiling. "I am afraid of doing something wrong. I feel like I've lost my good judgment. I have always been so decisive; what happened to me?" My eyes are wet, and I look at Thomas, hoping that he will say something —that he will somehow save me. Why can't he just make this decision for me? But that is probably what Thomas is alluding to. I am caught up in my past and everything that comes with it.

"Well," Thomas looks at me, "are you ready, Eva? A new guest has arrived. Will you come with me and greet a new arrival?"

"Sure, why not? I can't see clearly anyhow." My tone is resigned, and I exhale.

Thomas laughs, "Come on, you." He takes hold of my hand and pulls me. I can't help but laugh. It is a relief to laugh, and I am astonished by the way he can allow sorrow and joy to be present at the same time and that he doesn't start to feel sorry for me. Interesting.

28

THE FIRST GUEST

The room appears smaller. The last time I was here was when I arrived at In-Between myself. It feels like an eternity since then. Now, I am back but on the other side. Sweat is running down my back, and my heart is pumping furiously. Days and memories flash in front of my eyes like a film montage—the flight, the crash, and my first meeting with Thomas. Those were probably the most disturbing days of my life. And now, my time is almost up, and it is just starting for the young man lying on the floor.

"Come in," Thomas gestures with his arm. "He's just about to wake up."

I halt in the doorway and look at the room. It is a deja vu experience to see the hovering walls again, the pale floor, and how the soft, warm light affects me. I smile. In-Between is familiar to me now, and I have the home-ground advantage.

Thomas is sitting next to the man who is just arriving. There is a shift in the floor. He is lying on a light, mat-like bed that is set into the floor and is flush with the rest, which is made of marble. A bit of a Japanese-inspired style, I think.

THE LIFE

My memories from the day I arrived are blurred. It was all so overwhelming and intense; everything seemed to happen so fast.

The young man is tall with prominent cheekbones and a ring in his right ear. His face is covered with razor stubble, and he looks rather haggard.

"What happened to him?" I squat down just behind Thomas.

"He's been using drugs and has given up. Our job is to get him to believe that he can get off drugs and take care of himself, and also that giving up is not the easy way out."

"Why? You just said that everything is as it should be." I keep a little distance between Thomas and me and the young man.

"It is." Thomas is sitting in the lotus position and resting his hands on his thighs. "He shouldn't go back at any price, but he has an opportunity to learn something, and he gave himself this challenge before he was born because he thought that he could handle it."

"How do you know that?" I whisper, which isn't necessary because I don't need to be afraid of waking him.

"It's in his file. There is a log file for all souls, and it includes such information as what they have entered their mortal lives to learn from and transform."

"What's in my file?" I ask eagerly, and I scoot closer to him.

A loving laughter fills the room. "I knew that you would ask me that." He moves a bit closer. "His name is Ken, and he has pushed himself to the limit without knowing why. It isn't certain that he'll wake up. He's unconscious, and it's touch and go. He could die. But, if he awakes, we'll talk to him. Until then, we'll shine some healing white light on him."

Thomas walks over to one of the computers and turns on a sharp white light that only shines on Ken's body. "This is a healing, life-giving light. Observe his face and hands. You see them change gradually from being entirely white and lifeless; they'll begin to take on a healthier color."

Ken moves slightly.

"Thomas," I turn toward him, "he's waking up." I move back, and Thomas sits in front of me.

Ken opens his eyes and jerks up into a sitting position. He starts scurrying back and holds his hand out against us, attempting to disassociate himself from us. "WHO THE HELL ARE YOU? WHAT'S GOING ON?" He puts his other hand in front of his eyes and backs up until he can't get any further away. Thomas remains seated quietly and calmly, and I am sitting right behind him, not so calm.

"WHO ARE YOU?" Ken's voice is rough and sounds rusty. "WHERE AM I? WHAT HAVE YOU DONE TO ME?"

It is fascinating to watch Thomas project serenity, which eventually begins to affect Ken without Thomas having to say anything.

"*Who are you?*" Ken curls up his legs. "What the hell is this place?"

Thomas cautiously moves a bit closer to Ken, who is now backed up against the opposite wall. "This is a place in between life and death." Thomas's tone and radiance get Ken to lower his arm a bit. He moves a bit closer, and Ken rests his head on his fist. He finds it hard to sit still, and his hands and right leg are shaking. His eyes are darting around the room, and he is uneasy.

Thomas looks at him. "You have pushed yourself to an extreme in your life on Earth, and you need to choose whether you would like to return or if you will give up."

For some reason or other, what Thomas is saying makes sense to Ken. He leans back against the wall and rests his head. "I know it. I've gone too far, and now I've hit the wall."

Thomas looks at Ken appreciatively and smiles. "That's right."

"I want to go back, but I can't deal with this shit by myself. I'll get back on the needle again. Everything inside me is dark. Know what I mean?"

"I understand." Thomas nods. "I can offer you the chance to go back with some healing light and strength. But we don't have much time. Your condition is critical. Can you walk?"

Ken shakes his head. "My legs are shot. I can hardly feel them."

Thomas turns toward me. "There's no time to spare. Eva, go over to the switchboard and enter 1223."

I get up and hurry over to the switchboard and enter 1223 without knowing what it means. A lot of windows come up on the screen, asking for a code. I raise my hands from the keyboard. "Thomas, I need a code."

He pulls a device out of his pocket, pushes on it, and says, "Enter 1221XY29HJ8098." I enter it as he reads it out loud. Then a section of the wall slides open, and a new room appears. This can't be true. Tell me it isn't real. I squint to see better, then look at Thomas and back to the room that has just been revealed.

Can I have been so close this whole time?

Thomas smiles as though he is reading my mind.

The dispatch room.

"Here, grab hold of him. We have no time to waste." Thomas calls me over, and I run to him. Together, we move Ken to the couch that is sitting in the middle of the dispatch room.

"This is my card. Run it through the machine up there, quickly. Ken is about to lose consciousness." Thomas hands me a thin, rubbery, transparent card. I hurry, but it isn't easy. My hands are shaking. There is a narrow slit I have to get the card into. Come on, get yourself together. I tighten my grip on the card and hold it next to the machine.

"Now, hold it completely still...." Thomas is composed, but his tone is firm, "or it won't work."

I hold my wrist with my other hand for support. Why is it taking so long? Come on.

Ken has passed out. He is lying on the couch, completely pale. The machine starts up with a suspended, nearly silent movement. The light is so powerful that I have to cover my eyes. Thomas pulls me back. "We need to keep our distance, or we'll get too much light on us."

When we step back, a screen rises from the floor. I look down; there must be sensors on the floor that have registered our movements. We are standing, still observing Ken. "Will he make it?" I fight to keep my voice calm.

"We'll find out soon. First, he needs to be exposed to the right amount of light so that he'll have the strength to return to his life. If he can take in the light, he will be able to disintegrate and leave here to return to his body on Earth. This process involves the pure transformation of energy." Thomas looks at me. "I'm afraid that it may be too late—that he cannot take in enough light to wake up again."

It doesn't seem like Thomas is shaken by this situation, but of course, he has experience. My legs are like jelly, and I am pressing my hands over my mouth. *Calm down*, I say to myself. If Thomas can stand there peacefully, so can I.

It is extraordinary to watch Ken. The light is powerful. An icy blue color is shining through, and his white skin is slowly changing color, not much, but enough that I can make it out.

The dispatch room only contains the couch and the screen we are standing next to. It isn't very big. I notice a dark point on the ceiling and wonder what it is for.

Thomas touches the screen in front of us. It is built into the glass screen that rose from the floor. Several graphs and numbers come up.

"This is where we can monitor how he is doing. This shows that his heart rate is rising. It was down to ten percent, and now it is up to fifty-four percent. We were very close to losing him. The percentage is rising slowly, but steadily. It looks as if the light is working."

I look at Thomas. "You said that those who are in the red category are the easiest to handle, but receiving Ken requires an incredible amount of experience and knowledge."

Thomas returns my gaze. "Yes and no.... This duty can seem overwhelming, but you will also have a stronger connection with yourself when you are ready to take on these assignments. You will, of course, be familiar with the system so that you will have no doubt about what needs to be done. Remember that we can only do our best. We are not superhumans just because we work at In-Between. Humility is properly one of the most important virtues."

I look over at Ken. He is lying completely still and looks dead. It is silent here except for the humming of the machine that is emitting light. I still don't understand how Thomas could know that Ken shouldn't stay here. Maybe I'm a little slow on the uptake. If I don't ask, I won't get an answer. I swallow and turn back toward Thomas.

"But," I hesitate for a second, "I have to stay here for forty-two days. How do you know that Ken shouldn't?"

Thomas smiles at me. By now, I know his smile so well. There is never the slightest sign of irritation or tiredness in response to my questions. I feel his love and solicitude toward me.

"There are several factors that are conclusive. One of the most important is that I can see in his profile that he was in the middle of a process on Earth that he can use toward his development. The highest priority is to support that, but since he was also physically affected, it was important to help him with that here and now."

Sixty-four percent. Ken's heart rate keeps rising.

I am bubbling with excitement. "I am so glad to be here today." I can't help smiling. "This is so exciting. There's something else I've been wondering about." I hold back for a moment, but Thomas says nothing. "In a way, I think that time goes so quickly here. I only have a few days left, but when I realize that I have been here for thirty-eight days, it seems so unreal. On the one hand, it seems like I just arrived; on the other hand, I've had so many experiences. It's hard for me to explain."

Seventy-two. The graph on the screen is steadily rising toward one hundred percent.

Thomas places two fingers on the middle of my chest. "Your spiritual heart lies here. In my experience, the heart knows nothing of time. It is only when our hearts are closed, and we are living in our minds that we measure time, and it can seem long." I feel warmth rushing to the spot where Thomas has his fingertips. "When the heart is open, we lose our sense of time because it is not relevant to the heart. When you neglect your heart, you may feel a longing for these moments, if only they could last longer, maybe forever." Thomas looks at me mildly and tucks my hair behind my ear. "There is something about you, Eva. You have a very special fragility, and at the same time, you have the strength that could inspire many. A lot has happened inside you in the time you have been here. You are like a flower that is about to blossom."

Seventy-eight percent.

Hopefully, I don't lose everything I have learned here when I return home. Will those who know me also sense that I have changed? Will I be strong enough not to fall back into my old ways of being? I hope so. I take a deep breath and run my fingers over my lips. Thomas sees me as no one else has seen me. If only I could take him with me.

He places his arm around my shoulders. "When Ken is over eighty percent, he will begin to return to Earth. He is so close now; it almost can't go wrong. He will experience it as a dream. It is only because we caught him before he had completely let go of life on Earth that it is possible to send him back."

We stand there watching Ken and checking to ensure that his heart rate continues to rise. His body gradually fades and disappears. "Back on Earth, he will return to consciousness and have another chance. Whether he uses it or not, we cannot know."

"What now?" I ask.

"Now, we can wait for the next soul that needs our help. We just need to close this file." Thomas goes over to the switchboard. "Look. You go in here and write a brief description of what has happened and then endorse it. Then Ken's file will be up to date. While you are doing that, I'll go get us something to drink."

Before I can protest, Thomas is already out the door. I'd better make some notes in Ken's file and finalize his case.

The second I press the button to endorse the file, a message appears saying that I am now active as a receiver again. What do I do? I can't receive someone on my own. But it is too late. The machine that sent Ken off is already processing the next soul for reception.

29

BAPTISM OF FIRE

I run into the other room. The wall to the dispatch room slides shut behind me, and I stand there fixed in place. A new soul is about to arrive. I look at the closed door. Where is Thomas? It can't take that long to get something to drink. If only the person won't wake up. Now, I must focus on the task at hand and not let myself panic. How did he bring up the profile?

Decisively, I walk over to the large screen and drag some of the windows that Thomas left open. All kinds of images come up. I try to move them around in the hope of recognizing the file that has the information I need.

It is not to be seen anywhere. There is a red percentage scale that is rising; that must represent the percentage of the manifestation's energy that has arrived. It's up to seventy-eight percent. The person will be here soon, which means that there's a risk that the person will awaken.

"Thomas, come on." I stomp my heel on the floor. Where is he? My face is tense, one fist is clenched, and I am pushing buttons with the other hand, frantically trying to find the profile.

Eighty-two percent!

"Come on, where are you?" I need help here. There must be some kind of inbox or something. There... That looks like it could be a profile. It is. Kate is forty-eight years old and... suicide? Suicide can't fall under the red category. The very thought of suicide hits me like a punch in the stomach and brings my shoulders up to my ears. What should I say to her if she wakes up?

"Hi, my name is Eva. How nice of you to stop by."

Eighty-eight percent.

Now, this is getting serious. I reach for my Skycon in my pocket and try to call Thomas. His Skycon rings on the table next to me.

Okay. I have to make a plan. It can't be too hard. "Hi, my name is Eva." I clear my throat. That didn't sound very satisfactory. I try saying it while smiling. "Hi, my name is Eva. Welcome to In-Between." Yes, that was better. Whew, it's up to ninety-two percent. Kate's body becomes faintly visible on the mattress behind the screen that encircles the mattress during the arrival phase. The outline of her body is there, but she is still almost transparent. I look over at the door. Would you please come, Thomas!

Ninety-eight percent. At first, her skin was all white, and now it is beginning to gain a warmer glow, and she is breathing steadily.

The screen begins to lower into the floor, and there is nothing that separates us. I look upward, shut my eyes, and take in a deep breath. Serenity comes to me from where I do not know. I take a step forward to her side and kneel next to her. I have one eye on the screen and one on Kate.

Ninety-nine percent.

Now, it is so close to her arrival. I have no idea what will happen next. It says in her profile that she is married with two children who still live at home. Her husband has been unfaithful to her several times, and she has just been fired from her job. All her life, she has been struggling with low self-esteem and always attracted people who took advantage of her. That must have been the last straw. She is lying on the floor with her legs extended and her arms along the sides of her body. Her smooth brown pageboy falls back from her face. Her nose is small, and her cheeks are plump. She looks so relaxed and refined. Her blue suit seems expensive, and she is wearing a diamond wedding ring.

Suicide. I feel a lump in my throat. That is so egoistic. I bite my lip, and the pain makes me focus on the present. Why does life have that emergency exit? Why do we have that possibility? Several times in my life, I have felt as if I didn't belong—that no one understood me. There have been times when the pain was overwhelming, and this emergency exit came to mind, although I've never seriously considered it. But if someone else does it, then it seems suddenly legitimate; the back door of life becomes visible.

One hundred percent. Kate can wake up at any time now. I am kneeling in an upright position. She is lying so still and has a burdened facial expression. If Thomas came now, it would be totally perfect.

I bend forward and stroke her hair. She is warm. I don't know what I had imagined. Her eyelids begin to move, and slowly, very slowly, they open up, and she looks at me. I smile at her. She smiles back and shuts her eyes as if she just needed to see that she is safe and can relax again. She is completely still.

I move a bit closer to her and place my hand on her arm so that she can feel that I am there. I don't know how long I sit there, but it must be a while. It feels lovely just to sit next to her and give her the time that she needs.

A warm sensation builds up behind me, and I look over my shoulder. Thomas is there.

"Hi," he whispers. "Are you thirsty?"

I take the glass. "Where have you been? I... I thought that you had forgotten me."

He chuckles and shakes his head. "Have you missed me?"

"Actually not. At least not right now, maybe earlier. Yes and no."

"It looks like everything is going fine."

I nod. "There isn't much to do right now. I think she's fallen asleep."

Kate's breathing is deep and slow.

Thomas looks at me and whispers, "There's a lot to it. Don't underestimate the support you are giving her by sitting patiently at her side without having an agenda." He sits down next to me. "How many people do you think have experienced that? Most people feel pressure from others to do or achieve things, to be different than who they are or to do things that basically, they do not want to do."

Kate looks like she is at peace.

"Kate can sense that you are there for her, with no expectations or reservations. She can feel the unconditional love flowing from you to her, a love that comes from an open heart." He puts his hand on my shoulder. "Most people have no idea what that means and, therefore, cannot imagine it. It isn't until we experience it for ourselves that it arouses something inside us, and we begin to understand."

I am enjoying the tranquility and silence here.

"Eva," Thomas looks into my eyes, "you have a big heart and so much love to give."

I am touched. No one has ever said that to me before. And even though, in some way, I think that I have a lot to give, I've never truly dared to share it. I've always been afraid that others would not want it or that I would not give what was right.

Kate begins to stir. She turns toward us slowly and opens her eyes. I smile at her and say, "Hi."

She responds the same way, "Hi."

"My name is Eva, and this is Thomas. We are here to receive you here at In-Between."

Kate's eyebrows are wrinkled, and her eyes wander. It is overwhelming. Not long ago, she decided to leave Earth and thought that it was all over. She must have spent days, weeks, perhaps even months preparing to die, and now she is waking up anyhow.

"I'm thirsty." Kate smiles at me. The lines around her eyes are so delicate, and they get a bit more distinct as she speaks.

"Here." Thomas pours her a glass of water.

She takes it and drinks it all. "Oh, that was wonderful. I don't remember the last time a glass of water tasted so good."

We all laugh. It is incredible to be sitting here, receiving another person, a soul on its journey. At this moment, I think, what now? I am sitting closer to Kate and have the primary contact, and Thomas isn't doing anything. Then I remember what the Master said to me.

The heart always has the answer.

I try to become aware of what I would like to do. What would I need if I were lying there? I would like to know where I was. Slowly, I begin to explain to Kate where she is in a very simple manner.

I look briefly at Thomas and finish by saying, "You have all the time you need to take proper leave of your life on Earth and prepare for your soul's further journey."

Kate looks at me. It doesn't seem to put her off. When I pause for a moment, she says, "Thank you; I have never felt blessed before. What an opportunity. It seems too good to be true." She shakes her head.

I smile at her. She's right. It is fantastic.

"Would you like to get something to eat? Are you hungry, Kate?" I tilt my head sideways and feel like I am beaming all the way down to my belly. She nods, and I put my hand on her shoulder to assist her so that she can sit up. Her entire body is shaking and needs to be supported so she can get onto her feet. Coming here is very hard on the body. The air is different, and the whole transferring process is so intense and powerful. Afterward, there can be several days with sore muscles and tiredness. I remember it well.

Thomas stays in the background. It suddenly hits me that I am being tested. Am I doing it well enough? Am I doing things right? I've been so absorbed by everything that is happening that I haven't given it any thought.

"I'd like to wash my face. Is there a restroom nearby?" Kate looks at me questioningly, and I turn toward Thomas.

"Right this way." He presses a button on the screen, and a section of the wall slides aside so that a small room with two doors appears.

My arm is under Kate's. She seems to be at ease. We walk slowly toward the restroom. Her legs are a little stiff, but she is managing it surprisingly well.

"Would you like me to go with you?" I look at Kate.

"No, you don't need to. I can take care of myself from here." Her pronunciation is exact without sounding snobbish. I don't let Kate out of my sight until she has gone into the restroom and shut the door behind her.

I'm totally impressed by her when I think back to how I was when I had just arrived. But, unlike me, she has been preparing to leave.

I turn around to face Thomas. He looks back at me, "Yes?"

"When do I find out if I've passed the test?"

"When would you like to know?"

Can I decide?

"Now."

He laughs. "Tomorrow."

"That's a long time to wait—a whole night."

He smiles teasingly at me.

Kate exits the restroom, and I walk over to her.

"Could you use an arm for support?" She nods and takes hold of my arm.

I have the feeling that Thomas already knows the result of my test and is just keeping me waiting. First and foremost, I must take care of Kate. I don't know how much she needs me, but she seems like someone who can say what she needs or object if necessary. That makes it much easier.

"If you two go on ahead, then I'll log off for today." Thomas makes it clear that he feels secure, leaving Kate to me.

"Are you coming to the café, Thomas?"

"I don't know. Maybe."

"If we don't see each other, then see you tomorrow." I wave at him.

He waves back. "That's a date."

Looking at Kate, I feel warmth in my heart spreading throughout me, filling every little cell in my body until even my hands are warm. Thomas once told me that hands are an extension of the heart, and this is the first time I have experienced it first-hand. We walk slowly down the hallway. Kate is very quiet. She is looking around, taking in impressions.

I am walking with a new soul. My breathing is steady. How incredible that I am allowed to experience this.

30

THE CIRCLE

A well-known sound is coming from my pocket. I pull out the Skycon; there is no picture from the caller.

"Hello," I say loudly and clearly. A deep voice offers me a polite greeting.

Quickly, I turn around to see if anyone else is here, but there isn't. I'm standing on a secluded ledge that I found on one of my many walks. The wind is lifting my hair into my mouth, and I spit it out before continuing.

"This is Eva." Curious, I look at the Skycon. An image of an older man with a worn face appears.

"Please be at X17 this evening at 6 p.m. Do not ask any questions." The image of the man disappears again.

"Excuse me?" I tap on the screen with my finger.

Why would someone contact me in that way? X17 doesn't mean anything to me. I sit down on a white bench and look out at the sky. Clouds are drifting underneath me at a glacial pace, and out on the horizon, a flock of small birds is enjoying themselves. Fortunately, it doesn't seem like anyone else is aware of this little nook. Behind me is a wall of bushes that provide shelter. I take in a deep breath. My body feels almost electric. I have been searching in vain for Thomas all day long, and he hasn't answered my calls. I want to know if I've passed the test, not that it would affect my decision, but just out of curiosity. Kate is dealing very well with her arrival, beyond all expectations. She has already started meditating and seems happy to be here. I lean back on the bench and let my sight drift into infinity. I have grown fond of my walk by myself. It is so strange; when I was on Earth, I was always busy with something: work, cooking, or planning the next day. Doing nothing seemed like a punishment. During the time I have been here, I started to appreciate the silence and time just to be without any agenda or direction. Strange how you can judge others for what they do, and then one day, you realize that you were the one off-track.

IT IS APPROACHING SIX O'CLOCK, and I'm heading toward the X Department. In fact, I don't know what kind of place I am to meet up at. The X Department houses offices and administration. There are some places that I can't go because there are different levels of security clearance, and this is one of them. It is quite interesting that I could make my way to the Master, but I can't get into Department X.

I look at my Skycon, and I'll be there in seven minutes. That means five because I am always a bit quicker than the time estimates. It is very still here; most people are probably eating dinner now. The hallways are the same as everywhere else, bright and simple. The main difference is just a very pale strip of light on the floor that indicates this section with an X and a discreet shade of purple.

The soft lighting on the ceiling turns on automatically as I walk along. The sun is gone, and I can just make out the edge of the clouds outside the large windows on my left.

One more door, then I'll arrive. They must have put a clearance

THE LIFE

on my Skycon; there is no trouble getting into the area today. Eleven, twelve, thirteen, fourteen, then seventeen must be over here. Fifteen, sixteen. I can't see seventeen; this is eighteen and nineteen. It makes no sense. Where is seventeen? Looking more carefully, I go back and forth, but there is simply no seventeen to be seen; the numbers just skip from sixteen to eighteen. I hate this sort of thing that makes me feel stupid. I pull up my sleeve and look at my watch. I'm right on time.

Perhaps there is a secret door like the one near the Master's residence. I go right up to the wall and examine it carefully, inch by inch. Is there a circle somewhere that I have overlooked or some sort of motion detector? Is this a part of the test? Slowly and silently, I let my hand glide over the entire wall, thoroughly covering the surface. Nothing happens. I walk over to the other side of the hallway and do the same there. What is it that I can't see? Why was I asked to come here when no one is here to meet me? Is this a part of the test, or is there something that I've completely misunderstood? Maybe he didn't say X17. Could I have heard wrong? I rub my hands over my face several times and try to see if it brings clarity.

It's past six now. I hate being late, but it isn't my fault. I am here, in a way, yet not really. The frustration starts to build inside me, and I keep running my hand over the soft and a bit cool surface.

"Come with me."

The voice startles me, and I let out a halfhearted scream that sounds more like a hoarse hen. I recognize the voice that asked me to meet here, coming from behind. I turn around to see a well-groomed man dressed in a long black coat. He only has a fringe of hair on the sides of his head and a narrow face. I'd better follow him.

We walk down the hallway and around to the other side of this department to be in a hallway parallel to the one we were in before. When we get to the middle of the hallway, a wall slides open, and I step into a small, well-lit room with no people or furniture. The door slides shut behind me, and I am standing there with the still unfamiliar man. He doesn't say anything and doesn't invite any questions. His face is locked in a serious expression.

The room is sealed, with no windows, doors, nothing. It appears much bigger than it is with the bright white soft walls. I stand quite still and wait. There is nothing else I can do right now. It is like standing in an elevator, just with greater pressure. I can't tell if we're moving upward or downward; somehow, it seems to be horizontal. A fine, red square frame runs around the wall opposite the one we came through.

The man goes over to the wall, places his hand on it, and a section of it slides open. A large room filled with huge candleholders in all corners comes into view. It is octagonal with a pitch-black floor and light walls. Some people are inside, standing and talking, but there isn't very much light, so it's hard to see who they are. Some of them have their backs to me.

I look at the man who escorted me. He moves his hand, signaling that I should enter. The door shuts behind me, and I am standing alone in the room, or at least that's how it feels. In front of me are stairs leading down to the others. There are no other doors to be seen, but I know by now that all is not what it seems. My jaw drops open as my eyes observe everything in the room. The floor is made of stone with a shiny surface so that the glow of the candles is reflected. The walls are illuminated, and red banners hang loosely from the ceiling, decorated with symbols I don't recognize. The roof slants upward into a glass pyramid with a view of the evening sky.

The others are very engaged in their conversations and haven't noticed that I have come, or perhaps do not even know that I should come. Isn't there anyone I know who could help me feel a little more welcome? I cringe on my toes and try to move forward, but nothing happens. I just stand there, trying to find a point to fix my gaze on to look more natural. Looking around, I catch sight of something that looks like a bar counter with some high chairs in front of it. I can take a seat over there until someone notices me. Of course, I could introduce myself, but to whom?

An older man approaches me. He's not very tall and walks with a slight limp. I don't think I recognize him. Judging by the deep wrinkles on his face, I estimate that he is about seventy years old. He smiles in a very friendly and inviting way and reaches both arms out to me.

"Eva, welcome. We are delighted to have you here." He lays his hands on mine; they are soft and warm. Something about him is incredibly pleasant, and that inspires confidence.

"I am sorry. I did not see that you had arrived. I was so absorbed in the conversation. We will start in just a moment. Come and meet the others. By the way, my name is Gabriel." His voice is deep and a bit rusty.

He takes my arm, and we walk toward the center of the room. Tall candlesticks with a rustic look and six arms are burning in all corners, emphasizing the room's octagonal shape. There are several alcoves in the walls with more candles, creating a fascinating effect.

In the middle of the room, seven chairs are placed in a circle on a large, red carpet with a golden ring printed in the middle. The chairs are made of a dark wood that I do not recognize at first glance. Various animals and symbols are carved into their arms and backs. The upholstery is flaming red, rather awe-inspiring. The position of the chairs reminds me of something I can't remember.

We walk over to another three people who are in the middle of a conversation. I can make out the faces of the two whose profiles I can see, but not the third. Most likely, I don't know them, even though something about them seems familiar.

"Excuse me, everyone. Eva has arrived." The two whose profiles I can see turn to face me, and then the third man with his back to me turns around.

"Thomas," I exclaim.

He smiles. "Eva, it is lovely to see you here. How nice that you could come."

My mouth drops open, and I'm about to ask a question, but Thomas puts his index finger in front of his mouth. "Not now. We have to have our meeting first."

Gabriel nods appreciatively at Thomas. I look at the other two, and they introduce themselves.

"Shiva."

"Yoge."

Shiva has thick, black hair. She is slight and has the most maternal eyes I have seen in ages. Yoge is tall, well over six feet, with a wide nose and a rather square-shaped head with hair wisps on both sides.

"Eva." I reach out my hand to greet them. They smile, put their palms together in front of their chests, and bow slowly. I look at Thomas, and he just grins back. I'm getting the feeling that they already know who I am.

"Come." Gabriel looks at me. "The time is nigh."

Thomas nods at me. "Just follow along." He gestures toward Gabriel with his open hand. I ought to feel secure now that I know Thomas is here, but my body trembles inside. I don't know where I am or what is going to happen. Luckily, they all seem friendly and harmless.

"Here." Gabriel points at the chair with an eagle carved on the back of it. "That is your chair."

My chair? A warm sensation rushes through my body, making me feel a bit honored. The whole atmosphere around the arrangement of the chairs looks rather holy and ceremonious. I am wondering what they want from me. I sit down. It isn't the most comfortable chair on earth, but I don't expect that we have gathered here just to sit and relax. There is Gabriel, Thomas, Yoge, Shiva, and me, and then two empty chairs. I look around. It doesn't look like any more people will be joining us.

Suddenly, a thought occurs to me. Where it comes from, I have no idea. It's like a flashback. *My dream.* It is my dream from the mountain, that day I was so ill. I look at the others and recognize them from my dream. They look a little different because their clothes are not the same, but I know it is them. And the two who are missing—who was it who sat in those two places? I try to recall the images from the dream. There was a woman… I'm sure. Or am I? I bite my lower lip.

Gabriel looks at me and smiles. "You remember it now. It is beginning to come back to you."

I move my head in small jolts.

"That is a good sign."

It is tranquil here. Everyone is patiently waiting and looking at me.

I try to remember more from the dream. We were sitting in a circle, and then there was a conversation. That's right. It is beginning to dawn on me. Gabriel. It was Gabriel who said that we should meet when the time was right. And I said that I needed some more time before I was ready….

It is clear to me that Gabriel is the one leading the meeting. He is the oldest one, maybe that's the reason. The others shut their eyes and sit in silence. I follow their example and close my eyes. Something about the atmosphere in the room is charged. There is a high energy level. Perhaps the pyramid form of the ceiling has something to do with it. I am sitting calmly, trying to stop the stream of my thoughts. Slowly, I gradually succeed, and my mind is still, at peace, and filled with space. I'm breathing deep down into my belly, in through my nose, and out through my mouth, going deeper and deeper inside myself. I can feel our circle becoming more powerful, as if we are united without touching each other physically. It seems like we are creating an inner, communal space as we sit here.

Images begin to appear in my inner vision. I can still hold back the stream of thoughts. Inside, I am completely calm, just watching images. There are very brief glimpses that last a second or perhaps even less. What I see makes no sense, and it is hard to deduce what it is: a silhouette of a woman, blood, and children playing. My thoughts come rushing, and the images disappear instantly.

I open my eyes. The others are sitting completely still with closed eyes. But they must be able to sense that I have broken the circle because, one by one, they open their eyes.

Gabriel looks around at the others and nods serenely. He shuts his eyes briefly and begins to speak when he opens them again. "Eva, first of all, I must ask you never to tell others about this meeting or name those who are present to anyone else other than those who are here. Whatever is said or done here must never leave this circle. Can you accept that?"

I nod solemnly, "Yes, I can."

"Good, then we may begin. The meeting today will be very brief. We are holding this meeting to give you a glimpse of something that you are a part of and that you have been part of for many, many lives. It is not certain that you remember us or your promise, but your soul does. It will lead you on your journey and do whatever is necessary so that the right circumstances occur when you are ready, such as the airplane crash, for example."

I listen quietly. The notion that everything is planned is not new to me. However, I am not completely convinced because that would mean I could just lean back and let matters take their course.

"Eva," Gabriel keeps looking at me, "it is not a question of whether everything is planned."

My stomach tightens. Can he read my thoughts?

"It is a question of whether there are some opportunities you have given yourself. If you are open to them during your life, you will be given help to realize them. Not everyone reaches the targets they set for themselves. Some become afraid, and others are so fascinated by their earthly lives that they completely lose themselves and their focus."

I shift my weight in the chair, beginning to feel uncomfortable. Carefully, I look around. They are all looking at me with soft and kind eyes, and it doesn't seem like the hard chair bothers them.

Gabriel continues in his steady voice. "But, as you know, we all give ourselves challenges and opportunities before we assume a new life. Some old souls have lived through many lives; others have just started on their journeys." Gabriel pauses. The room is dead quiet. There are no sounds to be heard from outside. "Whatever happens, your development can only advance. It is not possible to go backward. At most, you can take another ride around the carousel of life with the same challenges. Once you are incarnated as a human, you cannot come into other bodies than human ones."

I look over at Thomas. He has taken off the cloak and is wearing a shiny black shirt with a thin golden thread that runs around the slightly open collar and down the front. What is that? I look intently. The purple necklace! Now, I remember it. He gave me that Sugilite necklace in my dream, but now he has it again. I blink a bit frantically and turn my attention back to Gabriel.

"While you have been here, you have gained many insights. You have seen the spiritual quality of your life and have understood some of the challenges you have faced. Life is a long school, and you have reached the point where you can begin to pass your insight on to others. You have had the opportunity to leave, but you have remained. Something has kept you here."

I hear what Gabriel is saying. He knows that I have been offered to leave. Scary. Is there surveillance everywhere? Or is it supernatural powers? Until now, everything that he says makes sense to me. It is a subject that Thomas has talked about too. The part where we challenge ourselves and decide our souls' challenges. It still seems a bit frightening and distant, and yet also reassuring. Clearly, I can see some parallels to my own life. My curiosity arises; there is something fascinating about it—life and death, a soul's journey. My heart starts beating faster, and I sit bolt upright.

"As you can see, there are still two empty chairs." Yoge leans forward slightly and looks pointedly in their direction. His long, slim body can't fill out the chair.

Our eyes meet.

"We do not know exactly who they belong to, but we do know that they are not here yet. The knowledge that we once shared and chose to pass on many years ago cannot be accessed until we are all here." He pauses, and everyone sits still. "We have waited for thousands of years to reunite, for everyone to be ready. It looks as if we can succeed in this lifetime. It requires incredibly precise timing for seven souls to meet and be prepared to open up to the energy stream from the space where the knowledge is kept."

I am in awe—what he is saying sounds unbelievable. He blinks slowly and continues in a gentle voice.

"This can only succeed when the same seven souls are gathered so that the Ring can be closed. You only have three days left at In-Between. It is your choice whether you will stay or leave. We ask that you consider this very carefully."

I know what Yoge is saying. If I go back, it is not certain that the Ring can be made complete in this lifetime. It is up to me; I am a part of it, and they cannot access the knowledge without me. What is this knowledge? Why is it so important? And what about those who are missing?

After what seems like forever, Gabriel continues. "Eva, remember that if the Ring is meant to be completed in this life cycle, then you will stay. If this is not the time, then you will leave. We all know this. It is your choice, and you will know when the time comes."

As if that makes it any easier. They are just putting in a claim for my empathy. I look around at all of them. "What is this knowledge or insight you are talking about? Do you know?"

Gabriel nods. "It is the knowledge that we must bring back to Earth so that humans can reach the next stage of development. The knowledge that will change how the world operates. With this knowledge also comes very powerful energy that our bodies need to be prepared to receive."

His voice reminds me of the Master, incredibly composed and with long pauses between each sentence.

"The energy from the source that we can open up to is so forceful that it will help us return to Earth with higher awareness and clarity, helping people all over the world transform the way that they think and live." He keeps his eyes fixed on me. "Children will be born with greater awareness, with the energy of the new era, and everyone else will begin to absorb it and be lifted to a higher level of consciousness."

That certainly makes my decision easier. I nod a bit mechanically and pull my eyebrows together. They may be saying that I have a choice, but I feel pressure on my shoulders. I straighten up and lift my head. "How can you know that the other two will come in time?" I make eye contact with each person in the Ring—one by one—just so that they will know that I'm not afraid to confront them, and I don't buy into all this because they made up a fascinating room.

Thomas begins to speak. "We cannot know. However, we have never been closer. The other times we have gathered, we have been three at the most, and now we are up to five."

There is something about his charisma that impresses me and warms my heart. With him here, I know that it is not all bogus. But still, should I be a part of a unique Ring? It sounds a bit farfetched, even though the thought is appealing.

"Think it over." Thomas keeps looking at me. "You have three days left. We would like you to give us your answer Thursday evening at ten o'clock. If you choose to stay, we will meet again. If you choose to return to your mortal life, then you will wake up on Earth the following morning and will not be able to remember anything that has happened here."

My state of uncertainty must be evident. It feels like my brain has short-circuited. Nothing makes sense. I stiffen and stare without seeing anything.

"Eva."

My head jerks and I blink a couple of times. Thomas nods slowly. "Use these next few days to free your mind from confusion. We encourage you to avoid talking with others. Instead, spend your time alone so that you are not disturbed in your decision-making process. Do what you need to clear your mind, and remember, there is only one right decision, and that is the one that you will make."

"B-but," I stammer, "I don't know if I am prepared to make this decision. Are you sure that you've found the right person? You could be mistaken." My voice is shaking slightly, and my heart is pounding inside my chest.

Gabriel looks and me, and his voice is even. "Eva, our impression is that you are prepared to make this decision. Otherwise, we would not request that you do so. Right now, all your defense mechanisms have been activated. You will be tested to the utmost."

I listen intently, taking in every word and feeling the others' gaze fixed lovingly on me. At first, I thought that there would be a certain amount of pressure from the others. They must be eager to succeed, but I can sense their sincerity. Their faith is so enormous that they do not doubt for an instant that I will make the right choice. Not the slightest trace of mistrust exists inside them. They know that whatever is right will happen. A sense of peace grows within me, as well as the belief that they are right, that I am a part of this Ring.

Gabriel nods at me. "You must listen to yourself. Right now, you are affected by us, sensing that we are waiting in suspense and you would like to make us happy. But ask yourself what you are doing for others and what you are doing for yourself. If you choose to stay, is it because that is what you truly desire, or is it because you want to please us, or because you feel that you ought to stay?" He looks at me with a firm but very warm expression.

I look down at the floor. That is a good question. What am I doing for myself, and what am I doing for others? Actually, I don't care for the question because it compels me to examine several episodes in my life where I have definitely not been true to myself.

"Eva, life is full of crossroads, and you are standing in front of one of them right now."

I keep nodding and try to smile. Did I really think that life would become easier with age?

"One more thing," Thomas leans forward in his chair and smiles at me, "the test."

That catches me unaware—the test. I had completely forgotten about it. I'm not sure I can cope with anything else now.

"We needed to test you to find out if you are the one we thought you were."

"Well... does it mean?"

Thomas beams, "Yes, you have passed." His eyes radiate immense warmth.

Deeply touched, I place my hands over my mouth.

Gabriel speaks again. "Eva, the rest is up to you. You have a place in the Ring. If you decide to stay, our mission has the highest priority." He presses his palms together in front of his chest and bows slightly. I smile and place my hands like the others. We stand up, and I walk over to the door where I entered.

Thomas comes over to me. "It isn't certain that we will meet again."

I look at him. Somehow, I knew this.

He places his hand on my shoulder. "I will stay here. I have been relieved of my duty to receive people for the time being."

I stand still and look into his eyes. A lump forms in my throat. It feels like a boyfriend is breaking up with me, and I am inclined to cry and throw my arms around his neck. But I hold myself back. I am speechless. Words are inadequate to express my feelings anyhow. I lean forward and kiss him on the cheek, turn around, and walk out. The door closes behind me, and I am completely alone.

31

THE LAST DAY

Today is my last day at In-Between. Right now, I am the only one who knows it, and I shudder at the thought of saying it to the others.

I have waited for this day for such a long time, and now it is a reality. Although it is incredibly tempting to take part in the Ring's mission, I belong back on Earth with my family, not here. There is no doubt in my mind that I should go home. However, I realize that I have spent a great deal of time thinking about the Ring since our meeting. In a way, the notion of leaving In-Between seems unreal, just as unreal as arriving seemed. The difference is simply that this has become my life. I've become used to watching my family on a screen. I've forgotten how they smell and what it is like to touch them in anything but two dimensions.

My steps are quick and light as I walk to the control center. It is a joyful day. The sun ought to be shining, but it isn't. It will probably come.

I smile at everyone who crosses my path. If they only knew that I am going home tonight. Suddenly, a huge flash of light appears outside the window. I stop and wait. Five, six, seven, eight, nine. I walk closer to the window and wait for the crash of thunder. At once, the floor seismically shudders underneath me, and I am brought to my knees. An enormous clap of thunder makes all of In-Between vibrate. The sky is as black as coal. After a moment, another flash cuts through the sky right above us.

Someone places a hand on my back. "Are you all right?" It is a woman who has a shaved head and a ring in her nose. She reaches out her hand to help me back on my feet.

"Thank you."

"I've seen you before." She looks at me.

That's right, but I can't place her. I see so many people here, but there is something about her. In a way, she seems reserved, yet it also seems that she would like to talk with me.

"Now, I know." She smiles. "You were sitting next to me in the café the other day. Weren't you talking with Frank?"

"I'm afraid that I have to go now." I look at her and think that if I were meant to stay here, she would be someone I would like to get to know. She has a powerful personal magnetism and gives the impression of being very lively, and at the same time, a little mysterious.

"That's all right. Maybe we'll meet again."

I smile. After all, she doesn't know that I am going home tonight.

THE CONTROL ROOM is half empty, which is nice. I take a seat in front of a screen and log on. Sometimes, it can be overwhelming when all the stations are being used because everyone is experiencing a wide range of emotions, and people often give way to them.

I pull up a live feed of my mother. She is playing with Luke in her garden. The sun is out, and they are building some kind of castle out of empty boxes. What if my mother knew that I would wake up tomorrow morning? It is a special feeling to know something that she and Luke don't know yet, especially when it is such a crucial milestone in their lives. It is tempting to give them some sort of message. But I'd better behave myself. I am so looking forward to seeing their faces when I wake up.

"*Eva.*"

I recognize the voice immediately. It's Lucy. I haven't seen her or spoken with her since our clash about leaving early. She is approaching at a quick pace. Immediately, I'm on guard; I don't want to be scolded.

"Eva, how nice to see you. Where've you been? I haven't seen you in ages." Lucy opens her arms so that the pattern on her clothes stretches out.

I let down my defenses and smile. She is so sweet. It's always so difficult when people have different expectations and when they get mixed with emotions too. That doesn't make it any easier.

"Hi, Lucy." I stand up, and we hug each other, and our eyes meet.

"Eva, I am sorry if I was unreasonable. I can see now that it was my project, my ambition, that affected you. I was so enthusiastic on your behalf that I couldn't separate the two."

"It's absolutely fine. I know very well how that is."

Her eyes are gleaming, and she can hardly stand still. "What have you been doing? I'm leaving tomorrow. Now is the time. I would have left already, but the code didn't work after all." She casts up her eyes and sighs.

To be honest, I am not inclined to talk with anyone, but I don't feel like I can just get rid of her. It isn't certain that I will see her again—ever.

"Lucy, today is my last day. I'm leaving at ten tonight." A shiver runs down my back as I say it, and it makes me shake my body a bit.

"Wow. I'd completely forgotten about that," Lucy bursts out loudly and almost jumps for joy. "Time has just flown by. I thought that you were leaving sometime next week!"

I shrug my shoulders and pull a smile.

"That's awesome." She claps her hands. "Aren't you just thrilled?"

"Yes, I am definitely. Just the thought of seeing Luke again is indescribable." I stick my hands in my pockets and stand there awkwardly, swinging my hips.

"Honestly, what are you doing here? Shouldn't you be getting ready? There must be loads of people you have to say goodbye to. It seems like whoever I talk with knows who you are."

That's strange. Why do people know who I am? I keep to myself and haven't had contact with many others. I am finding it a little challenging to talk with Lucy. She is in a very different place than I am. It seems like we are running on two different frequencies that do not intersect.

It is nice to see her, and again I am reminded of her bubbling cheerfulness that is so contagious. Even the most negative person or someone who gripes all the time would not be able to resist her charms. Her joy and energy are infectious.

Maybe I can share her happiness and simultaneously be in touch with my own emotions and sustain my sensitive openness. This is interesting. In fact, right now, it feels surprisingly good. I realize that it is no problem for me to speak with her and give her my support and love while at the same time maintaining my integrity and remaining aware of my feelings. Eye-opening! I have never experienced this before. I almost always lose myself in the company of others.

Lucy stops her torrent of speech. "Are you here, Eva?"

"I'm sorry. I am here, and I'm listening to you, but I have to move on. As you said yourself, there are several things I have to see to today."

"One last thing—how do you feel about leaving?" Lucy looks at me seriously.

"I'm afraid. That's the truth. Although I'm looking forward to it, I am also afraid."

"I am too," says Lucy, and at that moment, her whole body settles down, like when the air seeps out of a balloon, and it falls to the ground. We gaze into each other's eyes. Hers are shiny and have many patterns in them.

I stand there, remaining aware of my groundedness. My body feels heavier, and my arms longer. I stay completely still and observe.

Lucy holds onto my gaze. I am about to reach my limit. If I move a bit, perhaps she will release her grip. I blink and then close my eyes for a couple of seconds to indicate that this exchange has ended.

Lucy understands. "Thanks. That is a fascinating place you got there. By the way, are you going to bid everyone farewell in the café this evening?"

"I don't know, but I will definitely have my last supper there." I laugh. "Maybe we'll see each other."

"That's a date. I don't like to say goodbye." Lucy pats me on the shoulder.

"How can we even know that it's goodbye? Just look at how we met here!"

32

BREATHE

Several nurses are standing around my bed. They are occupied with something, but I can't see my body. A couple of punches on the control panel, and the angle is adjusted to view my bed. One nurse with short, curly, highlighted hair is standing next to the respirator. She and the others are looking at each other very gravely, but nothing is said.

At that very moment, she removes the respirator from my mouth. But I can't breathe on my own! Have they given up on me? What's happening?

"*STOP IT!*" I yell at the screen, totally forgetting that she can't hear me. Quickly, I put on the headset that is hanging next to the screen. What are they saying? They must be talking about it. But they are silently watching my belly with great concentration.

The monitors beside my hospital bed begin to beep shrilly. I try desperately to make my body move, to give the medical staff a signal that they are making a mistake—that they can't give up on me yet. I put every bit of energy I can into reaching out to my earthbound body, but nothing happens.

Nothing.

A tall, thin female doctor with long, frizzy red hair looks at the nurse standing by the respirator and signals. She puts the respirator back in my mouth—the numbers on the monitor next to my bed change. The oxygen saturation level in my blood rises, and I can see that my blood pressure is stable. What is going on? I breathe freely again.

THIS IS the first time in all my days here that I am all alone in the control room. It feels a little ominous. Several of the large screens are shut off, and the atmosphere seems dead without any people.

I look back at the screen. Where is Andreas? I push on the screen in agitation. And where are my mother and Luke? Where is my family?

Have they given up on me?

"TAKE IT OFF," says the red-haired doctor, her chiseled features tightening. The respirator is removed again. The numbers on the monitor begin to fall. They are all watching me intently. There is no movement; my body remains perfectly still. Suddenly, my blood pressure drops drastically. The doctor signals my respirator to be put back in place, but my blood pressure continues to dive. "Increase the dopamine," the doctor insists. "Her heartbeat is dropping too." The atmosphere in the room is tense; everyone is deeply concentrating, and not a lot needs to be said.

"NO. You're not going to lose me. I'm going to wake up tomorrow." I'm talking to myself. "Take it easy down there." I laugh half-heartedly. It's a good thing that no one can see me talking to the screen.

A little window comes up with an image of Andreas. He is standing outside the door to the hospital, talking on the phone while smoking. Has he started smoking again? I press on the image, and the sound comes through.

"Don't worry. They know what they're doing." He is pacing back and forth quickly alongside the building. "Yes. The doctor said that it's standard procedure. They're trying to get Eva to breathe on her own by temporarily removing the respirator."

The only one he can be having this conversation with is my mother. I switch back to my room.

THEY ALL SEEM VERY CONCERNED. The red-haired doctor on my right is looking at the others. "Any suggestions?" Her brow is wrinkled, and she holds onto the bedrail to hide that her hand is shaking slightly.

It is tranquil, and I find myself humming a bit to fill the silence. They are all watching me, and it is clear that the situation is not as they had hoped.

"We have to increase the dopamine again." The doctor looks at the nurse next to the respirator. The numbers on the screen continue to fall. She nods back and turns the regulator.

"Get help." The doctor looks decisively at a young woman with long blonde hair, who then runs out the door.

THE SERIOUSNESS of the situation gradually dawns on me. I can't die. I'm here. This is impossible. I lean back in the chair that rocks steadily. Still, no one is here but me. I keep staring at the screen while my breathing becomes heavier.

"...NO MORE DOPAMINE." The nurse by the respirator is shaking her head. "We've exceeded the maximum dosage already." The situation clearly moves her, and her eyes are glassy.

"We don't have a choice. We have to increase the dosage." The red-haired doctor runs her hand over her forehead in quick jerks and signals to the nurse.

The nurse looks at the doctor severely but adjusts the IV as directed.

The blood pressure is still falling, and the oxygen saturation level is too.

"If we don't get it back up this instant, there is a risk of brain damage. Come on now, Eva. Come on. Fight!" The red-haired doctor places her hand on my chin and caresses it. She keeps whispering to me, "Come on, fight."

I'M FIGHTING against the weariness that tries to swallow me. I shut out everything except the viewing screen in front of me. I close my eyes hard, then open them.

Something is stirring inside me, something that seems to be trying to awaken. I close my eyes, and a picture of Annabel's sweet face appears at the same moment. I hear her lovely voice telling me that there is a place within me, like an uncut diamond, where I can access the most delicate energy that will set me free when I'm ready.

I am ready now.

I shut my eyes hard and feel my heart open. Suddenly, it is like a bright light breaks through the darkness—like I have accessed my inner diamond, my source of energy. I'm sending all the light down to my body, and I focus one hundred percent on my physical body on the hospital bed—light, energy, everything I have.

"YES! IT'S WORKING," shouts the nurse who is watching the numbers.

"Her heartbeat is approaching normal."

The nurse by the respirator nods. "It's stable."

The red-haired doctor looks up, and her lips move without words.

"Blood pressure eighty over forty and rising," says the nurse next to the respirator.

The young nurse is back with a younger doctor. He starts to ask all kinds of questions. They all have their eyes locked on my body.

EXHAUSTED BUT RELIEVED, I shift over to Andreas's window. He is still outside the hospital.

"We agreed on this yesterday, and I have discussed it with the doctor again." His voice is rather tense. "I'll call you when we know something." He snaps his phone shut, looks up at the sky, and takes a long last drag of his cigarette.

"BLOOD PRESSURE IS STABLE, and the oxygen saturation level is normal again."

The younger doctor goes over to the red-haired doctor and exchanges a few words. She looks at the nurse stationed by the respirator. "Remove the respirator again."

Everyone in the room is shocked.

"...But we almost lost her."

"I know. I have a feeling that she is ready to start breathing herself."

The atmosphere is charged. No one dares to say a word. I recognize the younger male doctor by my side because he is considered an expert, one of the country's most talented and experienced doctors, and he has appeared on television many times. He has performed miracles with patients, sometimes because he has gone to extremes. He nods at the red-haired doctor.

"Shut it off." She looks toward the nurse. Her hand is resting on my chest, and she is observing me closely.

SHOOTING PAINS STRIKE MY WOMB, and I bend over. It feels like my lungs are collapsing when the nurse removes the respirator from my earthly body.

I hold my breath—

And then slowly release it as I see my chest begin to rise and fall, slowly and raggedly beneath the hospital sheets as they replace the respirator.

THE YOUNG DOCTOR shines a light in my eyes, listens to my heartbeat, and takes my pulse. He grabs a printout from one of the many machines next to my bed.

"There is nothing more we can do for her now. If her blood pressure doesn't stabilize during the night, then it doesn't look so good. I can't see any kind of contact or reaction."

The red-haired doctor clenches her teeth as she nods to the younger doctor, accepting his evaluation.

I CLICK on the image of Andreas. The door opens, and the red-haired doctor comes out to him. She lets her long red hair down, runs her fingers through it a few times, and gestures toward a bench against the wall.

"It didn't go as we had anticipated. As I told you already, there is always a risk involved when trying to provoke someone in a coma to breathe on their own. We have had good results in the past."

Andreas bites his nail and kicks at some pebbles. "Is there still hope?" He presses his lips together and brings his hand up to his mouth.

The red-haired doctor takes a deep breath. "There's always hope," she looks intently at Andreas, "and miracles do happen. But let me be frank. It's a quarter past ten. By this time tomorrow...." She holds back; it is hard for her to get the words out of her mouth. "The next twenty-four hours will be critical. If she hasn't dramatically improved by this time tomorrow, I fear that she never will."

"Twenty-four hours for a miracle," Andreas says softly.

I LEAN FORWARD and switch off the viewing screen. I'm exhausted but also exalted.

Twenty-four hours is exactly what I need.

Twenty-four hours from now, I will wake up again. My soul will find its way back into my earthly body.

In twenty-four hours, I will give them their miracle.

33

LISTEN TO THE HEART

Heavy clouds are suspended above and below me. Rain is striking my face, and I spread out my arms and tilt my head back. I am standing alone in my secret spot, and I am thoroughly soaked in no time. The T-shirt clings to my body, and my pants are dripping. If only I dared to kick off my boots and stand barefoot. I open my mouth and let the raindrops hit my tongue. Slowly, I lower my arms and let them hang next to my body. The rain is dripping from my fingertips.

My Skycon rings and breaks the silence. Why haven't I shut it off? Who's disturbing me now? I shake my shoulders and open and shut my hands a couple of times so that my joints crack. I start blinking and feel how the blood begins to circulate in my body. The Skycon rings again.

"Take it easy. I'm coming." I fish out the Skycon and wipe off some water from the display. It's Thomas.

"Hi," I say in a quiet voice.

"Hi. Are you almost ready?"

"I don't know." That is the most honest answer I can come up with. I don't know what's right or wrong any longer. I feel like I'm in a centrifuge. One moment, I am happy and full of energy, and the next, I'm about to go insane and lose control completely.

"Is there anything you need in order to come closer to being ready?" Thomas is standing in the octagonal room. I can see the circle of seven chairs behind him.

I don't know what that could be. Actually, I would prefer to have it all over with so that I can be at peace.

"Thomas, when I am back on Earth, will I be at peace then?" My wet hair is clinging to my face, and raindrops are running down my cheeks. Black clouds surround me, both above and below.

He doesn't reply, and that's an answer in itself. I take a deep breath and try to wipe the rain from my face.

"...Eva, the reason I am calling you is to tell you where you should be tonight. At ten o'clock, you need to give us your answer. If you choose to go back to Earth, then the departure will take place immediately afterward. You should go to the dispatch room. Do you remember where it is?"

"Yes, I remember. Is there anything I should bring?" The rain tickles my skin, and the drops keep dripping from my nose.

"No. You cannot take anything from here. If you choose to leave, all you will have is your personal experience, no memories of people or In-Between. Is there anything else you need to know or that I can do for you?" His expression is calm. Still, I get that this is not an informal call for old times' sake.

"Are you coming? I'd like to see you one last time." I bite my lip.

It will be hard for me if I can't bid Thomas a proper farewell. I run my hand through my wet hair numerous times.

"I don't know, but I will do what I can to be there. It's not for me to decide." His voice is composed, but I can still sense that he is also affected by its uncertainty.

"Okay. I hope that we'll see each other there. If not, take good care of yourself. And thank you for everything." My voice begins to break, and I cannot say another word. I squeeze my lips together and let my head fall forward.

"You, too." He smiles at me.

My heart is breaking, and my eyes are welling up with tears. Neither of us wants to say anything else, and no words can change how I feel anyhow. But I can't let go of him. Right now, it feels like he is my only hope, and if I let him go, then I'll be alone with my internal division again.

"Eva, I know that this is difficult, but remember, we are not given greater challenges than what we can handle." He bows toward me with his hands folded in front of his chest.

"Thanks." It becomes quiet on the other end, then the image disappears, and the screen goes black. Thomas is gone.

There is still time. It is only two in the afternoon. I shake my head, slapping my hair against my face and spraying water. I sweep a lock of hair off my face and use my wet arms to try to dry it off as well as I can.

Can I be at peace now? I can't handle it anymore. I just want to go home.

There is one thing I have to do before leaving tonight. I've promised the Master to bring him my answer, which is the next point on the agenda. But first, I want to stop by my room and put on some dry clothes.

The Master told me that the answer lies in the heart. I know that I want to go home, but have I felt it deep in my heart? I am not sure. A mother should be with her child. No, I have no doubt whatsoever. I seem very convincing to myself, but the thought of going to the Master makes me nervous. What if he doesn't believe me? What can I say that would seem convincing? Will he understand that, as a mother, I have a duty to my child? He doesn't have children; at least, I don't think he does. I have some relatively fixed ideas as to what the Master is like… He never eats candy, doesn't have children, and doesn't have sex. That sounds somewhat redeemed. Maybe I should just ask him.

A sense of uneasiness runs through my body. Maybe I should just drop visiting him. No, it's no use. I've promised to give him my answer, and I don't want to be a coward.

I find a black skirt and a pink blouse in the closet. I don't need any of my gadgets. This time, I have an appointment, an invitation from the Master. I feel honored and very pleased.

It doesn't take very long to reach the mirrored hallway. As always, it is deserted. I open the door and go over to the section of the wall where the door is. For some reason, I can't find the little circle that opens the door.

I roll up my sleeve and try to push the section that constitutes the door, but nothing happens. I knock cautiously. Nothing. Maybe I should just wait. The last time it took a while before he let me in.

There are no other openings and nothing that looks like a switch or a camera. I look up and down the hallway and walk back and forth. After ten minutes, I begin to become impatient. Could it be that he isn't here or that he doesn't want to talk with me? Maybe I should try again later.

A profound disappointment overwhelms me, and I realize that my hope was pinned on meeting him again. By telling him that I am leaving, my decision would be made legitimate. I would like him to approve of my departure and give me his blessing. A blessing from the Master would have finally brought an end to the chaos that roils my thoughts and tears at my heart. Being a journalist, I can't help my curiosity from being interested in the Ring. What a story that could be. Then I would definitely get the Pulitzer Prize; it is hard not to smile.

As I walk the length of the hallway, I catch more than one inadvertent glimpse of myself in the mirrors but recognize none of them.

34

FAREWELL

Somehow, the hours pass. I wonder if they weighed as heavily on my mother and Andreas. Their vacuum is for sure more challenging than mine. At least I know that I will wake up. They don't.

It is almost six in the evening. I have four more hours left at In-Between. It is somewhat distressing. In-Between has left a great impression on my life that I will never forget, I hope—all the opportunities here, everything I have learned about myself and life—not to mention the challenges.

If I could choose an ideal scene, I would prefer to eat a farewell dinner with Thomas and Annabel, but neither is available. I take my tray of food and sit down at my favorite table in the back corner. Just then, I hear someone approaching at a fast pace. It is Frank, the last person I want to see right now.

"Hi, Eva," he says in an insinuating voice.

I give him a forced smile. "Hello, Frank."

The sun still hasn't broken through the clouds, and now the time is running out.

"Lucy's coming in a minute." Frank sits across from me. "She said that you'd be here." His smile is exaggerated. "This is so nice. I hear that you are leaving tonight. Good for you. You must be feeling tender now. You have a child, don't you?"

I nod and cross my arms. So much for wishful thinking. I may as well try to get the best out of the situation because I can't get out of it. "When are you moving on, Frank?"

He smiles confidently. "The way things look now, I have a couple of weeks left, but I am expecting them to offer me to stay. I am well-connected with some influential people, and they could use someone like me in reception."

I shudder at the thought, pitying anyone who would be received by Frank. He would try to brainwash them into thinking that he is God himself. With his excessive kindness, they won't stand a chance. He will catch them in his net. Not in my wildest fantasies can I imagine that the inner circle around the Master would give him the option of staying. I force another smile.

Lucy is standing at the bar, ordering food. It suits me fine that she is coming because I could use some distraction. Frank leans toward me and puts his hand on mine. "Eva, what's the first thing you'll do when you go back to Earth?"

I pull back my hand and lean back on the sofa. "That's obvious. I want to see my son, Luke." I take a bite of my food. It is a wonderful, zesty dish that was stir-fried to perfection. The sweet taste expands in my mouth.

"Here you are." Lucy comes to the table. "That's great. I was beginning to think that I'd missed you because I was running late."

I look at my watch and see that it's twenty-past six. Soon, there will only be three hours left. I move to the edge of the seat and notice that my right hand is tapping on the table.

"Eva, are you ready to leave? You must be so nervous."

"Yes, I am definitely."

Frank leans forward and gazes to the sides to make sure no one is close enough to listen in on our conversation. "There is something I'd like to share with you, but you must promise not to tell anyone else." He looks straight into my eyes.

Lucy can hardly sit still on her chair, filled with excitement. "Of course, Eva won't say anything. What is it, Frank?"

"Eva?" Frank keeps his gaze locked on me.

I nod once. It's probably just another attempt to make himself interesting.

He lowers his voice and moves even closer, if possible. "I cracked into the system last night, and something is going on."

My mouth drops, and I freeze inside.

Frank's gaze doesn't diminish. "I don't know exactly what, but I sense it is something big."

"What, Frank? What is it?" Lucy's voice is nearly out of control, and Frank shushes her. "That sounds so exciting, don't you think, Eva?" She places an elbow in my side.

I nod reluctantly.

"Have you heard anything, Eva? You are a journalist, right? You have the ability to nose it out if something is going on." Frank is staring at me.

I try to lean back, but it's like Frank has a grip on me. Instead, I reach for my glass of water and take a sip. "No, not really. Why would anybody tell me anything?"

I want to change the subject, but then again, I don't want to share any of my experiences with Frank, which means that Lucy can't hear about them either. I pick at my food for a moment but don't have much appetite anymore. Lucy is sitting next to Frank, all but shoveling food into her mouth. She has an enormous appetite and eats as if this is her last meal.

I can't take any more of Frank. And I'm certain he doesn't know anything. This is just one of his attempts to make himself interesting. It is such a shame that Lucy is buying it all—jumping right in with both feet.

"Nothing, Eva? Has no one said anything to you?"

"No, why would anyone tell me anything?" I repeat.

Frank narrows his eyes and runs his hand over his mouth.

"I need to straighten up my room. I'd better see to that now." I smile at Lucy. "So, this is the last goodbye."

Frank and Lucy look at me. It is sad and great at the same time. I'm just not very good at goodbyes. I have always tried to avoid them when possible. Right now, there is no way around it. This is the final farewell.

I stand up and give each of them a hug. I have no desire to speak.

Lucy looks at me and breaks the silence anyhow. "I'm so happy that we met again. Let's get together on Earth."

I can't help but laugh. "Yes, that's a good idea. Let's make a date and see if we can remember it once we're there." It seems absurd somehow, but on the other hand, why not? What if we could help each other recall some memories of our stay here, although Thomas says they will be erased? The brain is like a hard disk. It's hard to delete files one hundred percent, with so much information saved in backup files. I smile and feel the excitement bubbling in my veins. What if there is a trace of In-Between that won't get erased? It is possible. Maybe I will run into Lucy back on Earth, and perhaps that can awaken some memories.

I look at Lucy and say, "Well then, see you."

I DON'T NEED to take anything with me. All I have are the clothes I was wearing when I came, but I don't even need those because my body is in the intensive care unit. My hand runs through the clothes hanging in my closet, and I straighten a few items. I take a step back and feel deep gratitude. One last touch on the red button and the closet slides shut.

In the morning, I will wake up on the hospital bed on Earth and not in this room at In-Between. It seems so incredible that it's almost impossible to imagine. I let myself fall onto the bed, and it gives, so I bounce a little, taking one last look around my room. It has been a place where I have felt secure. I am humbled by all that I have been allowed to experience here.

One by one, I take the pictures of Luke down from the wall. I stroke his image. The paper is cool and feels stiff. Tomorrow, I'll be able to feel his soft, warm skin and smell his beautiful scent.

As I remove the pictures and my personal touches from the room, I can feel how much I have come to care about In-Between—all of its marvels and even its unexplained mysteries. I have grown accustomed to being here and feel good here. In-Between has nourished my personal development—I know myself much better now. The values that are in focus here: respect, tolerance, and love, are so important. In-Between has made a difference in my life, and it has enabled me to make a difference in other lives. I think briefly of Ken and Kate, then more lingeringly, longingly of Annabel.

The memory of Annabel fades away, and I remember. The Ring. I can see their faces, individually and as a group, and from both perspectives, their eyes are filled with hope. They can't go any further without me. I press my hands together and lean against the bare wall. I don't feel obliged to stay because of them. Still, I am aware of a fragile sensation tugging at me from a place deep inside me where something is about to awaken. What if it were a greater insight into my life? What if I am not meant to return?

I stand up and begin to pace back and forth. It is impossible for me to stand still. An explosion of anger fills my body. I scream and grab the nearest pillow and start beating it on the wall. I go on and on until I am exhausted and sink onto my knees. I sit there for a while before lying down on my back, looking up. Why can't life be easy? If I have chosen this challenge, then I must have been out of my mind at the time. An image of Luke appears in my inner vision. My fingers are fixed behind my neck, and tears start to build up in the corner of my eyes. Luke. That little boy with the blue eyes, blond hair, and long thin legs. The way he talks. His words aren't perfect yet, but the things he says... he is so wise. His small feet and warm hands. The way he hugs me and says he loves me. I am sobbing, and my whole body is shaking. Tears are running down my cheeks, and I can't stop them. I am crying like I will never stop, like a river about to overflow its banks. Why can't I just die or live? Why? Why do I have to make this decision? It seems so unfair.

I close my eyes, and slowly the tears disappear. My body rests on the floor. I am lying still, all alone.

IT IS ten minutes before ten. It is time to leave for the dispatch room. I know the way and need no map. But I don't know who will be there. I take one last look around my room, silently thanking it for the time I have spent here. I shut the door behind me. It locks, and a message appears on the touch screen.

"Time completed," is written with small letters followed by a heart, "meet at the dispatch room."

I no longer have access to my room. It is a special feeling, knowing that I am no longer a part of In-Between. I feel sure that the room will care for its next inhabitant. I step away from the door.

I am homeless.

Luckily, it's only here in In-Between that I'm homeless. My real home is waiting for me, or at least the hospital bed is.

The Skycon is in my pocket. I take it out. There are no unanswered calls, no messages. I must admit, I had hoped to hear from Thomas, but he hasn't contacted me. Perhaps he will be in the dispatch room. I walk slowly down the hallway that I have walked through hundreds of times before. Now each step carries a great significance, as this is the last time I'll walk here. "The last time," I whisper to myself.

In-Between's corridors and décor are beginning to lose their reality for me. For the first time in weeks, the thought of it all being a dream occurs to me. Maybe I'm reaching the end of the dream. Perhaps all this has been created by the coma and the blows my head got in the crash. Soon, I will wake up, and everything will go back to where it was.

It's dark outside. The sky has cleared and is filled with stars. I stop at one of the large windows and look out. There is a falling star. I close my eyes and send a wish into the universe.

May I learn to listen to my heart.

I stand still for a moment to take it in. In five minutes, I have to be in the dispatch room. I place my hand on the window. It almost seems like I can touch the stars. "You are so beautiful," I whisper and then keep walking.

Two minutes before departure, I am standing in front of the door to the dispatch room. I don't need to go through the reception area. There is a little circle with a green light indicating that I can enter. I put my finger on the circle, and the door slides open.

Inside, the room is nearly empty.

The screens are on one side, and the raised couch is in the center.

A shiver runs down my back. The floor looks like smoke and isn't solid. It looks exactly the same as when Thomas and I sent Ken back the other day.

I step inside cautiously.

It is now.

The time has come.

35

THE DECISION

It is precisely ten o'clock.

I'm standing all alone in the middle of the dispatch room. The stars are shining through the large, square window on the ceiling. It's a bit chilly, so I pull down the sleeves of my blue knit shirt. I decided to wear my casual clothes. "I might as well be as comfortable as possible," I mumble.

One wall is covered with screens. Next to me is the couch that almost floats above the floor. I run my finger over its surface.

Someone turns the door handle, and I look to see who it is. I don't recognize the guy who enters. Quiet, I sigh and feel a pang in my stomach. It's impossible to hide that I had hoped that Thomas would come. Maybe he didn't want to risk influencing my decision.

"Hello, Eva. My name is J.T. I am the one who will hear your decision."

J.T. Doesn't he have a real name, I wonder. He is big and powerful, with a deep cleft in his chin and a large cross hanging from his right ear.

"Eva." I reach out to shake his hand. That form of greeting is atypical here. Maybe I'm already adjusting to earthly mannerisms again.

J.T. stands in front of me and nods slowly. "According to the protocol, I must ask you if you have made your decision." He has a folder and a pen in his hand.

"Yes, I have."

"What is your decision?"

Silence fills the room. He watches me. I do not reply.

"What is your decision?" J.T. asks again.

I just look back at him. Inside my head, I am saying that I want to go home, but nothing comes out of my mouth.

"Eva, I need to know what your decision is." J.T. is beginning to look troubled.

I am standing perfectly still. I want to move my mouth, but still, nothing happens. The words can't come out. I'm just looking at him. *I want to go home*; I say again inside my head. My tongue runs over my lips. I bite my lower lip and clench my teeth together. My mouth is sealed, and I simply can't open it.

"Eva, I need to know your decision now. If you are going to leave, we only have an open slot at quarter past ten. If you don't make it, then I have to book a new time for you." He crosses his arms.

I look into J.T.'s eyes. He seems more forceful, stronger. Maybe it's needed to do his job. I'm sure many people come to this room who can't decide or don't want to go. In a way, life here is appealing. There are no earthly challenges, like obtaining food or earning money. He must be faced with many who have to leave against their will, as very few are allowed to stay and work....

I manage to open my mouth and look at his chest.

"I want to leave," I say so softly that the words hardly make any sound.

"Sorry, can you repeat that?" He bends toward me to hear better.

"I want to leave," I say again a little louder, quickly looking down to the floor.

"Are you sure? Once you're on your way, there's no turning back." J.T. opens the folder and skims the piece of paper in front of him. "I would like to draw your attention to the fact that you have been awarded the highest clearance level. There are no duties assigned to you, so I don't know what you are meant to do here...." He raises an eyebrow and regards me. "Not that it is any of my business, but this is the first time that this has happened while I've been on duty. I don't know who you are, but you can't just be anyone."

I raise my eyes to meet his. I shrug my shoulders and sigh.

"What is your final decision?"

"I want to leave," I say through clenched teeth, forcing myself to maintain eye contact.

"Fine. Then lay down over there on the couch. You have to lie on your back and relax. It doesn't hurt. You will fall into a deep, deep sleep, which will erase your memory of everything that has to do with In-Between." He makes a gesture like he is wiping his face. "When you wake, you will be back inside your body on Earth. You may feel uncomfortable for the first few days. Although you have been active here, your body has been lying motionless for a long time and will need some physiotherapy. You can count on coming out of intensive care immediately and going directly into rehabilitation. After that, it won't be long before you are back in your own life again."

I walk over to the couch. "Should I take off my clothes?"

"No, that isn't necessary. You can even keep your boots on." J.T. laughs.

I pull an indulgent smile.

"Do you have any objects that belong to In-Between?"

I nod against my will.

"You can place them here." J.T. points at a small tray next to the table.

I set down the Skycon and watch. "Too bad. I've enjoyed having them." I try to smile.

The couch feels hard. I sit on it and swing my legs up.

"You can lie down now. We'll get started with the transfer in a couple of minutes. Here's a blindfold you can wear; it can help you relax." J.T. hands me a black cloth and goes over to the wall with all the screens.

"Thanks," I mumble. I don't want to lose sight of In-Between yet and squeeze the blindfold in my hand.

I lie on my back, looking up at the ceiling—the spot. Now I realize that the small black spot up there is to help people focus. It is impossible not to look at it. Everything here is done with intention.

"If you shut your eyes, then we're ready to get started. Take care and have a good trip." J.T. turns to me and nods.

I look out from side to side and then up and down. There's nothing else to see. Then, I shut my eyes, put on the blindfold, and it becomes dark, totally dark. *Farewell, In-Between. Thank you for everything*, I think, and take a deep breath.

One of the machines clicks on, and then a low humming sound begins.

I can feel heat reaching my feet. It's hard to relax. I am not at peace and would like to move but remain completely still. The heat strikes my feet and continues up my legs. I have an urge to pull up my legs, but it is too late. I'm being scanned. The machine needs to analyze what I am made of to calculate how the transfer should be programmed. The heat progresses over my belly and chest, neck, nose, and forehead.

There is a regular clicking sound, and then it stops, and all is quiet again. I sense that the space around me is being sealed. I watched what happened to Ken when he was sent off, but it is something entirely different to be lying here... then a whizzing sound begins. A large machine is moving toward me, starting at my feet. Shouldn't I be sleeping? Maybe that is what the machine is going to do, anesthetize my whole system.

It's over. I will never see Thomas or the Master again. I'll never find out what the Ring should accomplish. It's no longer my responsibility and never has been. Shortly, I will be on Earth and wake up in the hospital. Then Luke, my mother, Andreas, and the doctors will get their proof that miracles do happen.

Living proof.

Living proof of...

My life.

My real life?

Or only my old life?

"NO!" It feels like my chest explodes, and instantly, I pull my feet up toward me. The movement is so forceful that my body is in a free-fall off the couch, and I hit the floor hard. I rip the blindfold off my eyes.

"I can't! I can't! I can't go!" I shout as I thrash around the cold floor, ignoring the pain from the fall. Managing to get up on all fours, I crawl over to and bang on the window to the control room. The icy blue light is blinding me, and I can't see J.T.

"Stop," the sound of my voice cuts through the room as I beat on the glass. "I don't want to leave."

Thomas comes rushing into the room, waving urgently at J.T. The machine shuts off, leaving the confined space inside the glass silent. He hurries over to me, kneels, and puts his palms on the glass that separates us. I place my palms on top of his.

The glass lowers down into the floor. I throw myself into his arms and press against him.

"I can't go; I can't go," I say, again and again, beginning to cry.

"It's all right." Thomas holds me in his arms.

"Why?" I stammer. "I should go, but I can't. What's wrong with me?"

"There's nothing wrong," he whispers in my ear. "You simply cannot betray your inner longing anymore. You have listened to your heart." His embrace is full of love and comfort. I press my nose against his shoulder and try to breathe without gasping for air.

J.T. comes over. "What happened there, woman? What are you

doing here? You just about gave me a heart attack. I thought that something very wrong happened in there." He laughs a little but realizes that it's inappropriate for the situation.

"Come," says Thomas, and he squeezes me. "I think it is time to talk."

I nod. "It is."

36

IT'S OVER

"Tomorrow, the respirator will be shut off." Thomas is holding my hand. "The doctors will report that they can't keep your blood pressure up and that any further treatment is therefore meaningless." He's wearing the same blue tunic that he was wearing the day I arrived. It has stains from my tears on the left shoulder.

I sit and stare into the wall of books in front of us. We left the dispatch room and went over to the library, where we can talk uninterrupted. I sink into the big sofa and tuck my legs under me. The light is dim, and the candle on the table has almost burnt down. It all seems so unreal.

Thomas speaks quietly, peacefully, with no insistence to his questions. "Are you sure you would like to stay?"

I am breathing evenly. "Yes, I'm sure. Something inside me is becoming more and more powerful, and, although I don't understand it, I have to stay." My voice is more profound than usual and more relaxed, despite everything I have experienced in the last few hours.

The glow from the candle gently lights up Thomas's face. The rest of the library is nearly dark. We are sitting front to front in what feels like a small safe space of love.

"You don't need to explain. I know. I've been there myself. And you can't expect that others who haven't felt that same longing will understand you. You need to have access to that place in yourself to understand a choice as radical as the one you have made."

I feel the warmth from his hands against my cool skin as he holds my hands in his.

"Thomas, what is this longing inside me that is so powerful that it can make me choose myself over my child?" It frightens me that I have made this choice. I look up and through the skylight and see stars hanging like a spangled canopy.

"For me," Thomas pauses and shuts his eyes briefly, "it is a yearning to find my own truth, to find out who I am. It is very banal, and at the same time, infinite. Being here at In-Between, I feel like I have been given the opportunity to get closer to my true self."

The candlelight is flickering, struggling to continue burning. I can feel Thomas's eyes resting on me, but I keep looking up as if the stars can lead me with greater clarity.

"For you," I begin, then select the words carefully. "For you—and each member of the Ring?" Then I turn my head, and our eyes meet.

Thomas shakes his head. "I can't speak for them any more than any of us could speak for you."

"We can only make the right decision, true?" I say, hoping I don't sound cynical. The weight of my decision and the responsibility that accompanied it is beginning to settle upon me, like being trapped in an avalanche where the light disappears with the air, and everything goes dark.

Thomas showers a sweet, slightly sad smile on me. "There are still so many people on Earth who are in doubt, who think that it is a question of believing in something, and who are living a life far removed from what they long for." He moves a bit closer to me so that I can see him better. "Most people do not know who they are or what they desire. Not that they should be changed or become different— that will happen when the time is right. But, for me, it was very hard to thrive on Earth once I began to work with myself. I became very sensitive, and all of that negative energy became too much. In a way, it took the life out of me."

"Have you ever regretted your decision?" I try to breathe, but it is hard.

"I have had to examine my doubt and guilt many times, but I have no regrets. There have been moments when I have been severely challenged, but I have always come back to my heart's desire."

"If you had second thoughts, would there still be a way?" I take one of the pillows on the sofa and squeeze it in my arms.

Thomas shakes his head slowly. "The life I left behind on Earth has continued without me. I could go down in another body. In principle, that is possible, but no one has ever been permitted to do so. You have to leave here and move on to the next phase of transition to get back to Earth. Are you having second thoughts?"

He looks at me with a gleam in his eye, and we both break out in laughter.

I shake my head and throw the pillow at his head. "No, I'm not. Well, you know, maybe a bit—like small lightning bolts that strike me. I am glad to be here and excited to see what In-Between offers me." I straighten up and close my eyes slightly. "What is extremely difficult for me is the sense of guilt I have about Luke and the consequences of my choice." I press my lips together and reach for Thomas's hand and press it against my heart. "I hope that Luke can handle it!"

Thomas pulls me close to him. "You have done what you feel is right. It cannot be any different."

The candle on the table goes out, and an almost transparent trail of smoke rises. Thomas pulls out a drawer from under the table and puts in a new candle. He lights it, and a tall warm flame starts to cast a radiant glow in his eyes.

I can't help wondering how many others—Andreas, my mother,

Luke—would consider what I have done to be the right decision. At least they will never know that I could decide.

"You will find that everyone will have an opinion about your choice. When we judge others, it is often because we are afraid of getting to know them, of putting ourselves in their situation, or that we lack awareness." Thomas sits back and puts his arm around me. I lean toward him and let him embrace me. "Try to think back to the time you were on Earth. Imagine that you are driving along in your car, and the car in front of you is driving too slowly; you start to become irritated. There is not enough space to pass it, and you are in a rush. Even though you drive right up behind it, it doesn't change its speed. You are just about to lay on the horn, but then the other driver pulls over to the side. As you pass, you roll down the window to say a few choice words, and at that moment, you see that it is your best friend's mother driving. How do you react? Think about it." Thomas pauses and gives me a moment to reflect. I don't comment. "When we know others, then we have sympathy and tolerance. If we don't know them, we get angry and judge them. No one but you can know what is right for you. You don't know what challenges Luke has chosen to give himself or if this will make him strong. I'm not saying that it is easy to grow up without a mother, but the fact is, we don't know the entire truth."

As I listen to Thomas, I fall into a deeper state of relaxation. My body occasionally trembles in reaction to what I have just been through, but it is subsiding. I can see all the spines of the hundreds of books on the tall shelves around us. They are like wallpaper.

"One of the most important things I have learned is to forgive others and also myself." Thomas moves a lock of hair away from my face. "It can be easier to forgive others than to forgive yourself. But, when we begin to forgive, then both we and others have the opportunity to move forward. We release the emotional bonds that hold us fixed."

I take in what he is saying and am aware that my inner judge is prepared to sentence me with a guilty conscience for staying.

"There are some practical things that I have to tell you." Thomas squeezes my shoulders and turns so that we are facing each other. "You have been given the highest level of clearance by the Master. That is to say; you can log on and access the personal files of those you receive to see what challenges they have given themselves. However, there is one soul's file you can't look at." He raises his eyebrows playfully. "Your own. It will remain closed. The same rules apply to everyone who gets to stay."

I turn up my nose. I would quite like to see my profile.

"This is based on the Master's evaluation. He has determined that it may influence our development too much if we know it."

The sound of footsteps in the hallway, along with voices speaking, comes closer. The door opens but is quickly shut again.

"You still have access to old recordings from Earth and can continue your personal development program if you wish. But there will probably be some new assignments that have to do with the work of the Ring. We will know more when we meet tomorrow."

I sit quietly and listen to Thomas as the silence around us begins to feel heavy.

Thomas continues. "Your primary work will come to take place in the Ring, but if you wish, you can also receive new souls. You know how that works." He smiles at me. "Of course, you can also see what Luke is doing and watch him grow up, but you can't interfere or intervene. Do you agree with that? No contact, no hints, no influence."

I can't hide a smile. I knew that he would say something like that and was already prepared for it. It is seldom that Thomas has that serious, rather strict school-teacher attitude. It is not easy for him to act severe. He winks at me.

"What happens if I break the rules?"

He bursts out laughing. "You won't!"

I keep on smiling and give him a nod.

"By the way, there's one more thing. You've been moved to the corridor where I'm staying."

"Is it corridor D?" I have never visited Thomas there, but he told me about it some time ago.

He shakes his head. "I stayed there until recently, but now that more members of the Ring are here, we've relocated so that we are all gathered together. We won't be neighbors, but almost; there is an empty room between us. Everyone in the Ring is staying in our corridor, and we are the only ones there."

"That sounds a little exclusive." I smile and rub my hands together.

"Call it what you will. It is a lovely place. I've arranged for your private things to be moved there, and I want to give you this back...."

Thomas puts his hand in his pocket, holds his hand toward me, and slowly opens it to reveal my Skycon.

"Thanks. I was already beginning to miss it." I take it between my thumb and index fingers and look it over.

"It's been upgraded with more functions, maps, and information. You can try out the new functions later."

Thomas moves as though he's about to get up.

"Do you have to go somewhere?" I say with a curious tone.

"Yes, I do. I'm tired. Shall I escort you to your new room?" He leans over to blow out the candle.

"I would be honored." I place the Skycon in my pocket and stand up to stretch so that my bones reply with soreness.

We walk together down the light corridors surrounded with white moving walls as if living in In-Between is the most natural thing in the world.

37

ANGELA

I wake up wide-eyed with a loud gasp. Where am I? What is this unfamiliar room?

A deep breath does wonders.

Now, I remember.

I am in my new, larger room, with the most enchanting panorama that provides a stunning view. I can look out at the clouds and down on Earth. Space extends as far as the eye can see. Otherwise, it looks like my old room, bright, light, simple, and very pleasant.

The pictures of Luke that I had in my old room are hanging on the wall here. I am moved when I see his image and put my hand over my mouth as I sit quietly and admire him, knowing that I will never be able to hug him again or put my nose into his hair and smell him. It was my decision, and I can only blame myself. But I don't. My mind is taking a break from hitting me with a guilty conscience. Slowly, I place both my hands on my heart and feel a stream of warm energy flow through my body.

This room is more spacious and the atmosphere more tranquil. It is evident that I am in another section of In-Between.

I get up, shower, and dress quickly in silence, taking everyday clothes from my new closet.

"THERE IS NO LONGER any hope. I've spoken to her relatives." It's the young doctor speaking to the nurse who is standing next to the respirator. "Her brain activity ceased completely last night at ten-fifteen." The doctor flips through the papers in his hands and finally puts them on a small table.

It is evident that he does not wish to give up on me—and an inhuman decision he has to make.

"Would you please shut off the respirator?" he says with no feelings attached.

Only the hospital staff is present. No one says anything. A woman with her hair pulled back in a ponytail and wearing narrow-framed glasses reaches out for the machine.

The red-haired doctor looks at the young doctor. "Are we absolutely sure that it is over?" She places her hand on my forehead and gently strokes my hair.

The little water fountain has run dry and somehow it seems that the pictures have faded too.

I CALL up an image of my mother in the garden. She is weeping but appears to be at peace. She reaches out...

I widen the perspective and catch my breath.

Andreas and Luke are in the garden with her, and the three link hands and bow their heads.

I glance at my mother's log: the red light is gone, replaced by a green light.

THE LIFE

"SHE'S GONE," the doctor says, removing the stethoscope from his ears. He gives the time of death and signs some forms that the nurse passes to him.

The red-haired doctor picks up the phone and places a call.

"I'm so sorry..." she begins.

THERE IS a feeling of total emptiness inside me. I shut off the screen, allowing my mother, Andreas, and Luke some privacy. I can't bear to watch anymore.

I am dead.

The door to my old life is permanently closed.

I am completely empty inside, not even able to think.

Am I still Eva?

Am I still myself?

I don't know...

There is some unfinished business that I want to see to. I still haven't given my answer to the Master. Now, I have the chance. I leave the control room and head straight for the section that is now mapped. Thoughts are spinning around in my head, and I need to focus on something other than Luke and my mother.

I don't look at my reflection as I walk down the mirrored corridor but catch a glimpse of myself smiling when the secret door that hadn't budged yesterday now opens instantly at the slightest touch.

Is it because he knew that I didn't have the answer yesterday?

I enter.

It's wonderful to be here again. I like the atmosphere. A wave of excitement rushes through me and makes me forget Luke and my mother just for now. This time, I'm expected. I am honored and humbled to have this opportunity. Slowly, I walk toward the door to the Master's room. Someone is speaking inside. It's not a voice that I recognize. Hopefully, I'm not interrupting. The door is ajar, and I peek in through the crack.

"Come in," says a deep, calm voice.

I've been discovered and step carefully into the room.

He is sitting in his chair in the corner. It looks like he is watching a TV show.

I cover my mouth with my hand and laugh. That must be the last thing I would have imagined. "What are you watching?" blurts out of me.

The Master turns in his chair, looks at me, and smiles. "Eva, I am watching to see how the world is coping." He is wearing a long yellow garment that goes all the way down to his feet.

I nod. "And how is the world coping?" He gazes into my eyes. I can feel the force from his inner being. His eyes are totally incredible, shiny, and almost transparent. There is an endlessness, a depth that I have never before encountered with anyone else. I fight not to take a step back.

"Tell me your answer." He doesn't bat an eye.

Small talk must not be his cup of tea.

One deep breath replaces another as I get ready to say. "I have chosen to stay."

"Good. Then we can continue. You have come a long way, and you still have an intense period ahead of you. It is important that, no matter what happens, you must remember to be true to your heart. It will always tell you the truth and will never compromise with the truth. Your heart will bring you home. Go now. You shall meet with the Ring."

A warm sensation is pouring through my body. "Thank you." I place my palms together in front of my chest. He does the same, and I leave full of energy.

THE LIFE

IT IS the first time we will gather in the Ring since I decided to stay. I take my place in the chair with the eagle crafted on the back.

The light is dim, and there is a faint, sweetish scent. The octagonal room doesn't seem as overwhelming today. Everyone seems relieved to see me. Although they said it was my decision to make, I can see that they had inwardly hoped that I would stay because they sense that the time is right.

Gabriel begins to speak and welcomes everyone. He looks at me. "Eva, welcome back. You have chosen to stay here at In-Between. We appreciate that very much. Your decision confirms our feeling that the time has come. You are a key person, and the fact that you have chosen to join us now gives us all hope. We have been waiting for you."

There is something unique about him that I have never seen in a man before, inner calm and acceptance. He has an incredibly masculine personality, and at the same time, a very delicate fragility.

"We are facing a challenge. As we all know, we can only access the knowledge that can raise the consciousness of people on Earth to the next level when everyone is present in the Ring."

Gabriel turns his head and looks directly at me. His words affect me, and I straighten my back.

"Eva, we need your help. You are the one who has arrived most recently, and, for that reason, you are the best one to travel on Earth. We are asking you to return to find the two who are missing from the Ring."

I must resemble a huge question mark. What are they saying—that I should go back to Earth? It was just a few hours ago that I decided to stay. And I am dead... I mean....

Gabriel leans forward in his chair. "There is no time to waste. The Ring must be closed so that we can access the essential information. Developments on Earth are going downhill faster than we had calculated. We need the last two members to come here, and you are the only one who can bring them here."

"But," I stutter, "how?" I look around at the others to see if I am the only one who isn't following his train of thought.

"We will manifest a body for you to use on Earth, not the one you just left. You will be able to contact us to get assistance, but the objective is for you to use your abilities to find the two who are missing. We have some hints for you, and we can all help with different fragments from our memories that have become clear."

My mouth is hanging open as I stare at Gabriel.

"It is possible that you have already had some glimpses of people or images."

I am totally perplexed, and my body feels like an empty shell.

Thomas joins in. "None of us can remember the names or the precise appearance of those who are missing."

I raise my index finger, moving it back and forth as I look at Gabriel. "But I've seen how we can affect people's lives by stopping a train or helping them win the lottery. Why can't you just pick up the two who are missing and bring them here?"

Gabriel looks back at me without responding. Judging by the reaction of the others, I suspect that I've touched a sore spot.

Shiva leans forward. Her long black hair falls loose around her face. "Eva, if it weren't necessary, we wouldn't ask you to leave. I understand that it must be overwhelming." Her voice is soft as a morning breeze and bright, and her manner is very considerate.

Gabriel takes over. "The fact of the matter is that we cannot confirm that someone belongs to the Ring until they are here, and we have the opportunity to test them. As long as they are on Earth, their frequencies are not strong enough for us to know for certain."

"Well, what about the people I find? How will I know that they are the right ones?"

Gabriel shakes his head slowly. "You cannot know. You will need to rely on your judgment. But when you are on Earth, you will be able to come close to them and more easily sense whether they are the right ones."

I shake my head despairingly and mumble to myself. *This can't be true....*

"You will also have the possibility of trying to generate images or coincidences involving them in a natural way so that they do not arouse suspicion. In the same way that you experienced your dream here...."

I squeeze my eyelids together and tuck my hair behind my ears. "How am I supposed to get them here?" I hold my breath. "Are you saying that I have to arrange for them to get into a sudden accident?"

"We will leave that up to you. Time is running out. If we want to help humans evolve and nature to survive, you must leave tonight." Gabriel speaks slowly and clearly, and the others listen silently.

"But I thought that I was going to stay here." The chair feels significantly harder than before. I swallow. This is so unanticipated. They can't force me to do it. Again, it is my free choice. I close my eyes and breathe deeply, losing sense of time. And when I open my eyes again, I realize the others haven't moved at all.

They are waiting for me.

They trust me.

They believe in me.

I take in a breath that goes all the way to the center of my heart, to the place where Annabel's diamond is buried. "If this is what I must do, then I will do it. I will go back to Earth. I will find the two missing members of the Circle." My gaze goes around the circle, falling on each member in turn.

Never before have words felt as heavy as these.

The other members of the Ring lower their heads as though bowing to me.

"Thomas will gather all the information we have, and you will also have contact with him while you are away."

"I will find them," my voice is determined, "no matter how long it takes."

Gabriel raises his hand. "One last thing. You only have forty-two days on Earth before you must return yourself. The body that we are creating won't be able to carry energy to last any longer than that. If you don't make it back in time, the door to In-Between is closed. We only have this one chance."

"I will find them," I try to erase any doubt by repeating it. I'm not sure if I do it for my sake or theirs.

Gabriel looks around the circle. "Good. There is no time to waste."

We conclude our meeting by rising and pressing our palms together in unison.

I GO OUTSIDE and look out over the horizon. It is infinite. The sky is light blue, and there isn't a cloud in sight.

"When I get down to Earth," I look at Thomas, who is standing by my side, 'I'm going to look up to see if I can catch sight of you up here."

Thomas puts his arm around my shoulder.

"And, it might not be part of the plan, but I want to ride an airplane through the clouds to see if I can find you. Will you wave if you see me?"

Thomas smiles. "Definitely. I'm going to keep an eye on you."

"How is it going to happen?" I cover my mouth with my hands in suspense.

"We've never tried it before. This is the first time that anyone has been permitted to go back to Earth in another body and retain the knowledge of this place."

I feel a shiver of excitement down my spine. "So, I'm the guinea pig." I try to laugh but don't when I see the gravity in Thomas's eyes.

"It is important that you do not reveal our existence to anyone on Earth. It could disrupt our work if people found out that we exist before they reach the next level of consciousness."

"Why?" I put my hand around his waist.

Thomas releases his hold on my shoulder and turns to me in seriousness. "If people hear about In-Between, it is possible that many, particularly young people who feel lost in society, would be tempted to come here in the hope that life here is better than that on Earth, or in the hope of being saved."

I breathe slowly and feel pressure inside my chest.

"There are many young people who do not get the attention and love they need as they grow up and who feel overlooked or lost. But when the new knowledge comes through to them, I am sure that they will be capable of bringing the human race further."

I sense Thomas's sincerity.

"You will go down in a woman's body, and your new name will be... Angela. Remember to have fun while you are away. You'll be back at In-Between before you know it."

This feels like a significant event. Soon, I will be back on Earth. A subtle shiver tickles under my skin; hopefully, I will succeed.

Thomas unbuttons the top button of his shirt. "You should have this. It is yours." He unfastens the purple necklace and hands it to me. I'm standing still, filled with reverence, reminding myself of the dream. Ceremoniously, he hangs it around my neck.

"Come," he begins to walk. "It's time."

I LIE DOWN on the table. It is less than twelve hours ago that I was here last. Now, I have a mission to find the two people who are missing from our Ring.

This is so far out that my mind has given up trying to predict the future. But I can't help wondering how it will feel to be back on Earth. I am tense and tingling with excitement.

Thomas is standing by my side.

"See you... Remember that it is you who must establish contact when you get down there. We can't do it from up here."

"Tell me one more time what I should do." I turn my head and look at Thomas. He looks at me with caring eyes and places a hand on my shoulder.

"You will have your Skycon with you. You are going to land at exactly 12:00, and at 13:00, we will have an opening so we can establish a connection."

I look at the watch and see that it is now 11:33.

"Remember that we only have this opening for sixty seconds and that we only have one chance."

I nod to indicate that I understand. "Can't we just say that if I can't make it at 13:00 that you make an opening again the day after?"

Thomas shakes his head. "Unfortunately, it doesn't work that way. We have to reach the same frequency, and it can only be used once. Right now, our Skycons have the correct settings, but once we make the opening, our system frequency will change after one minute so that the system cannot be misused. And if we don't get it right the first time, the settings will no longer match up, and we will not be able to communicate."

"All right." I feel my throat tighten.

"And one last thing. When it is 13:00, you enter 7777, and then you will be in contact with me."

I feel inside my pocket to be sure that I have my Skycon. I confirm, 'Seven, seven, seven, seven at 13:00." I can remember that and reach for Thomas's hand and squeeze it hard.

"Are you ready?"

"I'm as ready as I'm going to be." I give his hand one last squeeze and release it. Our eyes meet one final time. He walks over to the screen, and I find the focus point on the ceiling.

This is it.

I hope that I can carry out the mission. I wonder what I will look like when I land on Earth and where I will land. I hope that I find the right two people in time.

I am no longer Eva.

I am Angela.

The machine comes to life.

"See you, In-Between," I whisper. "I'll be back soon."

I close my eyes.

That low humming sound starts up, and I feel the heat on my feet, legs, stomach, and face.

I am on my way back to Earth and see a powerful white light from my inner eye.

I feel lighter than air.

The humming is gone, and I cannot feel my body.

I'm sailing in silence.

My thoughts dwindle as the light becomes more powerful.

I fall and fall until I merge with the white light.

There is an immense, empty space.

No time, no place, just white light, and silence.

GRADUALLY, heat spreads from my feet and upward through my body.

I am beginning to feel something soft underneath me that is becoming more solid. I move my finger, and something thin, a little stiff, and smooth tickles my hand. I put my thumb and index finger around it and let them glide up and down. It's long, flimsy, and pointed at the end. Can it be? My hand slides down again, feeling the object's emergence from the earth in which it has sprouted.

It's a blade of grass.

I open my eyes very slowly.

The light is still powerful, and my heart is beating rapidly.

The sky.

I'm lying on grass, looking up at the sky.
Low clouds are hanging above me, no longer below.
I am back on Earth.

Want to know what happens next?
Get Book 2 in the IN-BETWEEN Series,
THE RING here:

readerlinks.com/l/2170851

AFTERWORD

Dear reader

I was on my way home from a trip to India when I felt my body starting to shiver and energy rising my spine.

My eyes were open, but what looked like a huge screen appeared in front of me.

I could see a woman, a plane crashing, and a gorgeous man reaching out for her.

It was like watching a movie, so real that I could feel it in my body. I looked around the plane to see if anyone saw what I was seeing. People were either asleep or watching their devices.

I don't know how long it took, but after what was properly no more than 10-15 seconds, it disappeared again.

I sat completely silent.

Then I reached for my laptop and started to write down what I had just seen.

Only four-month earlier, I had sold my business and asked the universe to guide me in what I should do now.

AFTERWORD

At that moment, I knew. I closed my eyes and felt a vast calmness inside the space of nothingness.

This was the story I was going to pass on.

Take care

Sagar Constantin

ABOUT THE AUTHOR

Sagar Constantin is a bestselling Scandinavian author with more than seven books. She writes stories that are both captivating but also highly inspirational.

The In-Between series came to Sagar on her way home from a business trip to India, and she instantly knew that this was a story that she had to share with the world.

She has a great ability to make psychological issues easy to understand and comprehend, and through her reading, it is possible to grow inside and at the same time be highly entertained.

Sagar is also an international speaker and lecturer for businesses. Every year, she trains thousands of people in subjects like personal development, change management, EQ, and High-performance teams.

When she is not writing and teaching, she loves to spend time with her family and enjoys nature walks. Sagar lives in Denmark but travels the world with her work.

To be the first to hear about new releases and bargains —from Sagar Constantin—sign up below.

(I promise not to share your email with anyone else, and I won't clutter your inbox.)

To sign up to receive the NewsLetter go here: https://books.sagarconstantin.com/news

---

Follow Sagar Constantin on BookBub here: https://www.bookbub.com/authors/sagar-constantin

Follow Sagar on BookBub

Connect with Sagar online:

https://www.facebook.com/SagarConstantinAuthor
https://www.instagram.com/sagar.constantin.author/
https://twitter.com/ConstantinSagar
https://www.goodreads.com/sagarconstantin
https://www.linkedin.com/in/sagarconstantin/

Website: https://livingbetween.com
Mail to: info@sagarconstantin.com

Printed in Great Britain
by Amazon